Morten Ramsland, born in 1971, has a degree in Danish and Art History. He is married, with a young son and daughter. *Doghead* is his first book to be published in English. It became a huge bestseller in Denmark, where he won Author of the Year, Book of the Year, the Reader's Prize and the most prestigious prize for literature, the Golden Laurel Prize.

DOGHEAD

Morten Ramsland

Translated from the Danish
by Tiina Nunnally

BLACK SWAN

TRANSWORLD PUBLISHERS
61-63 Uxbridge Road, London W5 5SA
A Random House Group Company
www.rbooks.co.uk

DOGHEAD
A BLACK SWAN BOOK: 9780552773430

First published in Great Britain
in 2007 by Doubleday
a division of Transworld Publishers
Black Swan edition published 2008

Addresses for Random House Group Ltd companies outside the UK
can be found at: www.randomhouse.co.uk
The Random House Group Ltd Reg. No. 954009

The Random House Group Limited supports The Forest Stewardship
Council (FSC), the leading international forest certification organisation.
All our titles that are printed on Greenpeace approved FSC certified paper
carry the FSC logo. Our paper procurement policy can be found at
www.rbooks.co.uk/environment

Typeset in 11/13.5pt Giovanni Book by
Falcon Oast Graphic Art Ltd.

Printed in the UK by CPI Cox & Wyman, Reading, RG1 8EX.

2 4 6 8 10 9 7 5 3 1

Contents

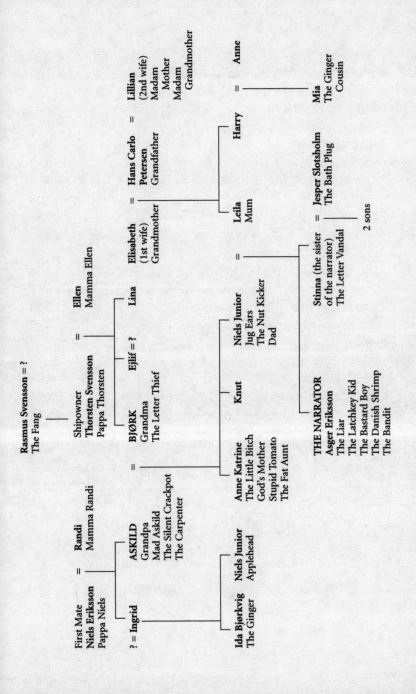

PART ONE

PART ONE

A Plain in Eastern Germany –
5 March 1944

SOMEWHERE IN EASTERN Germany, my grandfather Askild is running across an open plain. The Germans are after him, and he has lost one of his shoes; it's freezing. The half moon casts a pale glow over the landscape, transforming it into a ploughed field with frozen soldiers partly buried in mud. Less than three hours ago my grandfather said goodbye to his friend Herman Hemning. By running in opposite directions, they were trying to trick their pursuers into focusing on only one of the two tracks. My father has not yet been born. My grandmother Bjørk, who had arrived too late at the prison in Oslo and therefore never got to say goodbye, is not yet married to Grandpa Askild. Officially they're not even engaged. So my whole existence is hanging by a thread.

Askild pulls out pieces of bone that have been rubbed with rat poison and scatters them on the ground. A minute passes, two minutes. He stops to catch his breath before running again. Right now it's essential to get going, Askild Eriksson, because those could be bloodhounds howling in the distance. Or maybe that sound is the

Katarina blowing its horn in the morning fog outside Bergen: a memory that pops up of its own accord, threatening to knock his legs out from under him. Or it could also be his deaf ear, which has given him a sixth sense, now that the entire Eriksson lineage is at risk. Run, damn it, run! But Askild doesn't budge. With the rat poison and the bone fragments and the ship *Katarina* all around him, he is struck by this lightning flash of memory.

It doesn't look good. Grandpa Askild is standing paralysed on a German plain. Grandma Bjørk is in Norway, malnourished, with bleeding gums and a guilty conscience. The shipyard, which has been in her family's possession ever since her grandfather arrived in Bergen as a young man from Nordland, has gone belly-up. His seven freighters have been sunk by the Germans, the patrician family home has been sold, and Great-grandfather Thorsten is lying in bed, paralysed after a stroke, while his daughter Bjørk has to work at the Holst clothing shop, her bleeding gums dripping on to the fabric. 'The German torpedoes have sunk us all,' says Grandma Bjørk.

Now Askild wakes up. Those are bloodhounds howling.

A thought races through his mind: Herman will get away. The dogs have determined the fates of both men by focusing on Askild's tracks. He looks down and catches sight of a hole in his sock, where his big toe is sticking out. It's blue and filthy and looks like a little trapped fish. Askild has been in Sachsenhausen concentration camp for almost a year, and he refuses to go back there under any circumstances. It's Sunday, 5 March 1944. The time is eight minutes to two in the morning, and a gigantic *NO* grows in Grandpa's stomach and explodes out into his body, which finally – at long last – starts running down a slope. He stumbles, gets up, stumbles and gets up again.

The bloodhounds are howling. In the distance shots can be heard.

The *NO* echoes inside Grandpa. *NO* to the Germans and the bloodhounds. *NO* to Sachsenhausen's nightmarish winters. And that's how Askild runs, in a trance, in desperation, with a resounding *NO* inside his body, while everyone is breathing peacefully in the shut-up house of a former merchant on the outskirts of Odense, where the other two quarters of my genetic make-up can be found.

In Odense my maternal grandfather wakes up, puts on his slippers and goes out to the shed to piss in the cold night. Maybe he's thinking about a leak in the roof that needs repairing at the very moment that Askild, my other grandfather, stubs his big toe on a frozen clod of earth and bites a hole in his lower lip. My maternal grandmother is sleeping with folded hands after taking her daily medicine. My uncle Harry is sleeping with his hands under the covers, even though that's not allowed, and he's dreaming about all the horrible things that might happen to him. Bjørk, my paternal grandmother, is in Bergen dreaming that a sailor is pounding on her window and peering in at her with terrified eyes. At first she doesn't know what to do. She calls for help, but no one comes to her rescue. She shouts louder and louder, until she realizes that it's the sailor who is calling for help, and then . . . as Askild stubs his foot against the frozen clod of earth, she wakes with a start and sits up in bed.

The clocks are synchronized. Askild is running in the dark.

Before the sun rises, the Germans catch up with him. He's sitting in a tree in a nearby wood. The bloodhounds race through the early morning and stop at the foot of the tree. He is blue with cold when the Germans point the barrels of their rifles at him and order him down. They don't shoot him. A couple of months later Askild is sent to Buchenwald.

The Lunch

W E WOULD REALLY LIKE to know how Grandpa Askild manages to survive, preferably with all the details. We want to know how he paves the way so that I and my big sister Stinna can come into the world. But after Christmas lunch my grandpa shuts up like a clam and drinks another aquavit. Whatever it was the Germans did to him, he refuses to tell us.

'Plague or cholera,' he says instead.

He has just noticed a road sign down the street that looks like a German with a rifle. Grandma Bjørk shakes her head at him and talks about something else. Grandpa uses a cane when he walks and he has grown quite fat. Not like back then, when the white buses of the Red Cross brought him home from Buchenwald via Neuengamme, and he was nothing but a brush stroke in the air. I picture Grandpa Askild as a thin line topped by a big round head sitting on the seat in the back of the bus.

'What else happened, Grandpa?' asks Stinna.

But Askild would rather talk about all the times he stood on the dock as a child in Bergen, waiting to greet his father when the *Katarina* came into port after months at sea. The reunion always filled him with equal parts of terror and joy, because after the homecoming dinner, his mother would read aloud from the black book in which all of Askild's misdeeds had been neatly written down. Then his father would take the strap out of the cupboard to give Askild all the beatings that had been stored up for several months.

'Back then the world was real,' he says.

We can't get any more details out of him, so we run outside with our cousin Mia. The main thing is not to let the Little Bitch see us. The Little Bitch's real name is Anne Katrine, and she's our aunt, our father's fat sister. Luckily she's gone down to the basement, because she thinks that at some point we'll all go down there too. But the three of us dash out of the back door and discover to our great joy that there's snow on the ground. First we throw snowballs at each other, and then we play 'German shepherd'. My sister Stinna gets to be Grandpa Askild, Cousin Mia is the Red Cross, and I apparently have to be the German shepherd, even though I'm not wild about the idea. Being the German shepherd means crawling around on all fours trying to capture Grandpa's leg, and that's not much fun in slushy snow.

'Don't forget to bark!' shouts Mia as I rush around at my sister's heels. Mia knows a lot about dogs because she and Uncle Harry and Aunt Anne have a black Labrador. 'You have to bark properly!' she shouts, and I bark and throw myself in the snow at Stinna's shoes. She gives a loud shriek when I grab her legs and topple her over into the snow.

'Here's some rat poison,' gasps my sister, trying to stuff snow into my mouth while I, in turn, try to bend her thumb backwards. 'Ow!' she wheezes as Mia cheers Askild on and makes snowballs to give him, which is actually cheating.

'All right,' says Stinna suddenly. 'Now the German shepherd is dead.'

'No, not yet!' I protest, spitting out snow along with the words. Mia overrules me, saying that if the German shepherd is dead, then he's dead, and now it's her turn to rescue Askild. Actually we're supposed to pretend to torture him first, but the girls don't feel like it today, so Mia takes Stinna with her into the space in the back of the garage and shuts the door with a little smile.

'Go on inside!' Stinna shouts to me through the closed door.

'You can go and play with the Little Bitch,' Mia adds.

In the living room Dad is arguing with Grandpa. It has to do with the time when Askild stole Dad's coin collection with the valuable silver coins from way back in the sixteen hundreds. Dad had a big collection of coins that he got from American sailors who put into port in Bergen.

A huge ship, a supertanker with a whole soccer field on deck, sails past my inner eye. The sun is glinting off the gold buttons on the uniforms of the American sailors, who are very rich. And they all toss flags and coins down to the boys on the dock. That's how Dad collected a small fortune. But one day when he was outside playing, Askild sneaked into his room, nabbed the coin collection, and went off to the pub.

'Thief,' Dad snarls as Grandma Bjørk tries to change the subject.

One minute Grandpa Askild claims that Dad must have

17

forgotten the coin collection somewhere. The next minute he says that Dad gave him permission to sell it. Askild had one beer at the Corner and then gave the rest of the money to Dad.

'Liar!' shouts Dad as he leans across the table, his dark eyes blazing. 'We hadn't even moved to Denmark back then!'

Sweat has formed on Askild's brow, and he glances over at Grandma. Then he stands up. 'We're going now, Bjørk. We're not welcome here!' He leans on his cane, which he always keeps close at hand under the table, but Grandma Bjørk doesn't want to go home yet.

'It's only five o'clock, Askild. Good Lord, stop making such a fuss.'

Stinna shows up and says that Askild can just go on home by himself. Lately my sister has started getting a little too uppity. She's also started skipping her gym classes, and Mum doesn't know what she's going to do about her.

'Are you coming, Bjørk?' Grandpa persists. He has left the living room and is now standing out in the hallway, fumbling with the bottles of Giraffe beer that he has stuffed in his pockets to hide from Dad. The Little Bitch has run down to the basement, and Askild is looking around for her in annoyance. Even though my aunt is almost as old as my father, she has never moved away from home. 'Anne Katrine!' he shouts. 'We're going home now!' But Grandma Bjørk still doesn't want to go.

'We got a postcard from little Knut,' she suddenly exclaims, causing a big commotion.

Normally the grown-ups never talk about Uncle Knut, who is nine years younger than Dad and a real rogue who

18

never seems able to stay in one place. Months and even years can go by before anyone hears from him. When he finally does write, it's usually because he's got some unhappy young girl in trouble and he needs money, and what sort of thanks is that? He never even bothers to send a Christmas card, that scoundrel. Mum is always worrying about all the females left in the lurch by Uncle Knut, who ran away to sea when he turned fourteen and has hardly written a word to us since. Dad is the only one in the family with any financial sense. He's always the one who has to give Grandma money whenever Uncle Knut gets in trouble, because Grandpa Askild can't bear to hear the name Knut mentioned. His face grows stern and he says: 'Knut who?' He has never got over the fact that his son ran away from home shortly before his birthday and didn't give a damn about the three-speed bicycle that Askild had bought for him. The bicycle is still in the shed on Tunøvej, rusting and gathering dust. 'Don't touch it,' Askild always grumbles whenever we get too close.

Mum thinks that Dad is just plain stupid to fork out the money, and sometimes it's Knut that they fight about after we've gone to bed in the evening. Then Mum says that Uncle Knut will never learn to deal with the consequences of his own life if Dad keeps bailing him out, and Dad snaps that he's tired of always being the one who has to please everybody. Even though Mum likes discussing things more than Dad does, their arguments often end with her in tears. I can hear her sobs penetrate through the wall of my room. I go over and wake up my sister Stinna, who sleeps more soundly than I do, so we can spy on them together. Unfortunately, we almost always see the same thing: Mum sitting on the sofa, crying, while Dad stands at the window with his back turned to her, sighing as his cigarette drops ash on to the floor. Afterwards I'm allowed to sleep in Stinna's bed. Mum thinks I'm getting too old for that, but Stinna's bed is much bigger than mine, and she doesn't have anything against it, as long as I don't fidget.

Grandma Bjørk has taken the postcard from Uncle Knut out of her purse while Askild watches her in astonishment from the hallway.

'What does he say?' Stinna wants to know and hurries over to stand behind Grandma.

Normally letters from Uncle Knut are not something Grandma mentions out loud, so this must be a very special postcard. She puts on her reading glasses and reads the whole thing to herself without saying a word. Then she takes off her reading glasses and looks around at all of us.

'He's coming on 2 June.' Her voice cracks. 'That's a Thursday.'

In the subsequent silence, my outburst: 'He's coming!' sounds like a thunderclap. Everyone stares at me. Stinna says that we can take him with us to the beach. Cousin Mia thinks that's a good idea, but Dad remarks that we don't know whether Knut might have other things to do.

'Of course he'll come with us to the beach,' says Mum.

Grandma Bjørk is beaming. She has tears in her eyes, her hands are fumbling nervously with the postcard, and her gaze shifts towards the hallway, where Grandpa Askild isn't saying a word.

'Where is he now?' asks Dad, and Grandma tells us that Knut has been living in Jamaica for the past few years.

'Jamaica!' I shout. 'Jamaica! Jamaica!'

'He has his own business,' says Bjørk, but Dad doesn't quite believe it, especially since Grandma usually does quite a bit of embellishing when it comes to Uncle Knut's life and his means of earning a living.

'Well, we'll wait and see,' says Dad, having a hard time hiding his joy.

Grandma casts another glance at the hallway, where Grandpa Askild slowly comes into view. 'Look, he's been stealing beer again,' says Stinna, pointing to Grandpa's right pocket. Askild pulls a couple of Giraffes out of his pockets with a foolish grin. The coin collection seems to have been forgotten, and finally he sits back down. He wants a glass of rum, now that we're about to have a visitor from Jamaica.

Dad gets the rum bottle out of the cabinet with the translucent panes of glass and pours him a drink. Grandpa downs the rum in one gulp and pours another. Then he belches loudly and gives me a reproachful look. 'No belching at the table,' he says.

Bjørk and the Rose-Coloured Blanket

ASKILD AND BJØRK met each other in 1936 in a birch grove near the district of Kalfaret in Bergen. Less than seven years later, Askild was sent to Sachsenhausen. He was a sort of smuggler-collaborator who tried to cheat the Germans by selling them a load of timber that was actually their own.

Askild was friends with Bjørk's brother Ejlif, and he was a regular visitor at their house located on Kalfarveien. Sometimes he also came over when Ejlif wasn't at home. Once he kissed Grandma Bjørk out in the garden under the pale birch trees; later he kissed her numerous times in Assistentkirkegård, the cemetery in Bergen. And even though suspicions began to circulate in the house, they managed to spend time alone because Ejlif would cover for them. Askild was studying to be both a ship's engineer and a mechanical engineer; he was the son of a first mate, which was not the best match for a shipowner's daughter.

Grandpa Askild himself claimed that in the olden days his family had fled the French Revolution, and because of that he had blue blood in his veins. He was dark like a Frenchman, his eyes shone like coal, and his beard was so thick and black that he had to shave several times a day to get rid of the dark shadow. Back then Askild was a handsome man, even though the most visible signs of his blue blood were the blue circles which, over the years, became etched beneath his mahogany-coloured eyes.

It was a hard blow for him when the Svensson family refused to accept him – that is, until they went bankrupt themselves. Askild slowly began to despise everything that Bjørk's family stood for, and in the end he even refused to accept her inheritance: the elegant furniture and the silverware that my great-grandmother Ellen had hidden away when bankruptcy descended on them. Everything was left behind in Bergen when Ellen died many years later, and it finally vanished into the pockets of the removal company because Askild neither could nor would pay for the cost of transporting everything to Denmark. Back then – before the war, before the bankruptcy and the fateful years in Buchenwald and Sachsenhausen – he had to settle for calling the Svensson family a bunch of Nordland peasants who had grown big and fat at the expense of others instead of building something from scratch on their own. And there they sat in Bergen, in their white patrician house, surrounded by a swarm of servants, trying to act so Danish that it was enough to make him sick.

'They haven't even discovered that Norway is a free country with free people,' said Askild, who, with that type of remark, lit a little spark in Bjørk's heart. In his own way Askild was a revolutionary, completely different from the cultivated and articulate young men who usually came to the house. Pappa Thorsten was always trying to marry Bjørk off to one of them – and, in particular, he had his eye on young Doctor Thor Gunnarsson, who spoke fluent Danish because he had studied at Copenhagen University. The doctor also came from a good family with solid traditions and a great deal of landholdings.

Thorsten had previously had bad experiences with first mates and their buccaneer offspring. But the more disapproval Pappa Thorsten displayed in speaking of Askild, the more interesting he became in Bjørk's eyes. She was the youngest of the family's three children, and the only unmarried daughter.

Ejlif had met Askild at trade school, and at weekends they spent a good deal of time together in illicit bars around Bergen. Askild took Ejlif along to places where he had never been, and where the girls were much more willing and made no demands when the early light of dawn seeped through the draughty wooden huts near the harbour.

Askild was barely fourteen when his shipmates paid for his first prostitute in Amsterdam. They cajoled him into following a thirty-year-old woman with a feather boa and rouge on her cheeks up the stairs to a little room, where the sound of a crying child could be heard on the other side of the thin wall. She lay down on her back, moistened her vagina with spit, and peered impatiently up at Askild, who simply stood there without knowing what he was supposed to do. The woman sighed and said that most men took off their clothes, whereupon Askild tore off his trousers and to his horror saw his manhood dangling limp and useless between his thighs. His mind went completely blank, but then she rolled on to her side, smiled for the first and only time, and with a little sigh began massaging his balls until he grew between her fingers.

Then she lay on her back again. 'Lie down here,' she said, and Askild obeyed like a blind man being led through the dark. With a swift movement she rolled on top of him so he could squirt his whole fourteen-year-old load into her abused womb. Thirty seconds later he leapt off the bed and got dressed so quickly that in his confusion he forgot his underwear, and then he slammed the door behind him without a backward glance. Down in the pub the crew slapped him on the back, and one of the sailors bought him a whisky at the bar.

The next year, for the first time, and after he had turned fifteen, he paid for his own whore during a shore leave in Hamburg, and in the years that followed his self-confidence grew in direct proportion to the number of whores he visited. By the time he was twenty-one and studying to get his engineering certificate in Bergen, he was quite an experienced and self-confident young man. And it was not difficult for him to impress the far less experienced Ejlif. But Askild had absolutely no insight into the nature of love. When he met Bjørk, he once again stood with his trousers down around his knees, and had no idea what he was supposed to do.

In the beginning Bjørk often saw Askild in the house without really paying much attention to him. But Pappa Thorsten, on the other hand, did. He definitely did not care for the look that Askild gave his daughter the first time he saw her sitting on a bench in the garden under the big birch trees. It was in the autumn, and Bjørk had a rose-coloured blanket wrapped around her. She was reading a book by Sigrid Undset – this was years before she became obsessed with novels about doctors – and she had fallen into a reverie over a few sentences, just as Ejlif entered the garden with first mate Eriksson's son and shouted: 'Don't tell me you're sitting here again, you ninny!' Bjørk glanced up, smiled with embarrassment at her brother, and then let her gaze shift to the figure behind him. She looked right through first mate Eriksson's son with a dreamy expression on her face, and even though this glance, which was dreamy, smiling, and embarrassed all in one, had nothing to do with Askild, it struck him like a sledge-hammer all the same.

He stammered 'hello', but by then Bjørk had already gone back to her book. And there stood Askild: paralysed in a birch grove next to the patrician home belonging to Thorsten Svensson. Eight years later, when he fell into the latrine pit behind the barracks housing the dysentery patients in Buchenwald, it was that very image of Bjørk, wrapped in a rose-coloured blanket beneath the birch trees on Kalfarveien, that enabled him to pull himself out of the viscous water and clamber over the steep edge. Only one thing was clear: if it was the last thing he did on this earth, he was going to return to that bright birch grove where Bjørk, wrapped in a rose-coloured blanket, had smiled at him with a dreamy expression on her face.

Twenty metres from the latrine pit he collapsed again but was gathered up by Pork Face, a German homosexual whom Askild, less than seven years earlier, during a shore leave in Hamburg, had rescued from a beating by a gang of young Nazis. They were demanding proof of the proper sexual orientation of all the guests in the pub. At that time Pork Face was so happy to escape the beating that he invited this Norwegian sailor named Askild on a trip to Berlin. Together they made the rounds of all the pubs that, according to Pork Face, were worth visiting.

It was an irony of fate that Askild should run into Pork Face again in Buchenwald. Pork Face washed him off with a bucket of water and sent him back to the dysentery barracks, advising him next time to shit in his trousers and for God's sake not venture down to the latrine pit, which was a stinking gate to hell.

It was also Pork Face who saved Askild's black-market business and stolen-goods operation during the month that he lay in the sick bay with shit streaming between his legs. He was transformed into a skeleton as a green hue slowly spread over his gaunt skin, and forever after lent an acidic shade to his tattoos.

At that time, Red Cross packages had started to find their way to the camp. There were Swedish and Danish ones, but British and American packages for prisoners of war also arrived, even though there were few prisoners of war at the camp. It was the tobacco and cigarette rations in these packages that were especially worth their weight in gold. Askild had previously collected chewed-up butts that the guards tossed away. He mixed them with the scrapings from pipes smoked to the very bottom, along with withered leaves. Then he rolled them in bits of old newspaper and traded them for food and other necessities like blankets and medicine. Before the dysentery shattered his intestines, he was the one who had started 'reorganizing' the packages – which meant stealing them from the other barracks and dispersing the contents so they became used on an equal basis with the camp's other modes of payment. These included gold teeth – though they did not have a great deal of value compared with Chesterfields and Lucky Strikes, which could be used to bribe practically any guard – and coupons to the whorehouse of Polish women, which stood on the outskirts of the camp, as well as a network of fees and reciprocal payments so complicated that not even Askild could figure them out.

A single Lucky Strike, discreetly delivered each day by Pork Face to the block capo, ensured that Askild was allowed to lie in peace in the sick bay for a whole month, even though he just as well could have been anaesthetized to death with Evipan by SS Hauptscharführer Wilhelm. Each day Pork Face also went over to the sick bay to stuff scraps of food into Askild's half-open mouth – either out of gratitude or unrequited love, or maybe simply as a link in his own survival strategy, since Askild had put him in charge of administering his Red Cross packages. Up until now Pork Face had survived two years and one escape attempt, which was more than most. The threat of having to make it on his own if Askild died kept Pork Face sneaking over to the sick bay, even though the increasingly paltry scraps of food that he stuffed into Askild's mouth seemed more and more like an investment in death instead of the future.

On 1 February 1945, when the Russians reached the Oder River, Askild got up from his sickbed and staggered back to his barracks, which was reserved exclusively for criminal Germans, Russians, and Poles. There he intended to take back his place in the hierarchy that Pork Face had tried to preserve. But he never managed to regain his privileges.

Three weeks later, Pork Face disappeared during a bombardment. They were both working outside Buchenwald in a release command unit, a temporary labour camp, having been commandeered to dig for gold in Leipzig. It meant plundering corpses in bombed-out houses under the close supervision of the SS. Askild had just stepped aside to take a piss, and as he stood there with his dick in his hand, the Brits flew over the area in their Wellington bombers and transformed the already devastated town into an inferno of splinter and phosphor bombs. Not until the next day, after some semblance of order had been restored to the groups of prisoners, did the digging for gold continue. Askild was ordered to dig out the 4-metre-long tunnel where Pork Face had been working. After a couple of hours, when a hole was finally dug through and Askild suddenly stood in an almost untouched cellar room, he saw Pork Face sitting with his back against a wall, staring straight ahead without expression. At first Askild thought he was alive, but when he touched his hand, Pork Face disintegrated into a pile of bones and a few scraps of cloth that fluttered to the ground like dark powder.

Askild says that the violent generation of heat had vaporized all his fatty tissues: 'And that was the end of that faggot asshole,' he belches.

Mum says that's not something to be talking about in front of the children. By now she too is drunk, and so she starts smoking, which she normally never does.

'The phosphor bomb is a primitive predecessor of the napalm bomb and a diabolical invention,' Grandpa tells us. 'When the phosphorus comes in contact with oxygen, it starts to burn. Once a man gets phosphorus on his body, it doesn't do any good to immerse him in water. It just starts burning again when he comes out of the water . . . What a fucking invention, bang, bang!' Grandpa aims his index finger at me: '*Achtung, Achtung, weiter-marschieren, schnell, los, los—*'

Grandma Bjørk wants to go home, but now Askild doesn't feel like listening to her. She has got up and is standing there, shifting from one foot to the other, holding her purse with Uncle Knut's postcard inside.

Later Grandpa Askild goes into my sister Stinna's room, holding a meatball in his hand. My cousin Mia is going to spend the night with us, and she is given permission to bring over Bernard, their black Lab, who is going to sleep here too. Uncle Harry and Aunt Anne live only one and a half kilometres away, so it was no trouble to run over and get the dog.

When Askild sees Bernard, he goes over and holds out the meatball. 'Come on, you stupid mutt,' he says. Cousin Mia informs Grandpa that her dog's name is Bernard.

'Oh, is that right?' says Askild with a grin as he presses the meatball against the dog's snout. Terrified, Bernard tries to back away.

'I'm not sure he wants your meatball,' says Mia. But Askild tells her to shut up, and then he grabs Bernard's jaw and tries to force the meatball into his mouth.

Bernard whimpers, and Askild mumbles, 'Damned mutt', and tiny drops of sweat start appearing on his shiny forehead.

My sister tells him to stop scaring Bernard, but Askild just laughs and asks her whether her budding breasts have got any bigger. He removes one hand from Bernard and reaches out for her little breasts as he laughs so hard we clearly see his yellowed pirate teeth. My twelve-year-old sister doesn't like having them called 'budding breasts', and her face turns bright red with fury. She can't get a word out, just stammers something that we can't understand.

In the middle of the whole thing, Bernard pees on the floor out of sheer fright. 'What the hell!' shouts Askild, and he drops the meatball, which rolls under Stinna's bed. He yells at Bernard, saying the dog hasn't been properly trained. Then he grabs the animal by the scruff of his neck and presses his head down into the pee on the floor, to teach him a lesson. But the only result is that Bernard pees even more, and this time it strikes one of Askild's shoes.

'You – rotten – man – how – can – you – be – so – bloody – cruel – to – animals!' Stinna stammers.

'What?' shouts Askild, maybe because his deaf ear is playing tricks on him. 'What kind of language is that?'

I can't stand listening to them any more. I don't know how it happens, but suddenly I'm punching Grandpa hard on the thigh and calling him a stupid idiot.

'What!' bellows Askild.

'Get out of here, you stupid idiot,' I say.

Complete silence in the room. For a brief moment it actually looks as if I've stopped Grandpa cold. I hold my breath, feeling quite proud, because I've pulled it off. Then he kicks me in the behind, making me fall forward into Stinna's dressing table so I hurt my shoulder.

It really hurts bad, but I don't say a word.

Askild snarls at me, saying that's no way to talk to your grandfather. Mia runs off to get Dad, and soon my father is standing in the room and telling Askild not to kick his son in the behind. Askild replies that Dad hasn't brought me up properly. He calls me a latchkey kid because Mum, who has started studying to be a nurse, is no longer home during the day to take care of me. And nothing ever comes of that except brats, says Askild, who doesn't dare call me a bastard now that Dad is standing right next to him.

Stinna says that Askild should just go on back to his own house now. 'You've been talking about leaving all night, Grandpa, so why don't you just get going?'

After they head back to the living room, we hear the Little Bitch making a commotion out in the hall. Stinna hurries to lock the door to her room before she comes in.

A slight trembling ripples through my whole body. My sister cautiously touches my shoulder and asks me if it still hurts.

I nod.

'He should get a taste of his own piss,' she says spitefully. And suddenly we start hatching a plan. Before the night is over, Grandpa is going to taste, if not his own piss, then at least someone else's.

By 1938 Askild had become a shadow who ran around after Bjørk with an expression on his face that made Pappa Thorsten more and more nervous. And after a while Askild stopped inviting Ejlif out to pubs because he preferred to spend the evenings drinking tea and playing cards in the patrician villa on Kalfarveien. By this time Bjørk had, of course, begun to notice him – a couple of years had passed since he first caught sight of her sitting under the birch trees. She and her sister Lina often made fun of Askild's uncouth manner, his stammered remarks, and his awkward attempts to rid himself of his west-coast Norwegian dialect and speak a more genteel Bergen-style

Danish, as was the custom during those years in the Svensson family. Over time he had also grown quite clumsy. He would spill tea all over the table in the middle of a game of cards. Whenever they had elk stew for supper, he would drip big brown spots all the way from the serving dish to his plate.

'That's what happens when you open your door to all sorts of buccaneer youths,' said Pappa Thorsten, who complained to his wife Ellen about her hospitable invitation to Askild to join them for dinner. But she felt sorry for the young man whose parents, after a fight, had thrown him out of the house, forcing him to take lodgings with Captain Knutsson's widow in a room that was only ten square metres. So she refused to budge. If her house was open to all the other guests that Thorsten kept dragging home to introduce to Bjørk, then it had to be open to Askild too. Pappa Thorsten grudgingly agreed, while he listened with alarm to Bjørk's laughter whenever Askild made some new faux pas. There was something ominous about that laughter, even though Bjørk still regarded the young engineering student as nothing more than a source of daily entertainment.

Naturally, in the long run, it was not Askild's ridiculous attempts to acquire elegant manners that had an effect. It was not his imploring eyes when she occasionally caught him just standing around, staring. Nor was it his clumsiness or his stammered sentences. No, instead it was the things that he said when Bjørk wasn't present, when she happened to walk by a half-open door and in passing caught scraps of his conversations with Ejlif, remarks out of context that she had to complete for herself. She was surrounded by suitors, but she felt that no matter who she

33

chose, she would be forever chained to the patrician villa on Kalfarveien.

Late one night, when she passed Ejlif's room and heard parts of a conversation that smouldered with distant ports, sea foam, and tobacco smoke, she stopped in the hallway and stood there, utterly spellbound by the world that opened before her. Bjørk wondered how this young man, whom she and her sister Lina had dubbed 'Mad Askild' and 'the Silent Crackpot', could possess such depths. How could he be well-versed in the physical arts of love when he was so hopeless in a social setting that he couldn't even manage to compliment her on her dress without stammering and blushing? Soon she began sneaking out of bed at night, after her mother had gone to sleep and her father had shut himself up in his study. She would hover around Ejlif's room where a narrow strip of light crept out into the hallway along with fragments of tales from foreign shores.

The next time Askild spilled elk stew on the table, Bjørk put her hand on his arm and said, 'Never you mind, Askild. I'll take care of it.'

Askild muttered 'thank you' – it was the only thing he could think of to say, though Bjørk wished he would say something more to her. But Askild promptly clammed up, and that was how Bjørk slowly fell in love with his invisible self, while he, in turn, fell in love with all that was visible about her.

It was during this period that he gradually began dabbling in smuggling and black-market activities. During the summer holidays when he went out to sea, Askild, like the rest of the crew, had become accustomed to bringing home tax-free goods. At first just for his own use, but one day a sailor told Askild about a speakeasy called the Merry Circus Wagon, and he showed him how to hide 10 litres of whisky in the bottom of a lifeboat. That's when Askild slowly began to envision opportunities.

The next time he returned home from sea, he sold his secret cargo for fifty kroner. After the break with his parents, this was a much-needed cash injection for his ailing finances. But to make a real difference, fifty kroner once a year wouldn't be nearly enough. Askild sauntered around town as he hatched big plans for his future, and that very evening he sought out the red-haired sailor who had shown him how to hide the 10 litres of alcohol in a lifeboat. 'The Russian', who had been given that name because of his Russian heritage, welcomed him warmly, and they spent several hours together in their cups before Askild came out with his idea.

'You're crazy,' replied the Russian when Askild presented his plans. 'Why should I risk it?'

Askild smiled. There was plenty of money in it for both of them. 'Trust me,' he said, and that would be his mantra for the next couple of years.

'But where are you going to sell it all?' asked the Russian sceptically.

'Leave it to me,' Askild went on, since he didn't yet know who exactly was going to buy the smuggled goods. In general, the details of the plan weren't nearly as fully thought out as he led the Russian to believe. A month later, when the freighter sailed into harbour, Askild was standing on the dock, on the lookout for his new business partner, who was supposed to deliver seventeen bottles of rum, sixteen bottles of whisky, and twenty-one bottles of aquavit that had been across the equator and back, plus a considerable quantity of cigarettes. The fact that the Russian had drunk roughly a third of the alcohol and sang so loudly that everyone turned to stare was not exactly part of the plan. Even so, Askild made a small profit. When the ship again sailed into harbour a month later, the Russian had once again drunk a good share of the alcohol. Almost half was missing, but this time Askild was not nearly as furious. The week before he had made a deal with Erik Redbeard, a Swedish Finn with Danish roots, who was going to help Askild set up a more reliable business venture. Six weeks later, when Erik Redbeard put into port, Askild's customer base had been expanded to the Evening Room, which paid a better price than the Merry Circus Wagon, as well as the Meeting Place.

One of the first things that Askild bought with his money was an elegant suit. It never impressed Pappa Thorsten, and Bjørk, who was used to seeing that sort of attire, looked right through it in order to catch sight of Askild's invisible self.

Once in a while Askild would see his father's ship, which was no longer called the *Katarina* but rather the *Amanda*, when it put in at the Fortress wharf. Pappa Niels, with his grey hair gleaming in the morning sun, would be standing on the bridge – now slightly hunched over and no longer as terrifying as back when Askild was a child – while Askild's mother Randi would be waiting, as always, on the wharf along with his sister Ingrid and her young son, who had been named for her father and was now called Niels Junior or simply Applehead.

Askild never acknowledged his parents' presence. For many years their only communication consisted of a small monthly sum, discreetly delivered in a brown envelope by a maid. For safety's sake Mamma Randi had printed *To Askild* on the outside of the envelope. But instead of considering this monetary helping hand as the ultimate evidence that he was still his parents' son, he regarded it more as a monthly humiliation, which he, by God, was forced to sign for with the words *sum received on this day and this month, Askild*. And the maid would then take the receipt back to his mother.

But they shouldn't think that he was going to come crawling back to beg forgiveness just because one November night in 1937 he had brought a girl home to his attic room, where, the next morning, Mamma Randi had surprised her as she was putting on her knickers. And for the last time in her life Randi would scream so loud that it echoed through the whole house: 'Just wait until Pappa hears about this!'

A month later, when Pappa Niels returned home from sea – the black book was no longer in use, but Randi could remember the smallest details – Askild was given a choice: either apologize to his mother or move out. And since Askild, at the age of twenty-three, felt that he had already apologized enough in his short lifetime, he shouted, 'Damned if I will!' right in Pappa Niels's face. His father then took out the belt from the cupboard – it was so pathetic. Askild was a head taller than he was and ready to fight to the finish. Only the intervention of Mamma Randi had stopped Askild from committing violence against his own father. And God only knew what the maid had thought as she stood with her ear glued to the parlour door while Mamma Randi howled and Pappa Niels raced between the furniture with a furious Askild at his heels.

The next day Askild moved into a room in the home of Captain Knutsson's widow, and the silent war of nerves, which would last seven years, six months, and eleven days, began.

When Askild was unexpectedly called before the draft board in 1939, he bribed the doctor with a carton of cigarettes and two bottles of aquavit and was then classified as *unfit for military service*. Afterwards he walked down the street, whistling, and wandered around Fisketorget, the harbour marketplace where bright salmon, coalfish, and crabs glittered in the sunlight. He had a clear sense that something big was in the offing, which turned out to be true: the German blitzkrieg began against Poland, Soviet troops invaded Finland. And Askild was soon to become a very prosperous man.

He turned and continued towards the Kalfaret district to tell Ejlif about the fortunate outcome of his draft board examination, but when he arrived, Bjørk was standing on the garden path, in the process of putting on her white woollen gloves. 'Ejlif's not home,' she said, 'and I'm going out for a walk.' She was about to add some snide remark but changed her mind and headed down to the road while Askild remained on the garden path. When she reached the garden gate, she turned around and said, 'Are you coming, or were you just planning to stand there all day?'

That was the first time the two of them were alone together, except for those occasions on Kalfarveien when they happened to spend a few silent moments in each other's company. At eighteen, she was five years younger than Askild, and her fascination with him was more marked by childish curiosity than by any feelings of ardour. As they walked, she was overwhelmed by the physical sensation that he was observing her, but each time she glanced at him, Askild had his eyes fixed on the ground. He looked like someone who was afraid of stumbling, and Bjørk couldn't help being slightly puzzled by all the contradictory impressions she received from him.

After they had walked for half an hour, they reached the cemetery, and stopped in front of a memorial to her grandfather Rasmus. More than seventy years earlier, in the late 1860s, Rasmus had left Nordland behind to travel to Bergen, where he founded the family shipping business. And it was here that Bjørk, after she had finished telling Askild about Rasmus Svensson – also called Rasmus Fang because of his business methods – stood on tiptoe and kissed Askild on the cheek. That was all that happened. They didn't say another word about it. Twice Bjørk tried to pump Askild for information about the sea, but Askild answered evasively. It started snowing, and Bjørk made a snowball and threw it at the back of Askild's neck, which made him laugh and tell her that he had been rejected for military service. After that he clammed up again, and they walked back in silence. Bjørk had the awful suspicion that she was boring him, while Askild had a clear sense that today was his lucky day. When they once again stood in front of the house on Kalfarveien, he straightened his shoulders and took Bjørk's hand. She gave him a quick smile and then ran up the garden path, while Askild trudged home to his lodgings at the widow Knutsson's.

The following Thursday Askild again stood in front of the villa on Kalfarveien, wearing the dark frock coat he had bought with his smuggling money. It wasn't long before Bjørk came down the path, pulling on her white woollen gloves. They took exactly the same route they had taken the week before, stopping in front of Rasmus's grave where the trees swayed in the wind. And there they swiftly kissed before setting off back home. They would often exchange only a few words, but each week over the next couple of years they would walk the same route and repeat the same rituals, which slowly gave them a sense of having a shared history.

From 1939 onwards, not a single week did Askild neglect to show up at precisely three thirty in front of the patrician villa on Kalfarveien. All the while, Norway was invaded by the Germans, the battle of Trondheim sent shock waves through the whole country, and ration stamps and a scarcity of goods became a fact of life. Pappa Thorsten hastily reorganized his freighters so that they now operated a shuttle service between England and the free world. And after the invasion, Askild's father's ship the *Amanda* was downgraded to a passenger ship with specific destinations in the turbulent areas of northern Norway.

When war came to Norway in 1940, the market exploded, and even though shipping was suspended so that the only Norwegian vessels coming into harbour were passenger ships and fishing boats, Askild immediately found new ways of supplying the thirsty speakeasies. The Russian knew a man on Big Sotra Island who could deliver large quantities of home-made aquavit, and Erik Redbeard had a brother-in-law on Tysnes Island who could provide fake labels and the required tax stamps.

In this way Askild eventually became a wealthy man.

Every two weeks he would sew a small fortune into his mattress in his rented room on Håkonsgaten. The fact that his smuggling activities were developing into a risky business was something that only occurred to him whenever he woke in the night with sweat on his brow. For a few crazed moments he would consider covering his tracks and not showing up when the next ship came into port. But this feeling would last, at the most, only until the first rays of sunshine seeped in through the gap between the curtains on Håkonsgaten.

Those first years of the war were good for Askild. The bolder he behaved during his weekly walks with Bjørk, the more smuggling and black-market activities he would set in motion – and his plans for the future became even more grandiose. Quietly he was still slaving away at his books, studying under his reading lamp the framework and construction of ships. He found unused rooms, false walls, structural parts that could be pulled down and put back up in a matter of a few hours with the help of a red-eyed but no longer singing Russian, or Erik Redbeard, who, like Askild, preferred to work in silence. Askild had never before been shy about spending lavishly, but now that his income was growing in direct proportion to the destruction going on in Europe, he became more frugal, not to mention miserly. And he sewed almost all his money into the mattress on Håkonsgaten, with the vague dream that one day, after he married Bjørk, he would use the money to build a house on the outskirts of town.

Bjørk knew nothing about the house on the outskirts of Bergen or about Askild's smuggling activities. To the great amusement of her sister Lina and the doting Doctor Thor Gunnarsson, she was still capable of making fun of Askild whenever he wasn't actually present. She would imitate his imploring eyes and his clumsy movements. It was so easy for her to impersonate his unrefined accent. But on Thursday afternoons, when she went out to the garden path and saw Askild standing there in his dark frock coat, she would be seized by a feeling of having betrayed him.

Askild had grown pale during this time. He slept only a few hours each night because so much of his energy was spent studying or smuggling. Eventually Bjørk stopped making jokes at his expense. Instead she would sit in silence and stare into space whenever the topic of conversation was the comical son of the first mate. 'Bjørk is sulking,' Lina would then say as she gave Doctor Thor a resigned look.

'I wonder what the little miss is thinking about?' he would reply. Shortly afterwards they would start playing a rhyming game, the point of which was to guess what Bjørk was thinking, until Thor tied a handkerchief over his eyes and began looking for Bjørk's good humour under cushions and rugs.

'Just stop it!' shouted Bjørk when he bent down to see if her good humour was hiding under the cushion she had propped behind her back. 'You're driving me crazy!'

But Lina urged the keen young doctor to keep going. They started talking in riddles that were supposed to arouse Bjørk's curiosity. When Thor, with the elegance of a magician, fished a shiny five-øre coin from one of her ears – 'so that's where her good humour was hiding' – Bjørk couldn't help laughing, even though she was furious at Lina and annoyed with Thor. Bjørk told the doctor that he should try to get a job with a circus, and Thor solemnly proclaimed that if that was her wish, he would do it at once.

One evening not long after this, Thor invited Bjørk out to the garden under the birch trees and told her that he had plans to build a house. He had clearly been drinking. The sweet scent of cognac and eau de toilette rose up from his jacket, enveloping him in a melancholy cloud. The light green leaves gleamed in the last light of day as, arm in arm, they walked among the white tree trunks. Bjørk felt flattered when Thor asked her how she thought the house should look, and for fun she began listing the various rooms that she thought a young doctor might need: 'A consulting room, a waiting room, a laboratory—'

Thor smiled amiably as Bjørk went on to list a living room, a parlour with a fireplace, and a bedroom. He urged her to continue. 'An operating room!' said Bjørk with a laugh. 'And a lot of children's rooms!' Only then, as she noticed his expression, did she realize they weren't talking about a house but about the future. Bjørk cast an anxious glance up at the big windows of the second floor, where Lina was standing and watching them. Without looking at Thor, Bjørk managed to stammer that she wanted to go inside, but Thor held her back.

'Just tell me what you think,' he said. He reached out a hand to grab hold of her arm and pulled her a bit closer.

'Hey!' cried Bjørk. 'Let go of me!' But her cry only served to make him tighten his grip, and he leant forward to kiss her. With a swift motion, she tore herself free, which caused a ripping sound. And there stood Doctor Thor Gunnarsson with a piece of Bjørk's dress in his hand.

For a moment he seemed utterly hypnotized by the scrap of white fabric, but then he stared straight ahead and with a weary look on his face exclaimed: 'Damn it all.' Bjørk assured him that it would undoubtedly be a lovely house, but right now she was freezing and wanted to go in.

Back inside, Bjørk had decided not to say anything about Thor's behaviour; then she caught sight of her family, who had gathered around the coffee table, looking at her with anticipation. She realized that they had all been informed of her conversation with Thor. Without thinking, the words 'he made indecent overtures out in the garden' burst out of her mouth.

'Good gracious, Bjørk,' exclaimed Mamma Ellen, casting a glance at her husband Thorsten, who opened his mouth to offer a few conciliatory remarks while inwardly cursing his daughter, but the words got stuck in his throat.

'He tore my dress when he tried to kiss me,' Bjørk went on, giving her father an angry look. 'If I hadn't resisted, he might have started swinging his you-know-what.'

'What's that?' Mum asks when I come back to the living room and set a big glass on the table in front of Grandpa Askild.

'Er,' I mumble, feeling weak at the knees, 'it's beer.'

Mum gives the glass a strange look and starts to cough because she's smoking a cigarette, which she's not used to. My sister Stinna and my cousin Mia are out in the kitchen, giggling. That's how the job was divided up: Mia peed into the glass, Stinna added some beer to disguise the taste, and then I had to do the dirty work because I'm better at lying. Mum says that the worst thing you can do is lie. Mia says that I can tell all sorts of lies without even blinking. Grandma Bjørk thinks that I just have a lively imagination, while Grandpa Askild says that I'm as full of shit as

44

an old privy. Mum, on the other hand, never thinks I'm lying. Even so, she keeps staring at that glass. 'What an odd colour!' she exclaims, reaching out her hand towards it.

'It's Askild's beer,' I tell her stubbornly. 'He left it in Stinna's room.' Askild can't remember anything about a glass of beer in the other room. Quickly I grab the glass before Mum can pick it up. I put it down on the other side of Grandpa, where Mum can't reach it.

'Here you are, Grandpa,' I say. 'I'm sorry I called you an idiot.'

Askild's face lights up. 'That's my boy!' he says, pinching my cheek affectionately, which really hurts, but I don't say a word.

'All right then. Cheers!' says Grandpa and he raises the glass to his lips. He's just about to take a big gulp and the girls out in the kitchen are giggling loudly, when all of a sudden he stops. My whole body goes cold because I'm afraid that he can smell Mia's pee.

Not a sound is heard from the kitchen.

Grandpa Askild gives me a solemn look.

'How old are you now?' he asks.

I tell him I am ten. He smiles sweetly, and then it comes. 'Well, that means you're old enough to taste your grandfather's beer.' He puts the glass with Mia's pee right under my nose, spilling a little on his fingers. 'Come on, take a swig,' he says, laughing.

'Ugh, no! I don't like beer,' I shout, but before I know it, Grandpa grabs me by the scruff of the neck and forces the glass to my lips. When I take a breath, I get a big, warm mouthful of the stuff. It tastes salty and slightly bitter, and it makes me cough.

'Askild!' cries Mum, when she sees my expression. 'That's enough.'

Askild laughs out loud.

'Stop tormenting the boy,' exclaims Grandma Bjørk, but that only draws a scornful snort from Askild, who has no intention whatsoever of letting his wife dictate his actions. He leans back in his chair, raises the glass once again to his lips, and downs the whole beer in one gulp. Then the expression on his face changes; his smile freezes, and the furrows on his forehead deepen so that he ends up looking like a baboon. For a moment it seems as if he's going to say something, but he changes his mind and sets the empty glass back on the table without a sound.

Two seconds later the girls out in the kitchen explode with laughter. They scream and howl and double over, holding on to each other. Grandpa Askild casts a puzzled glance towards the kitchen and has no idea what's going on. He shouts to them that they should go to bed; it's late, for God's sake . . . The girls, still giggling, disappear into their room, while I stay where I am in the living room, completely stunned. I drank my cousin's pee! I have no idea what to do with myself.

When I slink back to Stinna's room, Mia puts her hand up to her mouth, trying to stifle a laughing fit.

'Here he is!' shouts Stinna with enthusiasm. They both collapse on to the floor, where they writhe with laughter, practically sobbing. 'Blech! He actually drank it!' I'm just about to leave when Mia sits up and snickers. 'That was damn good, Asger. He didn't notice a thing! Ha ha!'

I've turned out to be the hero of the day, although a rather unfortunate one, but still a hero who has sacrificed himself for the cause. 'That's what they did during the war too,' says Stinna. And for the rest of the evening, the girls look at me with equal parts awe and disgust – until two hours later, that is, when Grandpa Askild crashes to the living-room floor and we forget all about my heroism.

In early May 1943, when Askild received his engineering certificate, he put on his best suit, went to get a shave from the barber, who nicked his face twice because Askild couldn't sit still, and then continued out along Strandkaien. A short time later Askild knocked on the door of Shipowner Svensson's office on C. Sundtsgaten to ask for permission to announce his engagement to Bjørk. The first reaction was a paralysing silence. Thorsten drank his coffee, spilling a good deal of it on a stack of papers. Then he gave Askild a congenial smile and asked whether Bjørk, in that event, was supposed to live in a rented room belonging to Captain Knutsson's widow?

Askild, who had been convinced that his degree certificate would sweep aside all final obstacles, stood there as if frozen. But the recalcitrant shipowner jumped up from his chair and offered Askild a seat. Thorsten then called for his secretary, who served them big glasses of sherry. He opened his desk drawer and took out a cigar box made of reindeer hide, cut off the ends of two cigars and stuck one of them into Askild's gaping mouth. Then he leant back comfortably in his chair, congratulated Askild on finishing his degree, and began asking him about his future plans and job prospects. It shouldn't be hard for him to find a position, a young ship's engineer and mechanical engineer like him, with plenty of guts and his heart in the right place. 'You should go to Oslo. There are opportunities in Oslo.' Then he launched into a long monologue about flowers. The world was full of flowers, he said – roses, hyacinths, why, even Nordland was teeming with flowers. Bjørk was as good as promised to Doctor Gunnarsson, and he wasn't somebody they wanted to disappoint. Besides, Pappa Thorsten had contacts in Oslo. He knew several people who would be happy to hire a young engineer with such fine credentials, so why get stuck with the first flower he happened to encounter along the way?

Half an hour later, when Askild once again stood outside on C. Sundtsgaten, he was feeling small and weak-kneed. He was twenty-eight years old and had just passed his final exam with honours. A small fortune was hidden inside his mattress on Håkonsgaten, keeping him warm at night, and yet he had just been thrown out like a beggar. For a brief moment he felt an urge to take his degree out of his inside pocket and tear it to pieces. But then he decided instead to show these Nordland peasants that they couldn't get rid of Askild Eriksson so easily. And he decided to go straight to the patrician house in Kalfaret. No sooner had he stepped inside the door than the news arrived that one of Pappa Thorsten's ships had been sunk by the Germans.

'Message for Fru Svensson, the shipowner's wife!' shouted a sixteen-year-old boy who had run all the way from the harbour office. 'The *Ingrid Marie* has gone down off Plymouth.' And then he bent down, gasping for breath. 'The first officer was rescued, the captain has drowned, seven crew members are reported missing, eight were saved by British authorities. Excuse me, Fru Svensson, but could I have a glass of water?'

Shortly after that, Thorsten showed up and rushed

through the house in confusion with sweat on his brow and all manner of curses and oaths pouring from his lips. Mamma Ellen was more composed. 'We still have six other ships, Thorsten. Calm down.'

'It's all falling apart!' shouted Thorsten. 'Everything's falling apart. It's impossible to do business under these circumstances!'

'And what about the captain?' he groaned. 'And the crew – those poor families!'

'Let me take care of that,' replied Ellen, and she took the list of crew members out of the hands of the groaning Thorsten and disappeared out of the door.

By the time she returned, it was already dark. Pappa Thorsten had withdrawn to his study, where he was sitting in silence, staring straight ahead. The rest of the family sat in the living room, listening to the radio along with Doctor Thor Gunnarsson. Askild had been there all day, but he hadn't had a chance to talk to either Ejlif or Bjørk about his visit to their father earlier that morning. They ate supper in silence. Doctor Thor and Askild were both at the table, but no one uttered a word until Pappa Thorsten said, 'I need to talk to Askild.' Bjørk watched in surprise as the two men went into the study, and then she gave Doctor Thor a little teasing smile. Inside the study, which was decorated with ship blueprints and framed photographs of the seven ships, Askild was invited to sit down. No sherry was served, and not one kind word crossed Pappa Thorsten's lips. With a grave expression, he looked at Askild, who still had his new degree in his inside pocket.

'I think you know what this is about, Askild,' said Thorsten. 'We don't want to see you here again.'

That was all. Askild was shaken. He sat on the leather

chair across from Thorsten and couldn't believe his ears.

'Why not?' he asked.

Thorsten insinuated that surely Askild knew quite well what the answer to that was. And besides, he had enough problems right now and he didn't think Askild wanted to create any more. When Thorsten started to get up, Askild managed to stammer that wild horses couldn't stop him from seeing Bjørk. Thorsten, who didn't think there was anything more to discuss, asked him to leave, preferably in a discreet manner. He opened the door and shepherded Askild out of the study.

'Askild is leaving now,' he informed the others as they passed the parlour.

Out in the hallway, they very nearly came to blows. 'You Nordland rabble!' shouted Askild. 'You damned peasants!'

Doctor Thor stood up and went out to tell Askild to behave decently. But Askild told him to shut up or he'd end up with a punch on the nose; yes, he would. 'Damn it all and to hell with you,' he shouted, his footsteps pounding swiftly down the stairs of the patrician villa on Kalfarveien that early evening in May 1943. The birds were singing. Askild couldn't believe what had just happened and in all the confusion he had forgotten his jacket. He reached his room in Håkonsgaten and, feeling saddened, threw himself on the bed. He couldn't understand how this day, which had started with such promise, had turned out so disheartening. He had just decided to go down to the Merry Circus Wagon to drown his sorrows when Widow Knutsson knocked on the door.

'I've told you that I won't have any girls in the room, but since she's the daughter of Shipowner Svensson and all, well, only five minutes, Askild, and then she has to leave.'

Fru Knutsson was about to close the door when she stopped and gave Askild an inquisitive glance, adding: 'She says you forgot your jacket.'

After coffee, when Pappa Thorsten had withdrawn to his study to pace back and forth like a lion in a cage, Bjørk had slipped out of the kitchen door with Askild's jacket under her arm. She practically ran the whole way over to Håkonsgaten and now, for the first time, she stood in Askild's room, which she had pictured so often in her mind. She was a little disappointed, she had to admit, by its shabbiness: a bed, a desk, a few bookshelves, and a couple of nondescript-looking sacks in one corner, which immediately aroused her curiosity. 'What's in those sacks?' she asked.

'Nothing,' said Askild, moving to block her view. 'Just junk. A bunch of old junk.'

Bjørk wanted to take a closer look at those sacks, but then she remembered why she had come. With great ceremony she handed over his jacket before throwing herself into his arms. Bjørk couldn't understand what had come over her father. 'He's not usually like that,' she said, adding that it would undoubtedly pass. 'Just wait and see. He's bound to change his mind.'

'I'm not so sure about that,' said Askild, and he told her that he was considering leaving Bergen. 'You could come with me,' he added. 'We could run off together.'

For a brief moment, it all seemed as easy as that; 'But honestly,' Bjørk replied, 'how would that really be possible?' A newly minted engineer without a job or a single øre of income. And these were not the best of times, after all. The *Ingrid Marie* had been sunk by the Germans, and what would happen next?

'Don't worry about all that,' said Askild with a smile. In a couple of months he was going to be a rich man, but Bjørk couldn't interpret his vague hints as anything more than an expression of childish fantasies.

Askild decided to tell her the whole story. He took a deep breath. A blissful expression, which Bjørk mistook for lust, slid across his face.

'This mattress,' he whispered secretively, pointing to his bed where a small fortune had gradually collected, 'can make us forget all our problems.'

But when he urged her to go over and feel the mattress, it was too much for Bjørk. 'Askild!' she exclaimed, casting a nervous glance at her watch. It had been exciting to come and visit him, but now she had to go. 'I'll see you on Thursday, all right?' she whispered. 'At the foot of Kong Oscarsgaten. Don't wait in front of the house.'

But Askild insisted on seeing her home. She reluctantly accepted, and they walked most of the way in silence. Askild gave up the idea of saying any more. Some other day he would tell her the whole story.

Later, when he returned to Håkonsgaten, Widow Knutsson was still upset. 'This has got to stop, Askild,' she said. 'Two visits on one evening, and the man is drunk. He stinks like a pub! Five minutes, and then he has to leave.'

'Who is it?' asked Askild in bewilderment.

'He says his name is Karl.'

In Askild's room sat the Russian, waiting to tell him how they could steal a shipload of lumber from the Germans and then sell it back to them for a staggering price.

'It's easy as pie,' he exclaimed. 'I've already done it twice.'

Why the Russian would now need Askild's help, when

he'd already done it twice on his own, failed to rouse Askild's suspicions. He was too eager to make more money.

'Damn it!' he snarled three days later when he saw the German guards. 'You didn't say anything about them!'

The Russian had to admit that the Germans, after the two previous thefts, had assigned extra manpower to guard the lumber supply. 'But we can do it. Trust me.'

'Oh my God!' Askild later groaned when he caught sight of the shadowy figure that the Russian had struck on the head with a bottle. An unconscious German soldier was lying on the ground while a dark fluid seeped out of the back of his head. 'Is he dead?' moaned Askild. 'Did we kill him?'

'Of course not,' snapped the Russian. 'He just blacked out. Calm down. Take it easy.'

'Hurry up, for God's sake!' They could hear footsteps in the distance, and the Russian raised the bottle in the air again. But no one showed up, and the docks were once again silent. From far off came the sound of the crashing waves and the lazy sighing of the wind.

Askild and the Russian concentrated on their work, using a crane that the Russian had rounded up. At last they had the entire cargo loaded on to a rusty old tub named the *Karen*, and moved off into the night. Later they docked at a remote wharf, where they covered the cargo with a tarp and left it behind, swiftly slipping back into town as the birds began to sing from the rooftops. 'We'll wait at least two weeks before we sell it,' Askild insisted. And when they went into the Merry Circus Wagon to celebrate a successful first venture with breakfast and home-brewed aquavit, all their worries had melted away.

After the theft, Askild and Bjørk met two more times at the foot of Kong Oscarsgaten. They took their familiar route but no longer kissed each other in front of Rasmus Fang's grave. From the day that the *Ingrid Marie* was sunk by the Germans, the grave had been excluded from their route by silent agreement. On their first walk, Askild was in high spirits, assuring Bjørk that everything was going to work out. Several times he mentioned leaving Bergen, and with ambiguous phrases assured her that he had the whole situation under control.

The following week he was a changed man. He seemed distracted, and when Bjørk asked him what was wrong, he shouted, 'My damn ear is bothering me!' Otherwise he barely said a word, nor did he listen to what she was saying.

'I've tried to talk to my mother,' Bjørk explained. 'She also thinks that it's just a matter of time before Pappa changes his tune.' When Askild didn't respond, she pinched his arm and cried, 'Are you listening to anything I'm saying?'

And that prompted Askild to nod. 'Of course I am,' he grumbled.

'I'm not so sure about that,' she said. Afterwards they continued on in silence. When they had been walking for a while, Bjørk said that maybe they ought to go back, and Askild turned as if on command and followed her back to Kalfarveien. There he hastily kissed her goodbye before she continued up the path to the villa with the familiar sensation that she had bored him. And she didn't know that two years and twenty-seven days would pass before she saw him again.

The next week he didn't show up.

Bjørk waited for two hours at the foot of Kong Oscarsgaten. Suddenly she thought about those sacks in Askild's room, the dark circles under his eyes, and the new suit he had been wearing. She couldn't really add everything up. It all merged together into a strange feeling that sent cold shivers down her spine. She waited another fifteen minutes, but that merely served to link Askild's ambiguous phrases about his future and his spectacular financial situation with what she was thinking. *No*, she told herself, *there's no reason to panic.*

Yet she didn't go back to Kalfarveien. Instead, she began walking down towards Fisketorget. By the time she reached Torgallmenningen she had started to hurry, and at Ole Bull's Square, she set off running. At the corner of Håkonsgaten, her shoes skidded out from under her and she banged her knee on a cobblestone and scraped one hand when she tried to break her fall. When she reached Widow Knutsson's house, she was so out of breath that she couldn't utter a single word. She knocked five times before Fru Knutsson yelled, 'What now!' and tore open the door with a fierce look on her face. Then she broke into a mournful wail.

'They've taken him away!' she shouted. 'They arrested him last night. And that poor Herr Karl. It's true that he stank enough for a whole pub, but to shoot him down like that, just like a dog! Smuggling!' She put her hand to her forehead. 'Smuggling in blessed Peter's old workroom, Frøken Svensson. Well, I never! And to think you've been fooling around with the likes of him. A girl from such a respectable family. Think of your reputation!'

For a few seconds Fru Knutsson's wailing turned into a shrill snivelling. Then she exploded again.

'Those mongrels!' she shouted right into Bjørk's pale face. 'They have no respect for the property of decent people. They came in the middle of the night and went through everything.'

'Who?' asked Bjørk.

'The Germans,' groaned the widow, putting her hand to her forehead again. 'They took everything but the mattress. They even chopped blessed Peter's old worktable into kindling!'

Two hours after Grandpa Askild swills down a whole glass of pee in one gulp, he topples to the floor. His chair falls over backwards. He is red in the face and he's making an odd, rattling noise as he writhes around, clutching his stomach.

'Askild!' screams Grandma Bjørk, jumping to her feet. She stands there, suddenly frozen. Summoned by her scream, we come rushing into the living room.

'What happened?' asks my sister Stinna.

'What's wrong with him?' mumbles Cousin Mia.

'Why is he doing that?' I squeak, struck by a terrible suspicion.

'Grandpa has a stomach-ache,' Dad reassures us as he bends down over him. 'Say something, Pappa,' he says, slapping his face. 'Pappa, what day is it today? Can you remember?'

Grandpa utters another rattling sound and starts writhing around like a cod that has been pulled up on land to gasp in the sunshine.

'Pappa!' Dad shouts. 'Today is Sunday. Do you remember that?'

When Grandpa Askild doesn't respond, Mum runs to the telephone to call for an ambulance.

Uncle Harry pipes up and says that Askild should drink some water; it's good for ulcers. 'Just bring on the water,' he says. But when all of them crowd around to bend over Grandpa, trying to empty a whole pitcher of water down his half-open lips, I can't stand it any longer.

'There was pee in the beer!' I yell because I know what this is all about.

My sister gives me a sharp poke in the side because she doesn't think this is the right time for major confessions. 'Shut up,' she snarls, pinching my arm. 'Don't say anything.'

'Yes, but it's all my fault!' I go on.

Mum asks me what sort of nonsense I'm talking about. I shouldn't be standing around babbling about pee when Grandpa is seriously ill. Or else I should just go to my room.

Stinna nods in agreement. 'Get lost,' she whispers and shoves her elbow into my side. But I have no intention of leaving. I give her a shove back.

Fifteen minutes later the drive is filled with sirens and blinking lights that cast blue blotches over the pale face of my grandmother. Bjørk hasn't budged since Askild slipped off his chair, and it's only when the medics lift him up on to a stretcher and hurry down the hall with him that she wakes up. 'Good Lord!' Bjørk exclaims and rushes after them. 'I'm coming too!' She runs right past my fat aunt Anne Katrine and is allowed to sit next to the stretcher along with Dad. The doors are slammed shut in the back, and the ambulance roars off in a flurry of flashing blue lights. Back at the house I just manage to catch a glimpse of my fat aunt, who runs down to the basement to hide in the space under the stairs. I consider going down there to join her, but I don't dare do that any more, and Uncle Harry also thinks that it's long past our bedtime.

'Go to bed now, kids,' he says and waves us out of the room. 'Grandpa Askild is going to be fine.'

But we can tell from his expression that he's worried. He's almost as pale as Grandma Bjørk, and his voice sounds quite gruff. Mum pours him a cognac and tells him to take it easy.

'Did we kill Grandpa?' I whisper, in shock, when we're once again sitting on Stinna's bed and a strange silence has settled over the house.

No one answers.

PART TWO

PART TWO

Homeward Bound

I'M ON MY WAY home to Denmark. The train is soundlessly racing along. We have just passed Osnabrück when it occurs to me that the *stories* have also started to return home. For the past couple of months they have kept me awake at night, speaking to me via countless tongues. They have often been coloured by Grandma Bjørk's sweet whispers, which I remember from lying in bed in my childhood home. She would tell me stories for hours until my mother said it was time for me to go to sleep and would throw her out of my room. Grandma told me about Bergen, about all the naughty pranks the children played, and about her own summer holidays in Nordland, where the midnight sun gleamed like a big, pale pearl above the mountains and fjords. But other voices were also mixed in, and they all demanded their own version of the truth.

I actually held out for quite a long time. More than seven years have passed since I moved to Amsterdam in 1994, promising myself not to let old stories prevent new ones from emerging. At the academy I made sure that they

61

wouldn't sneak on to my canvases. I didn't want to paint the way Grandpa Askild did. So those stories went into hibernation. Even Doghead slid beneath the surface of my consciousness, with its invisible body of shame and guilt. The death of my father's fat sister Anne Katrine, my subsequent exile to the old homeland, and everything else that happened afterwards; all seemed to be forgotten until a couple of months ago when Grandma Bjørk broke our tacit agreement. After an interlude of ten years, she started bombarding me with stories again.

Dear little Asger, she wrote on a postcard that arrived at my flat in Amsterdam. *Somewhere in eastern Germany, your grandfather is running across a plain. I've begun to fear that he may never come back home.*

A few days before, in a phone conversation with my sister Stinna, I was forewarned. 'Things have got really bad with the old lady. She talks nonsense all the time. I've told Jesper that we should do something about it, but we can't get her to sell the house. Good Lord, that ramshackle old place that Grandpa mortgaged to the hilt.'

Stinna has never forgiven Grandma Bjørk for letting Askild's body lie in the bedroom for so long before they found him. Askild had started to smell. That was in 1997, almost five years ago.

'If the nursing home won't release her, she's going to have to sell the house. She's not exactly swimming in money,' I said in a subdued tone, because I know what Stinna's temperament is like.

'And that's the worst part! Here she is, a woman who never had a red cent because Askild always drank it all up, and suddenly she thinks that she's rolling in it,' shouted Stinna.

'Do you realize how bad things are?' she went on. 'Our old grandmother thinks she's a millionaire. She keeps on babbling about our inheritance that she buried somewhere or other—'

'Where?' I asked.

'Well, how inconvenient that she doesn't happen to remember where it's buried . . . Listen, you don't believe all that rubbish, do you? A secret treasure? A pot of gold at the end of the rainbow? Come on! And now she wants to send Jesper out with a shovel to look for it. And afterwards she wants me to pay off the mortgage on the house. She says that if Uncle Knut ever comes home from Jamaica, or if you come back from Amsterdam, that's where the two of you can live. Isn't that ridiculous? Who would want to live in such a dump?'

After I hung up, I felt worn out and confused. It wasn't often that I talked to my sister. I went back to my studio and cast a swift glance at the blank canvases. Soon all those old stories started jostling around in my head: the buried treasure, a legendary pot of gold at the end of the rainbow. Askild's smuggling money! Could it really be true?

All his life, Askild believed that the money had been taken by the Germans. After shooting the fleeing Russian and arresting my grandfather late one night in 1943, the Germans had forced their way into the home of Widow Knutsson on Håkonsgaten and ransacked the place. They smashed the desk belonging to the late Captain Knutsson, tore the bookshelves from the wall, and emptied the three sacks filled with smuggled goods. All the while Widow Knutsson stood in the doorway like a ghost, making little

63

whimpering sounds. But all they found were the three sacks, fifty or so labels and tax stamps, and nineteen Norwegian kroner, which Askild hadn't had time to sew into the mattress. Curiously, they didn't touch the mattress.

Back at the Bergen jail, they slapped Askild countless times in the face, wanting to know whether he was the one who had clobbered the German guard at the lumber-yard. But what were they talking about? Askild didn't understand any of it, he said. He was just helping the Russian unload some timber— Theft? He really didn't know anything about that— They asked him if he thought they were idiots, and Askild shook his head. No, of course not. 'But it wasn't me!' he bellowed when one of the Germans grabbed his balls and squeezed hard. Askild's deaf ear, which at that time had been screeching all week long, now switched over to a higher pitch, and he was nearly deaf when, hours later, he shouted: 'It was the Russian, for God's sake!' Everything went black, and for a moment the pain disappeared and a liberating weightlessness seized his body and carried him off into the dark.

After a week the anonymous interrogators finally decided they'd had enough of the criminal, and they shipped him off with a prison transport to Oslo. This wasn't exactly the way that Pappa Thorsten had imagined it happening, but in the long run, he did end up getting his way. Askild went to Oslo, and in the patrician house on Kalfarveien the daily routines were resumed: dinners in the bosom of the family, and card games in the evening. In Pappa Thorsten's opinion, an enchanting sense of calm settled over the household, until that calm was broken by an alarming pounding that made him leap to his feet.

'Message for Shipowner Svensson!' shouted a sixteen-year-old boy who had run the whole way from the office at the harbour. 'The *Jens Juul* has been sunk west of Land's End!'

'Again?' cried Thorsten. And then he grabbed his jacket and dashed down to the office, remarking bitterly that the world had gone mad. And while my maternal great-grandfather Thorsten was running through Bergen to get a more detailed report about the latest blow to the family empire, my paternal grandfather Askild was sitting in prison in Oslo, staring at the wall. The beatings had stopped. The purple bruises had turned yellow and disappeared. Under normal circumstances, he would have been sentenced to a certain number of years, but since there were imminent plans for a large transport of prisoners to Germany, Askild Eriksson could just as well be sent along with them.

'You won't get a single krone from me,' Pappa Thorsten remarked one afternoon when Bjørk told him that she had been given permission to visit Askild. All the same, the very next day she left for Oslo, took lodgings at an inn, and then didn't sleep a wink all night. She had permission for a half-hour visit at two thirty in the afternoon, but by nine in the morning she was already wandering restlessly through the Oslo streets. At eleven o'clock she started shopping. She bought herring, bread, and tobacco, which she wrapped up in a warm blanket along with a letter from Askild's mother, Randi, and a little note from herself. When the clock struck one, she decided to buy a new dress. She went to a dozen shops, and by the time she finally emerged on to the street again, wearing her new dress, it was later than she had thought. She hurried down Karl Johan's Gaten, but at the corner of Akersgaten, she suddenly started running, once again struck by a terrible feeling that grew even worse when she realized that she was lost. She had to ask several people for directions before she finally – at ten minutes to three – presented herself to the guard at the Oslo prison.

'I'm here to visit Askild Eriksson,' she panted as she placed her package on top of the small counter. The guard sat there for a full minute, immersed in his paperwork, before he deigned to give Bjørk the slightest attention.

'Now let me see,' he finally said, opening a folder to look inside. Then he once again raised his head and said, 'Askild Eriksson . . . No, my dear, that's not going to be possible. He's on his way to Germany.'

'What?' gasped Bjørk.

The guard went back to shuffling through his papers while Bjørk simply stood there, as if paralysed. The noise of lurching locomotives and railcars that were being shunted back and forth became mixed with the sound of her pounding heart. After a moment the guard patted her hand kindly and told her that there were plenty of excellent places in Germany where people could be rehabilitated if they happened to go astray.

The next evening, after Bjørk had returned to Bergen, yet another messenger arrived at the patrician villa on Kalfarveien. 'Message for Shipowner Svensson!' yelled the sixteen-year-old boy with sweat on his brow.

Later that night, as Pappa Thorsten sat in his study,

66

cursing, Bjørk sneaked over to Widow Knutsson's house. She drank tea with the widow in the parlour and then asked if she might have a moment alone in Askild's old room. *This mattress*, Askild had said two weeks earlier, *can make us forget all our problems*. A fleeting smile passed over Bjørk's lips. Then she pulled a big pair of scissors out of her pocket and slit open the mattress.

'Asger!' cried my big sister when she rang me the next morning, waking me up. 'You have to take some responsibility too. Can't you at least call her up and talk to her?'

'What?' I groaned because I wasn't used to her waking me twice in one week.

'I was thinking . . . Can't you come home for a while? Jesper and I will pay your way, and you can stay in our guest room. If you just talk to Grandma, I'm sure she'll come to her senses again.'

'I'll think about it,' I told her and hung up the phone.

A couple of months before Stinna began lobbying on the phone, Bjørk had started sending me mysterious messages. *I'm sorry, but I express myself not so good in Danish*, was the first thing she wrote to me, although she had lived in Denmark for forty years. At first I wasn't especially interested in her letters and postcards. They lay on the kitchen table for days before I could bring myself to read them. (The same thing had happened with letters from my mother.) But when I did finally start reading them, I was astonished to see how confused Bjørk was. Several times she called me Askild, other times Knut or Niels or Thor. I also noticed how she kept going back to the story

67

about my grandfather running across an eastern German plain.

I had no sooner hung up the phone before I happened to think about the time we almost killed Grandpa Askild with Cousin Mia's pee. On impulse, I punched in Stinna's number.

'You again?' she said. 'You're calling to say that you won't come home. Don't tell me that, Asger.'

'That's not it,' I replied. 'I just wanted to—'

'Bjørk is sick!' shouted Stinna. 'Don't you want to see your grandmother before she dies? There's something really wrong with her heart. How much more blunt do I have to be? Do you want me to spell it out for you? She's going to D – I – E, Asger. So you've got to come home and be responsible. I refuse to have everything dumped on my shoulders, like last time.'

'Something wrong with her heart?' I whispered. Grandma Bjørk hadn't mentioned anything about that. I didn't know what to say, and for a moment there was only a rushing sound in the receiver. Then Stinna regretted her tactics.

'I'm sorry. But won't you come home and talk to her? We miss you, you know, Sweetie-pie—'

'Sweetie-pie?' I said.

'I miss my little brother. Is there something wrong with that?' she shouted, and then once again she changed her tone of voice. 'Jesper can sleep on the sofa, and you can sleep in the bed with me. Like when we were kids,' she whispered with a laugh. 'Come on, you dope—'

I'm on my way home. Only slowly did it dawn on me that Grandma Bjørk was about to leave us. And her mysterious

68

messages were a way of calling me back before it was too late. After my conversation with Stinna, I sat down on the kitchen floor with Bjørk's postcards and brief letters spread out all around me. In the studio, my blank canvases gleamed. I should have paid attention to the warning signals: the blank canvases were babbling at me, making me extra sensitive to the continual pressure of the stories. Spread out around me on the kitchen floor lay fragments of our history. Disconnected episodes that all bore the mark of having been shaped by an ageing woman's confused thoughts. Anecdotes in which the names of the main characters kept changing places with each other. Tales in which the endings occurred in the wrong place, and the beginnings turned up where something had been definitively brought to a close. And as I sat there, sifting through all those pieces of paper, the old feeling of guilt began growing inside me. Ever since that summer when Knut came home from Jamaica, I've felt that I had a particular role in the misfortunes that finally made our family fall apart and scatter to the four winds. The idea of gathering everyone back together, not to mention the thought of my homecoming and the state in which I might find my grandmother, stripped me of all courage. I circled around the idea for several days until finally, this afternoon, I slammed the door to my flat and grabbed my suitcases to catch a train home, just as Stinna had decided I should do. I left behind a two-room flat, three-quarters furnished, along with fifty blank canvases and an unrealistic dream that I could make my living as an artist in Amsterdam. But right now, in this train that is rushing along soundlessly and has just passed Osnabrück, here I sit, the Bastard Boy, the Latchkey Kid, and the Liar, as Askild used to call me. And I'm toying with the idea that I've entered into some sort of secret barter agreement. In exchange for the blank canvases that I left behind in Amsterdam, new images have started popping into my head.

Meyer's Theatre

AFTER ALMOST TWO YEARS in Germany, Askild was going home. He was sitting in a white bus that belonged to the Red Cross. The Bernadotte Rescue Mission, which got Nordic prisoners out of the German camps before the final chaos of the war erupted, was in full swing. It was springtime in 1945, and flowers gleamed along the sides of the road. Cities that had been bombed to smithereens looked like a forest of scaffolding, in which only the load-bearing beams remained. Every once in a while it occurred to Askild that he really was on his way home. He was a free man who could stand up and get off the bus if he liked. But it had all happened so fast. First the evacuation from the release command unit at Buchenwald, then the arrival at the Scandinavian camp in Neuengamme, and suddenly yesterday the rumours that it was his turn next. Now, as he peered out of the window, everything slipped past like scenes from one of the films he used to watch as a young man in Bergen. That world seemed so alien now.

He had just noticed the screeching in his deaf ear when the bus stopped for a bathroom break. A couple of young children were standing at the edge of the road, staring with curiosity at the white bus as kindly nurses helped the weakest of the passengers out. The bus driver helped a dysentery patient over to the ditch and pulled down his pants for him. Askild, formerly a tall and broad-shouldered man, had been transformed into a skeleton. He weighed approximately half what he had before the failed scheme in Bergen. A nurse with big hips took Askild kindly by the arm and with a smile whispered something to him in Swedish that he didn't fully understand. Her touch made him dizzy, but then he abruptly pulled away from her. 'I'm not a baby,' he snarled, shuffling out of the bus.

'Watch out for the step!' cried the nurse as Askild's legs threatened to give way beneath him. 'Be careful,' she added before Askild fell. No one heard the soundless crack as Askild's left leg broke right above the ankle.

When they at long last crossed the border into Denmark, the whole world seemed different again. Here were no wounds from the war; no bombed-out cities. And each time the bus stopped, it was surrounded by crowds of shouting people. Askild, whose left leg was now wrapped in pieces of fabric and gauze, opened a window to take a rose from a girl who insisted on kissing him on the cheek. 'For all our heroes,' she whispered as she shook his hand.

The next moment she was shoved aside by three young men. 'What was it like down there?' they wanted to know. 'What were you in prison for?'

Thanks to Count Folke Bernadotte's Rescue Mission, my paternal grandfather survived. Askild escaped the death marches during the last days of the war, as he was now sailing across the waters of Øresund, which were clear and blue. In Sweden the landscape began to look familiar, but there were still several weeks before the war would end, and Askild was given quarters in Ramlösa, where he could have his leg tended to and get fattened up in the ward for malnourished prisoners. He ought to have felt relieved, but he didn't. Instead he started dreaming.

He began having those dreams that would torment him for the rest of his life. He dreamt about Herman Hemning, who had fled in the opposite direction when they ran away from Sachsenhausen together. It was Herman's terrified face that rode Askild like an incubus. Nothing else from their escape attempt. Not the bloodhounds that in the early morning hour came racing towards the tree he had climbed after his flight across that eastern German plain. Not the two uniformed figures, who more or less came sauntering across the plain, where the escaped prisoner could no longer get away. One of them was SS Rottenführer Meyer. The other was a mere private, a soldier he didn't know. Not even the dog that clamped its jaws around his ankle bothered him as much, or the blows he suffered from the rifle butts as they hurried him across the frozen hillocks of the plain, all the way up over a little slope to where two men were waiting. One of them was on his knees in the frost. He was battered and shaking with cold, just like Askild. The other man, yet another unfamiliar soldier, was standing with his gun pointed at the kneeling man's forehead. Askild was stunned when he realized that the man on his knees was Herman. All this time he had believed that Herman had reached safety, that he had managed to escape, since the bloodhounds had chosen to follow Askild's tracks.

'Let's see who has the greater instinct for survival,' Meyer proposed. 'A quick little duel. Or should we just kill both of them?' It's a dark story, and Askild never told us all the details, even though he always returned to the scene whenever he was drunk.

I imagine that yet another resounding NO grew inside Askild's belly. Meyer's shiny pistol gleamed in the dim light of the morning as two pairs of eyes stared at each other: Herman Hemning, who had run in one direction, and Askild, who ran the opposite way after they had come a certain distance from the camp, which they had fled together. 'Good luck, friend,' was the last thing they had said to each other. And now here they were, meeting again, beaten and shaking with cold; both of them prepared to fight for their lives in Herr Meyer's alternative theatre.

'Get going,' shouted Meyer.

'Los, ihr Schweinhunde,' shouted the private who was eager for some payback for a whole night of hard work.

Askild and Herman on an eastern German plain. For a brief moment each of them assessed his unexpected opponent, and Askild considered screaming his resounding NO at the face of SS Rottenführer Meyer, but he thought better of it. Instead he directed the NO at his former bedmate from Barracks 24, Herman Hemning, who had warmed him on cold nights and lifted his spirits with dirty jokes and cock-and-bull stories about growing up in Oslo's working-class neighbourhoods. Utterly terrified, Herman refused to strike out at Askild; he was already resigned to dying. 'No,' he whispered, 'no—' Then pistol shots began thundering over their heads. Herman took a

74

step forward and struck at Askild, who had long since prepared himself to fight. Askild avoided the punch and dealt Herman a decisive blow to the liver. Then he threw himself at him like a mad dog . . .

This was the moment when he always woke up. In the midst of the lunacy. He had been fleeing from bloodhounds, but now he had become a mad dog himself.

The day after Askild's arrival in Ramlösa, the nurse suggested that he write a letter home. He absentmindedly accepted the paper and pen without really knowing what he should write to Bjørk, his mother Randi, or his father Niels.

Later, when Askild handed a letter to the nurse, it was not addressed to his family in Norway but to Pork Face's mother in Oldenburg. He asked the nurse to send it at once, but she just gave him a suspicious look. 'Aren't you from Bergen?' she asked. 'What were you in prison for, anyway?'

'Nothing,' whispered Askild. 'But that faggot's mother should be told.'

'Faggot?' said the nurse.

'Yes,' he sighed.

The following week Askild wrote another letter, this time to Herman Hemning's wife in Oslo. But like the letter to Oldenburg, it was never sent.

Then came the liberation, and King Haakon VII and the Norwegian government returned from exile in England. But back home in Bergen, Askild's family still hadn't heard from him, not a single word, even though Pappa Niels had been pestering the authorities, and Bjørk had written letters to everyone she could think of. 'He probably died somewhere down there,' said Doctor Thor, but Bjørk told him not to talk like that.

'Is he ever going to come home?' Askild's little nephew Applehead asked his grandmother. And Mamma Randi replied that only God could know that. 'But is it true that he's a carpenter?' Applehead went on. He didn't know who his own father was, and for all practical purposes he lived with his grandparents while his mother, Ingrid, lived in a one-room flat in town. 'That's what they're saying down on the street. They say that he's a carpenter because he once clobbered a German on the head with a stick.'

'A carpenter?' said Mamma Randi. 'What sort of nonsense is that?'

'Askild!' shouted the nurse in Ramlösa as she leant over my listless grandfather. 'Get out of bed. Write a letter. Go home to your family. You can't spend the rest of your life here.'

And why not? thought Askild, giving her a vacant stare before he once again turned his back to her and retreated into himself. For two long years the image of Bjørk, wrapped in a rose-coloured blanket under the birch trees on Kalfarveien, had kept him alive, making him beat the terrified Herman Hemning to death on an eastern German plain and forcing him to climb out of the stinking latrine pit. But now, when he could finally go back as a free man, he simply refused to leave Ramlösa. The image of Bjørk in a bright birch-tree grove suddenly seemed to belong to a completely different life, one where Askild was young and naive, a boy with youthful dreams, a smuggler's dreams of wealth, sailing the high seas . . . No, Askild was in fact seriously considering staying in Sweden and starting all over again in a country where no one knew him. One day, when the terrified Herman Hemning did not keep Askild confined to his bed, he enquired about the possibility of staying. And the head doctor told him that it could be done. The following week Askild was given an address in Gothenburg where the doctor's brother-in-law lived. He might be able to help.

The next morning Askild sat on the edge of his bed, moving his foot up and down for half an hour. *Should I? Or shouldn't I? Yes or no?*

Then he went home to Bergen.

The Carpenter

KALFARVEIEN LOOKED exactly the same, but even at the train station people had started giving Askild strange looks. And when he limped up the garden path with the aid of his cane and knocked on the door of the house from which Pappa Thorsten, back at the beginning of time, had banished him, things didn't get much better.

'Is that you?' asked the astonished woman who opened the door and caught sight of the scrawny Askild. 'It's the Carpenter!'

'I'm an engineer, ma'am,' replied Askild, who couldn't remember ever having seen this woman before. 'I'd like to speak to Bjørk Svensson, please.'

'Well, I never!' she went on, staring with admiration at Askild. 'You certainly gave him a proper thump, that German dog.'

Naturally, Askild couldn't know that in his absence he had been given the nickname the Carpenter because of a news item in the paper about the unfortunate episode down at the harbour. 'Let's just cut out all this carpenter rubbish,' he whispered. 'Is she home?'

'No. Oh dear God, no,' exclaimed the woman. 'The Germans sank every last one of their ships, and then Herr Svensson had a stroke, the poor man. They live on Skivebakken now. They had to sell . . .'

Then, as Askild made a move to go, the woman said, 'Psst. So tell me, what was it really like down there?'

'Pure hell,' replied Askild as he headed down the garden path where he had once stood every single Thursday, waiting for Bjørk. A short distance away on Kalfarveien, he had to stop because his heart was galloping violently, and because he suddenly happened to think about his father. Had he too gone down with a ship? Impaled on a German torpedo somewhere in the Norwegian Sea? His left ear started ringing, and Askild considered going out to Skansen first to see his parents, but then he changed his mind. He set off again for Skivebakken as he pictured Bjørk sitting in a rocking chair in a draughty wooden house, staring straight ahead with a melancholy look on her face. But that was not at all what she was doing.

'Presto!' said Doctor Thor as he pulled a ten-øre coin out of Bjørk's ear. 'That's where her good humour was!'

Bjørk laughed loudly. Her gums no longer bled after she confided in Thor, who had immediately arranged for a daily vitamin supplement. She placed her hand on Thor's arm and told him to show her the trick with the hat. The trick with the hat wasn't something that was normally done in a parlour, but Pappa Thorsten was asleep on his sickbed, Mamma Ellen had gone into town, her sister Lina wasn't visiting, and as soon as the war was over her brother Ejlif had found a job at a sawmill in Børkersjø, so he had moved to Nordland.

'It takes a bit of preparation,' said Thor, and he slipped out into the hallway to get a hat as Askild was huffing and puffing like an old man, on his way up to Skivebakken.

'Abracadabra,' said Thor with a laugh, and he pulled a pair of white cotton knickers out of the tall hat, which Bjørk had first inspected for hidden spaces and loose flaps. 'And what do you say to that?' The trick with the hat was actually a pub joke. 'I wonder where your wife was last night?' asks the magician. Then he pulls the knickers out of the tall hat and exclaims, 'With the manager!'

Bjørk laughed so loudly that she didn't hear the faint knock on the door. 'Do it again,' she cried. And Doctor Thor said 'hocus pocus', as he knelt down in front of Bjørk, waving his hand in circles.

'Most people just go on in,' a little boy shouted to Askild, who opened the door and tiptoed into the hall. His whole body suddenly felt clammy. He couldn't hear a thing because of his bad ear, and he stepped inside the parlour just as Doctor Thor pulled the white knickers out of the hat for a second time, waving them right in front of Bjørk's nose. But to Thor's astonishment, instead of laughing, she screamed with terror at seeing Askild, who was so thin that he looked like the newspaper photos of European Jews that she had seen in *Bergens Tidende*.

'What the hell?' cried Thor, and in bewilderment he stuck the white cotton knickers into his inside pocket.

Bjørk stopped screaming, and a strange silence settled over the new house on Skivebakken. Then Askild turned around in the doorway, stubbed his big toe on the door sill, and left. He hurried down the road. Right now he just wanted to go home; he didn't want to listen to Bjørk, who came running after him. When she tried to tug on his arm, he even took a swing at her with his cane. Askild had had enough, and he wanted to go home to Skansen, although he hadn't been there for seven years.

'Askild! Where are you going?' shouted Bjørk. She followed him for a couple of hundred metres before she turned around and went back to the house on Skivebakken, while the little boy yelled to his pals, 'There goes the Carpenter! He's the one who clobbered that German!'

'What should I do?' whispered Bjørk when she got back to the house. Thor replied that now she was going to have to make a choice.

'So why not choose me?' he said and then cursed because he was tired of pulling rabbits out of his black hat, tired of waiting around and playing the well-educated clown. A dozen years had now passed since he saw Bjørk for the first time at a dinner given by the former shipowner and now quite demented Thorsten Svensson, who at that moment was drooling in his bed in the next room. Pappa Thorsten had heard the whole thing. *Choose Thor, choose Thor, choose Thor*, he wanted to say. But he had to make do with rocking restlessly in his bed because he couldn't get up and pound on the table, as the man he once was would have done.

Askild paused for a moment in front of the building in Skansen and looked up at the flat where his mother Randi was sitting and crocheting while his father Niels dozed in a rocking chair. The kids surrounding Askild had now swelled to a large group. 'Did you hit him hard?' they asked as they struck one another on the head with sticks to illustrate their question.

81

'Yes!' said Askild in a sudden burst of folly. And just for fun he swung his cane. 'I gave him a big thump. Ha!' The boys cheered with delight, but then Askild again happened to think about the unfortunate Russian who was shot down like a dog. He was the one, after all, and not Askild, who had knocked out the German soldier at the lumber-yard. 'Get lost, damn it,' he groaned, jabbing at the kids with his cane. 'Or else I'm going to beat you so hard that your mothers won't recognize you when you get home.'

'Yow!' shouted one of the boys. 'Yow! The Carpenter is fuming.'

'Yow! Wow!' they all started shouting as Askild shut the door behind him and struggled to make his way up to the third floor. From there, Mamma Randi could hear the shouts of 'yow' from the street below. 'What's all that noise?' she whispered to herself. She had just stood up to go over to the window when the door opened with a bang and in came her son.

'Askild?' Mamma Randi managed to whisper before she dropped her crocheting.

Pappa Niels leapt up from his rocking chair and ran past Randi to his son. But when he tried to take Askild in his arms, they bumped heads. It wasn't every day that two men in the Eriksson family gave each other a hug. Afterwards they rubbed their bearded cheeks against each other, and the first mate, now retired, muttered some incomprehensible words to his son, to whom he hadn't spoken for so many years.

'I'm back now,' said Askild after he had picked up his cane from the floor and sat down in the rocking chair. 'But don't ask me any questions.'

'No, of course not,' said Mamma Randi. And she ran over to the window to shout down to the boys on the street, telling them to run over to Fru Ibsen's place to give Ingrid and Applehead the news that Askild had come home. 'It's not every day that a mother's son returns from the dead,' she shouted as she was struck by a strange feeling that she had suddenly gone insane. Just to be on the safe side, she cast another glance at her thirty-year-old son, who was sitting in the rocking chair holding his cane like an old man in the afternoon light. 'That's right,' she yelled to the boys on the street. 'Oh yes, it's true all right!'

Then Ingrid came dashing through the door to throw her arms around Askild's neck, while Applehead stood in the doorway, staring with disappointment at this uncle who had come back home.

'Is *that* Askild?' he whispered, giving his mother a reproachful look. 'I thought he would be a lot bigger.'

Transformation

LATER THAT DAY, when Bjørk entered the flat in Skansen, only three sentences of any significance were exchanged between her and my grandfather.

'Well,' said Bjørk, placing her hand on Askild's arm, 'now he's left for the last time.'

'Who?' asked Askild.

'Doctor Thor,' replied Bjørk. 'Those tricks of his are really quite awful.'

With these words, Thor Gunnarsson, also known as the Dane because of his particular charm, disappeared from my family's official story. He had spent eleven years conjuring coins from Bjørk's enchanting little ears, and eleven years pulling rabbits out of his black hat, even though it was something else that he dreamt of pulling out to provoke jubilation. But unlike my grandfather Askild, he lacked that special kind of mystery when talking about himself or his past – the sort of mystery that makes room for other people's dreams. Askild, on the other hand, had acquired an aura of romance. An aura that would later become the putrid stench of alcohol and bitterness. But Bjørk did not know that as she sat in the parlour in Skansen, cautiously peering at the skeletal Askild. She was very anxious to tell him that she had actually gone to Oslo to visit him in prison.

'Let's not talk about that any more,' replied Askild, prompting a brief silence in the conversation, which Applehead, who had eventually got over his disappointment, decided to use to his advantage.

'So did you ever see him? Did you see Hitler? Did you?'

'Niels!' exclaimed Pappa Niels, and Applehead cast a frightened glance at his grandfather with the white hair and the big hands.

For a moment the threat hovered like a slap in the air, but then Askild intervened and said, 'No, but I've seen his bloodhounds, little Niels. I sure as hell have seen his bloodhounds.' Applehead stared with admiration at this strange uncle of his, about whom he had imagined so many different things. And gradually the rest of the family realized that Applehead was the only person in whom Askild was willing to confide. 'Stop pestering me,' became Askild's standard remark until his family finally gave up asking him anything; instead, they would get Applehead to do it.

'Go and ask Askild whether he was in Sachsenhausen the whole time,' the women would whisper out in the kitchen. 'Go and ask him why it took him so long to come back home. Go in and ask your uncle right now.' Applehead would march into the parlour to ask his uncle and then return to the kitchen to tell them that Askild had sat in shit up to his neck, and that he had apparently fed rat poison to Hitler's bloodhounds, but the dogs didn't like it. They liked Uncle much better.

'Sweet Mother of God!' was Mamma Randi's reply. After Askild's arrest, she had become a diligent church-goer, and every Wednesday she went to the nearby church to take part in the Bible circle for women with husbands at sea. It was conducted under the stern leadership of Dean Ingemann. It was also the source of her new habit of invoking the Virgin Mary. She was not Catholic; she had merely misunderstood the expression.

'What's going on out there?' they heard from the parlour. 'Can't we have a little peace around here? I'm trying to sleep.'

'Sorry, Askild, my dear,' whispered Mamma Randi as she went into the parlour to put a blanket over him so that he could have his afternoon nap. Suddenly she found herself humming the lullabies she used to sing to him when he was a little boy.

If it weren't for the fact that Applehead knew grown men couldn't cry, he later would have sworn that his uncle was crying right there in front of all of them as he sat in the rocking chair while Mamma Randi sang lullabies. And in the meantime, Bjørk stared absentmindedly straight ahead because Askild's homecoming hadn't turned out to be the homecoming of her dreams – even though after two nights she and Askild had slept together in his parents' bedroom while Pappa Niels and Mamma Randi slept in the guest room. During those first few months, nothing was too good for Askild. It was also taken for granted that they would be married as soon as he had enough meat on his bones to make a proper appearance in the wedding photos. Yet Bjørk felt, all the same, that something was missing.

On the first night they slept together, she had asked

Askild not to do you-know-what until the pastor had blessed them. Askild had nodded sombrely, and then he had merely lain down to go to sleep without attempting anything. But that wasn't the worst part.

The worst part was that he refused to tell her about his years in Germany, and so she had to make do with six-year-old Applehead's reports, which were quite disjointed, to put it mildly.

At the same time, there was so much that Bjørk was burning to share with Askild, including, for instance, the fact that she knew all about his smuggling activities. She had hidden the money at home in a box under her bed, and on quite a few occasions she tried to bring up the subject, but never with any luck. Askild didn't want to be reminded of his days as a big-time smuggler. He was so determined to make a new start and put everything behind him that he was in danger of forgetting how he had been struck with boundless yearning at the sight of young Bjørk, wrapped in a rose-coloured blanket, sitting under the birch trees on Kalfarveien.

In the weeks following his return home, he had very little urge to leave the flat in Skansen, but whenever he did, he was astonished by the mysterious transformation he seemed to have undergone. Boys flocked around him as if he were a returning hero.

'Here comes the Carpenter!' they would cry. 'Show us how you hit that German dog. Show us with your cane!'

Rumours about Askild Eriksson, the smuggler and criminal, had vanished like dew in the sun, and kindly looks were now directed at my grandfather. Admiring faces smiled at him whenever he walked around Bergen; proud nods and firm handshakes received him like a son and a liberator. 'Good day to you, sir. Welcome home, sir,' was on everyone's lips. It didn't take long before a friendly delegation of three men from the now freely patrolling home guard knocked on the door in Skansen to reward my gaping father with a Milorg armband, a badge of honour among the Resistance fighters, in recognition of his patriotic character and unselfish daring.

Over the course of the summer, two jug-ears began to stir. Two jug-ears that fluttered like wings and gave Bjørk an odd rumbling in her stomach. And finally it couldn't be put off any longer: wedding bells rang over Bergen and the surrounding area. Applehead had been given permission to be Askild's best man, while Ejlif, who had come all the way home from Børkersjø, escorted his sister Bjørk down the aisle, winking at his old friend and drinking companion, who now had enough meat on his bones to look good in the wedding photos.

At the sound of the church bells, Pappa Thorsten got out of bed and staggered out to the road, where he collapsed, only to be gathered up later by the noisy wedding procession. The bridegroom himself carried the old man back to bed, because he was now determined to erase the past; he no longer harboured any ill feelings. Bjørk smiled at her groom and was warmed by the glow of his magnanimous gesture. And then the wedding procession continued on its way to Skansen, and there was singing and dancing, and Germany was far, far away . . .

It was actually quite a splendid start to a new life, if it hadn't been for the pulverized Pork Face and the terrified Herman Hemning who, every night for many years to come, woke Askild at four in the morning with a pack of howling bloodhounds. In this way my grandfather was turned into a decidedly type-A personality. *'Get going,'* screamed SS Rottenführer Meyer; *'Los, ihr Schweinhunde,'* shrieked the private.

And Askild would jump up and eat breakfast in the dead of night while Bjørk groaned in the bedroom. 'Come back to bed, Askild!' she would yell. 'Come back here and be my husband!' Because, of course, there were limits to how many allowances could be made. Two years in a German concentration camp, but all the same . . .

New Life in the Old Privy

IT'S EVENING by the time my train stops in my home town. I immediately jump on to a city bus and ten minutes later I surprise my sister Stinna in the drive as she's taking out the rubbish.

'Better late than never,' she says, giving me a smile.

Even though it's been a couple of years since I last saw her, she hasn't changed very much. There is still something mermaid-like about Stinna. She tosses the rubbish bag into the dustbin and comes over to give me a kiss. For a moment we stand there, close together in the dark, and then she pulls me along into the living room where the parrot Kai is sitting on his perch, nervously flapping his wings. 'Who goes there?' he jabbers. A few seconds later Stinna's two children come running in carrying a prosthetic nose that has sparked a noisy squabble.

'That's enough!' shouts Stinna. 'Put down that nose and say hello to your uncle.'

'Are you the one who's scared of dogheads?' the older one asks, looking at me with curiosity.

'*Was* scared,' Stinna corrects him with an embarrassed

smile. 'He's not afraid of dogheads any more. He's a grown-up now. Right?'

I'm not exactly sure what I should say, but I like the use of the plural: dogheads ... It seems so wonderfully liberating. But there was actually only one doghead, and lately I've been thinking more and more about it.

'Can I have a look at that nose?' I ask.

The next moment I'm standing there holding a soft plastic nose that is so lifelike it's actually quite gruesome. 'Doesn't he wear it any more?' I say, weighing the nose in my hand.

'No,' Stinna replies. 'He smokes too much. It's turned all yellow.'

I put the nose down on a nearby table. Jesper is still at work. When we later sit in the living room to have a glass of wine, I catch sight of one of Grandpa Askild's old paintings hanging behind a door, in a spot that's as out of the way as possible. I give a little start because it's the same painting that once hung in our childhood home. Dad hung it up to avoid any trouble from Grandpa, and now it's the only one left. The painting depicts a human figure in Askild's plagiarized cubist style – a style he had seen in reproductions of works by Picasso, Braque, and Cézanne in the late forties. Grandpa Askild was particularly fond of Picasso's *Portrait of Ambroise Vollard*, which reminded him of himself; *Violin*, which reminded him of the vile screeching in his left ear; and *Bathers with a Toy Boat*, which eventually became a more conciliatory portrait of the *Katarina* in the morning fog. That's what he told me right before I moved to Amsterdam. Back then I was always going over to have coffee with my grandparents. At the same time, I would borrow art books to take back home.

Or as Grandpa Askild, naturally, would say: I just came over to borrow his books.

Maybe he was right. I wouldn't have gone to see them as often if it hadn't been for the art books, which I found so fascinating. Because there was something rather painful connected with those visits. When I was there I didn't like looking at the old photographs of Dad that hung on the wall, nor was I very happy about the presence of the blind and deaf old woman in my fat aunt Anne Katrine's former room. Askild's mother Randi did nothing but sit there with her few treasures from a bygone time: the black book containing details of all of Grandpa Askild's naughty deeds, and the family portraits on the wall. It wasn't so much Mamma Randi's unnatural presence that bothered me – at the time she was more than a hundred years old – as much as my fat aunt's absence and the feelings of guilt that her memory provoked in me. But worst of all was the uncertainty. Did they know that I had killed Anne Katrine?

I tell Stinna about those visits, but she doesn't seem especially interested.

'Tell me something about Amsterdam instead,' she says with a smile. 'I never get to hear anything about anything.' She gives me a look of encouragement, but I don't feel like talking about Amsterdam. Instead, I get up and go over to take the painting down from the wall. I can see that Stinna is now expecting some sort of lengthy lecture on cubism, but I don't give those kinds of lectures any more. I'm inclined to believe that it wasn't so much cubism that took up residence inside Grandpa Askild. Instead, it was Grandpa who discovered that he had a cubist soul inside him. Maybe this cubist self had always been there. Maybe it was released by his stay in Germany. Askild painted the same motifs almost all his life – people and shapes that were in the process of disintegration – until 1995, when he was diagnosed with stomach cancer and burnt nearly all his paintings.

After that he changed his style and started painting landscapes, so finally something did happen. But in the intervening fifty years, it was as if he projected the same theme on to his canvases over and over again. During that long period, his marriage to Grandma Bjørk wasn't much of a success either. Only during those first years when they lived with Mamma Randi and Pappa Niels were they ever truly close to one another, at least according to Bjørk. After their wedding, when Randi pushed their beds together and said, 'All right, now it's just a matter of getting started,' they had grown close to each other in a more wordless fashion.

'Close to each other?' Stinna asks with a refined smile. 'Were Grandpa and Grandma *ever* close to each other?'

'I think they were—'

'Listen to me,' Stinna goes on. 'All those times that Grandma sat on the edge of your bed and told you stories – surely you're not trying to make me believe that she was telling you about their sex life?'

In moments of doubt Bjørk did wonder what had happened to the silent seducer she had dreamt of in her younger days in the patrician villa on Kalfarveien. Askild didn't seem particularly experienced. 'He acted like a boy who was taking an exam,' she said a few weeks later to her older sister as she recalled his terrified face the first time she woke him in the night.

'Shouldn't we wait?' he had asked. 'After all, you told me to—'

But Bjørk thought quite honestly that she had waited long enough. Cautiously had she placed a finger to his lips and whispered, 'So show me how it's done.' And then Askild had reluctantly crawled over to her bed and mounted his future wife the way a man ascends an extremely treacherous mountain. He had slogged away with an obstinate look on his face until a certain soreness spread through her belly and the old suspicion that she was boring him nearly robbed her of courage. When he finally came, she felt disappointed. She remembered once when she was a little girl she had asked her mother where all the babies came from. Mamma Ellen had replied that children appeared of their own accord whenever a woman compromised her dignity and did her duty.

For the next eight nights she stayed away from Askild's bed. But on the ninth night she crept over there once more. 'Show me again how it's done,' she whispered, and then cautiously added, 'the real way it's done.' And she lay down at his side, closed her eyes, and waited for the miracle to happen. This time at least he didn't seem as scared. He looked at her body for a long time in the dim light as his hands went exploring, finding secret crevices and ticklish spots where no man had ever been before. A wave of well-being had made Askild shut his eyes, but when he opened them again, the sight of his hands crawling over Bjørk's naked body like two primitive and independent creatures had made all trace of desire disappear. These were the same hands that had once, on an eastern German plain, pounded the head of a terrified Herman against the ground. With a swift, frightened movement, he snatched them away, which made Bjørk think that he was teasing her.

'Hey,' she giggled. 'You naughty boy.'

When Askild unbuttoned the fly of his pyjamas and obligingly started rubbing his dick so that he might at least fulfil his duty towards his future wife, Bjørk couldn't understand what had happened to his enchanting mood. This time, too, he slogged away endlessly. Disappointed, Bjørk had gone back to her own bed and woken the next morning with a sheepish feeling because she had dreamt about Doctor Thor and all the wondrous things he could pull out of his black hat.

It was only when Randi pushed their beds together after the wedding that Bjørk decided to take matters into her own hands. Even though they had now had intercourse twice, she had still not touched him with her own fingers. As she started on her mission of discovery in the darkness of the bedroom, like someone playing blind man's buff, she noticed how strangely angular her husband's body was. When she later dared to explore his manhood as well, she couldn't stop herself from giggling a bit . . . What a peculiar thing it was, hard and soft at the same time. And those balls the size of dove eggs, which she cautiously rolled between her fingers, not knowing that the last person to have his fingers in Askild's secret spot was a German interrogator in the Bergen jail. 'Careful,' whispered Askild. As she caught his eye, it struck her that Askild was a child who had returned home after a long, dark journey. She put one hand behind his head, pressing it to her breast.

'There, there,' she whispered in his ear. 'Everything is going to be fine.' At the same time she continued her exploration with her other hand, encouraged by Askild's murmured sounds and his heated breath against her warm breast, until something hot and wet squirted along her wrist and made her laugh out loud. All of Mamma Ellen's remarks about compromising one's dignity were revealed to be nonsense when he gallantly suggested that they should trade sides so that he would be sleeping on the wet spot. That was a husband's duty, he told her. So what did it matter, thought Bjørk, that he said so little in the daytime and refused to tell anything, if they could reach each other in the wordless dark?

Their wordless games in the dark continued during the following months. Gradually Bjørk's curiosity about the male anatomy was satisfied, and she took pleasure in the conviction that men and women were two very different creatures who could reach each other only in darkness, with the shades pulled down.

Shortly after their wedding, Askild found a job at the shipyard in Bergen. Of course they could use a young engineer who had a Milorg armband and everything else. So Bjørk started getting up at five in the morning to serve coal-black tea to the pale Askild, who would sit in the parlour and stare straight ahead in such a lonely manner. He would sit there while she lit the fire in the woodstove, brushed his jacket, pressed his trousers, straightened his tie, and whispered to him: 'Have a good day at work, and come straight home.'

She didn't think about the way he often smelled of alcohol when he came home from the shipyard. They had their wordless darkness, after all. Alcohol also made him shake off his melancholy, as evidenced the day he came home drunk, bringing with him a jazz record he had borrowed from his colleague Ingolf Fisker. Askild started to dance in the parlour.

'What's all this hubbub about?' exclaimed Mamma Randi, who was simply speechless, whereas Askild's father was not.

'My son is listening to Negro music!' he shouted, which prompted Askild to say that Negro music was banned in the Third Reich, before he went back to dancing.

One day Askild brought home an easel and announced that he was going to be an artist, which made Pappa Niels say: 'My son is mad!' But with a mysterious expression on his face Askild pulled from his inside pocket a crumpled reproduction of Picasso's *Portrait of Ambroise Vollard*.

'Look at this,' he said, spreading it out on the dining-room table as if it were a secret treasure map. 'Can you see who it is?'

'Dean Ingemann?' suggested Applehead.

'Nope,' said Askild, patting his nephew on the head.

'Quisling,' suggested Mamma Randi, who couldn't recall ever seeing a more ugly painting.

'No.'

'Hmm . . .' said Bjørk and cast a swift glance at the title in the lower right corner. 'Could it be Herr Vollard?'

'Yes and no,' replied Askild as he kissed her on the cheek. 'Let me rephrase my question. Who does this represent, aside from Ambroise Vollard?' When no one came up with any suggestions, he went on, 'It's me. Can't you see that?' But no one could see it. Apart from Bjørk, that is. A terrible thought suddenly flew through her mind. Didn't the reproduction look like the image of Askild that she hadn't been able to piece together? And was it really true that there was no sense of coherence behind it? Merely an endless accumulation of fragments and sharp angles on which a person might cut herself? But then she wiped these unpleasant thoughts from her mind and said, 'Nonsense, Askild. You're not that old or that ugly.'

A wounded expression crossed Askild's face, and he had only one thing to say: 'How provincial you all are!'

After the family had made the acquaintance of Picasso's cubist period, the melancholy fragrance of alcohol and eau de toilette which shrouded Askild took on an acrid tinge. It was the smell of turpentine, which he poured into little metal pots when, after work and on Sundays, he would set up his canvases and start swinging his paintbrushes. Often he would frown and curse loudly because his was not a natural talent. And in the beginning Bjørk hardly noticed the few times when Askild stayed in the parlour in the evening with his easel, his paintbrush, and his odour of turpentine, so that she had to go to bed alone. It was only in the early morning, as she ironed his shirts, enveloped in the steam of alcohol, eau de toilette, and turpentine, that she would quietly note how different this scent was from the velvety soft fragrance she had encountered with Doctor Thor. There was something implacable about it, something that stubbornly refused to accept her love. And when she kissed Askild goodbye in the morning before he left for the shipyard, she thought: *What's happening to our wordless darkness? What's happening?* But as soon as he disappeared down the street with his cane, all her worries would vanish.

One night Bjørk awoke, sweating, in her bed because

she had dreamt that a sunflower had started to grow out of her navel. The next morning her stomach hurt, and after Askild had left for the shipyard, Randi called Doctor Heinz. He came over and placed his chrome stethoscope on Bjørk's big, round belly.

'Nothing to worry about,' he said calmly, giving Randi a confidential wink. 'Drink some water and sleep as much as you can. It's still three weeks until your due date.'

Bjørk nodded, because there had always been something reassuring about the sight of a doctor's brown leather bag. Even so, the pains grew worse, cold sweat began trickling from her forehead, and she had to lie down on the sofa. A short time later, a sparrow flew in through the open window and began flapping wildly around the parlour until it crashed into the windowpane and fell on to the sofa. Bjørk immediately took this as a sign.

'The baby's coming now,' she shouted. 'The baby's coming now! And I have gas in my stomach too! Call my mother!'

Terrified, Randi ran for the phone to put in another call to Doctor Heinz, who refused to keep running back and forth. 'If that girl has gas in her stomach, send her out to the privy,' he said, sounding annoyed. 'It's not time yet, for God's sake.'

So Bjørk was sitting out on the privy in a cold sweat, with piercing pains in her loins, when Askild came home from the shipyard. In his inside pocket he carried a crumpled reproduction of Picasso's *Violin*, which he promptly spread out on the dining-room table. 'What kind of foolishness is that?' he asked when he heard that Bjørk, following the advice of Doctor Heinz, was sitting on the privy. He picked up the phone to ring the doctor, who by now was getting quite tired of all these phone calls. He was in the middle of dinner, but when Askild raised his voice, he decided to indulge the prospective father and said, 'All right, I'll be there in an hour.'

Before an hour had passed, a horrible pain forced the air out of Bjørk's lungs, and something fluttering that wanted to come into the world began pressing its way farther and farther out. She wanted to get up and run back to the sofa, but the piercing pains made her feel faint. And while Applehead watched open-mouthed as the dead bird in the parlour began to stir – 'it flew right off', he would later say, 'I saw it myself!' – something formless came into the world between Bjørk's legs. It made the acquaintance of gravity and plunged into the privy's stinking morass of turds and chemicals.

'Askild!' yelled Bjørk as the walls twisted – and in stepped Askild with a wild look in his eyes. He stuck both hands down into the privy and began rummaging around, stirring up waves of shit around him. Then Askild grabbed hold of something long, which felt like an umbilical cord, and he tugged on it, fishing out the tiny infant with the expression of an angler who has caught a good-sized cod on his hook.

'A boy!' he shouted, since he was the first to examine the little creature's sex organs. 'It's a boy! My God, we're good, aren't we!'

Then Mamma Randi appeared and water was boiled, and the newborn was washed before Doctor Heinz stepped through the door and muttered, 'You must be kidding! Down in the privy!' But in spite of his premature and rather surprising introduction to the harsh realities of life, the boy was declared healthy and sound. He was wrapped in a blanket and presented to his parents in the parlour. They were both astonished when they saw his big ears, which until then had been hidden under the stinking foetal membrane.

'Did you see how he looks?' whispered Askild, but none of those present wanted to answer him.

'Wow!' Applehead kept saying during the weeks that followed as he repeatedly leant down to look at his cousin. 'Look at those ears! Where did he get those from?'

'Not from our family, at any rate,' said Mamma Randi.

'Hey!' cried Applehead, opening his eyes wide. 'They moved. I saw it myself!'

'Stop talking about his ears,' said Bjørk with a sigh. She was certain that there were more positive things to focus on. 'Look at his nose,' she said. 'See how handsome it is? Look at his eyes. See how adorable they are? I know he's going to be somebody great.'

And morning, noon, and night she would keep on singing, 'Mother's little boy. A bright future is ahead of you, you, you.'

'What do you mean?' Applehead wanted to know. 'Is he going to be a firefighter? Or maybe the prime minister?'

But Bjørk told everyone to be quiet. The boy needed to sleep. And when Askild came home from the shipyard in the evening, spreading a pervasive smell of alcohol, eau de toilette, and turpentine all around him, she would say, 'Shh . . . The baby's asleep. Try to be quiet, Askild. Can't you take your painting things out on to the landing? No, don't start tickling the boy. Stop teasing him.'

Askild, who thought he should be allowed to tickle his

101

own son under the chin, muttered a few feeble protests before disappearing out to the landing. There he went back to work on a painting that would later be titled *New Life in the Old Privy*, taking sips from his newly acquired hip flask, which, along with his cane, would become his trusty companion all his life. But not even the closed back door of the flat could prevent that rank smell from penetrating all the cracks and crevices. Bjørk sighed and opened windows to air out the place, but nothing helped. Later, when Askild came into the kitchen to watch her bathe the infant, she would say, 'Why are you standing there gawking?' If he wanted to sing to the boy, she would say, 'You're scaring him with your voice.' And if he leant over the cradle to give his son a kiss, she would say, 'You're scratching him with your whiskers, Askild. Stop it.'

At the same time, their wordless darkness had come to an end. Now there was someone else taking his place at her breast. Pushed out on to the landing, the alcoholic spirits that had possessed Askild began to take on a new dimension.

Askild's lungs, already weakened after his years spent in draughty barracks in Germany, suffered from the damp air on the landing, the turpentine fumes, and his increasing use of tobacco. Before long he had to retreat from the welding halls at the shipyard and the enclosed spaces on board ship where the gases from the welding hung in thick clouds, making him cough and gasp for breath. He shut himself inside the drafting room and spent all his time bending over the drafting table. He never emerged to see his sketches transformed into the iron and steel of reality. As a result, his designs for ships slowly began to change character. An element of fantasy slipped into them, receiving considerable help from the alcoholic spirits and the cubist paintings emerging on the landing. Askild felt that he was on the track of something absolutely new that would revolutionize the work processes at the shipyard. But not everyone agreed.

'Those damned engineers,' muttered the welders in the welding halls. 'They sit at their drafting tables and don't know shit about reality!'

'Damn it,' said the electricians. 'We can't make head nor tail of these drawings.'

'Shit!' exclaimed the shipyard foremen. 'What the hell is this?'

As the months passed, their dissatisfaction grew. One day a three-man delegation showed up to present their complaints to the boss, who listened sombrely for all of fifteen minutes. 'All right,' he said. 'We'd better fix those mistakes. Cheer up, men!' But their mission failed and, before the delegation could leave, the boss shut the door and whispered to them, 'He's the Carpenter, damn it all. What do you want me to do? I can't very well fire the Carpenter, can I? Do you realize what that would mean?'

But the boss did decide to have a talk with Askild.

'I know that you're good at your job,' he told him one day after work. 'But sometimes a person can be so good that he thinks he doesn't have to use his head.'

It wasn't until half an hour later, in a pub, that Askild put his frustrations into words. He was talking to his colleague Ingolf Fisker. 'Petty people, petty ideas, provincial nitwits . . .' Ingolf nodded sympathetically. He was the one, after all, who had introduced Askild to both jazz and cubism.

On the way home, it started snowing. Autumn had come to Bergen, it was 1946 and Askild recalled the feeling that had grown inside him when, as a young man, he had been ushered out of Shipowner Thorsten's office. He had roamed through the streets with his degree and an engagement ring in his pocket. It was a feeling of exodus, of new beginnings on the horizon. Back in Sweden he had almost gone to Gothenburg to start afresh, and as a youth he had felt the same sensation in his blood whenever a ship sailed out of the harbour and everything was showered in spray.

A month later, when Askild read a job advert in *Bergens Tidende*, placed by a shipyard in Oslo, he didn't hesitate for a second. He grabbed the phone, and by lunchtime the very next day, was knocking on the door to the boss's office to say, without faltering, 'I've found a job in Oslo. Maybe they'll appreciate my talents there.' The boss expressed his regrets that Askild felt it necessary to go, but at the same time he assured him that the shipyard would release him as soon as he wished. 'In that case,' replied Askild, 'I'd like to leave today.'

After work that day, when Askild took up his usual place in the nearest pub, he tried to convince Ingolf Fisker to go with him to Oslo. 'The wages are better,' he said. 'And they give you accommodation. We're going to be living like counts and barons!' But Ingolf Fisker could not be persuaded, so Askild finished his drink and went home to tell his family about his new plans for the future.

'To Oslo?' exclaimed Bjørk. 'What happened? Did you get fired?' Once upon a time, before the war, Askild's words would have sounded like sweet music to her ears. Back then, at the very centre of her emotional life, was a yearning to get away from the white patrician villa on Kalfarveien. But now she was feeling quite comfortable living in the flat in Skansen – with a husband who was either at work or out on the landing, so that she could pour all her love on to her little son, while she allowed Mamma Randi to wait on her.

'You can't be serious!' she shouted, and Mamma Randi interrupted her by saying, 'A man usually discusses this sort of thing with his wife first. Is this how you thank us for everything we've done? Is this how you thank us for sleeping in our own guest room? Sweet Mother of God! Is this how a son thanks his own mother?'

'This is just so typical!' shouted Askild. 'Go ahead and gang up on me! You old cows!' And while they squabbled out in the kitchen, Applehead's little body grew rigid with fear in the parlour, imagining that his grandfather Niels might resume his habit of hitting him again after the uncle who had returned home was gone.

The only one who didn't feel a need to protest on that evening was Pappa Niels. Later on he slipped out to see his son on the landing, staring for a long time at the cubist human figure that seemed about to fall right off the canvas. Then he patted Askild on the shoulder.

Askild gave his father a puzzled look, in doubt for a moment as to what the old man wanted. But then his face brightened and he pulled a crumpled reproduction out of his pocket. This time it was *Bathers with a Toy Boat*, and he asked Niels whether he could see what it looked like. Niels stared for a long time at the picture, which reminded Askild of the *Katarina* in the morning fog. 'It looks like a toy boat,' Niels said, and went back to his rocking chair.

In the days that followed, removal crates began piling

up in the flat, clothes were packed up, and pots and pans changed hands.

On the day before their departure, Bjørk went back to the house on Skivebakken to say goodbye to her parents, but by then Pappa Thorsten had slipped into dementia and lost all contact with his surroundings. She sat down on the edge of the bed, took his hand in hers and thought about her long and delightful childhood in a white patrician villa on Kalfarveien with its swarm of servants, a dream beneath the birch trees, and a doctor's gentle scent of melancholy. Mamma Ellen served tea, murmuring, 'Good Lord, Oslo.'

And then they departed. Askild, with his eyes fixed straight ahead on the future, and Bjørk, with her eyes turned towards the family waving to them from the train platform. The last thing she saw, before her view was blocked by buildings and trees, was the figure of little Applehead, who stood there, staring sadly off into space. Then she turned around and looked at her husband, who was restlessly pounding his cane on the floor of the train carriage. He patted her tenderly on the cheek and said, 'We should have done this long ago, Bjørk. Yes, by God, long ago!'

PART THREE

PART THREE

The Shitty Contraption

'THEY WEREN'T REALLY that big,' my sister Stinna says. But she's not looking very carefully at the photographs that I've brought from Grandpa and Grandma's house on Tunøvej, wanting to show her that I'm telling the truth.

I went out there this afternoon, after visiting Grandma Bjørk. The house is still fully furnished, except for the few things that Jesper and Stinna had taken over to Bjørk in the nursing home. I immediately opened the big cupboard in the bedroom and, with my heart pounding, started rummaging through it. My intuition turned out to be right: I found the old letters that Grandpa Askild had written in Ramlösa. On the outside of the envelope it says: *Please burn after my death.* But Grandma never did burn them, nor did she ever imagine that I would go rummaging through their possessions in such an inconsiderate way. I also found the shitty contraption and a heap of painting equipment, which I took back to Stinna's house. And I found the old childhood pictures of Dad. His ears aren't just well-developed. They're huge. I try to convince Stinna that they're out of proportion with the rest of his head, but she'd rather hear my opinion about Grandma Bjørk's condition.

'So?' she says. 'What do you think?'

'Doesn't she belong in a hospital?' I ask.

I was rather shocked at the sight of her. She was lying in bed on her back when I arrived. A long tube that ended in a little green hook under her nose ensured that she was getting enough oxygen. Her eyes were closed. Her skin was ashen. The air in the room seemed stuffy, and there was a faint smell of urine. I thought she was asleep, and I tiptoed as quietly as I could over to the bed to take her hand.

'So you finally decided to come home,' she whispered without opening her eyes. 'I was beginning to worry that you never would.'

It had been several years since I had last seen her, and I should have been more prepared. After all, I had watched Mamma Randi live well past a hundred, but the effects of old age on Bjørk shocked me: the countless wrinkles, the bones jutting out, her trembling lips.

'Why did you start again?' The words burst out of me. I was referring to her stories. I had intended to ask her this some time during the next few weeks, but now it was the first thing I said. And my voice sounded both reproachful and strangely relieved.

'Open the cupboard,' she replied.

I looked around in confusion. There were several cupboards that could be opened, but I went over to the largest of them, opened it, and they all came tumbling out. There must have been thirty or forty of them in all: empty tins like the ones used for sardines. Glued to them were various aerial shots of Grandma Bjørk's golden home town, and they all had the same caption: *Fresh Air from Bergen*. Norwegian stamps had been pasted on the back, and I immediately recognized Applehead's characteristic handwriting.

Stinna has now told me that Applehead sends a new tin every week or so. Maybe he thinks it will give Grandma Bjørk a laugh, but she takes those tins very seriously.

'Hand me one,' she whispered.

I quickly realized that she wanted to take a sniff of the fresh air. There were three little holes on one side of the tin. That was apparently where you needed to sniff. I removed the oxygen tube, supported her head with one hand, and with the other held the tin up to her so that she could take a deep breath through her nose. After inhaling the fresh air, Grandma slipped back down in bed with a dreamy look on her face. And then the magic effect of the tin set in. All of a sudden she sat up.

'It's that splinter of ice,' she whispered, putting her hand on her heart. 'That cursed splinter of ice has plagued me most of my life, but lately it's been getting worse.'

She talked a lot of nonsense. She repeated herself, couldn't remember people's names, and she kept being mesmerized by the big landscape painting that hung on the wall. But once in a while she was so lucid that I could coax from her important details and clear up various disputed points, for instance regarding the size of Dad's ears. Even Grandma Bjørk insisted that they were absolutely huge.

But when it comes to Stinna, an old lady's word isn't worth much. She wants more concrete proof, even though she refuses to accept the photos that I've brought.

'The angle can play tricks on you,' she says.

Stinna knows full well that most of Dad's childhood was marked by those ears of his, but right now all she wants is to be right.

'Even his first memory had to do with those ears,' I tell her.

'His first memory?' Stinna smiles, thinking that now I'm in deep water and I won't be able to touch bottom. 'That's not something I've ever heard about.'

The first thing Niels 'Jug Ears' Junior remembered was an open front gate bathed in magical light. To be more precise, a garden gate in front of one of the houses belonging to the shipyard in Oslo. Bjørk was hanging laundry at the back, and Jug Ears had gone into the front yard to play with his toy train when he suddenly caught sight of the open gate. Normally it was always kept closed, but on this particular day Askild had forgotten to shut it, and Jug Ears stared in astonishment at the road beyond. Until now it had been forbidden territory, not merely because he was only allowed to play inside the yard, but also because the possibility of venturing out beyond the gate had never occurred to him. Standing there, a witness to the abrupt expansion of his world, something began to sprout inside him. Something was calling him, something was singing a wondrous song and making him forget all about his toy train. He tossed it aside and went out into the world, filled with an enormous desire to shout – a desire that did not diminish when, out on the pavement, he caught sight of an enchanting creature. A girl about six years old was standing there with two younger boys, all of them having fun tormenting a mouse they had caught.

Jug Ears wanted to play too. When he had gone a few

metres along the road, the smallest of the boys noticed him and poked the enchanting creature in the side. She turned around, revealing an equally enchanting rosebud mouth, that clearly seemed to invite him to come closer. Then she shouted, 'Hey! You, with the ears!'

Jug Ears stopped.

'Yes, you. Jug Ears. It's you I'm talking to. I bet you can even hear the grass growing, by the looks of you!'

A strange silence began spreading inside him, and it did not diminish when the boys started to snicker loudly. 'What do you think? Isn't he a little fat . . . behind the ears!' And turning to Niels Junior they said: 'Hey, jet fighter! Watch out you don't take off!'

'Hey, you ugly little ear-creature. Shouldn't you run home to your mum?'

The three hollering children had hardly made their entrance into Jug Ears' life before they just as quickly left it. Little Niels turned around and ran back to the safe world on the other side of the garden gate.

A couple of weeks later Askild came home from the shipyard a bit more intoxicated than usual. In those situations, Jug Ears was in the habit of huddling up in the cupboard under the kitchen sink where the gentle rushing of the water in the pipes had a soothing effect on his body. There he would let his dreams carry him away as he drew little stick figures on the inside of the cupboard with the stub of a pencil, while emotions ran high in the parlour. On that particular evening, a specific problem was bothering Askild. In the parlour, after being pressed hard, he had to admit that he had been fired from the shipyard because of his unprofessional ship designs and a good deal of complaints from the welders, electricians, and foremen.

'Peasants!' mumbled Askild, pounding the floor with his cane. 'Uneducated swine!'

'Yes, but, good Lord,' said Bjørk with a sigh as she served her husband black tea. 'What are we going to do now?'

Askild had to admit that it had come to blows at the shipyard. Curses had been hurled through the air. And what good was his Milorg armband and all the rest when no one in Oslo had ever heard of the Carpenter, the famous freedom fighter from western Norway?

Removal crates again began to pile up. Little Jug Ears, as he had now been christened by the street's howling chorus, crawled around and hid in the boxes. He drew little stick figures on the insides and disappeared into mysterious worlds of books, pots and pans, and old clothes. One day he stuck his head up from a box and asked, 'Hey, where exactly are we going, anyway?'

And Askild, who was sitting with half a cup of aquavit, staring off into space, replied, 'Out into the wild blue yonder, sonny. That's what we should have done a long time ago.'

In front of the houses near the shipyard in Kristiansand, which was where the family moved a month later, there were also garden gates, children playing on the street, and a little Niels Junior who wanted to go out into the world.

'Hey! You over there! What a sight you are! A father with a cane and a son with a pair of ears that— Hey! What do you think they look like?'

'Hm – octopuses?' a squeaky voice suggested.

'Pancakes,' suggested someone else.

'No, damn it, he looks like an elephant! Can't you see that? He's Dumbo.'

Jug Ears had that same sense of stillness spreading inside him. He remembered it from before, but this time he was not going to run back to the safe world on the other side of the gate. Instead, he stayed where he was and watched the playing children, who for a moment forgot about his presence and went back to lowering a string with a hook on the end into the sewer. A little later, when they fished out an old sack, restlessness began to spread among the group. Once again they caught sight of little Niels Junior standing in front of the garden gate.

'Hey!' they shouted. 'What the hell are you staring at, Dumbo?'

Jug Ears opened his mouth. Something wanted to get out. And then he shouted his first message to the world on the other side of the gate. 'You're the Dumbo!'

'Ha!' laughed the biggest of the boys. His name was Per. 'Have you ever heard a flea growl? Have you ever heard— Hey! Come over here and show us your ears.'

'What are you doing?' Jug Ears wanted to know when he reached the other children.

And one of the boys explained that they were fishing for eel in the sewer. 'They get into the harbour, and some-times they come up through the toilets at the shipyard,' he went on with a sly look on his face. When Jug Ears asked them what they were going to use the eels for, they all looked at him in astonishment. 'He's not only ugly, he's stupid,' said Per with a sigh. And silence once again began spreading inside little Niels Junior, until the youngest boy took pity on him and said, 'We eat them.'

'Blech!' exclaimed Jug Ears. 'Don't you think they're disgusting?'

'Nope, not at all, Dumbo! Hey, weren't we going to take a closer look at your ears?' said Per. And he grabbed one of Niels Junior's ears.

'Ow!' yelled Jug Ears. 'Ow! Ow!'

'Who wants to take the other one?'

Standing there between two big boys, Jug Ears felt a terrible pain, and everything went black before his eyes. The earth vanished beneath his feet, and he was hovering around in an utter void. 'Let's see if he can really fly!' shouted a voice. 'Fly, Dumbo, fly!' Only when his eyes rolled back into his head and he began emitting a strange rattling sound did the boys release their grip and let him sink down on to the street.

'Hey, look at that!' shouted one boy. 'His ears are moving! He can move them, by God!' They all leant down to examine his ears, which, luckily, seemed to be unscathed. And they did possess a peculiar ability to move all on their own. The boys whispered and murmured, and then, after their surprise had subsided, Per patted Jug Ears on the shoulder and said, 'We're sorry about all that. How about if we help you make those ears of yours look more normal?'

'Could you really do that?' asked Jug Ears, sniffling. And Per replied, 'Of course! Hey, go get the sack!' The muddy sack, which they had hauled up from the sewer, was promptly brought over to little Jug Ears, who was sitting on the pavement with that strange silence inside his body. Per started talking quietly, saying that if you got eel blood in your eyes, you would go blind. But if you got eel sludge in your ears, they would start to shrink. And with his index finger he slowly fished a big clump of brown sludge out of the sack. 'Hey, who wants to treat his other ear?'

'I do!' sounded a squeaky voice. 'No, let me!' said someone else. And another minor argument flared up, until a little boy with green snot running out of his nose won the right to do it. Following Per's example, he scraped some stinking sludge out of the sack. 'Put it in his ears,' said Per. And Jug Ears felt something cold and gluey slithering into his ear passages.

'Er . . . are you sure this will help?' he asked, and the boys all nodded eagerly while Jug Ears shut his eyes and shivered.

'Hey, I want to do it too,' said a voice after the first treatment had been completed. 'Me too!' said another, and more sludge was fished out, and more index fingers bored their way into the big, bright red ears until Per said, 'Go on home now. If they don't shrink, we'll give you another treatment tomorrow.'

From that day on Bjørk waged a mighty battle with cotton swabs and soapy water, trying to keep her son's ears clean. But no sooner had she satisfied herself that they were clean, than sludge would begin pouring out of them again. 'Those ears, those ears,' Askild would say with a sigh when he came home from the shipyard and found his wife in the process of cleaning his son's ears at the kitchen table. 'He doesn't have an ear infection, does he?' They asked Niels Junior whether he was in pain. They smeared Vaseline on the thermometer and took his temperature, but there was nothing wrong with him. And as time passed, sludge was not the only thing that was fished out of his ears during the daily cleaning ritual. No, Bjørk also found tiny snails, greenish clumps that looked decidedly like hardened gobs of snot, pieces of dried leaves, and even tadpoles. One day she gave her son a grave look and said, 'You mustn't put things in your ears. You might end up going deaf.'

Jug Ears nodded and asked her if it was true that his ears were too big.

'Who told you that?' Bjørk wanted to know. But Jug Ears, who didn't want to say anything about the secret treatments he was getting every day out on the street, replied, 'Nobody.'

That day Bjørk drew her husband into the parlour, where they whispered and murmured for a whole fifteen minutes. After that Askild dashed out to the kitchen, seized hold of Jug Ears, and lifted him up in the air so that everything whirled before his eyes. Then he set him on top of the kitchen table. 'Be proud of your ears!' shouted Askild. 'They make it possible for you to hear things that no one else can hear. With them you can hear everything those damned Kristiansand peasants can't hear!'

'Er—' said Jug Ears after he had recovered from his fright. 'What can I hear, Askild?'

'Don't call me Askild, sonny. Call me Pappa. Do you understand?'

'Yes, Pappa. But what can I hear?'

Since Askild had no ready answer to give him, Jug Ears tried hard to listen on his own. He could hear the sound of his mother holding her breath in the parlour; he could hear his father's wheezing lungs; and he could hear a faint rushing and humming, which was due to the quantities of remedies stuffed deep inside his ear passages, put there by

118

imaginative children. With time Jug Ears would end up hearing some rather unbelievable things, but at the present moment he merely peered apologetically at his father and said, 'What do you want me to hear, Pappa? Tell me.'

'Those ears of yours are real, dyed-in-the-wool, manly ears! You're going to make women swoon because of them.'

After that Askild went out to paint, and Jug Ears stayed where he was, standing on top of the kitchen table, until Bjørk came in and lifted him down.

Jug Ears crawled inside the cupboard under the sink, closed the door behind him, and pulled a pencil stub out of his pocket so that he could continue drawing his little stick figures. Usually he just drew big heads and little feet, but suddenly the pencil stub slid between his fingers, and on the face of one of the figures he drew a triangle that looked exactly like a fang. After that he enthusiastically made the same scrawl over and over again, and the colony of stick figures that lived inside the cupboard was soon transformed into a colony of tiny little monsters. And there was something reassuring about creating his own monsters.

Before long the monsters moved out into the surrounding world. One morning, when Askild dropped his razor on the floor of the bathroom, he bent down to find three little monsters on the wall under the sink. When Bjørk was cleaning, she found monsters under the beds and between the lower shelves in the pantry. And one day when she was doing a major spring clean she broke into the very heart of the colony in the cupboard under the kitchen sink. The sight of all those monsters made a cold shiver run down her back. She scrubbed and washed but without much success, partly because Jug Ears kept drawing new ones, and partly because the old monsters would break through like spots of oil on the newly painted wall. It was virtually impossible to get rid of them.

'Monsters and ear dirt,' said Askild one evening. 'What kind of a boy is this son of mine?'

A few days later Askild came home with a macaw named Kai that he had bought from a seaman at the local pub. The bird could say 'Give me a sugar cube' and 'Bring in the aquavit'. It was the latter remark that had especially tickled Askild. Kai was installed on a perch in the parlour, with a metal chain attached to one leg so that he couldn't fly away.

'Is he really from America?' asked Jug Ears.

Askild nodded and lifted up his son so he could get a proper look at the bird with its hooked beak, its brilliantly coloured feathers, and its tiny, nervous eyes that looked like rotating glass marbles. Jug Ears stared with fascination at the creature, delighted by its exotic sounds and smells, until Askild shouted, 'Hey, watch out or it'll bite your nose off!'

After the initial shock had subsided, Kai became a favourite topic of conversation for the father and son.

'Should we give the bird some water, Pappa?'

'Have you talked to Kai today, son?' And like any beloved child in a family, Kai was given many nicknames. Pip Boy, Babble Head, and Yankee. Later, after the bird had taken lessons from Askild and started to imitate his sounds, it was called Demon Creature and That Damn Bird. Occasionally Askild would be seen staggering around town with Kai on his shoulder.

It gave Jug Ears a certain status among the boys of the neighbourhood that his father walked around with an honest-to-goodness parrot from America. 'Is that a real parrot? Can it talk?' Jug Ears would hear when he went out to the street for his daily ear treatments. And so he brought the boys inside the house to get a closer look at the marvel.

'Can we touch it?' asked Per.

'Of course you can,' Jug Ears told him, 'but only on the beak.'

Happily surprised by this generous gesture, Per took a step closer to the parrot, but when his index finger started to waver 5 centimetres from the bird's beak, Jug Ears yelled, 'Watch out! It's going to bite your nose off!' Terrified, Per yanked back his hand.

'Ha! You were too scared to touch it!' cried a squeaky voice.

With a single blow the parrot named Kai had upset the balance of power among the boys. Per vigorously defended himself, but in the midst of the discussion, when Jug Ears went over to the bird, lifted it down, and pressed his little nose to the parrot's enormous beak, there was nothing more to discuss.

But the ear treatments continued. To Bjørk's great horror, she kept on finding sludge, snails, and mashed insects inside her son's oversized ears. The consumption of cotton swabs increased astronomically, soapy water frothed in metal basins, and monsters erupted in the cupboard under the sink, even more frightening than before. 'It's an inflammation of the middle ear,' said Askild. And once again a Vaseline-smeared thermometer was stuck up Jug Ears' rear end, which seemed to him the worst humiliation of all. Every day his mamma would pull his trousers down to his knees, spread the cheeks of his bottom, and stick inside something cold and unpleasant while Askild yelled impatiently from the parlour, 'Does the boy have a fever?' The result was always the same. Jug Ears did not have a fever, but a certain sensation in his backside made him harbour mixed feelings towards his mamma. Up until then he'd seen her as the sweet angel in the house, someone who had to put up with his increasingly intractable father.

Things did not improve when one day Bjørk pulled her son's trousers back up, gave him a secretive smile, and dealt another blow by saying: 'You're going to have a little sister.'

'How could that happen?' asked Jug Ears. And Bjørk replied, 'That's not something you should ask me about, you naughty boy. Ask your father.'

'When your little brother gets here, you'll have to act like a big boy and stop peeing in bed,' said Askild, referring to the fact that Jug Ears had started peeing in bed much more often, ever since the parrot from America had lost its curiosity value in the neighbourhood.

'You have to be a model for him,' Askild went on, adding with a gruff look on his face, 'so pull yourself together.'

Jug Ears, who didn't really understand what his father was talking about, did sense a certain dissatisfaction with his character. Much later this same sensation would merge into Jug Ears' favourite expression: 'going downhill'. For instance, after a strained Christmas lunch, he would lean back in his chair, heave a big sigh of relief, and exclaim, 'Things have been *going downhill* for Pappa all his life.' Or at a business dinner, as he gloated over the unfortunate investments of a competitor, he might say, 'It's really *going downhill* for X. I bet you anything he'll have to sell before the year is out.' But as a four-year-old standing in front of his turpentine-smelling father, Jug Ears had a sense that he was the one who had been going downhill, and in a sudden fit of ill temper he exclaimed, 'But where is that damned baby going to come from?'

'When swine copulate, they produce piglets. When human beings screw, they produce children,' Askild said with a belch. 'Now go out and play.'

'Askild!' cried Bjørk. 'What kind of language is that!'

'I think the boy can stand to hear the truth,' said Askild.

But Bjørk disagreed. 'That man drives me crazy,' she later whispered to her sister on the telephone. 'Drunk as a skunk, a mouth like a longshoreman, and that horrible stench of turpentine. Lord, how I miss Bergen!' Lina, who over the past couple of years had become used to lending an ear to Bjørk's complaints, smiled smugly and let her sister vent her frustrations. 'I'm telling you, those words he uses! I blush just thinking about them,' Bjørk went on, shivering because certain words, hurled from a filthy mouth, came closer to home than she cared to acknowledge. Now, it was true that their sex life had stalled after Jug Ears' birth, but lately it had begun to re-emerge in a new form that was closer to screwing than to anything else. Askild, slightly tipsy, drunk, or completely soused, would crawl into his wife's bed and take her with a force that bore witness to pent-up frustrations, while fantasies about a doctor's gentle scent of melancholy would seep into Bjørk's dreams.

She did not mention any of this to her sister. 'That man is

driving me insane,' she complained instead, adding in an almost inaudible voice, 'Sometimes I wish he would drink himself to death.' After that she hung up the phone and went looking for little Jug Ears, who had disappeared into the cupboard under the sink.

Since a steady stream of stinking matter was still pouring from her son's ears, Bjørk decided one day to take him to see a paediatrician. She had to go into town anyway. The doctor's name was Pontoppidan, and he was an elderly man. Bjørk found herself surrounded by all kinds of medical implements – test tubes, blood pressure devices, and thick volumes about child masturbation, which was one of the doctor's specialities. At the sight of his physician's bag, and enveloped in a sterile scent that reminded her of something very familiar, Bjørk relaxed for the first time in a long while. Jug Ears sat quite still as the doctor studied his ears with interest. At first he seemed most preoccupied with their size and their perpendicular placement on the boy's head. It was only later that the doctor began taking an interest in the core of the problem, meaning the stinking matter that was pouring in a steady stream out of his patient's ears. That part of the examination took approximately one minute.

Then Doctor Pontoppidan leant back in his chair, lit his pipe, and let another minute pass in silence before he said, 'Inflammation of the middle ear? Is that what you think, my dear madam? No, let me say this loud and clear: the boy is putting things in his ears.'

'Yes, but I've told him not to do that. Niels! Didn't I tell you not to put anything in your ears?' cried Bjørk.

Little Niels Junior nodded. Bjørk, who had hoped for a

diagnosis and some curative pills, shook her head in resignation. 'So I suppose there's nothing you can do,' she whispered.

'Don't be so sure about that,' said the doctor, and he summoned his nurse, who took little Jug Ears out to the waiting room. 'You see, my dear madam.' He meticulously tapped his pipe on the desk, and then went on, 'There are certain methods. May I ask you . . . er . . . do you ever use corporal punishment on your son?'

'Not very often,' replied Bjørk, who wasn't quite sure what kind of answer the doctor was expecting.

'Then it's quite clear, my dear madam! The strap! Use the strap whenever he puts anything in his ears, and preferably at once. Immediate punishment, you see. So the little boy won't be confused and so he understands why his parents have to use necessary means!' said the doctor, giving her a triumphant look.

'But aren't there any other options?' asked Bjørk.

Pontoppidan again leant back in his chair and relit his pipe. At first he seemed annoyed by Bjørk's hesitation, but suddenly his face brightened. He dashed over to one of the big oak cupboards and rummaged through some out-moded apparatus. He pulled out something that looked like a mini-version of a suit of armour, but let's just call it the *shitty contraption*, as Jug Ears did a short time later. The shitty contraption landed on the doctor's desk as he exclaimed in a voice that could not entirely disguise his enthusiasm, 'Here's our solution!'

In front of Bjørk lay a steel corset constructed some time before the First World War by Pontoppidan himself after careful study of apparatus used by Doctor Daniel G. M. Schreber and other like-minded physicians. The devices were all for the sole purpose of preventing children from masturbating or carrying out any other indecent games, so the corset was an antiquated device, even in the early 1950s. Bjørk whispered in astonishment, 'What on earth is that?' Somewhere deep inside she could feel a sense of resistance, but she was tired of ear sludge and cotton swabs, she was depressed about the problems of her family life, and she was bewitched by the authority of the brilliant doctor. Gradually she allowed herself to be persuaded.

'Naturally, he can still play as much as he likes. He just won't be able to lift his arms up past his shoulders,' the elderly doctor explained. He added, 'Whenever you or your husband are present, the boy doesn't have to wear the corset, of course.'

A few adjustments had to be made. Since the corset was not going to serve its original purpose, the lower section could be removed. Only the upper portion, which would be fastened to the boy's wrists in order to limit his freedom of movement, was required.

'His habit of putting things in his ears is not driven by the same monstrous forces that characterize masturbation,' the doctor went on, showing a spark of the all-absorbing interest for his profession that he had felt in the past. Besides, for a brief period he had used the corset on his own children, and with excellent results. His son was now a practising physician, and his daughter was married to a naval officer in Oslo.

'Well,' said Bjørk, 'at least it's preferable to using the strap.'

Jug Ears was then called back in, after having left three monsters and a single fang on the wall under his chair in the waiting room. At first he was happily unaware of his fate as the doctor took measurements and even ventured to tease the boy. But then: screaming and howling. A startled nurse, who had to be summoned to help hold the boy; a resigned Bjørk, who turned away; and a doctor who suddenly began cursing loudly. 'He bit me, confound it!' Three drops of blood trickled from the doctor's hand. And then: the *shitty contraption*.

On the way home through the streets of Kristiansand, Jug Ears muttered, 'Stupid Mamma', with his eyes fixed on the pavement. 'Stupid, stupid Mamma.'

Breaking Through

'WHAT ON EARTH has the boy got on!' bellowed Askild when he came home from the shipyard and found his son under the sink. 'What the hell kind of armour is that!'

Whimpering, Jug Ears crawled out of the cupboard so his father could get a closer look at Pontoppidan's corset. 'Pappa, I don't want to wear this. I don't *want* to! This *shitty contraption*!' he protested.

He cast a pleading glance at his father, who rubbed the black stubble on his face in bewilderment until he abruptly made up his mind and shouted, 'Take off that piece of shit!'

Askild, as mentioned before, did not share Bjørk's faith in authorities. He especially didn't trust those doctors who pulled cotton knickers out of their black hats. 'My son can't be running around looking like that!' he groaned and began fumbling with the corset. But for some reason Bjørk decided this time to stand her ground.

'It's on Doctor Pontoppidan's orders. And it's only for a couple of months,' she shouted as Askild began tugging at the straps and belts to free his son from the doctor's torture instrument.

'I don't give a damn,' said Askild as he loosened one strap and then another, but Bjørk refused to budge. She threw herself between father and son, practically toppling Jug Ears over.

'Or else I'll go back home to Mamma!' she yelled.

There was a moment of utter silence. Jug Ears looked at his mother in dismay.

'"Mamma, Mamma, I want to go home to Mamma,"' Askild mimicked his wife in a sarcastic baby voice.

'I mean it, Askild. I'll leave!' Bjørk went on as she gave her husband a good shake.

'This place is a loony bin!' shouted Askild, who had other things on his mind, including a certain grumbling that had started up in the corners of the shipyard. Always the same old trouble. This very day a few kindly suggestions had been made with regard to his imaginative ship drawings and his cubist inspiration.

Askild retreated to the parlour, making his betrayal clear to Jug Ears, who was left all alone in the kitchen with his stupid mother. Over the following days shouts of ridicule could be heard on the street.

'Hey! Have you seen Jug Ears? He's got armour on!'

'Hey, Dumbo, today's not Halloween!'

And of course the ear treatments continued. This time with no possibility for Jug Ears to defend himself, since an elderly doctor's corset was restricting his freedom of movement. And Bjørk kept on mucking out the sludge and bits of snail from her son's ears. A month later, when she showed up at Pontoppidan's office to complain about the negative results, the doctor looked ten years older and stared at her with a distracted air.

'Hmm,' he said. 'Is it the warts on his feet again?'

'Warts on his feet?' said Bjørk, giving the elderly doctor a look of astonishment. 'It's his ears. You're going to have to examine them again.' But the doctor didn't think that would be necessary.

'We need to wait and see how long this continues. Everything in good time, my dear madam. One day you'll wake up, and the whole thing will be over,' he recited absentmindedly.

Feeling slightly confused but, in spite of everything, still reassured by the sight of the doctor's brown leather bag, which never lost its magical attraction for my paternal grandmother, Bjørk took her son by the hand and walked back home through the city streets. 'You heard the doctor,' she said. 'One day everything will be fine.'

Askild still didn't care for the sight of Pontoppidan's corset, but during this time he had other things on his mind, as he would for long periods for the rest of his life. Since he did his best thinking in the local pubs, the family didn't see much of him. And after Bjørk had threatened to go back home to Bergen, she and Askild communicated only when absolutely necessary. At the same time, they developed a habit that would haunt them for the rest of their lives.

At six o'clock Bjørk would eat dinner in the kitchen with Jug Ears. Then the food would be reheated, the pots would be wrapped in newspaper, and everything would be placed under the quilts in the bedroom to keep the food warm until Askild came home to eat around nine. Their bedroom, which had previously been a breathing space with a wordless darkness, was now transformed into a storage room for fish balls, boiled coalfish, and cabbage stew. An oppressive odour of food began to cling to the quilts. I can still remember that smell whenever I, as a child, would step into their dark and stuffy bedroom on Tunøvej. Also dating from this time was Askild's characteristic expression: the bitter lines around his mouth and his remote, dark gaze that could make people think he looked slightly mean. What in the past had been a more diffuse smell of alcohol and turpentine fumes now began, in the early 1950s, to mark the face of my grandfather, who was no longer quite so young.

Problems were starting to pile up around Askild, until one evening when he read an advert in the newspaper. Or was it the other way around? Did he read the ad later, after he, in a rage, had chased his boss through half the shipyard, swinging his cane and shouting that he was going to give the man a good beating? Half an hour later his boss showed up in the payroll office to have Askild Eriksson stricken from the books, effective immediately. What a crazy man he was! The next morning two policemen knocked on the door to give Askild an official injunction against returning to the shipyard. Bjørk stared in shock at these two representatives of the forces of law and order. Either before or after this incident, Askild happened to read a brief ad in which the word 'Stavanger' imprinted itself on his consciousness.

No one in the family objected when one evening he proclaimed that they were done with Kristiansand, that shithole. They would now be heading off to golden Stavanger, where they would live like counts and barons.

Bjørk thought, *Stavanger? At least that's in the right direction – halfway back home to Bergen!* And she looked forward to the day when, for the last time, she would slam the door on this house populated by her son's monsters and her husband's ghosts.

Others were more sceptical. 'So why not come home to Bergen? Good Lord, couldn't he get his old job back?' said Lina on the telephone. In the meantime, removal crates began piling up in the house, along with sacks and all manner of junk. 'Hey, Jug Ears!' came the shouts from out on the street. 'What's happening? Where are you going?'

'Away,' was Jug Ears' reply. Then he ran into the house to disappear inside the cardboard boxes and start exploring all the exposed intimacies of his family: the underwear, the faded photographs, and the old letters, not a few of which were from a certain Doctor Thor. He managed to cover all those removal crates with tiny monsters in such disturbing numbers that they disconcerted the moving men and turned the removal process into sheer chaos. And of course it didn't help matters that Bjørk was very pregnant. Nor did it help that Askild, in high spirits during the days prior to their move, kept pouring shots of home-brewed aquavit for the removal men. He also played poker with them into the wee hours, and at three in the morning decided to introduce them to the joys of jazz.

And what a sight it was for the neighbours and the children playing on the street when the family arrived at Havnebakken in Stavanger. At the train station Askild fell in love with an old horse that was standing on the other side of the platform, chewing on a piece of cardboard. Ignoring the protests of the removal men and Bjørk's half-hearted attempts to talk some sense into him, Askild decided that this horse should pull the removal wagon all the way up Havnebakken.

In the back of the wagon, which was wobbling dangerously, lay three dead-drunk removal men who had fallen asleep and were snoring loudly. Up front sat a surly-looking man. In one hand he held a cane, in the other he clutched the reins, and on his left shoulder sat a parrot alternately screeching 'Damn it to hell!' and 'Who goes there?' Next to the man sat a very pregnant woman who hadn't slept a wink all night. And on top of all the removal crates, like the pinnacle on a marzipan cake, perched a funny-looking little lad with gigantic ears, wearing a strange armour that prevented him from lifting his arms.

All the neighbours gathered in the doorways, while children came running after the wagon. A few of them were disappointed when they realized that the circus had not, in fact, come to town. Others were excited simply because the similarity to a circus could not be denied.

But Stavanger was not the golden city after all, and the family was not received like counts and barons. It's true that the children of the neighbourhood were eager to help move the furniture, and they were sorely needed, since the removal men could not be roused from their stupor. But the grown-ups stayed indoors, and when a neighbour from across the street finally decided to go over and welcome the newcomers, he quickly retreated. 'And he calls himself an engineer! What language! He's nothing more than a dock worker, in my opinion.'

It was not as easy to offend the neighbourhood children. With the greatest enthusiasm they seized hold of boxes and cupboards, and before long old letters from Doctor Thor were scattered all over the garden path, canvases were torn, and the china was clattering. The children seemed especially interested in little Jug Ears. 'What's wrong with him?' they asked Bjørk. 'Is he a spastic? Is that why he's walking around with that thing on?' Bjørk patiently explained to the inquisitive boys that her little son had a habit of putting things in his ears. The corset was not a form of armour but rather the invention of a highly intelligent doctor. Over the next few days shouts of ridicule could be heard on the street.

'Hey! You over there! Can we call you Jug Ears? Come here and show us how you put things in your ears!'

Even though Jug Ears wasn't too keen on going out into the world any more, he never failed to comply. 'A big boy has to go out and play,' his father had always told him. 'Only mice live under the kitchen sink.' So Jug Ears would waddle out to the street, wearing his impossible corset that would forever mark him as a spastic and oddball in Stavanger. And when he stood in front of his potential tormentors, he would say without hesitation, 'I can't do it myself, but if you promise not to tug on my ears, I'll let you do it for me.'

'That's a deal. What shall we put inside them?'

'Leaves,' suggested Jug Ears as he calculated how long he would need to stay outside on the street in order to satisfy his father.

Not long after they moved, Bjørk started having ominous dreams that nearly scared her out of her wits. One night she awoke after dreaming about a huge bird that landed on her bed and began to peck holes in her swollen belly.

Another night one of Askild's cubist figures climbed down from the wall and approached, threatening her with a big scalpel. When she awoke from this last dream, it was three in the morning. She got out of bed, and a strange pain sent her rushing for the toilet. But just as she was about to sit down, she realized what was happening and ran back to the bedroom and shook Askild awake. 'The baby's coming!' she shouted. 'Call my mother!'

Askild pulled on his bathrobe and dashed for the phone to call his mother-in-law, who told him that Pappa Thorsten's condition had grown considerably worse during the night, so she wouldn't be able to come to Stavanger. 'Oh no,' whispered Bjørk. 'We have to go home to Bergen.' But Askild ordered her back to bed and forbade her to go anywhere near the privy.

'If things go as fast as they did last time, we can still make it to Bergen,' he reassured her. Then he called the midwife.

The first labour pains that washed over Bjørk woke Jug Ears, and shortly afterwards he found his father out in the kitchen. 'Your little brother is on his way,' said Askild. 'Remember what we agreed.'

'Yes, Pappa,' murmured Jug Ears. Then he crept into the cupboard under the kitchen sink as soon as he got the chance. And there he sat for the entire forty-eight hours that his mother was in labour. Unlike her big brother, the baby girl was in no hurry to come into the world. There sat Jug Ears while the midwife's optimistic chatter slowly became a worried whispering. There he sat as the young doctor was summoned. A big commotion followed, with voices that were distorted and muted by the stinking sludge inside Jug Ears' ear canals. Later on came the sound of his mother's shrill voice, saying: 'No, I won't! No! I can't do it any more!'

And inside the cupboard with all the monsters new alliances were being forged: it's hard for someone to replace their son with a younger and more perfect child. *Those ears, those ears! They make it possible for you to hear things that no one else can hear. With them you can hear everything those cursed Kristiansand peasants can't hear. But what can I hear, Pappa? Listen! But what do you want me to hear, Pappa?* And while Bjørk screamed from her bed, Jug Ears tried with all his might to listen as hard as he could, so that for once he would be able to satisfy his parents. Deep inside his ear canals something began to stir. Childish dreams and ideas were fermenting in there; the accumulation of years of sludge and snails grated against his eardrums until finally – as his mother's screams grew too intense – Jug Ears stuffed a finger in each ear and everything went quiet. Not because Bjørk's screams had stopped, because she would keep on for another twenty-four hours, but because Jug Ears had broken through. In short, he had tuned in to other frequencies.

A different drama was overshadowing the drama of childbirth; voices other than those belonging to his mother and father, the midwife, and the doctor began making themselves heard. There was a terrible jumble until a hoarse voice abruptly separated out from the others. *Hey, sonny, are you awake? Hello! Hello!* Then everything was quiet again, but before long the voice was back, this time talking about bed-wetting and humiliations and *a great inheritance that was lost because seven torpedoes took it down into the deep.* Later the voice sounded more conciliatory: *To hell with all that! The moment is approaching – you've been lying here, an invalid, for seven years, pissing in your trousers and acting like a baby – let's take off, now. Nothing is so bad that you can't escape from it. Are you coming, sonny?* And later he also heard another voice, which he recognized as belonging to his maternal grandfather Thorsten.

Yes, Pappa, said Thorsten's feeble voice, *I'm coming.*

The Fang Sings

THE NEXT MORNING when Jug Ears woke up inside the cupboard, he could hear weeping. He got to his feet and ran to his parents' bedroom, where Bjørk had given birth to a little, blue-tinged girl barely an hour earlier. 'Well, well,' was the first thing that Askild said when he saw that he had been cheated out of a second son. 'It's not her fault, after all.' Over the years he would adopt a clear double standard in the way he treated his three children. 'You two,' he liked to say to his sons, 'need to pull yourselves together, or you're really in for it!' But about his daughter he would merely say, 'Good Lord, she's doing the best she can.' And whenever he was drunk, which he usually was, his heart would overflow and he would put the little girl on his lap and murmur along with the peculiar sounds that she made.

Bjørk treated her daughter with great love right from the start, humming tunes about a brighter future and protecting her as best she could from too much fatherly attention. Then, a couple of years later, a doctor explained to Bjørk what everyone else had known for a long time.

The girl was brain-damaged and most likely would never learn to speak. After that, a cold wind swept through Bjørk's heart. This didn't mean that she neglected her daughter; outwardly nothing had changed. 'No one could ever fault me for the way I brought her up,' she said many years later, 'but my heart has always been with my boys.'

'Come and say hello to your little sister,' said Askild, lifting up Jug Ears so that he could give the newborn a kiss.

'No, I don't want to,' protested Jug Ears. But Askild refused to be deterred.

'Come on,' he grumbled. 'Give her a kiss on the cheek!'

'No, I won't!' howled Jug Ears, flailing around so fiercely that Askild had to use all his strength to force the boy's head down towards the newborn's cheek. Only when Jug Ears was back standing on the floor did he remember the voices he had heard in the night.

'Grandpa Thorsten has gone home to Nordland to be with his pappa!' he exclaimed proudly, giving his mother and father an expectant look. 'I heard it with my very own ears!'

'What did you say?' asked Askild.

'Oh God,' moaned Bjørk, who in the heat of the moment had forgotten all about Pappa Thorsten in Bergen. 'Oh no. Askild, please be a dear and call my mother.'

A short time later, when Askild called his mother-in-law, he was told that Pappa Thorsten had passed away during the night. Thorsten had died in his sleep and was put on ice until Bjørk could regain enough strength to travel to Bergen to take part in the funeral. That took two weeks, and in spite of being kept in cold storage, Thorsten started to smell, just as Askild would one day start to smell, although Dad never did, because he ended up frozen in the cold ice of the permafrost.

This oppressive smell hovered over the church and over-shadowed the fragrance of the flowers. Bjørk had gone to Bergen alone, taking the newborn infant with her, and she sat in the front row with Mamma Ellen. In the midst of the olfactory chaos, she was also aware of a velvety soft fragrance. In short, a doctor's gentle scent of melancholy, which was rising from the third row in the church, where Doctor Thor Gunnarsson was sitting in the pew reserved for old friends of the family. If the truth be told, most of their old friends had fled when the ships went down in the deep. Thor was sitting all alone in that row, but even so, Bjørk had a feeling that he somehow managed to fill it up.

The next day, after Pappa Thorsten had been laid to rest, she once again encountered that scent of lost oppor-tunities, this time at Fisketorget in the afternoon sun, and later while sitting over a pickled herring sandwich in a local restaurant. Doctor Thor, who had already achieved a certain renown because of his dissertation on neuro-surgery, behaved like a perfect gentleman, as usual. He conversed attentively and wiped his mouth carefully on the cloth napkin, in contrast to Askild, who had acquired the filthy habit of using his shirtsleeve. The doctor was so kind in every way that it was enough to make a person weep. Only when Bjørk glanced away did a certain hunger come into his eyes, and if she was com-pletely honest, he also seemed a trifle dreary in appearance, although he had by no means lost his sense of humour. 'Presto!' he said with a laugh after the food was eaten, fishing the familiar coin from her ear with his usual aplomb. 'That's where her good humour was!' He then took his leave, and they kissed each other on the cheek a little more intensely than was proper for a married woman and an old family friend.

A strange agitation made Bjørk's heart gallop, and on her way home aboard the ship to Stavanger, she thought: *Why don't I just go and get my son and come back home to Mamma? What am I really doing in Stavanger?* When they docked in Stavanger, and Askild failed to show up, even though he had promised to do so, the restless churning continued inside her: *How did things get to this point, where my own husband is starting to disgust me?* But when she finally arrived home and found her forgetful husband less drunk than expected and her neglected son – who leapt out of his hiding place under the sink and ran to meet her – beaming with joy, she thought: *Oh, what was I thinking?*

'We met completely by chance!' Bjørk later claimed when Askild tried to probe into the matter. 'That man has always hounded me.'

But many years later, in the kitchen of my childhood home, she was whistling a different tune. Grandma Bjørk made remarks that implied meetings that were more than just chance encounters.

'Back then I was really quite bold. I jumped right in with both feet. But now I've been married for over thirty years to that drunkard, and I still can't bring myself to leave him.' This was followed by a meticulously rehearsed comedy in two acts.

Act One: Mum would go into the bedroom and get out the divorce papers from the bureau. Then she would come

141

back into the kitchen and place the papers in front of Grandma Bjørk, telling her where to sign and which sections to fill out. With a shaking hand, my grandmother would obey, and when the completed divorce papers lay on the table between them and Grandma Bjørk's eyes were brimming with tears of relief, she would thank my mother with all her heart. Then they would drink tea, and Grandma Bjørk would take long puffs on her low-tar cigarettes.

Act Two: After tea, Grandma Bjørk would get cold feet. She would say she didn't want Mum to send in the papers after all. She would just take them home to give the whole thing a little more thought and then send them in herself in a week or two. 'I swear I will,' she would say with conviction before she scurried down the drive with me at her heels. She would tell me a couple of stories and kiss me goodbye at the corner of Tunøvej. And the divorce papers? They would disappear into thin air, and a few months later Grandma Bjørk would be back, and the whole scene would be repeated.

As mentioned, Bjørk had started to feel a certain loathing for her alcoholic husband. Dreams straight out of romantic novels about doctors now haunted her at night. Even in her waking hours, these novels were gaining a hold on her. She bought them at the nearest bookshop and compulsively devoured them whenever she had a free moment. Askild had nothing but contempt for his wife's new literary inclinations, and he tried, without much luck, to interest her instead in art books and jazz records. But it cannot be denied that in this whole matter Bjørk had already made up her mind. In cubism she saw nothing more than her husband's madness, and in jazz she heard only his clinking penchant for the bottle. This lifelong battle between Askild's so-called refined cultural interests and Bjørk's more popular tastes was the crux of their relationship. The conflict was only partially resolved when Bjørk, in her old age, developed a passion for the joys of gambling dens. At night, every time she heard a creaking from Askild's bed, Bjørk would wake up, dreading that he might come over to her to demand his conjugal rights. Her heart would begin pounding, and she would feel a very real sense of anxiety. On those rare occasions when he did come to her, she would merely close her eyes and imagine the soft hands of a doctor and an idyllic pastel scene, the kind that adorned the covers of her collection of medical romances and story magazines, which by now had become quite extensive.

In a weak moment I ask myself whether it could really be true that my father, at the age of five, heard voices. That he had a telepathic contact with Pappa Thorsten when he was in his death throes. Or that no less than Rasmus Fang, the 'grand old man' of the Nordland rabble, after leading his son across the river of death, returned to his great-grandson to spew gibberish in his ears whenever the boy sat in the cupboard with his monsters. *Riches will flow, coins will rain down, and gold will find its way into your hands*, he would chant. Yes, I also ask myself whether it could really be true that fragments of the Fang's simple philosophy, his teaching and screeds, began to appear, such as: *It's important to know your weaknesses, but it's even more important to know the weaknesses of others. Strike first, ask questions later. Rumours are worth their weight in gold: go get something on those swine!* Did remarks like that really begin to echo in the cupboard under the kitchen sink? It's certainly possible. In the beginning Jug Ears received them in a strange state of scepticism and terror. But later on, as he grew more familiar with the Fang's gruff voice, he started to long for them, receiving them with admiration and childish joy.

After the birth of Anne Katrine, the Fang became a frequent visitor to the cupboard under the sink. When he wasn't reeling off his screeds and instilling in his great-grandson the basic elements of his repellent philosophy, he would indulge in nostalgic homages to Bergen, that golden city, a Mecca for buccaneers and gold-diggers. Bergen soon became equivalent to the big X on a treasure map, and Jug Ears started asking his parents about the town. 'Is it true that there are so many crabs in the sea near Bergen that all you have to do is go out on the dock and shovel them up? Is it true that everyone gets rich in Bergen?'

'What kind of gibberish is the boy spouting?' snapped Askild.

But Bjørk's reply was, 'That could very well be, my dear—'

In spite of good advice from a gruff phantom, it cannot be denied that the family's stay in Stavanger was in many respects one long period of *going downhill*. Even the baby girl, who was the absolute bright spot of Stavanger, gave them more worries than joy. At first a persistent jaundice set in, followed by colic. When all her howling had finally stopped, whooping cough descended on them, and the doctor became a frequent visitor to their home. But after

Askild was once again fired, and in a desperate drunken binge admitted that Norwegian shipyards didn't exactly grow on trees, Bjørk decided, for once, to set wheels in motion.

'Fired again! That man is going to be the death of me! Oh, my dear sister, if you only knew what I've been going through down here in Stavanger,' Bjørk complained to Lina on the phone. 'So now it's going to have to be Bergen. Couldn't you have a little talk with X? Couldn't you get your husband to ingratiate himself with Z?'

And that's why her sister Lina's husband one day strolled down to the shipyard in Bergen. And in the office of the boss the myth about the Carpenter was once more revived after a lapse of seven years. All things being equal, a small favour for a friend wouldn't hurt the shipyard's reputation, and as for the imaginative ships' drawings, the Carpenter had undoubtedly outgrown that habit.

The Fang's hoarse voice was heard to say: *Oh, wondrous city faraway; oh, marvellous city close at hand*. And when all his talk about Bergen was suddenly replaced by real people saying real things about the city, Jug Ears burst out of the cupboard and ran into the parlour, where he found Bjørk fumbling with a piece of paper as she stood in front of her drunken husband.

The paper was, to be more precise, a letter which had arrived that day from the shipyard in Bergen, offering Askild his old job back.

'Just read the letter. See what I've arranged for us?' Bjørk said, unable to keep a certain pride out of her voice.

But Askild refused to accept the offer with a simple 'thank you'. He had no use for a helping hand from a deceitful woman who went behind his back and spread

145

rumours about him having problems. He could solve them on his own. 'So what's this all about?' he grunted suspiciously. And after he read the letter, he tore it into pieces.

'But Askild,' Bjørk objected, 'you've been offered a job in Bergen. And a man in your situation can't afford to turn it down.'

'Bergen!' shouted Jug Ears, jumping up and down. 'Bergen! Bergen! Is it true? Are we going to Bergen?'

'Yes,' replied Bjørk, patting her son on the head as she kept her eyes fixed on Askild's face. 'That's where we're going, little Niels.'

'Ha!' shouted Jug Ears a short time later out on the street. 'We're going away. Back home to Bergen!'

It was nearly impossible to restrain him during this time.

'Is it true that we're going to catch crabs in Bergen? Tons of crabs?' he kept on asking his parents, who had no idea where the boy had got these obsessive ideas.

'Is it true that we're going to be rich now?' he babbled, and Bjørk told him, 'Well, we'll have to wait and see about that. You know how your father is and how he handles money.' But Jug Ears' enthusiasm could not be quelled. And there were others who were more than thrilled when the family, after seven years in exile, stepped back into the flat in Skansen.

'Sweet Mother of God! Back home again! What good was all that flitting about anyway?' said Mamma Randi, who had put on more than 20 kilos since her son had gone off to Oslo. They all lined up to kiss the matriarch: Jug Ears with a strange tickling in his stomach, Bjørk with the intoxication of a homecoming roaring in her blood, and Askild with a tired and resigned expression. Then Applehead, who was now fifteen years old and had fuzz on his upper lip, came running in through the door. 'Hi, Uncle! Hi, Cousin! Hi, Aunt! Have you seen my new bike? Come on and I'll show it to you!'

'Take it easy, everybody!' groaned Pappa Niels from his rocking chair. A little while later he added, 'All right, I know the tune: I'm banished to the galley once again.'

The Nut Kicker

FROM 1954, FOR TWO years, the family lived once again in the flat in Skansen with Mamma Randi and Pappa Niels. The bedroom became filled with the family's junk, the landing was taken over by painting equipment, and little monsters broke out from the cupboard under the sink. Nevertheless, Randi and Niels were both satisfied with the arrangement. And the day after the family's arrival Jug Ears was invited to take a tour around Bergen on the back of his cousin Applehead's new bicycle.

'What kind of weird shirt is that you're wearing?' asked Applehead before they got on the bike.

Jug Ears told him that it was something an old man had invented a long time ago. And when Applehead wanted to know why he didn't just take it off, Jug Ears stared at him wide-eyed.

'Could I do that?' he said.

'Geez!' exclaimed Applehead. 'Of course you can!'

Before Jug Ears could even count to ten, his cousin's filthy mitts had torn open the straps and pulled the shitty contraption over his head. 'So get on,' said Applehead. 'Don't just stand there gawking.'

Astonished, Jug Ears climbed on to the bike and off they went, all over Bergen.

After two weeks Jug Ears had seen most of the city, and of course he was a bit disappointed to discover that the sea was not boiling with gigantic crabs and gold was not glittering on the mountain slopes. The Fang had really laid it on thick. But his disappointment quickly left him, to be replaced by an enthusiasm for the bike rides. Not to mention his delight over the fact that his cousin had used his pocket knife on the shitty contraption so that Jug Ears could now remove it and put it back on by himself whenever he liked. A feeling of freedom was bubbling in his blood, because no one ever made comments about his ears when he was with Applehead. But when his cousin wasn't around, the situation was different.

'Hey, you over there. Yes, you. Cousin Jug Ears! Come here so we can take a closer look at those ears of yours!' he heard one day on the street.

'Hell, no,' shouted Jug Ears.

'What? What did he just say? Is he trying to be rude, that ugly little monkey!' And before he knew it, he was surrounded by a bunch of Bergen boys, who didn't look very different from the boys in Kristiansand or Stavanger. 'Wow, those are some ears he's got! By God, he's ugly!' they said, laughing. Then hands seized hold of his arms while others took a firm grip on his ears. Once again Jug Ears heard feet pounding the asphalt as a blinding pain spread from his ears through his whole body.

'Ow!' he howled. 'Stop it. Let go of me!'

And the whole episode might have gone full circle

except that suddenly the loud clanking of a bicycle was heard as it came roaring around the corner. 'What the hell is going on here?' Applehead said before he rammed into the group at high speed. In the confusion someone's foot was run over, and two of the boys landed on their backsides before they all fled in a wild panic.

'Did anything happen?' asked Applehead in a grim voice.

'No, but they didn't like my ears,' said Jug Ears, whereupon Applehead had these wise words to say: 'If anyone says anything about your ears, just kick them in the nuts.'

'Er— the nuts?' said Jug Ears.

'Yes, damn it all, a good kick that will really make their bells ring.'

After moving to Bergen, Niels Jug Ears Junior acquired a new nickname: the Nut Kicker. *Strike first, ask questions later*, the Fang had whispered. And inspired by Applehead's words about a ringing bell, Jug Ears set about carrying out his first major plan: to kick people in the nuts. He was often seen on the street, a wildly kicking eight-year-old boy who frequently came home for dinner with a black eye and split lip. But one day, when Applehead was inspecting his cousin's newly acquired shiner, it became clear to both of them that a different strategy was needed. 'Who was it this time?' asked Applehead, and Jug Ears replied that it was Niller with the freckles from Øvregaten.

'That goat,' cursed Applehead. 'Let's go over there and have a talk with him.'

So they biked over to Øvregaten where the freckled Niller was playing ball by himself. Before Jug Ears knew it, his cousin had disappeared into a dark courtyard at the back, leaving him all alone in enemy territory.

'Pssst!' he heard from the dark. 'Yell something at him. Get him to come over here.'

'Hey you!' shouted Jug Ears, making obscene gestures. 'Hey, Niller! Spot-face! You ugly idiot!'

'What the hell?' cried Niller, dropping the ball he was playing with and making a dash for the insolent brat. But as he stood in front of the newcomer from Stavanger, a fifteen-year-old boy with fuzz on his upper lip emerged from the dark courtyard at the back, seized hold of the terrified Niller, and pulled him into the darkness. There the older boy pinned his arms behind his back and shouted to his little cousin: 'Come on! Kick him!'

For a moment Jug Ears hesitated, but then he kicked Niller in the groin, making a tiny hollow sound escape from the boy's lips.

'No, damn it!' said Applehead. 'Aim for his nuts, not that sissy weenie there!'

Jug Ears took aim again, and this time he hit home. In other words bells rang, blood seeped out of Niller's lips, and he collapsed on the ground. Applehead, to emphasize that they meant business, gave him a kick in the rear end and added, 'We're not going to have any more trouble from you, are we?'

'No, no,' gasped Niller. 'Never again.'

Out on the street Jug Ears realized that he was shaking, and he was amazed that his cousin could be whistling, apparently unaffected. 'All right,' said Applehead when they had climbed back on his bike. 'Who's next on the list?'

'Ow! Ow!' could be heard in the back courtyards of

Bergen. 'No! No!' echoed through the dark alleyways. After taking turns to work over every bully in the neighbourhood and having developed a good technique, Jug Ears succeeded in winning a certain respect among the boys.

'Hey, there he goes, the Nut Kicker,' they now whispered. And even though Jug Ears never managed to make the boys stop teasing him completely, for the first time in his life he was miraculously left in peace. This was largely thanks to Applehead, about whom a rumour began circulating that not long ago he had given his grandfather Niels a punch in the jaw when the old man had taken the strap out of the cupboard.

Pappa Niels hadn't actually attempted any further blows with the strap since a young Askild had chased him around the dining-room table after the episode with the slutty girl. Truth be told, he was now going senile. On some mornings both Askild and Mamma Randi had to block his way when he waxed his moustache with Vaseline, doused himself with Old Spice, unbuttoned his shirt so everyone could see the white hair on his chest, and tried to leave the flat to sign on as a seaman with the *Amanda*. On a few occasions they were unable to hold him back, and he wandered around the harbour docks, offering his labour to any skipper he happened to meet, until some kind soul took pity on him and gave him a glass of beer before escorting him home to the flat in Skansen. There he had to come clean and listen to the overweight Randi bawl him out.

While Jug Ears zoomed around Bergen with his cousin, making bells ring, Bjørk was on her way to see the doctor with her daughter, who at the age of two and a half still hadn't learnt to walk. Nor could she utter a single word. 'It'll come,' Askild was in the habit of saying, but eventually Bjørk began to have her doubts. And one day she slipped unnoticed out of the flat, taking Anne Katrine with her, and knocked on the office door of . . . no less than Doctor Thor, who in addition to his studies in neurosurgery, had started a small medical practice.

Surrounded by all manner of medical paraphernalia, and stimulated by the memory of fifty or more glorious illusions from medical romances, Bjørk sat down in Thor's office and let it all pour out. Not just her own concerns about her daughter, but also her problems with her alcoholic spouse. She hinted that their sexual relationship was sheer torture, and that the marriage had quite simply been a mistake. The whole long diatribe left Doctor Thor breathless. In reality he had always pictured Bjørk as happy. She had been given a real choice, and she had chosen the gloomy human skeleton who had suddenly appeared in the doorway. A dizzy lightness spread through his body, and after he had regained control he leant across the desk and took her hand.

Now, Thor had always been conscientious about fulfilling his obligations. While he examined the little girl, studying her reflexes, trying out various intelligence tests, and asking Bjørk about the child, it gradually dawned on him that it would be quite tasteless to think about his own pleasure in a situation like this. He examined the girl three times to be completely sure. Then he took a deep breath, and after he had pronounced his diagnosis, a window flew open. A cold wind swept through the doctor's office and into my grandmother's heart, where it remained like a splinter of ice until her dying day.

Gone was the enchanted mood. On her way home through the streets of Bergen with little Anne Katrine, it was clear to Bjørk that she would now have to give greater thought to her son. One doomed child in the family was more than enough.

'Who told you that?' grunted Askild when Bjørk told him about the diagnosis that evening.

'Doctor Thor.'

'That knicker magician!' cried Askild.

'He's the best doctor in town, Askild. Good Lord, does all that really matter any more?' But her answer didn't seem to satisfy Askild, who went over to the playpen and lifted up his daughter. 'Brain-damaged? An idiot? Retarded? Like hell she is!' he shouted.

'Hey! What's going on?' asked Jug Ears, who had just come rushing in the door.

'Look at your sister,' replied Askild. 'Does she look like an idiot to you?'

'Huh?' said Jug Ears in bewilderment.

'Exactly! That's what I'm talking about,' exclaimed Askild. 'Your mother's so-called doctor wants to lock up the child in some institution for idiots.'

'But why?'

'God only knows,' he grunted while Mamma Randi murmured 'Sweet Mother of God,' and Pappa Niels stared vacantly straight ahead, sitting in his rocking chair.

And with that all further discussion of the subject was over, and even Mamma Randi was amazingly silent all evening, as was Bjørk. After freezing most of the afternoon, she closed her eyes and fell asleep on the sofa next to Pappa Niels. And while Bjørk dreamt about the cold splinter of ice that had pierced her heart, and Askild puttered around on the landing, painting one of his least successful pictures – later called *The Doctor and the Scalpel* – Jug Ears went over to the playpen and looked down at his sister, who lay there sucking on a wooden block. And he, who had stubbornly refused to give her a welcome kiss in Stavanger, suddenly hopped into the playpen and began playing with the mute little girl, who drooled with delight. He sat there for the rest of the evening, playing with his sister, until Bjørk woke up from her dream, sent the children off to bed, and ensconced herself under an extra blanket before once again floating off into her dreams.

Over the next thirty years Bjørk developed a fear of open windows, a manic preoccupation with draughty rooms, a penchant for woollen sweaters, and an almost patho-logical obsession with scarves. 'Don't forget your jacket or your scarf. Take care that you don't catch cold,' she would admonish all her family members by turn whenever they went outdoors. *She's the frigid type*, the Fang would have whispered. I've chosen to look on it a little differently: it was a fear of the cold, of what she had sensed inside her-self when Doctor Thor, back in 1954, made his diagnosis. The next day no one in the family could see anything different about the way Bjørk treated her daughter. The only apparent change from the day before was that the tune about a bright future was once and for all omitted from her repertoire of goodnight songs. Yet through my fat aunt's eyes I can see a certain distance, though I'm not going to spend any time dwelling on it. But as far as Askild was concerned, the changes in his emotional life were obvious to everyone. That very

155

evening he tried with all his might to get his daughter to walk, and in the weeks that followed, he attempted with growing ferocity to teach her to say 'Pappa'. At first the only result was tears, but when Anne Katrine, at the age of six, actually did start to walk, and when she, as a seven-year-old, uttered that magic word, 'Pappa', Askild regarded it as a personal victory, even though by that time he had given up teaching his daughter anything.

While Bjørk's love for the girl suffered from the presence of the cold wind inside her heart, and while Askild with all his might tried to prove that there was nothing wrong with *his* daughter, Jug Ears' love for his sister began to flourish. He started joining in with her wordless games, and sometimes he would take her with him out to the street. There Jug Ears noted with satisfaction that his former tormentors would cross over to the opposite pavement whenever he and his sister came walking down the street. Occasionally he dared to shout after them, but in the long run it proved to be a rather lonely occupation. The real triumph occurred when Jug Ears' former tormentors stopped crossing to the opposite pavement and instead came over and snapped a boiled crab claw in two, giving him half of it.

'Want to go with us to catch crab tomorrow?' a thin boy named Thorbjørn asked him one day. And that's how it happened that Jug Ears was initiated into one of the boys' great passions: catching crabs on the harbour docks, using crushed clams for bait, tied to a piece of twine. And even though the sea wasn't exactly boiling with crabs as the Fang had promised, there were still considerable numbers of them hiding in the rock clefts and under the seaweed along the Bergen docks. While the crushed clams did their work in the deep, the boys would keep themselves entertained by gathering up cigarette butts, extracting the remnants of dank tobacco, rolling them up in newspaper, and finally lighting them as they told lewd jokes. Later on they would head over to Fisketorget, where they delivered their crabs to Svein the fishmonger, who exchanged every live crab for one cooked crab claw. The crab claws were often eaten on the spot. But in spite of his enthusiasm for the grand adventure with the crabs, Jug Ears watched with a certain scepticism as his five giant crabs were transformed into five measly crab claws. 'Er—' he muttered on the way home with his mouth full of crab meat. 'Why should that fat tub of lard make money off us?' But none of the other boys could see anything unfair about this long-standing barter agreement.

It was on the evening after Jug Ears' tentative complaints about Svein the fishmonger that Bjørk noticed something miraculous. Sitting on the sofa, once again pregnant and growing tired of the domineering Mamma Randi who treated her like an invalid and forced her to drink greenish vitamin concoctions that smelled disgusting, Bjørk cast a weary glance at her son, who was sitting in the playpen with his sister. For a brief moment her eyes rested on his ears, and then surprise made her pregnant body tremble. She leapt to her feet and approached her son in amazement.

'Stop it,' cried little Niels as she started prodding his ears. 'That tickles.'

But nothing could stop Bjørk now. She took a firm grip of both ears, examined them carefully, and then ordered her son to stand under a lamp. There she continued her examination until she came to the miraculous conclusion that his ears were quite simply sparkling clean.

'Askild!' she yelled, running out to the landing. 'Askild! His ears . . . I don't know what happened!'

In came Askild, and it cannot be ruled out that he may have repressed the whole story about ear dirt, because after casting a swift glance at his son's ears, he merely said, although with a certain relief in his voice, 'Well, how about that.' Then he returned to the landing.

After that Doctor Pontoppidan's loathsome corset was stowed away at the bottom of a cupboard, consigned to the oblivion of the deep. It was only in the wee hours of the morning at family parties that the matter of the corset, many years later, would come up – and it was Bjørk, as always, who had to take the blame. 'You and your doctor novels,' Askild would jeer. 'You'd play the fool for any man with a stethoscope!'

PART FOUR

PART FOUR

Applehead Runs Away

APPLEHEAD WAS NOT even seventeen when he ran away to sea in 1955. Six months earlier, you could already see certain peculiar changes in the boy, who up until then had been hunting down his cousin's former tormentors, mostly for the fun of it, and long after they had stopped plaguing Jug Ears. Often it was Jug Ears himself who had to step in and talk some sense into his incorrigible cousin when Applehead got on his bike to chase after the terrified members of the crab club, uttering the dreaded words: 'Are you trying to be clever? Do you want a fight?' But suddenly this stopped. Applehead began riding past the boys without paying the slightest attention, whistling into the blue. One time he rode right into the milkman's truck, which was parked on the street.

On the home front his behaviour also gave cause for alarm. The boy who had previously been so vocal had become almost mute, and several times the family caught him sitting quietly, writing words on a piece of paper. Mamma Randi made him take cod-liver oil, and she cooked up disgusting vitamin concoctions for him to drink. But nothing did any good. Applehead continued to look pale, and he devoted more and more time to his writing habit. And when no one was looking, he covered the back of the paper with crudely drawn hearts. Then he would bike all the way out to Lange Woods, go over to a very specific pine tree with a huge hole splitting its trunk apart, and place his letter inside. After making sure that no one was around, Applehead would retreat to a nearby thicket, light one of the cigarettes he had pinched from his uncle, and wait there with a pounding heart until a red-haired creature came into view among the pine trees. From a distance he would watch as Ida Bjørkvig approached. She was the daughter of the city's most vocal teetotaller, who the very next year, in collaboration with Dean Ingemann, would see to it that the Meeting Place was shut down. Later they would also put the squeeze on the Merry Circus Wagon and the Evening Room. Purposefully, but with a look of feigned resignation, Ida would walk over to the pine tree with the split trunk and pull out the letter. She would unfold it hastily, and after she had read it an irresistible smile would cross her lips. Then she would once again vanish among the trees of the forest.

It was that smile that kept Applehead coming back, because whenever he attempted to talk to her, she sang quite a different tune. 'Keep away from me, you jackass,' she shouted if he followed her on his bike. 'I've heard some ugly things about you. Did you know that?' she would say if he, with puppy-dog eyes, tried to follow her home from school. But every time he shouted the secret code words from his bicycle: *the postman's coming*, she would faithfully show up at Lange Woods to read his hopeless declarations of love, driven by curiosity and by something else that she wasn't too keen on putting into words.

'Good Lord,' she would say many years later. 'No one could resist that jackass.'

Only after making her way through fifty or so letters did she decide not to vanish among the trees of the forest. Instead, she went right over to the thicket where Applehead was hiding. 'What are you doing lying under there?' she asked. 'Give me a cigarette.'

She didn't want to sit down. In seven long puffs, she smoked the whole cigarette as she told him that he could walk her home from school the next day. After she had left, Applehead picked up her soggy cigarette butt and put it in his pocket.

'Hey!' was occasionally heard on the streets when Applehead, who had quickly lost his awe-inspiring aura, bicycled around Bergen in a state of distraction. 'That ass is sleeping with the teetotaller's daughter!'

In such situations some of Applehead's old self could suddenly reappear, and he would chase after the insolent members of the crab club in a rage. But everyone could see that he no longer did it with the same cool perspective as before.

'My God, what a doormat your cousin has become,' Thorbjørn told Jug Ears. Applehead had recently been seen walking three paces behind the teetotaller's daughter, carrying her school-bag with a look in his eyes that made the neighbourhood boys cringe. 'And she's a ginger!' they said, as if referring to a particularly disgusting breed. But along with scorn there was a flourishing curiosity, and wild rumours began circulating about what the pair might be doing in Lange Woods. Sometimes the boys would go out there to spy on the couple, and one time a boy managed to pull a letter out of the old tree and read a few words that were unbearably asinine, before Applehead came racing over, his face white with fury. Another time a shocked boy saw a naked breast in the thicket.

'She was lying there completely naked, smoking cigarettes,' was the gossip that circulated among the boys of the neighbourhood. 'Hey! They're screwing in Lange Woods – and they're smoking cigarettes at the same time!' they said. 'Do you know what she was doing? She was down on all fours saying, "Come on, give me your fat dick!"'

Pursued by the boys of the neighbourhood, the young couple had to flee farther and farther into the forest. They soon spent entire Sundays wandering among the pine trees, stopping in small clearings where cushions of moss served as a velvety bed. And there, far away from Bergen's screaming choir of boys, the spirits of the trees began whispering strange stories, and voices from the earth sang peculiar songs. The feelings that gradually arose between Applehead and Ida were marked by a certain uneasiness, prompting them to move closer together; and by an effervescent lightness of spirit that inspired them to do things that couldn't be done anywhere else. Things that filled both of them with a certain anxiety when they returned in the evening to the bustling life of Bergen. But the expeditions continued, deeper and deeper into the woods – during that summer when the weather, by Bergen standards, was amazingly fine. They ended abruptly when Ida, three weeks after the start of the new school year, came rushing over to their old thicket and shouted, 'I'm pregnant, you jackass. Look what you've done now, you stupid beast!'

She turned around and ran off. But the next time Applehead saw her, she wasn't nearly as crude in her choice of words. In a low voice she bemoaned her lot, concluding with the horrifying remark: 'I'm going to have to tell my mother.'

After that Applehead suffered not only from all the physical signs of love, but also from an unpleasant form of cold sweat that would come over him whenever he thought about Ida the Ginger and what they had done in those enchanted woods. For the next three weeks he saw nothing of Ida Bjørkvig. She seemed to have been swallowed up by the earth, and if the truth be told, he was no longer quite as eager. He still rode his bike around Bergen, but he was even more distracted than before. He became a mere shadow of his former, awe-inspiring, self.

He biked around and around as if in a trance, until the day when a big black car pulled up beside him and forced him into the kerb, nearly toppling him to the ground. And out of the car climbed the teetotaller Arnt Bjørkvig with a furious look on his face. Applehead instantly understood that you didn't argue with a man like Bjørkvig, and, pale as a ghost, he got into the black car. Even though this was the first time Applehead had ridden in a car, he couldn't muster any enthusiasm. And after they had driven for a quarter of an hour without exchanging a single word, he discovered, to his horror, that the teetotaller was heading for Hell's Cliff. It was a high ledge some distance from town, and in his mind's eye, Applehead pictured himself being driven up there and pushed off.

'Er,' he managed to stammer, 'I didn't do it on purpose.'

Bjørkvig told him to shut up, and only when they were actually parked at Hell's Cliff did the teetotaller take a deep breath and turn to look at the boy. 'I don't much care for you,' he said. 'I don't like your sort. Too bloody clever by half, but it doesn't matter, because next Saturday you're going to marry Ida in Mariakirke.'

The teetotaller stared at him with his tiny round eyes, and Applehead felt, once again, that this was not a man he could argue with. So he merely stammered, 'Yes, well, of course.'

'Good,' said the teetotaller and nodded at the car door. 'Now get out before you make me sick!'

The next moment Applehead stood alone in the road as Arnt Bjørkvig stepped on the accelerator and roared off towards town. Finding himself in a cold sweat again, Applehead decided to have a talk with Askild. Applehead was the only one in the family who ever considered asking Askild for advice about anything. A few hours later he reached the pub where Askild liked to go after work.

'There he is, my favourite nephew,' exclaimed Askild. 'Have you started frequenting pubs?'

Still plagued by a cold sweat, Applehead managed to say that he needed to talk. So Askild led him to a table in the corner, ordered an aquavit for his nephew, and seemed to be in high spirits. He jabbered and babbled left and right, shouting rude remarks at the waitresses. And it suddenly occurred to Applehead that his uncle had a whole other life in this place.

'All right,' said Askild, giving Applehead a serious look after he explained his dilemma. 'As I see it, you have two options right now: marry the girl, or run away.'

The latter option, in particular, had a positive effect on

166

the cold sweat. 'Run away?' Applehead repeated. 'But where would I go?'

'To sea, you numbskull.'

'But what about Ida?' stammered Applehead.

'The girl made her own bed, so let her lie in it,' replied Askild and ordered another aquavit. 'It's not your fault, under any circumstance.'

This last comment was delivered with a confidential smile that opened a world of possibilities. And in the company of his uncle and his drinking buddies, who were telling tall tales from the sea, the enchanted woods slowly lost their grip on the boy. The terrifying teetotaller paled and shrank, and even the Ginger, who only a short time ago had spilled her desperate tears at his breast, became a hazy dream. Instead sea foam and breakers began to appear on the horizon, along with shore leaves in distant lands, merry evenings spent in exotic ports, and whores who cost ten øre for a whole night and had no inhibitions whatsoever. Before Applehead said goodbye to his uncle and went to find his bicycle, the cold sweat had vanished like dew in the sun, and everything seemed so simple.

One morning soon afterwards, Jug Ears awoke to the sound of Mamma Randi running around the parlour and crying as she waved a letter that Applehead had written in his characteristic handwriting.

'Sweet Mother of God!' she wailed. 'He's just a child. Are you the one who put such ideas into that boy's head, Niels?'

Pappa Niels, who had become accustomed to getting up at four in the morning, only to sit down in his rocking chair and sleep until five thirty, awoke with a start and peered in terror at his enormous wife. That's when the commotion began. 'The South Seas, the Philippines – they're all crazy savages down there, cannibals, they eat people, that cursed boy—'

Randi quickly realized that Niels had actually spoken to Applehead that very morning and, out of her mind with rage, she showered the senile man with insults because he hadn't tried to stop the boy. Askild's sister Ingrid was hastily summoned home from her shift at Haukeland Hospital. And standing in front of the furious Randi and his older sister, who was on the verge of tears, Askild finally had to admit that he was the one who had advised Applehead to run away to sea.

'What!' shouted Ingrid and Mamma Randi in unison. 'You didn't!'

I've had enough! thought Askild that morning on his way to the shipyard. *I'm supposed to bow and scrape, even go down on my knees, it's always the same old story* . . . And as he walked along in the raw chill of the morning, an old vision began to appear in his mind: a house on the outskirts of Bergen, a view of the sea, peace and calm in his family. It was the same dream that had captivated him as a young man in his room at Widow Knutsson's – a dream that he had vaguely shared with Bjørk.

Before long he had chosen a plot of land, and a short time later he managed to raise enough money for the deeds, which he did by persistently referring to his good job and his old reputation as a great freedom fighter. Now, every single Sunday he went out to the site to work at the hard Bergen bedrock with dynamite. The explosions often echoed far away, and the family was tormented by thoughts of a drunken Askild fumbling around with sticks of dynamite while his portable gramophone played jazz. This meant that he always received a hearty welcome when he came home. Bjørk too was looking forward to escaping from her tyrannical mother-in-law, and occasionally she would take the children out to the property to see how the work was progressing.

'So how long are we going to live there?' Jug Ears asked one day, nodding towards the blast-shattered building site.

Bjørk cast a swift glance at her son and said, 'Forever.'

Jug Ears never forgot this promise, and later it would become the most tangible proof that his mother was a liar. But there were other things that pointed in the same direction. For instance: why was she always going to the doctor when there was never anything wrong with her? And why did she say that she was going shopping and then return home empty-handed several hours later? But I'm getting ahead of the story.

The Saturday after Applehead's disappearing act, there was a knock on the door of the flat in Skansen, and in came a furious Arnt Bjørkvig with the Ginger dressed in a modest wedding gown. At first no one could understand a word the man was shouting, and the girl was so dissolved in tears that she couldn't say a single word. Only little by little did they understand the reason for Applehead's disappearance. 'I'm going to kill him!' bellowed the teetotaller, and he seized a bewildered Pappa Niels by the collar. The parrot screeched, Mamma Randi shrieked, and only Askild's decisiveness prevented the visit from disintegrating into utter farce. He grabbed Herr Bjørkvig by the arm, pure and simple, and shoved him outside, telling him that the bridegroom had gone to the South Seas and wouldn't be around for the next couple of years. And while Ida the Ginger was deciding never to shed another tear, Applehead was lying underneath his hammock in the bottom of a ship, retching. That was the only form of solidarity with the pregnant Ginger that he could muster, even though the memory of her in those enchanted woods continued to haunt him at night beneath foreign skies, pursuing him all the way into the darkest alleyways of Manila and Singapore.

The following year when Ida, who had quit school, could be seen walking around Bergen pushing a baby pram with not just one but two ginger girls inside, the Eriksson family developed a habit of hurrying away. In spite of the gossip at Fisketorget, Mamma Randi denied any connection with the twins. Askild would look right through them as he staggered to and from the shipyard with his pockets filled with dynamite, on his way out to the building site. And his sister Ingrid followed Askild's example. Only Bjørk, who had now become a mother for the third time, went over to Ida, patted her hand, and picked up each of the infants in turn, praising them to the skies.

'Hey!' said the boys in the neighbourhood. 'Did he really run away? Just like that?'

Jug Ears nodded.

'No shit? Wow!' they said. And in this way Applehead succeeded in regaining his reputation among the neighbourhood boys. They quickly forgot that the idiot had ridden his bike straight into the milkman's truck; they forgot how 'the boy with puppy-dog eyes' had carried the school-bag for the red-haired girl; and they forgot those asinine words that they had once read in a stolen letter.

The Crab Episode

WHILE APPLEHEAD was bicycling through the streets of Bergen in a state of distraction, Jug Ears made up his mind that he was no longer going to settle for a single crab claw in exchange for a whole crab. But the first time he voiced his objections to Svein, the fishmonger looked at him with an indulgent smile.

'Is that right? So what would the fine gentleman like instead? A dead herring?'

The other members of the crab club stared at their comrade in astonishment when he replied without blinking, 'I'll take cash.'

This was met with loud laughter from Svein. He doubled up over the counter, making the blocks of ice slide down, and when he had finished, he gave little Jug Ears a cold look and snarled, 'Get out of here!'

Ha! What a nitwit. But that man isn't the only fishmonger in town, the Fang whispered that evening under the sink. The very next day Jug Ears roamed around Fisketorget on his own, talking about crabs, big fat crabs, alive and kicking and ready to display on blocks of ice, only ten øre apiece and no problems with delivery. 'Just say the word,' he whispered. Before long he had come to an agreement with fishmonger Hundrik, whose stall was on the outskirts of Fisketorget. After that, whenever the crab club went over to Fisketorget to exchange the day's catch for crab claws, Jug Ears would slip away unnoticed and go over to Hundrik's stall where he would deliver, with no problems, crabs at ten øre apiece. Soon he began buying up the other boys' crabs too, for seven øre apiece. 'But don't tell anybody,' he whispered.

'It's my own personal agreement with Hundrik,' he would insist whenever the boys wanted to know why they couldn't just go over to Hundrik and deliver the crabs themselves. 'Nope!' shouted Jug Ears. 'Make your own deals with your own fishmongers!'

But it was the actual fishing for the crabs that interested the other boys most, and so no one objected when Jug Ears dropped the price for crabs to five øre apiece. Or later, when he offered to buy the whole day's catch for a sum that was far below what Hundrik was willing to pay. 'Okay,' they said simply, 'but then you have to carry them to the marketplace by yourself!' And so a group of boys could be seen heading towards Fisketorget, but one of them clearly stood out because he was lugging the entire day's catch of crabs.

For the first time Jug Ears knew what it felt like to have money, which was the fulfilment of a prophecy. *Riches will flow, gold will find its way into your hands*, the Fang had whispered. But it can't be denied that, over time, Jug Ears began making use of rather questionable practices. 'Oh no!' he would say, patting his pockets. 'I don't have any cash on me today.' Instead, quite by accident, he would find a couple of liquorice whips in his back pocket or a few cigarettes he had snitched from his father. 'I guess that's all I've got,' he would say apologetically. And his comrades would turn over their crabs to him, wondering a bit what he was using all the money for.

He wasn't saving up for a bicycle, nor was he paying out any cash to a girl called Lewd Linda to get her to take off her knickers. No, he bought money. With new money he bought old money, mysterious-looking coins that made his heart pound. He could often be seen staring at the smudged display windows of Ibsen's coin shop. Ibsen frequently had to wash the greasy marks from Jug Ears' nose off the windowpane. And the coin dealer would come rushing out to chase off the boy. 'Stop drooling on my windows!' he would shout, threatening him with a swing of his cane. No one knew how old Ibsen was, but it was common knowledge that he had a screw loose, and was probably the oldest man in western Norway. It was not until Jug Ears one day slipped inside the shop, placed a handful of change on the counter, and asked the price of a specific coin in the display window that Ibsen became more kindly disposed. With a sly expression, he led the boy over to an old bureau and fished out a shiny wooden box. After a dramatic pause, he pried off the lid. What was inside? Gold coins from Czarist Russia, silver coins from the Prussian empire, old misprinted banknotes from before the monetary union, and a lot of other obscure items.

'Ivan the Terrible,' said Ibsen, pounding his fist solemnly on the counter. 'He came here to my shop. He stood right there where you're standing now, you young pup. Wipe that grin off your face. Where do you think I got these coins? Ivan was in my shop! But I suppose you don't believe me? Go on then, get out of here!'

And Jug Ears replied, 'No, no, I believe you!'

'Good,' said Ibsen. 'Mention anyone you like, and I'll tell you they were in my shop. Come on, go ahead and think of a name!'

'Er, the king,' said Jug Ears. 'King Haakon.'

'1913! He wanted to refurbish his collection, and he personally gave me an anniversary coin. He had his son with him. You don't believe me? The old kings had more style. Nowadays people are interested only in dollars. Haven't you seen how they all crowd around the American warships out at the Skoltegrunn dock? Bought and sold for the big man's dollar. Ha! Haven't you seen how those Yankees toss coins from the railing as if they were sticks of chewing gum? Brand-new coins with no soul, just as shiny as the body part they use for sitting on. And the people, ha! They sell their souls for the big man's dollars—' While the coin dealer rambled on, Jug Ears picked up a big gold coin and stared intently at the portrait of Ivan the Terrible, who by some miracle seemed to be winking at him.

'Hey!' cried Ibsen. 'Keep your mitts off that coin! Not everything can be bought with money, you young pup.' Ibsen pointed to a small silver coin from Czarist Russia, and this time it was Czar Nikolai who winked at Jug Ears before his hand closed around it.

'Hey, what's the rush!' shouted the coin dealer as Jug Ears raced out of the door with the coin in his pocket and vanished down Allikegaten. Back home in Skansen, he found an old wooden box among Askild's painting supplies and placed the coin inside. He hid the box under his bed before he went into the parlour to see to his little brother Knut, who was now almost six months old. But in spite of Ibsen's admonitions, that very same afternoon Jug Ears ran down to the Skoltegrunn dock to have a look at the American warship that had arrived the day before. On deck a bunch of blue-and-white-clad sailors were hanging around.

'Hey!' shouted Jug Ears to the blue-and-white-clad sailors. 'Give me a dollar. Or just a half!' And a shiny coin floated through the air and landed on the dock at his feet, exactly as Ibsen had predicted. Jug Ears picked it up and stared at it, spellbound. He couldn't understand why the old coin dealer refused to handle dollars. Nor could he understand why the blue-and-white-clad sailors had tossed the coin down to him without a second thought. So he tried it again.

'Hey!' he yelled. 'How about another one, just a little one, please—'

Another coin was tossed down to him, accompanied by laughter on board ship. When he bent down to pick it up, he felt something hard strike the back of his head and he heard even louder laughter from the ship. Instinctively he put his hand on the stinging spot a couple of centimetres above the nape of his neck, and as pain spread over his head, he felt a sharp jab at his throat and then another smack as a coin struck him hard on the knee. Standing there in a shower of coins, it occurred to Jug Ears that the blue-and-white-clad sailors were not just giving him a bunch of coins. No, they were trying to *hit* him, and he couldn't figure out whether he had landed in heaven or in hell. Instead, he ran around the dock in bewilderment, gathering up the coins. *Riches will flow, coins will rain down, and gold will find its way into your hands*, the Fang had whispered. But in the midst of this inferno, a coin hit Jug Ears hard on the forehead, and he howled and fled the dock . . .

Back home – with bruises all over his body – he saw to it that Czar Nikolai found himself in the company of George Washington, several times over. The laughter from the bridge still haunted Jug Ears. *Have I sold my soul for the big man's dollar?* he thought as he remembered the coins still lying on the dock beneath the huge ship. But the next day when he ran back to the dock, hoping to find the rest of the coins, they had all vanished along with the warship and the blue-and-white-clad sailors. Besides learning something about the big man's dollar, this episode also taught Jug Ears that coin-collecting was no bed of roses. Whenever he wasn't out fishing for crabs or being castigated in the White School and bowing politely to Deputy-Headmaster Kramer, he would visit Ibsen the coin dealer on Allikegaten.

'Ha! You young pup. Are you back again? Where do you get all this money from?' Yet concealed behind Ibsen's implacable facade was a passionate collector who was grateful to have a loyal disciple.

'Christian IX,' grunted the ageless old man. 'You don't know who Christian IX was? Good Lord! What do they teach you at that school of yours? King Christian was in my shop! Ask me when. In 1864. A statesman with style, but also a real miser! A transaction with him could take several days. But what do you know about things like that? Ha! You don't believe me?'

Jug Ears nodded.

'Ha! You think King Christian is a city in Russia. You think Friedrich Wilhelm of Prussia is a crab dealer at

Fisketorget! Ha! Have you no sense of history, you green-horn? Ask me whether Wilhelm of Prussia was ever in my shop. Ask me whether 16 skillings make 192 pence. The answer is yes!!'

This was how Jug Ears learnt about the Lübeck monetary system, about pennies, skillings, marks, dalers, about the monetary union of 1873, and about various forms of deception, such as mixing too much copper into gold and silver coins. In the box under his bed Czar Nikolai was eventually joined by Carlos III of Spain, by Friedrich August I of Sachsen, by Wilhelm of Prussia, and by various Danish kings in silver and copper.

But the number of big man's dollars also increased con-siderably, and of course Jug Ears never told Ibsen that he would faithfully show up every time the American war-ships put in at the Skoltegrunn dock – now wearing a pot on his head as a helmet and using a pot lid to shield him-self from the hail of coins.

'Give me a dollar! Just a half!' shouted Jug Ears, flailing his arms and legs wildly at the blue-and-white-clad sailors on deck.

'Give me half a million!' screamed the other boys, also equipped with pots and lids, as they stood waiting for the blessed shower of coins. Often a great scrum would break out at the Skoltegrunn dock when coins and pieces of chewing gum rained down on the boys, shattering any sense of solidarity they might have had. A wild panic would erupt. Fierce brawls followed by jubilant howls of victory were the order of the day as the boys threw them-selves at the big man's missiles. Even the previously chewed lumps of gum had a certain value because they could be mixed with sugar and chewed again. The situation at the Skoltegrunn dock didn't get any better when boys from the nearby slums got wind of this special sport that the blue-and-white-clad sailors on the American warships had thought up to pass the time. Soon the slum boys began showing up to stake their own claim to the bounty. When arguments didn't get them anywhere, they had to turn to other methods, like scornful taunts: 'Look at that boy with the ears! My God! How come he doesn't just fly right up to the ship?' Or, directed at skinny Thorbjørn: 'Watch out you don't snap in half, Daddy Longlegs!'

This quickly led to spitting and fistfights, and lumps of dog shit being skewered on sticks and tossed through the air. Eventually something else became obligatory whenever the blue-and-white-clad sailors came into harbour: clubs cut from pine trees up in Lange Woods, carved with the owner's initials and adorned with formidable monsters.

A rivalry had always existed between these two groups of boys in the neighbourhood. But after the blue-and-white-clad sailors had developed and refined their favourite sport, encouraged by the entertaining mass brawl going on below them, things really began to get out of hand.

The presence of the American warships had the unfortunate effect of making Bergen smaller; the city quite simply shrank. It was no longer safe to frequent some neighbourhoods alone. North of specific street corners and west of certain blocks of buildings, you never knew when you might run into a mob of slum kids wielding clubs. And if you got lost one day – as happened to Daddy Longlegs Thorbjørn – you could be sure of receiving the same sort of treatment that he did. First they dragged the terrified boy through the streets of the slums, which prompted an ever-growing crowd of jeering kids to gather round him. Afterwards they led him into an abandoned shed, where they tied him to a pole while one of the smaller boys was sent out to find some dog shit. By the time the boy returned with a piece of shit on a stick, Thorbjørn had already peed in his trousers with fright, and his wails could be heard all over the neighbourhood and beyond. But when he caught sight of the dog shit trembling with menace on the thin stick, he suddenly fell silent. Nor did he say a word when the piece of shit was divided in half. Or when one piece was shoved down his underwear and the other half was smeared all over the seat of his trousers. He was also completely silent as they led him through the slums, and he had to put up with humiliating taunts.

When they finally released him, Thorbjørn didn't dare go home. No, instead he ran over to Skansen pond to wash his trousers in the cold water. The next day everyone in the neighbourhood around Skansen agreed that this time the slum kids had gone too far.

Jug Ears certainly didn't care for the way things had developed. Askild was now the only one who would stroll unconcerned through the slums whenever he headed out to his property to work the hard Bergen bedrock with dynamite.

At the local school, which was called the White School because of its white buildings, Jug Ears learnt that neither his reputation as the Nut Kicker nor his family ties to Applehead could spare him from the humiliations of the educational system. It's here that Deputy-Headmaster Kramer comes roaring into the picture – with his red goatee, bald pate, and a few scraggly wisps of hair behind his ears. He had one blue eye and one brown; the boys called him either the Rainbow or the Palette.

In the last row at the very back of the classroom in the White School sat Daddy Longlegs Thorbjørn, who had acquired a nervous tic under his left eye after his involuntary tour of the slum district. In the next to last row sat Niller with the freckles, otherwise known as Spot Face, who had been the first victim of the art of nut-kicking. But he was now a loyal soldier in the battles at the Skoltegrunn dock. At that time Jug Ears was seated in the front row, largely because of the enthusiasm of Magnus, the newly hired history teacher, for the boy's knowledge of history. Jug Ears was familiar with the lineage of the Russian czars, with Wilhelm of Prussia, with Friedrich August of Sachsen, and with the succession of Nordic kings. All the facts that Jug Ears had at his fingertips had initially prompted the history teacher to conclude that the boy was a walking encyclopaedia, and he had instantly promoted him to the first row. Later the history teacher realized that the boy's knowledge of history was highly coloured by misunderstandings and imaginative rewritings. For instance, Jug Ears obstinately claimed that Christian III, who made Norway a Danish province in the sixteenth century, had paid a recent visit to Ibsen the coin dealer on Allikegaten, and that George Washington was the biggest baby of all time. Even so, the history teacher showed a certain indulgence for childish fantasies, and that's why Jug Ears was currently sitting in the front row, feeling bored.

The only view he had was of the blackboard, and so he would often fall into a reverie in which the Fang's hoarse voice converged with that of Ibsen the coin dealer. Enchanting coins would glitter, big fat crabs would be pulled from the deep . . . and in the midst of this day-dreaming, Kramer the maths teacher would appear, foaming at the mouth. The deputy-headmaster would already have called his name several times.

'Niels, why don't you tell the others what I just said. Niels, is anyone at home?' But not until Kramer roared *Niels!* at the top of his lungs would Jug Ears awake from his daydreaming.

'Ow!' he cried this time, staring in terror at Kramer, who stood less than a metre away, bellowing, 'Are you paying attention, boy? Pardon me for saying so, but how can you possibly avoid hearing what's being said, considering the sort of equipment you possess?'

'Er, I don't know, sir,' replied Jug Ears with a guilty expression.

'What did you say? Did you hear that, gentlemen? He said he *doesn't know*!'

'Ha, ha, sir,' said the other pupils. 'Very funny, sir.'

'Okay, you hooligan,' raged Kramer as he took a firm grip on Jug Ears' left ear, forcing him to stand up. 'Let's hear what you're sitting here thinking about. Or maybe *that's* not something you know, either?'

'No, sir. I'm sorry, sir. I don't know, sir. Ow, ow!'

Deputy-Headmaster Kramer turned to the class and said, 'Give me some suggestions. Come on, boys. What's our clever little donkey-ears sitting there thinking about?'

'Er, the world situation, sir?' came the first suggestion from Niller with the freckles. Relief showed on the faces of the other pupils. *At least it's not me!* they were all thinking.

'Excuse me, sir. A certain girl by the name of Linda?'

'Herr Kramer, maybe Niels is thinking about his crazy sister?'

'No, boys!' exclaimed Kramer triumphantly as he yanked on Jug Ears' ears so hard that the boy had to stand on tiptoe. 'Wrong! Our model student, this child prodigy, the student teacher's pet, our very own donkey-head *was not thinking about anything at all.* His head is empty, completely empty. He's the type who's going to end up at the bonemeal factory, gentlemen!'

'Is that true, sir? Does Herr Kramer mean that Niels is going to be turned into bonemeal?'

'Am I right?' Kramer thundered at Jug Ears.

'Yes, sir,' howled Jug Ears. And when the deputy-headmaster ordered him to repeat after him, the boy added:

'My head is empty, ow, ow, I'm incapable of thinking, ow, ow, they're going to make bonemeal out of my ears, ow, ow, I deserve to be made into bonemeal, yes, sir, I'm a donkey and a beast!'

By this time Jug Ears' ears were in imminent danger of coming loose from his head, but suddenly an odd change seemed to come over the teacher, who always insisted on teaching in the physics lab. The pupils knew why, but the other teachers did not. Later they would discover the reason, and Deputy-Headmaster Kramer would be sentenced by the municipal court to a fine commensurate with eight days' pay at fifteen kroner per day. He let go of Jug Ears, patted him affectionately on the head, and went

182

to sit behind his desk. There he propped up his legs and said in the most charming of voices: 'The ball, you baboon.'

A ripple of excitement passed through the physics lab. Standing next to the teacher's desk was the feared electricity machine, a permanent part of the inventory in the physics lab where Deputy-Headmaster Kramer always insisted on teaching. It generated static electricity by means of a small crank, and it went by the nickname of 'the ball'. It was well known among the boys at the school that the electricity machine was not used for educational purposes. It was used instead as a means of punishment. First they had to take off their shoes and socks. Then they would go over and stand on the cold metal plate, which Kramer had nailed to the floor next to the machine to make the unruly kids extra conductive. Finally, they had to turn the crank until the air flashed with static electricity and their hair stood on end.

'Fate has not been merciful to me,' Jug Ears repeated after Kramer as he turned the crank like a man possessed. 'Fate has equipped me with a pair of enormous donkey-ears, but fate has also filled my head with snot, so that I can't listen to what's being said. I'm going to end up in a bonemeal factory – if they even have any use for me there.'

So Jug Ears turned the crank, the way other boys in Kramer's physics lab had, as they confessed their shameful shortcomings to the class, until Kramer pounded his key ring on the desk three times and said, 'Kiss the ball.' With those words the most deafening silence in the whole Norwegian school system descended on the physics lab, because it was a well-known fact that sparks would enter your brain if your lips touched the electric ball, and that this would often make you pee in your trousers.

So what did Jug Ears do? He bent down and kissed the ball.

'I've peed in my trousers,' he later repeated after Kramer. 'I'm a filthy little baboon.'

A Stray Roof Tile

M Y SISTER STINNA CAN VIVIDLY recall Dad's stories about Deputy-Headmaster Kramer, and she still shudders at the memory. Afterwards she sighs and looks out of the window, where her husband Jesper is going around with a hedge cutter, trimming the bushes. He's missing some fingers on each hand and has a hard time holding the hedge cutter. He's friendly enough towards me, but he still seems a bit reserved. He never comes into the guest room. He just knocks politely and waits outside until I open the door. I've lugged all Askild's old painting supplies into the room. I've also gone out and bought new things. Even though it took me less than twenty-four hours to travel back to Denmark, it's taking a long time for the stories to return home. They arrive separately, in the night; or in pairs, in dreams and visions that appear in my mind's eye.

'Did you go out to visit the old lady again today?' Stinna asks, turning her gaze away from Jesper.

I nod.

'Is she still just as crazy? With all those stupid tins?' she goes on. 'Have you noticed who she thinks is sending them?'

Again I nod. Grandma Bjørk thinks the fresh air from Bergen is coming from Dad. She never talks about the actual sender as someone who's still alive, even though she's very taken with all the stories about him. I also found a couple of letters from Mum among the tins, and a single letter from Uncle Knut, but it was over a year old. And Grandma's expression turned gloomy when I took it out.

'Is he still only sending letters when he needs money?' I ask Stinna.

'Knut, my ass,' she says. 'I dare him to write again. If he does, he'll have me to contend with.'

Knut had become a very real member of the family by the time they moved out to the new, almost finished house in the recently developed neighbourhood. Before anyone knew it, he had overtaken Anne Katrine and started to walk. First he stole Pappa Niels's pipe and threw it out of the window. Then he pinched Mamma Randi's crocheting and sent it the same way. That's how he got into the habit of tossing things out of the window, and before long no object under a certain size was safe. Knick-knacks, cutlery, coins and cigarettes, even Askild's tubes of paint had to be regularly gathered up from the street. In the beginning there was nothing to indicate that Knut would turn out to be the family's problem child, but his obsession with throwing things out of the window soon developed into a form of hyper-activity. At the same time, his level of energy made five-year-old Anne Katrine, sitting in her playpen, look even more retarded. The family had become accustomed to regarding her as a slightly oversized infant, but the puppy-dog look had vanished. She now had transparent skin and moved in a helpless manner. She resembled a sort of human plant that had been deprived of light. Eventually even Bjørk began to think there was something eerie about her; a coldness in her daughter's eyes that she could not separate from her own guilty conscience or from the splinter of ice in her heart, which she fought as best she could with good Norwegian sweaters and woollen blankets.

Shortly before they moved, little brother Knut was seized by a new obsession. He liked to run off or – as he later would have said – go out exploring. And Jug Ears was quickly assigned a number of new chores, such as gathering up the things under the windows and going out to find his little brother whenever he'd run off. 'Knut!' he could often be heard shouting as he walked through the neighbourhood. 'Where are you?' Jug Ears would frequently find Knut in the far corners of the back courtyards, hunting for cats, or in dustbins where he was digging for gold. Or Jug Ears might find his little brother several kilometres from home, in the process of working out just how far he could go.

'What would we do without you?' Bjørk would tell Jug Ears whenever he came home with his missing little brother.

These chores increased Jug Ears' sense of responsibility and sowed in his mind the idea that he was the one who had to hold the family together. This was later given expression in the countless envelopes containing crisp Danish five-hundred-krone notes, which he sent to his brother on the other side of the Atlantic.

When Jug Ears, shortly before they moved, showed his mother his impressive coin collection for the first time, she gave him an admiring look. She said that with such a treasure in the house, they were never going to lack for bread on the table. Bjørk's willingness to play the game of 'big-brother-is-the-light-of-the-family-and-much-more-reliable-than-his-father' incited Jug Ears to fight ever more zealously at the Skoltegrunn dock. And since he knew how unpopular the American coins were among genuine coin collectors, he often traded them with the other boys for much more valuable coins. In school he would draw a chalk line on the tile floor and challenge the others to toss coins. The one whose coin came closest to the chalk line won the entire lot. And at many of the docks in Bergen younger boys had started catching crabs for him.

With his treasure box under his arm, Jug Ears perched on top of the first of three removal wagons that drove out to the new house where they were going to live forever. Except for a few minor details, Askild had designed and built the house all on his own, and it was impossible to deny the cubist inspiration. 'Why is the dining room hexagonal? Why did you make the hallway so crooked?' asked Bjørk when she entered the house for the first time. She refrained from commenting on other details. Certain doors refused to close, the roof leaked, the insulation was deficient, and the wood floors had been so poorly planed that the family got splinters in their feet. But not even the cubist inspiration could dampen their joy, and Bjørk was relieved to escape from her domineering mother-in-law with her disgusting vitamin drinks.

Even Jug Ears was impressed. He had his own room! All day long he ran joyfully through the house, and in the evening he went in to inspect the cupboard under the sink. He closed the door after him, automatically reached for a pencil stub, and began drawing monsters on the inside of the door. He fell into the reverie that always claimed him whenever he sat under a sink, and he again heard the Fang talking about treasure chests filled with coins that made willing maidens break into song. Even though by now he was quite familiar with the Fang's universe, he still had a hard time understanding the meaning behind all those young maidens. The only person he knew who bore any resemblance to this sort of young maiden was Lewd Linda. The other boys were always talking about her. Once she called after him: 'Hey, Niels! They say you kissed the ball today!' But Jug Ears hurried off. He was certain that there was something snide about her comment, and he shuddered at the thought of all the things she did with the other boys in various sheds in the back courtyards. He had heard plenty of rumours. The most absurd of these was that she took their dicks in her mouth.

'Pretty soon I'm going to be so rich that Linda will beg me to put it in her mouth,' Daddy Longlegs Thorbjørn had said after a successful battle at the Skoltegrunn dock. And even though Jug Ears was sure that it was too absurd to be true, the imagined image of Lewd Linda with a dick in her mouth still prompted a storm of speculation. *Do they pee into her mouth?* he wondered before he dismissed the thought from his mind and went back to drawing his monsters. When he looked at them later on – Bjørk was calling him because little brother Knut had run off again – he couldn't understand why he had drawn them. So Jug Ears quickly crawled back out, feeling slightly sheepish.

'Knut!' he shouted outside the house. 'Where are you?'

'Up here,' he heard from the mountain slope overlooking the house. When Jug Ears climbed up to join him, Knut was pointing at a ship. You could see the sea from up there, as well as most of Bergen.

'Sips sail far 'way,' Knut prattled, jumping up and down with enthusiasm. 'Apphead far 'way.'

'Yup,' replied Jug Ears, taking him by the hand.

Ever since Askild first took Knut down to the shipyard to see one of the newly completed vessels, the boy had been totally obsessed with ships. And from Mamma Randi, who suffered from constant nightmares in which Applehead's ship sank in a fierce storm, he also knew a great deal about Applehead's dangerous journeys across the seas of the world.

'Apphead back!' said Knut on his way down the slope.

'Yup,' replied Jug Ears, taking his little brother back to the house, where he was praised to the skies by Bjørk. 'What would we do without you?' she said, patting the proud rescuer on the cheek.

Without me everything would go downhill, thought Jug Ears. And he went to his room to look at his coin collection.

Except for the fact that it had now got easier for little brother Knut to run off, no one in the family could see anything negative about their move. Bjørk and Askild both seemed enamoured of each other again, and the first weekend in the new house passed in an amazing mood of exaltation, right up until Sunday evening. Suddenly it occurred to Jug Ears – *why didn't I think about this before?* he moaned – that the road to the White School and his comrades in Skansen now led straight through the slum district, where mobs of club-wielding slum kids restlessly roamed, always on the lookout for a victim.

Downhill, thought Jug Ears. *Things are going to go downhill after all.*

The next morning he ate breakfast with the family and then went to his room to get his school-bag and homemade club. He kissed Bjørk goodbye and went out of the door, but 50 metres down the road he opened his schoolbag, took out the club, and set off at a run. He didn't stop until, drenched with sweat, he stood in front of the White School. He had covered the route to school, which was several kilometres, at a furious pace. He raced past a group of gaping slum boys, who hadn't seen a kid from Skansen in their neighbourhood for a very long time. He zoomed past Lewd Linda, nearly toppling her in his flight. 'Hey!' she yelled. 'Are you going up there to kiss the ball?' Even old ladies had retreated in fear from the club-wielding sprinter. Milkmen cursed, dogs barked, and morning-weary bicyclists practically tumbled over their handlebars when eleven-year-old Jug Ears crossed the streets at a furious clip. Even after he reached the safety zone on the other side of the slum district, his adrenaline had been pumping at such a rate that he couldn't stop, and it was not until he stood in front of the White School that he collapsed with his back against the high wall.

'You there!' resounded Deputy-Headmaster Kramer's familiar voice. 'This isn't some kind of rest stop.'

'I'm sorry, sir,' gasped Jug Ears, who was actually quite pleased with himself and his run. *Maybe everything isn't going to go downhill after all*, he thought.

* * *

191

Over the course of the next few weeks, Jug Ears quickly got into top form. The milkmen, bicyclists, and old ladies gradually got used to the sight of him. But there were others who did, too, meaning the slum kids, whose initial stares soon vanished. Several times a piece of dog shit on a stick came flying after him. At other times pebbles hit him, accompanied by shouts.

'Hey! It's the kid with the ears. Hello, Jug Ears! Lost your way in the city?'

'Do you want to try the same stunt as your friend?'

'Get out of our neighbourhood, buster!'

Soon they began lying in wait on street corners, hoping to stick out their legs and trip Jug Ears up as he came racing past. The first time he landed on his stomach in front of four slum kids with outstretched legs, Jug Ears leapt to his feet and started swinging his club so wildly that they immediately stepped back. But Black Per, Ugly Leif, Fat Hans, and Red Pig now surrounded him, blocking any possible escape.

'Take it easy,' said Red Pig. 'We just want to talk to you.'

'Like hell you do!' yelled Jug Ears.

'Yes, like hell we do, buster,' said Black Per.

Jug Ears had been planning for a situation like this. He took a step closer to Red Pig and raised his club to threaten him, but Red Pig didn't retreat. Instead, he fixed his eyes on the club, ready to dodge a blow.

'Take it easy,' said Ugly Leif when Jug Ears started swinging his club.

'Take it easy,' repeated Red Pig, reaching out to grab the club, but that left his crotch vulnerable – just as Jug Ears had anticipated.

The next second the super sprinter was tearing down the street before Ugly Leif, Black Per, or Fat Hans could react, while Red Pig lay crumpled up on the pavement, bright red in the face and with bells ringing in his ears.

'A direct hit! He really got you, didn't he, you fat pig!' yelled Linda, who had suddenly come into view at the end of the street.

It was during this time that Bjørk bought her two-hundredth medical romance. Askild, after a lengthy period of inactivity, took up cubist painting again in the entrance hall. Little brother Knut repeatedly lit small fire beacons on the mountain slope behind the house, eager to communicate with the distant ships in the fjord. And one Sunday Anne Katrine pulled herself up in her playpen and took her first step. Bjørk, who was in the midst of doing the wash, suddenly caught sight of her daughter over by the coffee table. She was standing there with her hands in an ashtray, chewing on a cigarette butt.

Holding a bundle of laundry in her arms, Bjørk wondered for a brief moment whether she ought to praise the girl because she was walking or scold her because she was chewing on a cigarette butt. This was a typical reaction for Bjørk, whose relationship with the child suffered from constant analysis. But this time all her speculations suddenly vanished. The laundry slipped out of her hands, and she ran out to the entrance hall to find Askild.

'What did I tell you!' exclaimed Askild, when he caught sight of his daughter chewing on the butt. 'There's nothing the hell wrong with Anne Katrine! She's just not as quick as the others.'

'How did she get out of the playpen?' whispered Bjørk, giving Askild's arm a little squeeze.

'She jumped. Like a filly,' Askild whispered back. And for a long time they stood there like that, arm in arm, looking at their daughter. *Just like any other ordinary couple*, thought Bjørk with a lump in her throat, until Anne Katrine abruptly grimaced and spat the butt out on the floor. Then she turned round and noticed her mother and father.

'Tootily-toot,' said Askild, giving her a cautious wave.

'She can walk!' he whispered a short time later into the telephone to a bewildered Pappa Niels, surprised at his own voice, until Mamma Randi tore the receiver away from the old man.

'It's Anne Katrine. She can walk,' Randi explained as she took Pappa Niels by the hand and hurried down the stairs and right through the slum district to see the miracle for herself.

'Ingrid?' asked Niels.

'No, you idiot. Not our daughter! Our granddaughter Anne Katrine!' declared Randi, casting an annoyed glance at her husband, who retained very little of his former swagger. *Sweet Mother of God, how the years have flown*, thought Randi. Then she caught sight of a little blond boy who was standing on a street corner, rummaging through a rubbish bin, and was filled with dismay. *What a horrid neighbourhood*, she thought.

She gave Pappa Niels a little push to pick up the pace, but she couldn't stop looking at the boy, who had now crawled halfway into the rubbish bin. There was something familiar about him. She was positive that she had seen him before. *But where?* she thought. Only after the boy had practically disappeared all the way inside the bin did it dawn on her who he was, and she let go of Pappa Niels to dash over to the boy.

'Ugh! Stop that. What do you think you're going to find in there?'

'Gold and scalps,' replied Knut pulling some old bones out of the rubbish.

'How disgusting,' said Randi.

'Is that little Niels Junior?' cried Pappa Niels.

'No, it's Knut, the younger boy. What's he doing here?' snapped Randi, and she dragged the boy along with them.

By the time they reached the house in the newly developed neighbourhood, Bjørk had also phoned her mother, even though Mamma Ellen seldom came to visit. Askild had never forgotten the way he had been treated as a young man in the white patrician villa on Kalfarveien and, as the years passed, bitterness settled into his veins. His animosity had not diminished even though Bjørk's family had rescued him from the embarrassing situation he had been in when he lost his job in Stavanger. And when Bjørk's sister came roaring up with her splendid husband in their new Volvo, gratitude did not exactly flow from my paternal grandfather.

Underlying the whole wretched affair was the vague notion that if only the Svensson family had received him properly so many years ago, he probably would not have thrown himself into the risky business of stealing an entire load of lumber and been arrested by the Germans. He never lacked sarcastic remarks when the conversation happened to turn to Bjørk's family, and so Bjørk preferred to meet her mother elsewhere, most often at Skivebakken or at her sister Lina's house. Yet Bjørk felt that her mother and sister shared a bond that did not include her, and, if the truth be told, Lina was also getting a bit tired of Bjørk's constant complaints.

But now the whole family had showed up, and for the first time in ages Anne Katrine was the centre of everyone's attention. When the family arrived, she was sitting on the floor in the parlour, playing with Knut's rubber ball. She shoved it away, waited a moment, and then crawled after it.

'Come on,' said Askild. 'Show us what I taught you.' But Anne Katrine refused to stand up and walk. She said 'toot, toot', chewed on Askild's hand for a bit, and then crawled after the ball, only to shove it away again. Half an hour passed in this manner. Askild set her on her feet several times, but each time he let her go, her legs gave way and she would stare in bewilderment at the family, who were waiting expectantly. After more failed attempts, Askild said, 'Let's have some coffee, Bjørk!'

But they drank their coffee in a gloomy mood, while Pappa Niels tried to figure out where he was. 'Are we visiting someone?' he asked several times. Annoyed, Randi told him where they were. Then Niels, in a moment of clarity, snickered at his wife and said, 'Of course I know where we are. We're in the skipper's cottage in the new development!' And he carelessly tossed his cigar stub at the windowsill. Randi started scolding him. Mamma Ellen thought, *Good Lord, what a family!* And in the midst of it all, Anne Katrine got up and tottered towards the windowsill and the smouldering cigar, which had landed in a potted plant. Naturally she was a bit startled when the whole family abruptly began to clap and cry with admiration. 'What did I tell you!' shouted Askild. 'She's practically *floating*!'

A moment later Pappa Niels stood up and said, 'Afternoon nap, disembarkation; unfortunately, I must go home now.'

'What!' wailed Mamma Randi as Anne Katrine walked from one person to the next. They all praised the girl to the skies, kissed her on the cheek, and patted her on the head. 'But we've only just got here!'

'Goodbye,' said Niels, shaking his wife's hand. 'It's been a pleasure.'

'Let Pappa go,' said Askild as Mamma Randi kept on objecting.

'Niels can't go home alone, not in his condition!' she said.

'If he doesn't make it home,' said Askild, 'we'll send Niels Junior after him. Niels is a master at finding people who are lost.'

'I may be old,' said Pappa Niels, 'but I'm not an idiot. Of course I can find my way home.'

At that moment he seemed amazingly lucid. The family made him tell them what route he would take home, and, sounding a bit offended, he described it down to the last detail. This recitation convinced Mamma Randi, who reluctantly let her husband go after warning him about the loose step on the stairs.

'Goodbye,' said Pappa Niels again as he bowed to his wife. 'It's been a pleasure.'

That very afternoon Jug Ears was on his way home through the slum district. He was sprinting through the streets, holding his home-made club and feeling utterly invincible. In his mind he was replaying brief clips from the movie that he had seen with Thorbjørn and the other boys from the neighbourhood. John Wayne, the lone cowboy, arrives in a hostile town. He rides straight across the prairie, Indians pursuing him on stolen horses, six-shooter gleaming brightly in his hand like a home-made club. And then John Wayne, galloping on his imaginary horse, comes to an abrupt halt when he spies seven Indians standing there doing NOTHING!

'Damn it!' swore Jug Ears before turning on his heel and racing off in the opposite direction. But the slum kids had already caught sight of him.

'Hey, Jug Ears! We want to talk to you!'

Jug Ears zoomed off with his heart in his throat, the six-shooter (*if only it were a real six-shooter*, thought Jug Ears) feeling clammy in his hand. He darted down a side street where he witnessed the same disturbing sight: Indians who were doing *nothing*, standing in the middle of the street. Again he turned on his heel, but now the seven Indians he had first seen came into view at the other end, and any sort of movie scene vanished from his mind. He was no longer John Wayne but rather Niels with the jug ears; and the Indians were not Indians but slum kids with a penchant for dog shit. In other words, there were slum kids on all sides of him. He ran over to an abandoned shop and crawled up on to the roof, but he couldn't get down the other side.

'Damn it!' he swore again, biting his lip as the two groups of boys gathered below him.

Standing there, above and in full view of twenty slum kids, he tried at first to be diplomatic.

'I'm a slum kid now, too – I practically live in your neighbourhood,' he shouted at the bunch of boys.

'No, you're not. You live out on the development, in the fancy houses. Don't you think we've heard about you riding around in your uncle's car? You really think you're something, don't you?'

'No, I don't,' howled Jug Ears. 'It's a stupid car! I don't like it at all— Really! And my uncle is stupid too!'

'But he's still your uncle. Bloody fancy, eh?' the boys shouted from down below. 'Listen here! Come down. We want to have a little talk with you!'

'No!' yelled Jug Ears, giving up being diplomatic and pelting the boys with stones.

'Ow!' he heard from below. 'All right, you asked for it.'

The boys began climbing up to the roof. Hands gripped the eaves as Jug Ears danced on any number of fingers and uttered shrill war whoops. At first everything went fine, but then two hands grabbed him by the ankles and pulled him down.

'Cut it out!' howled Jug Ears as he was hauled right through the slum district and shoved inside an abandoned shed. 'Cut it out!' he howled when they bound him with a rope to the same pole where Thorbjørn had been tied up earlier. 'Stop it,' he went on as the youngest boy was sent out to get some dog shit.

'Shut up,' Red Pig told him with a grin. 'Or we'll cut off your nuts.'

Pappa Niels, who only minutes before had been amazingly lucid, grew confused a short way down the road. Where was he? And even worse: Where was he going? He felt as if an invisible hand had seized hold of him, tied him in a knot, and tossed him at random into his past. One moment he was on his way home through the bright

199

morning streets of Bergen – Randi, Ingrid, and little Askild were supposed to have been waiting at the dock, but apparently they had been delayed. The next moment he was convinced that he had been sent out to get cigarettes for his father and had lost the money. But then the ramshackle buildings in the slum district convinced him that he wasn't in the Bergen of his childhood at all – he was in Amsterdam. Little Sprout, the youngest cabin boy, had disappeared in the red-light district and had to be found at all costs. Otherwise the skipper would be impossible. A familiar irritation surged through his mind, mixed with worry about the missing cabin boy and confusion because the light was so bright in the evening.

'Little Sprout?' a passing boy heard him mutter. 'Where are you, Little Sprout?'

Looking for Little Sprout, Pappa Niels hurried through the slum district, growing more and more nervous and annoyed. He couldn't find his way through the streets, and a vague premonition about the condition in which he was bound to find Little Sprout made him step up the pace. His heart was pounding, sweat was dripping into his eyes and making everything look hazy – so hazy that a dilapidated shed standing on a building site that he happened to pass suddenly looked like the shed that he had entered seventy years earlier. The red paint was peeling off and outside someone was standing guard. That must be the seaman, thought Pappa Niels, and he hurried over to the shed. Of course he was surprised when neither the seaman nor the laughing woman was inside. Nor did the sight of the cabin boy's bare ass strike him with fear and disbelief. What he did see was Little Sprout, tied to a pole, and wagging in front of his head was not the seaman's dick but something that looked unmistakably like a piece of dog shit on a stick.

'It's me!' shouted Little Sprout when he saw how confused Pappa Niels looked. 'It's me, Niels Junior, your grandson!'

Even though Little Sprout had clothes on, Pappa Niels recognized the expression of relief and deep embarrassment that had once been stamped on the face of the missing cabin boy. And even the slum kids looked confused. Red Pig tried to throw away the stick, but the dog shit fell off and landed on Pappa Niels's shoe. Black Per was already on his way out of the shed. For a moment the others considered overpowering the old man and tying him up to another pole, but that might have been going too far.

'It's me!' Little Sprout kept repeating.

And suddenly something dawned on Pappa Niels, and he replied, 'I know that, but why the hell are you tied to a pole?'

With that, all the slum kids vanished from the shed. Some fell over one another. Some cast a swift glance at the dog shit on the old man's shoe and ran away as fast as they could, while Pappa Niels silently untied Jug Ears. On their way back to the house in the development, a new memory swept through the old man's mind, and he now spoke to Jug Ears as he had often spoken to his own son: 'Don't go home with strange men, don't be fooled by their stories.' Jug Ears nodded as he cast surreptitious glances at the dog shit that was still stuck to the top of the old man's shoe.

'I can go the rest of the way by myself,' said Jug Ears as they approached the development. 'You won't tell anyone about all this, will you?' he went on, giving his grandfather a pleading look.

Once again Pappa Niels thought he recognized the voice of the missing cabin boy. 'No,' he replied, 'of course not.' A strong gust of wind made his hair stand up like a halo around his head, and an almost blissful expression slid across his face as, without warning, he bowed as deeply and gallantly as his old back would allow.

'It's been a pleasure,' he said, and shook hands with his astonished grandson.

Then Pappa Niels disappeared once more into the slum district. No one in his family ever saw him alive again. A couple of slum kids heard him trying to console Little Sprout: 'Don't cry, Little Sprout, nobody's going to find out . . .' A butcher saw him bend down, take off his shoes, and continue barefoot through the streets. Later a cabin boy heard him humming a sea shanty, a fisherman heard him swearing to himself and a couple of little boys who were fishing for crabs for Jug Ears, were, the following day, convinced that they heard the old man say, 'I damn well saved him. The first mate never managed to spear his ass.'

On his way out of this life, and on the lookout for the *Amanda* in the morning fog, Pappa Niels wandered around the docks of Bergen. A strong wind was blowing, and as he passed the former offices of Shipowner Thorsten Svensson on C. Sundtsgaten for the third time, a fierce gust blew through Vågen and tore off a single roof tile. The tile floated down 15 metres and struck Pappa Niels on the head.

'Misfortune,' said Askild many years later, giving my paternal grandmother Bjørk an angry look. 'Your family has brought us nothing but misfortune.'

'I told you!' cried Mamma Randi later that same evening. 'Askild! You were the one who said that he could go!'

Mamma Randi didn't get home until dusk, and when Pappa Niels was not sitting in his rocking chair, as usual, Niels Jug Ears Junior was sent out to look for his grandfather. Later Askild also went out to join in the search, but he stopped abruptly when he found his father's shoe in the middle of the street. 'How typical,' he snapped after examining Niels's shoe. 'Normal people step in dog shit, but of course my father, impossible as he is, has to get shit on *top* of his shoe!'

It was already dark by the time Jug Ears – after having run everywhere searching the docks – stumbled over the lifeless body on C. Sundtsgaten.

A Sailor Returns Home

BARELY A YEAR after the death of Pappa Niels in 1957, someone knocked on the door of the house in the new development. Outside stood an imposing-looking man with a big moustache. Anne Katrine, who was home alone with Bjørk and Randi, opened the door and stared in fright at the man, who was almost 2 metres tall. He smiled, showing a black gap where he was missing a front tooth. A big scar ran across his temple. His hair was short and bristly. His enormous biceps were adorned with colourful tattoos, including a parrot so lifelike that Anne Katrine wanted to touch it. A gold earring glittered in one ear, and his skin was unbelievably tanned.

'Apphead is back!' shouted Knut, up on the slope above the house. From there, using Askild's telescope, he had been following the extraordinary man's passage through town. The man matched perfectly his image of his long-lost cousin. But now Knut seemed to be a little scared of coming down, and he stayed where he was on the slope. In front of the house the giant picked up Anne Katrine by the waist and tossed her into the air three times as he laughed loudly. After that, Bjørk appeared in the doorway and stared in fright at the man. Then he grabbed her, too, by the waist and tossed her up into the air. 'Niels!' she cried. 'Is it really you!'

'Yup,' replied the man, grinning. 'Is it really you?'

At that moment Mamma Randi appeared in the doorway. At the sight of the huge man she uttered a little shriek, and then it was her turn to be tossed into the air.

'What a lot of nonsense,' she said afterwards, brushing off her clothes.

Then a brief lull ensued, which the two women used to make calls to Ingrid at Haukeland Hospital and to Askild at the shipyard. Little brother Knut first saw his aunt Ingrid come running towards the house. Shortly afterwards, Askild appeared. He dropped his cane and bumped heads with the giant when he was tossed into the air, but to Knut's great surprise, he didn't get mad or upset.

Little brother Knut still didn't dare go inside the house. Not until his older brother came home and was tossed several times into the air did Knut gather his courage and run into the parlour, right up to the imposing-looking man, and said, 'My name is Knut, and I want to be tossed in the air too!'

For the rest of the afternoon Knut clung to his cousin, feeling his biceps and insisting on poking his finger into the black gap in his top front teeth. He also made Applehead take off his reddish-brown T-shirt so that he could examine all the tattoos. He tugged at his cousin's earring, pulled on his huge moustache, and cautiously slid his finger along the thrilling scar on his right temple. 'Not a fair fight,' Applehead told him, using the English word for 'fair'. He had become accustomed to throwing in

English words here and there. 'Seven slant-eyes against one. But I thrashed the lot of them!'

Jug Ears was a bit more reserved, secretly staring at his cousin's enormous biceps. He couldn't really understand how such a transformation could be possible, but he was looking forward to taking Applehead down to the slum district soon. That would show them!

Later that day the two brothers took Applehead to see their rooms, and that's when Applehead asked them if they'd like to see something wild.

'Yes!' shouted Knut, jumping up and down. 'Something wild, something wild!'

With a sly expression, Applehead closed the door to the room and pulled down his trousers. A big, dark green tattoo crept up his thigh, and both brothers assumed that was what he wanted to show them. But with a swift movement Applehead also stripped off his underwear to expose his dick, making the brothers gasp. Not just at its size – it hung to mid-thigh and was as thick as a salami – but also because the strange stripes of colour covering the long dick and making it shimmer brightly took their breath away.

'Ow!' whispered Applehead when little brother Knut pinched his dick to see if it was real. It was. Not until they came close could they see the reason for the shimmering colours. Red and blue letters spelled out the words: FOR MY BELUVD IDA. The tattoo artist in Singapore hadn't been very familiar with the Latin alphabet – a couple of the letters were backwards while others were missing entirely – but that didn't seem to bother Applehead.

That evening he took a long bath and spent an hour and a half brushing his teeth, combing his hair, applying

Vaseline to his moustache, and drenching himself with Askild's Old Spice. Then he kissed all his family members goodbye and went over to the teetotaller's house on Hutomsgata. Along the way he stole three roses from a garden he happened to pass, whistling loudly like a man who's quite sure of himself and revelling in all the covert glances he encountered on the streets. Standing in front of the house on Hutomsgata, he knocked so hard that the walls shook. When the door opened, he dropped to his knees and proposed to Ida, who stared in horror at the strange man. At first she couldn't figure out who he was, but when she finally recognized him her cheeks turned red and she replied to his proposal with two stinging slaps: smack, smack! And then she slammed the door in his face.

No longer whistling or enjoying the glances of passers-by, and still carrying the wilting roses which he slapped against the corner of every building he passed, Applehead returned home to the flat in Skansen.

By the following day he had resumed his old ritual. He took his bicycle out of the cellar, oiled the rusty chain, and pounded the fender into place. Then he began pursuing the red-headed girl through the streets of Bergen whenever she went out for a walk with the twins. Applehead was once again a familiar sight as he rode around town in a state of distraction. Instead of asking to carry her school-bag, he now begged her to let him help with the groceries. He frequently offered to push the stroller with the two-year-old twins, and he even suggested digging a garden for the teetotaller and working for free as an errand boy at his elastic-band factory. But none of this did any good.

'Get lost, you jackass!' Ida would say whenever Applehead

crossed the 20-metre boundary which she had designated as her personal space. Soon Applehead became so desperate that he found it necessary to revive yet another ritual. 'The postman's coming!' he shouted with a smirk as he wobbled past her on the bicycle, which was now much too small for him. But Ida the Ginger never went to Lange Woods, and the letters piled up inside the old tree.

Instead, she began showering him with criticism. 'Take off that earring. You look like a pirate in a bad movie,' she shouted after him. 'Get your tooth fixed. Shave off that moustache. Throw out that duffel bag. Do you think I want to have anything to do with a stupid sailor?'

Over the next few months Applehead obeyed like a well-trained dog. And Knut noticed with disappointment how his imposing-looking cousin shed one thing after another. Applehead started wearing shirts so that the tattoos were no longer visible. He went to the dentist and had a false tooth put in. He shaved off his moustache and stopped inserting English words into his sentences. His suntan faded, the earring was put away in a drawer, and before a month had passed, Applehead was running errands for the teetotaller every morning. He made coffee, swept the floors, and in this way began preparing for his future career in the elastic-band business. 'Yes, sir!' Applehead said over and over, and he would always salute Arnt Bjørkvig, who saw an opportunity to restore his family's honour by browbeating the runaway groom.

Askild tried many times to get Applehead a job at the shipyard, but he wasn't interested. Instead, he started walking about with elastic bands around his shirtsleeves, to emphasize his loyalty to Bjørkvig Elastic Bands, which bore the slogan: *Bjørkvig Elastic Bands – Best in All the*

Lands. After work – still wearing a dozen elastic bands around his sleeves – Applehead would continue to pursue the teetotaller's daughter. Once he was seen walking 3 metres behind her, carrying two big grocery bags. Another time Thorbjørn saw him fixing a wheel on the stroller while Ida impatiently urged him to hurry up.

'What an applehead!' said Thorbjørn with despair to Jug Ears. Being an applehead became synonymous with being a knucklehead. But in spite of Thorbjørn's despairing tone, his indignation was only skin-deep because Applehead was now a grown-up, and everybody knew that grown-ups were fools. Even Jug Ears realized that his cousin, although he was 2 metres tall, wouldn't be much help in the slum district. As a representative of Bjørkvig Elastic Bands, he couldn't run about kicking boys in the nuts. So Jug Ears would have to handle things on his own, or with the help of his friends. Only Knut was deeply disappointed by his cousin.

'Stupid Applehead!' he muttered. And he stole one of Askild's old fountain pens before barricading himself in his room. Later that day Bjørk found him there with his trousers off, his little dick completely smeared with ink.

Much later Knut would acquire his own tattoo. But back then, in the late 1950s, Applehead's disappointing behaviour and Bjørk's new habit of checking on her younger son's dick for inappropriate ink drawings at bedtime, made Knut even more impossible. He started running farther away and throwing bigger things out of the windows. A short time later, one of his little bonfires on the mountain spread at a furious pace and ended up ravaging the entire slope. 'Fortunately it was the right slope,' Askild used to say, meaning the slope that was uninhabited. 'If the wind hadn't been blowing from the south—' was how Bjørk liked to tell the story. Later, the tale of Uncle Knut's forest fire became one of our absolute favourites. 'Ask Grandma Bjørk to tell the one about the forest fire,' my sister Stinna used to say, since she knew that Grandma was more likely to relent if I was the one to ask. 'Tell us about Knut's forest fire,' I would say, and Bjørk would give us a sly look before she started.

But back then – as black smoke suddenly began pouring over the mountainside – it wasn't such a funny story because Knut had disappeared and Jug Ears had been sent up to the mountain to look for him. That's when Askild first caught sight of the smoke. He tipped over his easel, which he had brought outside, and dashed for the mountain without his cane. By the time Bjørk saw the smoke a few minutes later, Askild had already vanished into the haze, and she could hear him desperately calling to his sons. 'We thought they were up there,' Grandma Bjørk used to say.

So then she and a dozen neighbours set off running for the mountain, armed with water buckets and carpet beaters, but nothing worked. The fire refused to be tamed and an entire section of the forest burned. But what about Jug Ears and little Knut? Here Grandma always used to allow some doubt to creep into her expression. Would we ever see them alive again? Yes! Because Jug Ears and Knut were down by the harbour, and didn't notice the black smoke until they were heading for home. Knut, having watched the flames from his little bonfire start to spread, got scared and ran towards the harbour. And that was just where Jug Ears had gone to find him. He caught up with

Knut halfway there, but then he took him down to the harbour to buy the day's catch of crabs from some boys. Later they went over to Fisketorget, where they sold the crabs for ten øre apiece. That's why they didn't get back home until the rescue team had returned without finding them. Askild was black from head to toe, and he had just picked up his cane from the ground when his two sons came walking up the garden path. He turned pale at the sight of them. Gripping his cane tightly, Askild swung it so hard at Knut's face that he broke the boy's nose.

'Ow!' wailed Jug Ears, but Knut didn't make a sound.

'Ow!' wailed Bjørk and positioned herself between them. That's how the family stood for a long time, frozen in a sad tableau. The only thing that moved was the blood that came trickling out of Knut's nose . . . Then Grandpa Askild turned on his heel and headed for a pub without even washing off the soot, while Bjørk tended to Knut's broken nose.

Of course this last part was never included in Grandma Bjørk's version. The story always ended with her embracing her sons. 'If the wind hadn't been blowing from the south,' she liked to say, 'we would certainly have ended up homeless.'

The day after the unfortunate forest fire, Askild painted a big picture, one and a half metres square, and that very evening he decided to call it *Bergen Is Burning*. In my opinion, *Bergen Is Burning* is one of his most successful paintings. The billowing flames behind a cobalt-blue face, and the swinging cane, which upsets the balance of the composition, seem to me an example of his methods at their best. But Askild never cared for it. He was much more fond of *The Doctor and the Scalpel*, which eleven years later would bring my parents together. And once Knut's nose healed, and Applehead transformed himself from a box-office draw into a very ordinary big man, everyone forgot about the forest fire and Knut's broken nose. And the daily voices again took up their soothing chant:

Oh, wondrous city, coins have rained down, gold has found its way into your hands, chanted the Fang, who was singing his last verse, but by now he had laid all the groundwork.

'Fat crabs. Big, beautiful crabs. Alive and kicking, ready to display on blocks of ice,' shouted Jug Ears, showing his impressive coin collection to everyone he could.

'Ooh, how amazing,' exclaimed Bjørk as she leant over the shiny coins, which Jug Ears polished twice a week.

'Huh,' said Askild, casting a sullen glance at the collection, which weighed 2 kilos. 'What are you going to do with them?'

Jug Ears was about to tell him something that he had heard from Ibsen the coin dealer, when their conversation was interrupted by a voice that no one had ever heard before. 'Pappa,' they heard. And a cold shiver ran down Bjørk's back before it dawned on her that the voice belonged to her daughter. Yes, it was Anne Katrine. She was standing right behind them in Jug Ears' room, saying her very first word. Askild jumped up and down, Bjørk clapped her hands. And by the next afternoon Anne Katrine's first word was being repeated in Doctor Thor's office, where my grandmother's voice could be heard more and more often.

'She said Pappa,' Bjørk explained, perching on Thor's desk as the doctor hung a sign on the door: *Danger of*

212

infection – no admittance. Bjørk tried to imitate her daughter's peculiar voice for Doctor Thor as she brushed a speck of lint off his shirt collar. But she couldn't really do it, and at that time another voice was causing more turmoil in the family than Anne Katrine's. A lone voice was echoing through the streets of Bergen: 'Keep your fingers off me, you jackass! Don't touch me until we're married!'

As far as the wedding went, the family has always had long discussions about what actually happened on that night in early spring 1959 when Ida finally caught sight of Applehead's tattooed dick. 'She must have been over-joyed,' Askild liked to say, whereas Bjørk would merely remark, 'Oh, that horrid boy.' Yet she talked a great deal about it, and as the years passed, she grew more and more preoccupied with the story, which finally became one of her favourites.

'He loved her so much,' Bjørk liked to conclude her tale, 'that without hesitation he allowed a total stranger to manhandle his thing.'

'What does "manhandle" mean, Grandma?'

'It means "wreck", you idiot,' replied my sister Stinna. 'Crush, ruin, cause to malfunction.' Bjørk nodded in agreement. So for years I was under the misconception that Applehead had turned himself into a eunuch out of love.

Askild was Applehead's best man, just as Applehead, thirteen years earlier, had been Askild's best man. Jug Ears sat quietly in the pew and watched the ceremony while Knut stood on the porch and refused to take part in the festivities. He was deeply disappointed in his cousin, and he caused a terrible scene during the party in the newly

213

developed neighbourhood. When the guests weren't looking, he tossed the wedding gifts, one by one, out of the
window. He poured the aquavit down the sink – stirred to
action by the teetotaller Arnt Bjørkvig, who was not
thrilled about the crates of aquavit that Askild had bought
for the occasion. Knut even managed to topple the
wedding cake and rip the bride's veil when Ida lifted him
up to kiss him on his crooked nose. 'Cut it out!' howled
Knut, to everyone's great amusement, and then he tore off
a piece of her veil. 'Cut it out!' he howled again when
Applehead caught him and carried him back to Ida so that
he could be given his well-deserved punishment: three
more kisses from the bride. Even at his own wedding
Applehead wore a bunch of elastic bands around his
sleeve, along with a little metal pin on his breast pocket
with the slogan: *Bjørkvig Elastic Bands – Best in All the
Lands.* He kept on saluting his father-in-law, and several
times he actually tried to sell elastic bands to the guests,
who just laughed at him. They started telling jokes about
the similarities between the elastic-band industry and the
condom business (implying that Applehead should have
gone into the condom business before he, at the age of
sixteen, got the bride pregnant).

But as the evening wore on, the party ran dry, and Jug
Ears was sent over to the Merry Circus Wagon to get fresh
supplies. Since Askild didn't have any more cash – and
Bjørkvig refused to cough up a single krone for aquavit –
he first had to walk around and take up a collection. His
pockets were clinking and jingling as he darted through
the slum district in the early evening. Ever since the
episode with Pappa Niels in the shed, he hadn't had any
more trouble with the slum kids, and so he raced through

the streets undisturbed and bought seven bottles of aquavit, which was as much as his money could buy at the Merry Circus Wagon. On his way home – now creeping along the walls since the seven bottles made it impossible to run – he heard a loud shriek behind a wooden fence. At first he wasn't going to stop, but when he recognized Lewd Linda's voice he decided to find out what was happening. He sneaked over to a spot where a board was missing and peeked into a building site where Linda was fooling around with two boys. They had forced her down on all fours. One was clamping her head between his knees while the other was trying to kick her in the rear with his wooden clogs. Jug Ears recognized one of them. It was Red Pig. He didn't recall ever seeing the other boy before.

'No,' yelled Linda when the boy he didn't know pulled off her knickers and started kicking her bare behind. 'Stop it,' she wept, attempting without success to pull her dress down over her white backside.

For an instant Jug Ears stood there, as if frozen. Then he too shouted, 'Stop it!' And the boys turned their heads to stare at him in astonishment.

'What the hell? It's Jug Ears! What have you got there?' shouted Red Pig, pointing at the bags of aquavit.

'Nothing,' replied Jug Ears. 'Leave her alone.'

'Leave her alone, leave her alone,' jeered Red Pig as he let go of Linda. 'You're just jealous,' he went on, walking over to Jug Ears. Red Pig was clutching something in his fist that looked like a rock, but when he got closer, he hesitated. And that proved to be fatal. The next second Red Pig was lying on the grass, writhing and bright red in the face, with his bells ringing. The boy that Jug Ears didn't know now released Linda and started coming closer. He was at least a head and a half taller and didn't look especially amused as he said, 'We were just having some fun.'

'Get out of here,' replied Jug Ears. 'Get going.'

'Hey, listen, is he her *little brother*, or what?' the boy asked, turning to Red Pig, who was still unable to utter a word. 'Hey, is he a snotty *little brother* keeping guard over his sister's virginity? How touching!' he laughed. But his laughter quickly ceased when he collapsed next to Red Pig.

'Hurry up!' Jug Ears shouted to Linda, who was taking a long time to pull up her knickers. When they reached the other side of the wooden fence, he handed her one of the bags. Then they raced off through the neighbourhood with their hair flying and didn't stop until they were a good distance beyond the slum district.

'What a couple of idiots,' snarled Linda, leaning against a wall and gasping for breath. 'How does my make-up look?'

'Fine,' stammered Jug Ears as he tried to stand on tiptoe so he wouldn't seem so short next to Linda.

'Hey, listen,' she said. 'What exactly do you have in these bags?' Her hands were already reaching inside, and a big smile lit up her face. And then she said, 'Doesn't my rescuer want a kiss?'

That's how Jug Ears, who was almost thirteen, got his first kiss. Linda, who had to bend down slightly, stuck her tongue in his mouth and bit him gently on the lower lip, which made him take a step back. 'Oops! I forgot you were used to the ball,' she said afterwards. 'Shall we have a taste of the aquavit?'

Jug Ears followed Linda behind a hedge and sat down next to her to sample the aquavit. And there, half an hour later – roused by Linda, who kept on calling him her hero, inspired by the aquavit, and spurred on by his thirteen-year-old hormones, he asked her something that had been weighing on his mind for a long time.

'Can I ask you . . .' he muttered, 'is it true that you – I mean – that *some people* put it in their mouth?'

'Put what in their mouth?' asked Linda.

'Er, a willy,' replied Jug Ears, noticing that everything was spinning in circles.

'A willy!' she mimicked him. And suddenly there was silence. Jug Ears could hear his heart pounding. He regretted asking the question and noticed that a nervous twitch had started at the corner of Linda's lips. *What now?* he thought.

'Is that what you want?' she asked after a pause. He could see that she was also drunk. Her eyes were slightly crossed as she swallowed hard and added pensively, 'It'll cost you a bottle.'

'All right,' replied Jug Ears. 'That's what I want.'

'What now?' asked Jug Ears a little while later, staring in horror at Linda, who had taken his dick in her mouth and was just holding it there without moving her tongue.

'Am I supposed to – I mean – do I really pee in there?' he managed to stammer.

At the same instant, Linda gave a start and shouted, 'You perverted pig!' She pushed Jug Ears away and he landed on his back in front of her. 'Ugh, what a disgusting boy you are!' she howled, giving him a fierce glare. 'Get out of here!' she went on, bursting into tears.

'What's the matter?' asked Jug Ears, even though he would have preferred to leave. 'Are you sad?'

'It doesn't matter. Here, take your bottle and get lost!' she wailed, flinging the bottle after him. He barely managed to catch it.

'You can keep it if you want,' Jug Ears stammered.

'You're all alike! God damn it!' she shouted. And so Jug Ears, his first experience with the opposite sex interrupted, backed out of the hedge with five and a half bottles of aquavit, all the while trying to zip up his fly.

Back at the wedding party, no one noticed that Jug Ears had been sampling the aquavit until he threw up on the groom's shoes. 'Is he sick?' asked Bjørk, sounding worried.

'Blech!' shouted Applehead.

'Are you drunk?' asked Askild, giving the boy a shake. But in many ways Jug Ears was in another world.

'Oh God!' he heard his mother wail. 'He *is* drunk.'

And deep inside his ear canals the Fang's hoarse voice was whispering: *Cheer up! Who the hell cares? The girl was nothing but a whore, a ridiculous little goose—*

'Leave me alone!' Jug Ears shouted at the Fang. 'Get lost!'

Of course his parents thought that he was talking to them. 'He's out of his mind,' declared Askild and picked up his son to carry him over to the sofa. But before they reached it, Jug Ears threw up all over Askild, who spent the rest of the evening in his undershirt. Soon Jug Ears was truly lost in another world . . . He snored loudly and didn't wake up until the guests had started to leave.

By then the Fang had departed, and Jug Ears was actually feeling quite lively. He walked about among the guests with a smirk on his face, even though he couldn't

218

forget Linda's miserable expression. The bridal couple was about to leave, which led to a spirited discussion at the front door, where two big wheelbarrows stood waiting, decorated with branches and garlands. It was Askild's idea that he and Arnt Bjørkvig should use the wheelbarrows to transport the newlyweds over to the Mission Hotel, where a room had been reserved for the night. But the teetotaller had no desire to be seen out at night with one of the town's most notorious alcoholics. He offered instead to drive the bridal couple to the hotel in his car.

'Not on your life!' shouted Askild. And the sense of bad feeling growing among the guests would have escalated if Jug Ears hadn't offered to push one of the wheelbarrows. Arnt Bjørkvig smiled with relief. On their way through Bergen's night-dark streets, Applehead talked about the starry skies over the South Seas, and about those nights when he had dreamt of the enchanted woods. His bride snickered loudly, and Jug Ears thought it was quite pleasant walking along with the newlyweds and his father. But just before they reached the Mission Hotel, Askild began to hear the howl of bloodhounds. The street signs looked like Germans with rifles, and Bergen was suddenly transformed. 'Who goes there?' muttered Grandpa Askild, peering nervously at the dark streets.

Jug Ears knew what happened whenever Askild started talking nonsense like that. So he suggested to his father that he should go right back home while he, Jug Ears, helped the bridal couple carry their baggage inside. Askild disappeared into the dark with his wheelbarrow and his cane. 'Keep away from me,' he muttered. 'You fucking dogs.'

After Askild had left, Jug Ears shook his head

apologetically and was about to pick up the luggage when Applehead stopped him.

'Under no circumstances!' he said as he grabbed Jug Ears, then the bags, and last of all his bride. Standing there holding his bride, his cousin, and his baggage in his arms, Applehead straightened his back and staggered into the lobby, where a sleepy night porter handed over the key. On their way up the stairs, Jug Ears found himself dangerously close to the bride. Her breast was touching his face, and her red hair tickling his nose, but no one seemed to notice his sudden erection. Applehead was humming loudly, obviously pleased with his own show of strength. Up on the third floor he unlocked the door with one hand, marched into the room, and tossed his burdens on to the bed.

'One kiss from the bride,' he told his cousin with a grin as Jug Ears tumbled helplessly on to the bed. 'And then you take off.'

Again Jug Ears found that people apparently bit each other on the lips when they kissed. 'Aha!' he heard, and then Ida's teeth sank into his lip and she started to giggle. 'What amazing ears you have,' she went on, biting them too. Then Applehead shoved his bewildered cousin out of the door.

On his way downstairs, Jug Ears heard the night porter lock the front door, and suddenly he realized that the porter must have thought that he was part of the baggage. *Maybe he didn't see me at all*, thought Jug Ears, and he stood there for a full five minutes before he crept back up to the room and knelt down in front of the keyhole with an odd trembling all over his body. Before he went back home through the streets in the growing light of dawn, he had solved the mystery of Applehead's wedding night and heard what the bride said when she first saw her husband's tattooed dick.

She stared at it with fascination. She weighed it in her hand. Cautiously she slid her finger along it as she deciphered the inscription. 'Oh no, you jackass,' she said.

The next day Jug Ears had a hangover. He lay in bed most of the day, tormenting himself by thinking about Linda's miserable expression and his own idiotic question, which now made him cringe. Through the keyhole at the Mission Hotel he had witnessed the love-making of two grown-ups, and he now understood that he had been the victim of a childish misunderstanding. *Poor Linda*, he thought while Anne Katrine ran through the house saying 'Pappa', and little brother Knut tossed things out of the window as Askild yelled at him.

Jug Ears closed his eyes and slid all the way under the covers. For the first time he felt like a prisoner in his parents' house. And the shame that had come over him when Askild began babbling about bloodhounds in front of the Mission Hotel was also a new feeling. At any rate, he had never noticed the shame so strongly before, even though it had always been present. Because it wasn't just the slum district that prevented his friends from coming over to his house. Askild's uncontrollable moods and the fear that his friends might see his father at his worst also meant Jug Ears preferred to meet them elsewhere.

On Monday morning he was eager to talk to Thorbjørn. Even though it had been an embarrassing weekend, it had nevertheless been extremely eventful, and that's why he raced off to the White School. Unfortunately

221

Deputy-Headmaster Kramer's class began promptly, and so Jug Ears decided to write down the extraordinary news on a piece of paper.

Linda had me in her mouth, it said on the first note that Jug Ears passed to Thorbjørn.

I drank aquavit this weekend, it said on the second one.

I watched my cousin screwing with the teetotaller's daughter at the Mission Hotel, it said on the third.

Thorbjørn shook his head in disbelief.

That's a lie, it said on the note that Thorbjørn crumpled up and tossed at the back of his neck.

No, it's not, Jug Ears wrote back.

Did you come in her mouth? Thorbjørn hastily scribbled, even though none of them had ever tried to come. But Jug Ears never had a chance to read what he wrote. 'Aha!' he heard, and suddenly the deputy headmaster was standing there, angrily waving the note.

'Oh, so you're passing notes, are you!' he exclaimed, giving Thorbjørn a furious look. The nerve under the boy's eye began to twitch ominously. 'My dear gentlemen,' the teacher went on triumphantly as he surveyed the pupils. 'My dear gentlemen, believe it or not, our good Daddy Longlegs is actually sitting here and *writing*!'

'Ha, ha,' they all said. 'That's really funny, sir.'

'I didn't know that he was even *capable* of writing.'

'Ha, ha, sir.'

'Let's have a look,' Kramer went on as he unfolded the note. 'All right, listen closely, you little baboons, our bone-meal candidate, the lanky lout who calls himself Thorbjørn has written these deeply intelligent words—'

Silence, suppressed snickering. The nerve under Thorbjørn's eye, which had plagued him ever since that unfortunate trip through the slum district, went completely berserk as Kramer began to read. 'DID YOU COME IN HER—' That was as far as the deputy headmaster got. Then he stopped abruptly, and ominous crimson blotches appeared on his throat and spread all the way up to his bald pate.

'Go on, sir. What did he write next?' said some of the students.

'Why did Herr Kramer stop reading?'

'Excuse me, sir, but your face is all red.'

'Our bonemeal candidate,' snarled Kramer two minutes later, now safely ensconced behind his desk. 'Our good oh-so-intelligent-nose-picking-lout,' he continued as he squinted his blue eye and stared at Thorbjørn with the brown one, 'Let me have the honour of introducing you to the ball.'

While most of the other boys had endured several encounters with the electric lips, Thorbjørn had always managed to avoid it.

But now he stood up, casting one last look at Jug Ears, who was fumbling with his next note under the desk. It said: *I think I found out something really important this weekend*. But Thorbjørn never had the chance to read it. Instead, he began sniffling loudly as he took off his shoes and socks and stepped on to the metal plate to turn the rubber crank.

'I have disturbed the lessons with my smutty behaviour,' chanted Kramer. But Thorbjørn's lips were quivering so badly that he couldn't repeat the teacher's words. He simply kept turning and turning the crank.

'I'm going to end up in the bonemeal factory – if they can even find any use for me,' Kramer went on. But

223

Thorbjørn still didn't make a sound, and an uneasy feeling slowly began to simmer in the classroom.

'Sir, he peed in his trousers,' someone said as Thorbjørn kept on turning.

And it was true that a big wet spot was starting to spread across the front of Thorbjørn's trousers and down his thigh. Jug Ears noticed that a little pool of piss was getting bigger at his friend's feet.

'Excuse me, sir, but—' said Niller with the freckles.

'Sir, have you thought about the fact that—' someone else ventured.

But the deputy headmaster merely pounded his key ring hard on the desk, told the class to keep quiet, and then shaped his lips to speak the dreaded words: 'Kiss the ball, you baboon,' he whispered. And, trembling in his wet trousers, on the verge of fainting with terror, Thorbjørn finally stopped turning the crank, took a deep breath, bent down, and . . .

. . . *died the instant his lips touched the electrical machine*. That's what it said in the Bergen newspapers the following day. *Interviews with the other pupils in the class revealed that the deputy headmaster had apparently used the electricity machine as a means of punishment for many years.*

Let's not confuse the issue, let's not succumb to hysteria it said in a much discussed editorial. *Punishing pupils is not a crime; using an electricity machine in a slightly creative way is not necessarily a crime either. Who could know that the boy had a hidden heart defect? However, to install a metal plate on the floor against regulations, and to overlook, quite lackadaisically, that the pupil was*

standing in a pool of urine, is to shirk one's responsibility.
Therefore, it is exceedingly gratifying to note that the
deputy headmaster has been suspended, effective
immediately.

The course of events, it further stated, does not
demonstrate, as certain disreputable newspapers have
claimed, that our school system is barbaric. No, on the
contrary, it shows that our school system is still function-
ing perfectly.

'What a swine,' Askild used to say, because he *was* in the
habit of confusing the issue. 'I know the type.'

Out of the Cupboard

AFTER THORBJØRN'S DEATH, reality began knocking at the door in the form of butchers, grocers, and various messenger boys who would stick an impudent foot in the door, creep around the house, and poke their heads in the windows. 'Herr Eriksson,' voices said more and more often, 'we know you're in there!'

Askild was painting out in the yard when Jug Ears came home from school earlier than usual.

'Why are you home this early?' asked Askild, noticing his pale face.

'Why are *you* home?' asked Jug Ears.

'I've taken a leave of absence,' replied Askild, and then he stared, wide-eyed, as his son passed out cold on the grass.

'It's really not that bad,' muttered Askild as he carried the boy into the house. 'How the hell did a son of mine get to be so sensitive?'

That same morning, while Thorbjørn was still alive and turning the crank like crazy, Askild had been called into the boss's office. 'I know that you made a great

226

contribution during the war,' said his boss. 'I know that you've had plenty of things to cope with—'

'Cope with?' said Askild, uncomprehending.

'Yes, that you've had your problems.'

'Problems!' said Askild. 'Like hell I have!'

'The bottle,' said the boss.

'The bottle!' snapped Askild, pounding his fist on the desk. 'Is it against the law now to have a little nip at lunch?'

Sacked, thought Askild on his way home. *Thrown out by a bunch of peasants, petty personages, uneducated swine, damn it all!*

'I've taken a leave of absence,' was Askild's only explanation to Bjørk when he came home – and, of course, that wasn't entirely a lie. Naturally it was a matter of leave without pay, leave for an indefinite period of time, leave until the whole cubist stuff was knocked out of my paternal grandfather once and for all. But calling it a leave of absence was simply one last little kindness on the part of his boss.

When Jug Ears regained consciousness, Askild shook his head in resignation. He was just about to say, 'Pull yourself together, my boy', but Bjørk beat him to it with her anxious chatter. 'Oh God, what happened? Put your feet up, take a deep breath—' Jug Ears, who was used to Bjørk's melodramatic outbursts, gave his parents a sombre look and told them what had happened to Thorbjørn that day in school.

'Oh no,' moaned Bjørk, while four words began churning around in Grandpa Askild's head. *I know the type*, he thought when he went back to his painting a little while later. *I know the type*, he cursed as the alcohol and

227

turpentine fumes began to affect his perception. *I know the type* was echoing through his mind when he suddenly barged back into the house and declared that he was going up to the White School to have a few civil words with the principal.

It didn't make life any easier for Jug Ears that his father was seen arguing with the school principal. And according to the gawking eye-witnesses, he cut quite a comic figure, standing in the middle of the schoolyard as he showered the principal with all the insults that were actually meant for his boss at the shipyard. Finally a group of teachers and pupils, who had been roaming aimlessly around the school in the hours since Thorbjørn's death, formed a circle around the two men. Magnus, the history teacher, gently took Askild by the arm and tried to lead him away from the embarrassing situation. 'Get your mitts off me!' shouted Askild and pushed him away. But instead of toppling the teacher on to the asphalt, he was the one who fell on his ass.

'Where's my cane?' yelled Askild. 'Who stole my cane?'

In the period that followed, it also didn't make life easier for anyone that Applehead, whose visits usually put Askild in a good mood, was so infatuated with the ginger twins and the fine elastic bands that he rarely came to see his family. But someone who did visit was Mamma Randi, all 100 kilos of her. She would march into the house and offer unwelcome suggestions as to how the family might solve its financial problems. 'Why don't you try the bonemeal factory,' she was fond of saying. 'They're always looking for people over there.'

But it was beneath Askild's dignity to set foot in a lowly

bonemeal factory. 'I've seen enough cadavers,' he said with a wink to his son.

After the municipal court handed down its verdict regarding Deputy-Headmaster Kramer, the boys paid a visit to Thorbjørn's grave. They stood in a circle around his headstone, and each of them placed his biggest crab among the withered flowers. 'Rumour has it that Kramer is going to leave town,' said Jug Ears. Then he went back to his house in the newly developed neighbourhood. Ever since Askild had been given an involuntary leave of absence, Jug Ears had been charged with yet another time-consuming task: bringing his father home from various pubs at dinnertime.

Things are going downhill, he often thought as he walked home through the streets of Bergen with his intoxicated father, on whose shoulder Kai the parrot would shriek: 'Damn it to hell!' This bird, who had previously brought father and son closer together, now began to get on Jug Ears' nerves.

Knock, knock, they would hear at all hours of the day. 'We know you're in there.'

'Niels!' Askild would shout. 'The usual tactic. You open the door!' And then my grandfather would tiptoe into the bedroom and crawl under the covers.

'No, he's not at home,' Jug Ears would say. 'No, you'll have to come back another day.'

Heads would pop up in the windows, and patronizing letters would arrive demanding impossible sums. And by the time the crabs on Thorbjørn's grave had scattered through the whole cemetery and started giving visitors a fright by skittering back and forth on the pathways – and yes, a few months had gone by, Deputy-Headmaster

Kramer really had left Bergen, and the city newspapers had forgotten that a boy by the name of Thorbjørn had ever existed – Askild suddenly decided that he'd had enough of pushy creditors.

One morning while Jug Ears was at school and Bjørk was out shopping with the younger kids, Askild went into his older son's room, knelt down by the bed, and pulled out the pot of gold at the end of the rainbow: the family treasure, polished and tended for five long years, won in the bloody battles at the Skoltegrunn dock, defended with clubs and pieces of dog shit on sticks, weighed and appraised in Allikegaten, financed by crabs pulled from the ocean's deep, and foretold by a singing apparition: *Coins will rain down, and gold will find its way into your hands* . . . And as if it were merely an ordinary wooden box containing some old coins, Askild stuck it under his arm and went off to town.

Of course it was his intention to go over to see Ibsen the coin dealer on Allikegaten and get a fair price for the collection, but first he was just going to take a little detour to his usual pub. Unfortunately, he only had enough cash for a single beer, and after that was gone, it occurred to him that he could try to sell the coin collection there. What did that foolish old man on Allikegaten really know about the market value anyway? First Askild tried to sell the collection to the bartender, but he wasn't interested in useless coins. Then he tried to persuade a couple of semi-soused regulars, but they gave him such suspicious looks that Askild felt insulted. By the time he finally succeeded in interesting a Finnish seaman, he had cut the price in half.

'Worth a lot of money?' said the seaman and laughed.

'Well, at least it'll be a good souvenir for my son.' Askild got fifteen kroner for it, and then he thought, why not just stay here and have a beer, and maybe a couple more?

Two hours later, after he had spent all the money on booze, he began feeling a little guilty. The seaman had disappeared, and it dawned on Askild that he had made a poor trade. A short time later he was seen down at the harbour, asking for a nameless seaman who had apparently cheated poor Herr Eriksson out of quite a lot of money. But the earth seemed to have swallowed up that seaman, and when Askild's fury over being cheated didn't just evaporate into the blue, he decided to go past the shipyard and have a few civil words with his former boss.

The watchman at the entrance to the shipyard saw him coming, staggering along with his cane. The workers in the drafting room heard him cursing as he walked straight through the office building. The boss himself first heard the sound of a chair being toppled, and then the door crashed open with a bang. There stood Askild Eriksson, seething with rage and bursting with swear-words, which he immediately began showering on his gaping boss. Askild swung his cane in a threatening manner and shouted so loud that his words echoed all the way out to the welding halls. He said that they were a pack of country bumpkins, Nordland riffraff, incompetent amateurs, uneducated swine. He yelled that he wanted compensation for lost wages; that there was nothing wrong with his drawings, it was those hopeless welders who didn't know a damn thing— First kindly, and then more firmly, hands seized hold of Askild, who shouted, 'Keep your hands off me, don't touch me, you conniving reactionaries, you have no idea what this is all about—' Then they roughly dragged my grandfather out of the boss's office. All the while, he shouted: 'You owe me at least three months' wages, I demand an apology, damn it all.' Finally they managed to shove him out of the office, but just as the boss took hold of the door to slam it in the face of the rabble-rouser, Askild made one last effort to mobilize his forces. He tore loose from his former colleagues and grabbed on to the door frame at the very instant when the boss slammed the door with all his might. They all heard a strange sound, and the next moment the boss was staring down at a piece of finger, which lay on the floor, looking very out of place.

'See that!' Askild managed to yell before the fury seeped out of him. 'Now he's even disabled me!'

Then there was silence. On one side of the door Askild's former colleagues stared at his right index finger, from which a thin stream of blood was spurting, as if from a water pistol. On the other side of the door, the boss bent down and picked up the fingertip. The boss looked quite pale, but that was nothing compared to Askild, who simply stood there, staring dumbfounded at his finger while the boss and his former colleagues put on a makeshift bandage. Then the boss tried to persuade Askild to go to hospital, but he merely replied, 'No, I'm not going to any damn hospital.'

'Well, you should at least see a doctor. I know a very good one,' said the boss, and he led Askild down to his car in the car park and opened the door.

But again Askild resisted. 'No,' he said, 'I can walk there myself.'

So Askild tottered off, holding his cane and carrying the tip of his finger in a paper bag. Since the boss felt uneasy about the situation, he decided to follow. At first everything was fine, but as Askild approached the centre of town, he grew dizzy and had to sit down abruptly on the pavement. The boss looked around for help and caught sight of a boy with a handcart.

'In you go,' he said to Askild after paying the boy to push the cart for him. 'Now I'm going to take you over to see my personal physician, the best in Bergen.'

But before they started off, another boy came over to the cart. His huge ears were quivering nervously, and in one hand he held a net teeming with crabs.

'Pappa!' cried the boy in horror. 'What happened?'

It was Jug Ears, who had a day off from school. He promptly joined the procession. Askild had started whimpering a bit, and after they had walked for a quarter of an hour, it dawned on Jug Ears that they were headed for Doctor Thor's consulting room. An uneasy premonition seized hold of him, but Askild impatiently told the boys to hurry up, while his boss attempted to offer consoling words to all of them.

'That finger is going to be as good as new,' he said without conviction.

A short time later they arrived at the doctor's office and stared with amazement at the strange sign hanging on the door.

It said: *Danger of infection – no admittance.*

'Infection?' exclaimed Askild's boss. 'What's that supposed to mean?'

'Infection?' said Askild, who had placed his arm around his son's shoulder to keep his balance.

'Infection?' muttered Jug Ears. And he suddenly had a strong desire to find a different doctor for his father. A panicked commotion was taking place on the other side of the door because the voices of Askild and Jug Ears had been recognized. Knickers, garters, and socks whirled through the air. And into the tall mahogany cabinet in the far corner of the room slipped a hasty shadow at the very instant that Askild's boss threw open the office door and led his former employee inside.

'Doctor Gunnarsson,' he said with authority, 'I have a patient in need of emergency treatment.'

Askild glared in surprise at Doctor Thor, tore off his bandage, and pointed at the doctor with his sheared-off finger, making a little stream of blood spray on to the doctor's unbuttoned shirt. For a brief moment the doctor thought he had been shot by a jealous husband and that it was his own blood staining his shirt. But that, of course, was pure nonsense. In his confused state, he recalled the time when Askild had been a gaunt shadow staring at him in disbelief in the house at Skivebakken.

'So do something, man,' exclaimed Askild's boss. And while Doctor Thor dismissed those memories from his mind and began buttoning up his bloody shirt to look at the patient's finger, Jug Ears leant against the tall mahogany cabinet. He shouldn't have done that. There was a loud clicking sound, the lock came unfastened, and out of the dark interior tumbled Bjørk – wearing only one high-heeled shoe and a pair of garters. In her hands was her dress, which she held up in front of her in terror. This crazy sight, which had no place in that office, caused all of them to gape. Out of sheer fright Askild dropped the paper bag he was holding. Jug Ears uttered a little scream. The boss gawked and gaped, and the embarrassed doctor instinctively ducked, as if he feared that someone might take a swing at him.

But a moment later, after the shock had ebbed, Askild began bellowing: 'You're standing on my finger! Are you out of your mind?! Move!'

If there had ever been any hope of re-attaching the tip of Askild's finger, it was now gone. When his boss bent down to pick up the paper bag, it was an exceedingly flattened fingertip that he pulled out. The heel of Bjørk's shoe, which was no bigger than a centimetre in diameter, had come down right on it as she tried to regain her balance. And what a peculiar expression slid across Bjørk's face when she discovered that she had been standing on her husband's finger.

It must have been the same expression that I saw many years later in the kitchen on Tunøvej in Odense. Grandma Bjørk was washing dishes after dinner, and afterwards, when she opened the cupboard under the sink, which was no longer populated by tiny little monsters, a frightened mouse came darting out and raced around her feet. She jumped into the air in terror. When she landed, there was a strange squashing sound. And sure enough – under one of Grandma Bjørk's slippers was a crushed mouse. 'How typical of you,' snapped Askild, his voice sounding unexpectedly annoyed. It puzzled me, because it would normally have made my grandfather laugh to see a mouse squashed under someone's shoe. But back then I didn't know about his finger. I think Askild got a certain amount of sadistic amusement from terrorizing Bjørk with the idea that he might reveal her secret to the whole family, which he never did until many years later, when Knut came home from Jamaica.

But to get back to Bergen ... The fingertip was

examined. Bjørk struggled valiantly with her dress, while no one said anything to her, not even Askild, who behaved with astonishing composure. He didn't say a single word as he stared at the paper bag with the crushed finger inside. Doctor Thor stood up and, after realizing that the cuckolded husband was not going to punch him in the face, he gave the boss a furious look and said, 'Why have you come bursting in here with this man? It's a matter for the hospital!'

Nor did Jug Ears say a word. Nothing could be read from his expression, and he refused to even glance at his mother. But he did make a big production about supporting his father, helping him back to the cart, holding the sorry-looking bag with the now-squashed finger, and wiping the sweat from Askild's forehead when he suddenly began to perspire copiously.

Not until they reached the hospital did Askild seem to wake up. He refused any sort of anaesthetic and under no circumstances would he stay overnight, even though Bjørk tried to persuade him otherwise.

'No,' he said when the doctors were done. 'Now we're all going home.'

On the way back, no words were exchanged until Bjørk stammered that she would just run over to Mamma Ellen's house to get Anne Katrine and little Knut.

'Oh, so that's where you parked them!' exclaimed Askild, subtracting yet another point from the secret tally he was keeping on Bjørk's family. 'That's some mother-in-law I've got.'

So father and son walked home alone. Jug Ears tried to support the injured man, but Askild kept swinging his cane in annoyance. When they reached the house, he went straight to the telephone and rang his mother-in-law to tell Bjørk not to come home that night. The fact that Bjørk started crying on the phone didn't mollify Askild in the least. He slammed down the receiver and went into the parlour, where he stopped in front of the bookcase. Then he started on the medical romances. He tore them from the shelves, one after the other, and ripped them in half, tearing out the pages and crumpling them up before hurling them around the room. It was one thing for Bjørk to be hopelessly infatuated with these doctor stories, but the fact that she had tried to turn her own life into a romance novel was simply too much for Askild. In a blizzard of drifting book pages, in that chamber of horrors dedicated to his wife's trite fantasies, and thinking to himself *adulteress, whore*, Askild found release for his rage. Jug Ears cooked supper for his father, told him to be careful with his finger, and poured more aquavit when his glass was empty. Reprising his role as the one who held the family together, he later helped his father into bed.

But the next day my grandpa Askild's mood hadn't improved. It was Saturday, and at seven in the morning Bjørk was already calling to ask whether she could come home. No, she couldn't, Askild told her, and he slammed down the receiver. At half past eight the first representative from reality was knocking on the door. Askild tore it open and shouted, 'Get out of here! Leave me alone!' In the meantime, his thirteen-year-old son cleaned up the parlour, gathering up all the torn-up medical romances and stuffing them into big sacks, which he set on the terrace. *It's all going downhill*, he thought. *When human beings copulate, they become piglets themselves.*

Later Jug Ears heard his father muttering loudly in the

parlour, and he understood that Askild needed to be alone. That's why he went to his room, cautiously closed the door, and knelt down by the bed to occupy his mind with something other than family problems. Jug Ears was right: Askild did want to be alone, and that's why he was a bit annoyed when his thirteen-year-old son suddenly stood in the doorway. 'My coin collection!' he whispered. 'Where's my coin collection?'

Askild, who certainly had other things to think about right now besides some stupid coin collection, replied, 'It's gone. Go to your room. I want to be alone.' But Jug Ears refused to be content with such a vague answer.

'Where is it? What have you done with it?' he asked.

'Shut up,' shouted Askild, throwing an ashtray at his son. 'Get out of here! I sold it.' The flying ashtray made Jug Ears promptly return to his room, but a few minutes later he was back.

'What did you get for it?' he murmured. And Askild, who could hardly stand the sight of his blubbering son standing in the doorway, told him, 'Fifteen kroner. It doesn't matter. I'll get you another one.'

'Fifteen kroner!' howled Jug Ears.

'I said I'd get you another one,' yelled Askild, and he went out of the terrace door to lie down on the bench.

Coins had rained down and gold had found its way into his hands, but nothing had ever been said about this happening. In other words, the Fang was hopeless as a prophet. Nor had he predicted that a rage as violent as dynamite would explode inside the body of a thirteen-year-old. A little while later Jug Ears was standing in the hallway where sticks of dynamite – left over from Askild's building work – lay scattered among various painting supplies. Jug Ears gathered up all the sticks, except for the ones that were in the parlour, and swiped a box of matches too. Then he headed for the neighbour's privy, which had always been an annoyance to Askild.

'We finally get a place of our own,' Askild used to say, 'and then the neighbours put their privy right next to our terrace.'

You're going to get that privy smack on your head, thought Jug Ears. *You're going to get a taste of your own shit, yes, you are*, he went on, thinking and yet not thinking, since the fragmented images that were churning inside his head, at the age of thirteen, couldn't exactly be called thoughts.

Gold was promised, and the gold had been taken back. A pot of gold had appeared at the end of the rainbow, and now it had been sold at a pub for just fifteen kroner.

Inside the neighbour's privy – not far from the bench where Askild was lying and staring up at the sky – two thirteen-year-old hands fumbled with a box of matches while those broken images churned round and round in his mind. Two hands opened the privy lid, dropped in the dynamite, and closed the lid again.

Grandpa Askild heard the sound of racing footsteps. Then he heard nothing for several minutes, so it took a while for him to realize that he had witnessed an enormous explosion. Down in the slum district they heard the boom at once. But in Askild's consciousness the sound vanished as delusions popped up and made him think that he had fallen into the latrine pit outside the dysentery barracks in Buchenwald – because, yes, shit was falling from the sky, shit was raining down and landing on his body. Through the viscous watery surface, transported to Buchenwald's nightmarish winter, Askild rose up. But now countless scraps of paper began floating down from the sky, each with its own little message: *In the doctor's waiting room, Doctor X had always been a friend of the family* . . . Tattered scraps from the exploded medical romances, which Jug Ears had placed out in the yard, came drifting down on Askild like snow. *His authoritative voice made her swoon . . . his firm gaze bewitched her heart . . . I was unfaithful to my husband, but he deserved it, that beast . . .*

Only after several minutes did it occur to Askild that he had not been transported back to Germany in the winter of 1945. In fact, he was standing on the terrace of his cubist house in the year of Our Lord 1959, completely smeared with the faeces of the neighbouring family, and with the pitiful remains of his wife's roughly two hundred medical romances floating all around him. 'God damn it!' bellowed Askild, and then he did something that he had sworn he would never do. He cast a furious glance at his son, who was standing at the other end of the garden, staring at him in horror. Then Askild ran inside the house, opened the wardrobe, and took out the thickest belt he could find. And he ran after his son at a furious speed, down towards the slum district. Jug Ears had raced through the area countless times before, and he had an instinct for finding short cuts and vanishing unnoticed down hidden alleyways – but it did him no good. He slipped on the gravel outside Ejegaard's grocery shop. And there, in front of fifteen to twenty gaping spectators, including a bunch of slum kids who, in spite of everything, were quite shaken afterwards, Askild gave his son so many lashes with the belt that Jug Ears finally fainted in the arms of his shit-covered father. Only when he held the limp body of his son in his arms did Askild recall his old vow never to use a belt on his own children. An indistinct sound escaped his lips, and then he carried his son home, laid him on the sofa, and went in to take a bath.

When Bjørk, defying her husband's prohibition, returned home in the early evening, Jug Ears was sitting on the kitchen floor with a pencil stub in his hand, drawing the biggest monster of his life. He had started inside the cupboard but the monster, which he had begun to draw out of habit, had grown bigger than ever, and that was why he had crawled out on to the kitchen floor.

'Hi,' said Bjørk. 'What an ugly-looking fellow. How about drawing some cars instead?'

Anne Katrine and little brother Knut didn't care much for the new creature in the kitchen either. Anne Katrine refused even to enter the room, and Knut promptly asked his mother whether it was alive.

'Of course not,' Bjørk told him. But when she tried to pry the pencil stub out of her son's hand, Jug Ears howled so loudly that she immediately gave it back to him.

The monster kept growing, into cupboards and out of cupboards. Over the course of the evening it spread across the whole kitchen, and Bjørk had the feeling that she was standing in the middle of a spider web.

In the parlour, Askild was also busy, creating a painting – later called *The Butcher Arrives* – which I will confine myself to characterizing as a sloppy application of red paint. So sloppy that Bjørk didn't notice the other spots on her husband's shirt; so sloppy that she didn't even pay attention to the spots that were seeping through the back of her son's shirt. She merely thought that Askild had splattered his son with paint. Nor was the mood exactly conducive to a lot of questions. So Bjørk roamed back and forth between the kitchen and parlour, like a guest in her own house. In the kitchen the monster kept growing; in the parlour the familiar air of intransigence began to set in. And at no time did the name of Doctor Thor cross anyone's lips.

Around nine o'clock Bjørk poured milk into a pan, added some oats, and fed the younger children. Then she served her drunken husband, who, in a bad temper, knocked the plate to the floor. 'Dog food!' he shouted. A short time later Bjørk put the younger children to bed. Knut still believed that the monster in the kitchen was alive, and, in spite of several more attempts, Bjørk couldn't get Jug Ears to relinquish the pencil stub. And so it wasn't until he fell asleep on the floor with the pencil in his hand that she discovered the bloody stripes on her son's back. When she confirmed that the stripes really were what they looked like, Bjørk collapsed. The wind was completely knocked out of her. Sitting on the kitchen floor next to her beaten son, Grandma Bjørk made one of the few major decisions of her life.

In the Enchanted Forests
of Nordland

Have gone to Nordland with the children. Don't know when we'll be back, it said on the note that Askild found the next morning. The house was empty; Grandma Bjørk had packed quietly. Her stay with her older brother in Nordland would end up lasting four months, and that period is one of the least discussed in my family. No one cared to elaborate on the fact that the family nearly fell apart, and no one had any desire to be reminded that, shortly after their arrival in Nordland, Jug Ears disappeared and didn't turn up again until several weeks later. Even now, after all this time, Grandma Bjørk still evades my questions, but maybe that's because she doesn't really know what happened. He vanished as a boy and returned as a pubescent youth – that's the only thing she says over and over. Only once did Dad talk about his wanderings through the enchanted forests of Nordland, but I don't know whether his words are worth repeating. Doubt creeps in, and I can tell that my sister Stinna is starting to get annoyed with me.

'Well, then you'll have to come up with something

yourself,' she says, giving the white canvas a resigned look. 'You can't just come to a dead halt right in the middle of the story.'

Bjørk's brother Ejlif lived on the outskirts of a small town called Børkersjø. After the war was over, he had immediately found work at the sawmill. Several years later he took over the management and transformed the slumbering sawmill into a moderately successful operation. So at first the forest into which Jug Ears vanished didn't seem very intimidating. There were large areas of non-woods – whole landscapes planted only with tree stumps, as well as bare mountain slopes that initially had a depressing effect on the family. In general, Børkersjø, with its few streets, seemed like a dreary place, and none of the children could recognize Bjørk's rapturous descriptions of her childhood summers spent in Nordland. 'No ships,' muttered Knut, who was not especially impressed by the sight of the barges towing the surplus timber downriver.

Ejlif, who noticed the children's disappointment, tried hard to cheer them up. 'If you go out to the edge of the woods, you may see a lynx,' he liked to say. And if that didn't improve their spirits, he would give them a conspiratorial look and say, 'It will soon be time for the Northern Lights.'

One night when ordinary natural phenomena weren't able to measure up to the magic that had imbued Bjørk's lost childhood summers, Ejlif found it necessary to turn to tall tales. 'They say that these woods are haunted,' he told them. 'Lots of people have seen a figure roaming through the trees. One time it also went right through a man, making his hair turn white overnight. They say that it's the spirit of the forest who is now homeless because we've cut down so many trees.'

'Just like us,' said Knut and tossed his uncle's pipe out of the window.

Ejlif's two sons were also eager to show Jug Ears the mysteries of Nordland, so they took him out to the stump forests. There they quickly persuaded him to take off his shirt so they could examine the white stripes on his back. They raced to see who could run the fastest from stump to stump without touching the ground. They taught him which berries were edible, which mushrooms left a sweet taste on the tongue and which ones he should give a wide berth to because a single bite could put a person into a trance-like state for weeks.

'You know that story about the forest spirit?' Jug Ears' younger cousin said one day. 'I bet that man ate a bad mushroom and it made him nuts.'

But even though the cousins had intended to take Jug Ears out to the edge of the woods to show him a rare lynx, they never made it that far. The forest was always too far away. Several times, after they had been wandering for hours, they would see it in the distance, a wall of trees, a trembling organism in the fog. After being in Nordland for a couple of weeks, Jug Ears had the impression that the forest kept moving away. That it wasn't even possible to reach it, and his cousins seemed to have the same impression since they were constantly getting sidetracked by other things. For instance they would suddenly want to show him how to catch mice with a little trap. They also showed him how to sneak up on a grouse, and taught him how to imitate the mating call of a capercaillie. They were also preoccupied with another game. They would dig a hole in the ground and then the older of the two would yell: 'Now!' And they would unzip their trousers and tug at their dicks until one of them spurted a milky white blob into the hole.

One day the younger cousin managed to catch a grouse. 'Now we'll show you forest spirits!' he cried, and he gathered a handful of small mushrooms, which they forced down the throat of the terrified grouse by pressing hard on its crop. Afterwards, when they let it go, the bird began rushing around among the stumps in bewilderment, apparently no longer afraid of humans. On the other hand, something else seemed to be scaring the bird, something internal that made it shriek loudly. 'Tree spirits!' howled the younger cousin. 'Only the old folks believe in that crap!' They could hear the grouse shrieking for the rest of the afternoon, but the cousins didn't pay any attention to the psychotic bird. Instead, they told Jug Ears about the woodcutter who had seen a lynx the day before. The younger cousin was positive that the woodcutter had been scared, but his brother declared that only little kids had anything to fear.

'So you'd better get on home, Peewee!' he told his little brother, punching him.

'No lynx today,' the cousins told their father when they got home.

Ejlif threw out his hands apologetically and assured Jug Ears that some day he would drive him out to the edge of the forest in one of the sawmill's cars. 'But tonight,' he went on, 'I'll be darned if the Northern Lights don't wake us all up.'

By then Jug Ears understood that his uncle's sly talk about the Northern Lights was his way of saying: 'I'm sorry, but Nordland just isn't as exciting as your mother told you.' That's why he was astonished when that very night he was awakened by his two cousins.

'The Northern Lights are here,' said the older boy with a grave expression.

And it was true. Through the window Jug Ears caught a glimpse of a purple glow that rippled across the sky like a psychedelic Milky Way. He let the two brothers coax him into the parlour, where they begged their father for permission to go out to the stump forest to take a closer look at the Northern Lights. 'All right,' said Ejlif, giving his nephew a searching glance. 'But watch out for the tree spirits!'

'We won't let the tree spirits go through us!' the two cousins replied in unison. That was a standard remark in the family, and on the first evening that she sat in her brother's parlour, even Bjørk had joined in.

'Don't let the tree spirits go through you,' Ejlif had said, by which he meant dejection and despair. To let the tree spirits go through you meant surrendering to the dark, hidden side of your nature.

Outdoors the Northern Lights seemed even stronger, though not strong enough to light up the landscape. The cousins leapt from tree stump to tree stump – a trick they could do even in the dark – while Jug Ears dashed after them. Occasionally he would trip over the stumps; other times he scraped his shins on them and cursed, afraid that his cousins would leave him behind.

'Tree spirits, all you creatures of the forest!' they cried. 'We dare you to come out!'

Racing along beneath the phosphorescent sky, struggling with an unfamiliar obstacle course, and with his crazy cousins 50 metres ahead, Jug Ears soon lost all sense of direction. Suddenly his cousins disappeared, and he could hear only their voices, which he tried to use to get his bearings. For what seemed like hours, Jug Ears wandered around alone in the enchanted landscape, until he finally caught sight of the boys behind a small hill.

'If you spill it out under the Northern Lights,' shouted the older boy, 'your dick will grow several centimetres, and your sperm will be luminescent! BUT ONLY IF YOU'RE THE FIRST ONE TO DO IT!' he yelled, and before Jug Ears knew it, his two cousins had their trousers down around their knees. Bathed in the purple glow of the Northern Lights, each boy was slogging away at his dick, trying to be the first to hit the nearest tree stump.

'You're crazy,' Jug Ears just managed to say before the purple stripes in the sky underwent a strange transformation, rippling through all the colours of the rainbow until they were locked into a turquoise glow that lit up the whole landscape. Jug Ears gasped. At first he stood as if dazzled by the magical sight while his cousins cheered, but that was nothing compared to what met his eyes when he turned around. No more than 100 metres behind him loomed the forest, like a gigantic wall. In the midst of his own astonishment, he couldn't help thinking that the forest must have been surprised by their night-time assault and simply not had time to retreat.

'Wow!' shrieked the older cousin. 'There it is!' Jug Ears thought he was talking about the forest, but the sight of the dark woods didn't seem to impress the other boys. They were preoccupied with something else entirely. Right at the edge of the forest, no more than 20 metres from them, sat a lynx with long, brush-shaped ears, giving them a lazy stare. Jug Ears could feel the little hairs on the back of his neck stand on end, and his cousins quickly stuffed their semi-hard dicks back inside their trousers.

'Who dares follow it into the woods?' whispered the older cousin, giving his brother a challenging look.

'Let's just go home,' replied the younger boy, shifting nervously from one foot to the other.

'Wimp,' snarled his brother. 'Are you scared of a stupid cat?'

In the silence that followed – before Jug Ears suddenly stepped forward and said 'I'll do it!' – they could hear the grouse shrieking in the distance.

'No, don't do it,' said the younger cousin.

'Phooey,' said his brother. 'A lynx is afraid of people. If you go after it, it will just slip back into the forest. It's an ancient ritual: a boy follows the lynx into the forest and comes back out a man.'

'That's not true,' said the younger boy.

While his cousins argued, Jug Ears walked towards the lynx. As he got closer, the animal's ears quivered nervously. Then it got up, circled around a few times, and trotted back into the woods.

'Remember to keep your distance,' the older cousin said softly. 'Don't get too close.'

Jug Ears nodded.

'You have to go all the way into the woods,' yelled the younger brother. 'Otherwise it doesn't count.'

A moment later the lynx slipped into the forest, and Jug Ears could glimpse its body among the dark shadows of the trees. 'Don't let the tree spirits go through you!' was the last thing he heard. Then the forest closed around him. The Northern Lights were still making it possible for him to take his bearings, but after he had gone a few paces, something happened. The lights flared up like an exploding rocket in the night sky, giving him one last glimpse of the luminescent lynx. Then everything went dark, and after that he neither saw nor heard a thing. No more shouts from his cousins, only a faint rustling in the spruce trees as needles drifted down, taking more with them as they fell . . . He turned around and started heading back out of the forest, but after walking right into the first couple of tree trunks, he lost his sense of direction and began wandering among the trees in confusion.

'Damn it,' he swore. 'How did I end up here?'

Outside – on the edge of the forest – his cousins stood in the dark and yelled, 'Come on out, Niels. This isn't funny any more!' After an hour had passed, they sat down on a couple of stumps. The younger boy took his brother's hand, and they quickly agreed to wait until dawn before they headed in to find their cousin.

When Jug Ears awoke the next morning, he was lying with his head on a pillow of moss, staring up into the mighty crowns of the trees. He was hungry, and he set about looking for berries and other edible plants, just as his cousins had taught him. First he found some cowberries in a thicket near a grove of birch trees. Later he found blueberries; their bitter taste made him grimace. And after that a couple of mushrooms. He could hear the sound of engines in the distance. Convinced that it must be the woodcutters who had started work for the day, he headed in the direction of the noise. As he walked, he noticed that the trees were getting bigger, the rocks on the forest floor swelled to the size of small mountains that had to be climbed, the pillows of moss underfoot became so soft that he sank up to his knees in them, and since he was still hungry, he began picking an occasional mushroom, the type that his cousins had taught him were edible – but he might have mistakenly eaten the wrong kind. Maybe even those same mushrooms which, the day before, they had fed to the grouse. Because several hours later, when he finally reached the source of the noise, he saw a hunched figure standing next to a giant tree, fumbling with an electricity machine overgrown with moss.

'Get on back to the bonemeal factory!' screamed the figure.

Jug Ears stared in horror at his former teacher and raced back to the safety of the woods. As he ran, he noticed that countless crabs were scurrying about on the forest floor. And once again he heard the psychotic grouse shrieking in the distance, and he felt the forest take a firm grip on him.

That was how Jug Ears ended up surrendering to the enchanted forest. A surprised woodcutter had seen the missing boy retreat in fear, but after that Jug Ears was not seen again until he showed up in Børkersjø several weeks later. Living on a diet of berries, roots, and various mushrooms – including a considerable quantity of psilocybin mushrooms, which he mistakenly assumed were edible – Jug Ears got lost in his own inner forest. During the first couple of days, he roamed around like a prince with a cosmic vision of a pot of gold at the end of the rainbow, and as background music he heard his mother's song about a brilliant future. But soon the disgusting stench of faeces began to disturb his vision; bloodhounds howled in the distance, and at night, when the Northern Lights flashed, he saw an emaciated man who, with a horrified look on his face, was bending over him and accusing him of being the son of a murderer.

Even more bothersome than the emaciated man was the Fang, that lying prophet, who kept turning up at any opportunity to instil in his great-grandson the last remnants of his loathsome philosophy.

'Get away from me!' shouted Jug Ears, flinging branches and stones at the despised apparition. 'I never want to see you again!'

The Fang began speaking apologetically about coins that would once more rain down, about gold that would slowly find its way into his hands again. *You didn't really think it was all going to be so damn easy, did you!* he swore. But Jug Ears wasn't about to give his old friend a chance.

'Get out of here!' he screamed. And while he was yelling at the Fang, he noticed that his own member started to grow; hair burst through his skin; his muscles ached and his bones groaned.

Go ahead and paddle your own canoe, Peewee! the rejected apparition muttered, disappearing among the trees. After that, Jug Ears never saw or heard from his great-grandfather again until the Fang showed up years later on the cold summits of Mt Blakhsa. But before he dissolved completely in the glow of the Northern Lights, the Fang turned around and said, *Come on, admit it, Peewee: we had a damn good time, didn't we?*

'Get out!' shouted Jug Ears. The spirit had barely vanished before he saw two enchanting girls come dancing towards him. One of them, whose beauty was the most breathtaking, was as blond as a birch; the other had her brown tresses piled up in a strange coiffure.

'Not in the mood, is that it?' whispered the blonde. 'Say goodbye to your great-grandfather nicely. You won't see him again.'

And with that, the two girls disappeared as well, giggling loudly. But unlike the other apparitions, they kept coming back. They tickled the bottom of his feet with a feather while he slept. They sprinkled crushed leaves in his eyes. They offered him colourful psilocybin mushrooms that were as juicy as mangoes. Jug Ears soon discovered that the blond girl took the lead in all their pranks. She was without doubt the most elusive – a big tease – and she would disappear every time he tried to touch her. The brunette, on the other hand, would take him in her arms and let him sleep with his head in her lap. In the end a certain rivalry developed between the two girls. Each time Jug Ears placed his head in the brunette's lap, the blonde would appear behind the trees, calling to him in her teasing voice. Then the brunette would get so mad that she threw stones at her, called her names, and tore at her own hair in sheer frustration.

But if the brunette wasn't around, the blonde would bend down to his ear and whisper, 'Let's run away together!'

Jug Ears would nod eagerly and repeat, 'Let's run away together.' But the next instant the blonde would vanish. He would hear her ghostly laughter among the trees, often followed by the sound of a catfight whenever the two girls attacked each other. The rivalry between the girls soon got on his nerves. He urged them to call a truce, but at the same time he felt flattered they were vying for his attention. He told them to go somewhere else to fight, and yet he enjoyed the sight of them rolling around on the forest floor, pulling each other by the hair, pinching and spitting. But finally the mood in the enchanted forest grew so tense that Jug Ears began to dream of being back home in Bergen. He shuddered at the sight of his wild dream girls, he gasped when tufts of their hair drifted down around his ears. And one night, when the brunette woke him and urged him to walk in the direction of the rainbow racing across the vault of the sky, he obeyed without looking back.

'Don't let the tree spirits go through you,' she whispered. And before he disappeared among the trees, she added, 'OR THAT OTHER GIRL EITHER!'

Jug Ears followed the rainbow, and when the terrain began to change and he was once more walking through the strange world of the stump forest, he felt yet again like a prince with a cosmic vision of a pot of gold at the end of the rainbow. In the distance he could glimpse a glittering city. He walked out of the stump forest and into the streets of the town. The citizens were asleep behind the dark panes, but later, when he stopped in front of a window where the rainbow ended, he discovered to his great disappointment that there was no gold to be seen.

'Damn it all,' he muttered. And then he opened the window, crawled inside, and lay down in his bed before his cousins, who slept in the same room, had time to rouse the rest of the household.

As was the case with so many other things, Bjørk had tried

to keep their son's disappearance secret from her husband. She hoped that Jug Ears would turn up. That was why more than a week passed before Bjørk sent a telegram to her husband to tell him of the situation. The next day a sombre-looking man with a parrot on his shoulder was seen arriving at the local bus station. He spoke to no one, looked no one in the eye, and asked for directions only once before he picked up his suitcase and set off for the house of the sawmill owner. 'Damn it,' he said when the door was opened, 'he hasn't run off to sea, has he?'

'Of course not,' cried Bjørk. 'He's just a child, after all!'

And so Askild settled into the guest room, assuming a tone of superficial politeness whenever he spoke to anyone in the family. He insisted on taking charge of the search, which was rather trying for the woodcutters who went out to the woods every day to look for their boss's missing nephew. Askild drove them crazy with his superior attitude, and he taxed their patience by devising elaborate schemes for searching the woods. He quickly gained a reputation for being much less logical than he imagined he was. And it was obvious that he had never set foot in Nordland before. As the weeks passed, his sense of superiority flagged. He would often sit for hours on the trunk of the car, staring off into space. An alarming pallor began to invade his face, until early one morning he was awakened by his two nephews, who came rushing into the guest room in their pyjamas. 'He's lying in his bed!' they shouted.

Askild dashed into his nephews' room. Bjørk, who had not seen her husband cry since that afternoon in 1945 when Mamma Randi had sung lullabies to him in the parlour in Skansen, stood rooted in the doorway. At first she was a bit frightened by the sight of her husband, but then she was filled with self-reproach at the sight of her slumbering son, who was in a dreadful state. But after assuring herself that the boy had no hidden wounds or lethal gashes, she started to wonder about the way that his clothes, aside from being torn and filthy, were much too small for him. And the dark shadow adorning his upper lip could not be washed off with water.

Jug Ears slept for three days, raving deliriously as the last shadows of tree spirits passed through his mind. When he finally woke up, his older cousin looked at him and said, 'Didn't we tell you to keep your hands off those mushrooms?'

That same evening Askild summoned his wife to the guest room, and over two cups of coffee they set about negotiating a secret agreement. After an hour and a half it was boiled down to two demands from Askild's side and one demand from Bjørk. 'You will not see Doctor Thor again, and you will move with me to wherever I end up getting my next job.' Those were Askild's demands. 'You will never lay hands on the children again,' was Bjørk's demand. And the following day the sombre-looking man was once again seen at the bus station with a parrot on his shoulder. This time he seemed a bit impatient, because he had so many things to take care of: salary negotiations, ferry tickets, appointments with a removal company, a pilgrimage to see a weepy Mamma Randi, and family dealings with Applehead, who was eager to take over the cubist house. When everything was in place, Askild wrote a brief letter to Bjørk in which he outlined his plans for the future. The letter was extremely matter-of-fact, but when he was about to send it off, he couldn't help himself.

'Cheer up,' he wrote at the end. 'We'll be living like counts and barons in Denmark.'

PART FIVE

Riding a Bike Blindfolded

'GHOSTS?' MY SISTER Stinna says, giving me a look of astonishment. 'Enchanted forests? What exactly are you getting at with all this?'

She's willing to go along with the idea that someone's childhood might contain a magic universe. But she seems to think that pubescent crises camouflaged as a psilocybin mushroom trip and Great-grandfather Rasmus as a babbling apparition is going a bit too far. 'Besides, you've never cared much for all these stories before, and now you suddenly can't talk about anything else,' she adds.

I'm fully aware of this. I'm mixing paints and stretching canvases in the guest room. It's as if the stories have started taking control of me. They're driving me back towards my own birth and towards motives that I'm not sure I'm quite ready to confront. I slap a few more colours on to the canvas. The guest room is starting to look a real mess. And a few minutes later Stinna's two children come running in to see the latest creations.

'Is that a doghead?' asks the older kid, pointing at a canvas that I've hung on the wall. The boy is wearing a prosthetic nose in the middle of his forehead, held in place with an elastic band, and in one hand he's holding a sword, nervously fidgeting with it.

'No,' I tell him. 'I haven't painted that yet.'

'Phooey,' he says, looking at the canvas with disappointment. 'I want to see a doghead!'

I don't know why Stinna's kids are so interested in dogheads. When she mentions the dogheads to me, it's always with a certain hesitation. But apparently she must have told her children stories about their uncle, who as a boy was afraid of the dogheads under the stairs. He was also scared of the dark and a number of other things. And maybe their interest in dogheads isn't any different from my own interest in Jamaica, back when Knut came to visit. At any rate, my nephew keeps on demanding a doghead from me, while his younger brother squirts him in the eye with a water pistol. 'That's my nose!' the younger one shouts, and the next moment they're rolling around on the ground among the canvas stretchers and tubes of paint.

'That's enough!' cries Stinna. 'You crazy kids! It's time for bed.' She herds them out of the guest room. A little while later I can hear her singing goodnight songs on the second floor. An hour later, when she returns with a bottle of wine, she looks much more relaxed.

'That's looking good,' she says, handing me a glass. A sly smile crosses her lips before she comes to the point. 'But why don't you cut loose a bit? Why don't you go out and have a good time somewhere?' She could just as well have said: 'Why don't you find yourself a girl?' At regular intervals, ever since puberty, I've had to deal with that particular embarrassing question. Of course there have been girls in my life, and of course I'm not a virgin any more, even though it did take quite a while. I just haven't been in as much of a hurry as other people. For a long time I thought that my hesitation towards the opposite sex was due to a particularly sensitive temperament, just as I was convinced that it was because of this sensitivity that my fear of the dark continued well after puberty and even into adulthood. But now I think that it was more likely due to my fat aunt, even though I still don't know if it was because of what I did to her or what she did to me. In any case, all sorts of well-meaning people have tried to foist girls on me.

I'm just about to respond curtly to Stinna when I stop myself and promise to go out and have some fun very soon – there's just something that I have to finish first.

'And what about Grandma Bjørk?' Stinna says, referring to my visit to the nursing home that morning. 'Did the fresh air arrive today? The usual charade?'

I nodded. Applehead's weekly tin was always eagerly anticipated. 'I'll bet Niels is having a splendid time up there in the old house,' Bjørk said with a sigh after she had inhaled the fresh air through the hole in the tin.

I couldn't get myself to correct her faulty impression. I couldn't make myself say that it wasn't Jug Ears at all who now lived in their old house in the newly developed neighbourhood, or who was so concerned about his mother's health that he sent her fresh air from Bergen. The whole story about Jug Ears' second disappearance was the most difficult blow for all of us to accept, and I was afraid that any reminder would be the death of her. That was why I let her continue to float in her ignorance, which is the only privilege of a great age. And I encouraged her to keep fantasizing about Bergen.

Bjørk crossed the waters of the Skagerrak only once and never set foot in Norway again. While I sat beside her bed this morning, I pulled out of my pocket a photograph showing the family standing on the ferry deck in a strong headwind shortly before New Year's Day 1960. In the centre of the picture are Askild and Bjørk, arm in arm. It's clear that their relationship is still marked by a certain formality so soon after the revelation in Doctor Thor's consulting room. Next to Bjørk stands Jug Ears, wearing a suit that is too small for him. On his forehead it's possible to glimpse a couple of pimples, which he has tried to hide by pulling down his cap. At the very edge of the picture Knut is casting a restless eye at the waves, while Anne Katrine is clinging to the leg of her father's trousers. It appears to be a photo of a completely normal family, but anyone in the know would quickly notice an odd phenomenon. A closer examination of the thirteen-year-old Jug Ears reveals that while his body has started to grow, while pimples have appeared and hair has begun to sprout in hidden places, *his ears have not grown at all*. They stayed exactly the same, and over time they actually seemed to get smaller. That's when what I like to call a time of adjustment and harmonization began.

The trip to Denmark was, without question, the longest one Bjørk ever undertook. Especially because of the heavy seas which, shortly after the unknown photographer left the family to their own devices, forced her below to the ferry's toilets, while Askild, who had stronger sea legs, walked around with a foolish grin on his face. Yet in spite of the rigours of the sea voyage, Bjørk always dreamt of making that trip one more time – just a little holiday, a brief jaunt up to Bergen to visit her family. It was something she talked about all her life. For many years Askild wasn't crazy about the idea. Then, in his old age, when he finally started talking about doing it, the trip seemed too overwhelming to both of them. Even when Askild, at the age of seventy, one day came home with two ferry tickets, which he meticulously unfolded on the table and studied for a long time under a magnifying glass while Grandma Bjørk stood leaning over him, it was as if the trip had become transformed into a dream voyage that defied all sense. They talked about the preparations for several months, but a feeling of unreality continued to hover over their plans. Finally Grandpa Askild went over to the travel bureau to get his money back. At our next visit, we all expected to find them depressed, but instead of being disheartened by the weaknesses of old age, they both seemed relieved.

'No,' said Askild. 'What has Norway ever really done for me? I want to die in Denmark.'

Askild's assimilation into his new country had taken place without a hitch. Denmark's liberal attitude towards alcohol was especially appealing. No more illicit pubs for him. Now he could drink with his head held high, which he did on a grand scale, except during those periods when his increasing problems with his ulcer forced him to go on the wagon for weeks at a time, wreaking havoc with all the household routines.

But back to the photograph from 1959.

'Those ears,' said Bjørk, laughing. 'We've never had anything but trouble from those ears.'

The first time she noticed the more balanced proportion between her son's ears and his body was during the second summer they spent in Ålborg. She was standing at the kitchen window, watching Jug Ears ride his bike in an insane spiral out on the street, when it suddenly dawned on her that his ears looked perfectly normal.

Jug Ears had known this for a long time, but at that moment he was more interested in riding his bike – until he lost control of it, that is. As Applehead had done many years earlier, he rammed right into the milkman's truck, which was parked on the street. That's when he heard a voice whispering.

'Hey, you idiot. You can't talk properly, and now you can't even ride a bike.'

And a fair-haired figure bearing a striking resemblance to the blond girl in the enchanted forest of Nordland walked past him down the road. So, on top of the throbbing pain in his knee, Jug Ears felt an even bigger pain in his gut, which soon turned to nausea. The fourteen-year-old girl, whose name was Marianne Qvist, didn't realize that she had played a past role in the dream forest of her admirer. Nor did she know that she would later play a decisive part in the Eriksson family history – or that, more or less unintentionally, she would deliver the worst of many blows the family would suffer. No, in her fourteen-year-old world the mountain-monkey on the bicycle was merely an exotic element in her daily life in Ålborg. And it was with a mixture of curiosity and contempt that she regarded the crazy bicyclist, who kept riding around at her heels. He wasn't quite as pesky as Applehead had once been to the Ginger, because he'd already spent a year and a half in Denmark, and it had taught him to keep a low profile.

In the schoolyard – on a blustery January day in 1960 soon after they had arrived – Jug Ears had been forced to revive his nut-kicking skills. A mountain-monkey from Norway had a need for certain talents in a Danish schoolyard if he wanted to avoid a turn in the basement pissoir, which was otherwise obligatory for new pupils. But that same spring, when he joined the local boxing club in order to perfect these skills, he was thrown out because he resorted to crude methods, by kicking his opponents in the nuts. To his great disappointment, he also discovered that the crabs in Limfjord near Ålborg paled in comparison with the giants from the North Sea. Nobody wanted to buy the puny crabs that he fished out of the muddy fjord.

One night shortly after they had moved to the new house Jug Ears was sitting on his bedroom windowsill in the glow of the nearest street lamp, unable to sleep. Bjørk had once promised him that they would live in the cubist house forever. Now Bergen was light years away, and he missed Applehead's wild behaviour, as well as the peevish friendship of Ibsen the coin dealer, and all the boys from Skansen. Sitting there, imagining himself back in Bergen, and about to surrender for the first time to melancholy, Jug Ears saw a light go on in a window across the street. Their neighbour was a welder who worked at the shipyard, as Askild did. Jug Ears blinked sleepily and then straightened when he saw the figure of a girl get out of bed and totter out of her room. She hadn't closed the curtains, and the sight of his dream girl from the enchanted forest struck him with such intensity that suddenly all his anguish took on new meaning. The fact that the dream forest blonde had assumed the shape of the welder's twelve-year-old daughter clad in a nightgown, or that she obviously did not return his conspiratorial glances in the days that followed, was not enough to discourage him. Before long he had borrowed Askild's telescope and installed it on the windowsill. There he would now sit for half the night with his eye glued to the telescope, a silent witness to rituals which, to the uninitiated, might seem trivial. Marianne brushing her hair in front of the mirror before she went to bed. The welder coming in to say good night. The mother sitting on the edge of the bed to rub her daughter's back. He noticed that she enjoyed having her back rubbed, that she had a habit of pursing her lips and giving herself charming looks in the mirror, and that she always remembered to kiss a green teddy bear – the ugliest of all those sitting on the shelf – before the light was turned off. Six months later he noticed, to his great astonishment, that kissing was not the only thing that she did to that stuffed animal. Several times she placed it between her legs as she lay in bed and squeezed her thighs so hard that the bear practically disappeared.

The sight of the now thirteen-year-old girl with a green teddy bear between her legs made him dizzy, and he began making unrealistic and quite complicated plans for getting her to notice him. But without Applehead's self-confidence, without having mastered the flat monotone of the Danish language, and after his embarrassing experience with Linda in the hedge, even in the daytime hours he couldn't find anything better to do than be a silent voyeur. In the meantime, his body kept growing, his ears shrank, and the first notes of a Jutland accent crept into his speech. A pallor, due to lack of sleep, came over his face, and a dark ring – the result of close contact with the telescope – began to be visible around his left eye.

But one night in the autumn of 1960, the silent voyeur was distracted by something white fluttering in the dark. It was the laundry that their neighbour's wife had forgotten to take in; it was now hanging on the laundry line, flapping restlessly in the autumn breeze. He adjusted the telescope and caught sight of a pair of white cotton knickers, which undoubtedly belonged to the girl. In a flash he had jumped out of the window and run across the street to the welder's yard. Glancing nervously from side to side, he swiped the knickers and stuck them in the pocket of his pyjamas. He hid the knickers in the top drawer of his bedside table, often taking them out when he couldn't sleep at night.

In a semi-dream state he would imagine that he was a green teddy bear and that he was receiving a goodnight kiss from the girl in the dream forest, after which he was placed between her strong legs to sleep. The fantasies made him a bit uneasy, but he was even more uneasy at the thought that Bjørk might find the cotton knickers on his pillow when she woke him in the morning. He promised himself that he would soon get rid of them. And he wondered like crazy how in the world he was going to make the girl notice him.

The answer came during that second summer in Ålborg. It appeared in the form of a worn-out old bicycle lying in a thicket, which Askild passed every day on his way to work. After Grandpa Askild had seen that ownerless bike often enough, he took it home and gave it to his son for his fifteenth birthday. As he stood in front of his very first bicycle, it dawned on Jug Ears that he now had the answer to his question. In short, he was going to get her to notice him as a fearless bicyclist.

After that the fifteen-year-old Jug Ears could be seen on the street showing the same zeal for dangerous bicycle stunts that he had once applied to the art of nut-kicking. He was soon zooming back and forth without using his hands to steer. He learnt to ride wearing a blindfold, cheating only when absolutely necessary. He experimented with using his hands instead of his feet to pedal, storming the kerbs as he sat backwards on his bike. This is also why Bjørk saw her bicycling son riding around in an insane spiral until he was stopped by the parked truck of the milkman. Bjørk, who came running out of the house to tend to Jug Ears' knee, also noticed the neighbour's now fourteen-year-old daughter disappearing down the street, casting sly looks over her shoulder. *Crazy boy*, Bjørk thought with a smile. But when winter arrived, the sight of her bicycling son, who was now doing stunts over the frozen puddles in the street, made Bjørk so nervous that one day she suggested that he ask the neighbour's daughter over for tea.

'Tea!' shouted Jug Ears in alarm. 'But what if she doesn't like tea?'

For the rest of the winter Bjørk would repeat her suggestion at regular intervals, but Jug Ears always refused. Then she changed her tactics and tried, using vague phrases, to correct her son's mistaken idea that girls were attracted to reckless daredevils. Using metaphors taken from medical romances, she described to him the way sensitive men could make women swoon, how courtesy was more valued than daring, and warmth more treasured than the greatest feats. But through the kitchen window on Nyboværftsvej Bjørk saw, to her horror, that not everyone had the same view of daredevils that she did.

'Anybody can do that,' said Marianne Qvist when Jug Ears biked around the street in insane circles. Then, in a kinder voice and with a hint of sensuality, she added, 'I know someone who can do that standing on the handlebars.' And so he climbed up on the handlebars and flew right into the nearest hedge. And the giggling girl disappeared down the street.

'You're cheating!' she cried when he tied his muffler around his eyes. 'You can see out of the bottom!'

When Marianne came over to him for the first time to tie the muffler properly, Jug Ears noticed a rumbling in his stomach. But it was swiftly replaced by fear when he got on his bike and, completely blind, began veering down the street. He was fine for the first 10 metres, but then he suddenly heard the sound of an engine. 'Keep to the right!' shouted Marianne. He turned sharply to the left, which meant that the welder, who was on his way home from work in his car, very nearly acquired a fearless bicyclist as a hood ornament.

'Gypsy kids!' he yelled, rolling down the window. 'In Denmark we don't ride our bikes around in traffic blindfolded!'

The incident with the welder's car settled the matter. The next day Bjørk stopped the welder's wife on the street to invite her to tea on the following afternoon. And she urged her to bring along her daughter. Another reason for Bjørk's invitation was a realization that she was lonely in Denmark. It was not a new feeling, but in Denmark the loneliness was worse since the language barrier often made people look at her in alarm when she opened her mouth to speak. She thought the neighbour's wife seemed friendly, and Askild hardly ever invited anyone home. Not wanting to worry her son, she didn't say a word to him, and so he was dumbstruck when he was summoned into the living room on the following afternoon to say hello to the guests. The fourteen-year-old girl was sulking next to her mother on the sofa, and she refused even to look at him. Bjørk, too, was a little nervous, so she quickly began telling stories about enchanted Nordland.

While Bjørk talked, Marianne yawned ostentatiously. But an hour later, when Bjørk suggested that Niels Junior show Marianne his room, she seemed a bit more interested. Once inside his room she asked with an edge of irony in her voice what his family was doing in Denmark if Norway was supposed to be as marvellous as Bjørk had said. Then she asked him for some milk for her tea, and when Jug Ears went out to the kitchen, she started going through his things. First she found an old telescope on the windowsill. She looked through it and witnessed the disturbing sight of her own bedroom in daylight. An unpleasant feeling of having been caught out seized hold of her, but when Jug Ears came back she merely said, 'Sugar, please, if you don't mind.' And then continued her investigation. She looked under the bed, where she found nothing but dust balls. She cast a swift glance in the wardrobe, which held only the usual items. Then she opened the drawer in the bedside table and hauled out a white garment at the very moment that Jug Ears reappeared in the doorway, holding the sugar bowl.

'What!' she cried, staring at the stolen item. 'These are Mother's knickers! What are they doing here?'

Jug Ears dropped the sugar bowl in sheer terror. And the next instant the fourteen-year-old girl was racing past him with a look on her face that showed nothing but scorn. Even more sullen than before, she sat down next to her mother on the sofa and didn't utter another word until she said goodbye.

After the guests had left, Bjørk had the feeling that something had gone wrong, and she couldn't understand what her son saw in that ill-tempered girl. Jug Ears, on the other hand, was left with the feeling that he had just triggered a catastrophe. And that evening he noticed that, contrary to custom, the curtains in Marianne's room were closed. He adjusted the telescope but had to make do with the odd shadow play silhouetted on the white curtains.

After that Jug Ears went around looking more and more pale. Bjørk actually started to miss his bicycle stunts, and even Askild noticed that the boy seemed distracted and listless. But a couple of weeks later Marianne Qvist walked past him on the street. Without looking at him, she handed him a letter, stopping to see his reaction. The letter consisted of only seven words: *Did you really think they were mine?* Jug Ears swallowed hard and then suddenly burst out with all the secrets he knew: that she liked to have her back rubbed, that she practised smiling a lot in a certain kind of way, and that her favourite teddy bear was the green one. 'I've noticed,' he told her, 'that you like the ugliest bear best of all.'

During this whole speech – as a good two years of suppressed night-time voyeurism poured out of his mouth – an astounded girl could be seen on Nyboværftsvej, her smile getting bigger and bigger, until he mentioned the green teddy bear.

'You peeping Tom!' she shouted suddenly, turning pale. 'You perverted pig!'

The next instant she was gone, running down the street. She no longer challenged him to any more bicycle stunts, and she told people that he was just as stupid as his father's parrot. Two weeks later a sign appeared in her window. It said: *You should talk! What exactly are you doing with my mother's knickers?*

I threw them out, wrote Jug Ears on a sign that he put on his windowsill. *I'm sorry.*

After that the bicycle acrobat could once again be seen on Nyboværftsvej, and Bjørk couldn't understand how she could ever have longed to see fifteen-year-old Niels Jug Ears Junior letting the neighbour's daughter tie a black scarf around his eyes so that he could veer down the street at a furious speed like a kamikaze pilot. And Marianne would run behind to direct him around parked cars. No, with a trembling heart, Bjørk had to conclude that not all girls were content with sweet words, courtesy, warmth, and so on. On the contrary, the welder's daughter kept challenging Jug Ears to try more and more breakneck tricks, and Grandma Bjørk actually thought she saw a lascivious smile cross the girl's face as her son obeyed . . . *Dumb as an ox, obedient as a dog, crazy as a pubescent youth*, thought Bjørk.

Marianne was attracted by Jug Ears' stunts. She especially enjoyed anything dangerous, and soon she sowed the crazy idea in his mind that he should bike straight through Ålborg blindfolded. At least it was Bjørk's impression that Marianne was the one who thought up the idea. According to him, Marianne practically forced him to do it, even though she was more likely just a catalyst for the big scheme.

It was the third summer in Ålborg. When the sweethearts, as Knut had started calling them, weren't practising new bicycle tricks on Nybovaerftsvej, they were trying out the route through Ålborg without wearing a blindfold. 'Preparation is the most important phase,' said Niels Junior, and he told everyone who would listen about the daring plan. But one day Askild decided that he'd had enough of his son's foolishness. He pounded the table and forbade him to go through with his idiotic scheme. Bjørk had already forbidden him on numerous occasions, and on his sixteenth birthday, Jug Ears had received a card from Mamma Randi, which warned him in the strongest terms. *When the hormones increase*, wrote Randi, *good sense vanishes. I forbid you to bike through that disgusting city blindfolded.*

According to Grandma Bjørk, Marianne had caused her son to lose all connection with the earth. Even now, many years later, when I visit Bjørk at the nursing home, she still gets a gloomy look in her eyes when I mention the neighbour's daughter from Nybovaerftsvej. Even my sister Stinna gets upset when the conversation turns to Marianne Qvist.

'Why not just forget about that silly goose?' says Stinna. 'She's really not all that important.'

But I can't do that. Marianne can't be left out. And besides, Stinna's view of Marianne Qvist has also been coloured by Jesper's opinion.

'What a bunch of nonsense!' Stinna interrupts me.

But that's another story. And I'm not going to torment Stinna with it right now.

As a child, Marianne Qvist had always been wild. Even at

the age of three she was bringing home worms, snails, and other vermin. At first her father had urged her to go out and explore nature, to climb trees, to investigate puddles for insect larvae, and to throw mud at the birds on the street. Her mother would merely gape at her filthy daughter with an expression of disgust. In this way Marianne became first and foremost her father's daughter. He often said of her that she was a gypsy girl. As a child his closest neighbour had been a gypsy colony, and the sight of all those gypsies coming and going had elicited a certain interest, as had the postcards that arrived every Christmas from an uncle in Greenland. So there was affection in his use of the nickname 'gypsy girl', although his wife Karen couldn't see what was so charming about it.

'Don't call my daughter a gypsy girl!' she cried. 'And stop all that Greenland nonsense – why should we go up there and rub shoulders with those filthy Greenlanders?'

The welder knew that Karen shuddered at the sight of the insect cocoons and bird skeletons which he was always cramming into his daughter's room. She loathed it when he took their six-year-old Marianne on fishing trips on Sundays, returning home with a daughter who was smeared with bloody entrails and fish scales. Karen turned pale with fear when he nailed boards to the big elm tree at the back so that Marianne could climb to the top and sit there, perching like a monkey on the highest branch and shouting 'Look what I can do!' as she swung ominously back and forth in the wind.

Karen was worried about the poor girl, whom her mad spouse had quite simply decided to turn into a boy. When her daughter's first school day approached, Karen put her secure life in Nybovaerftsvej at risk and issued an ultimatum: 'Things have got to change or it's all over, *finito*! Our daughter is not a boy!' The welder listened to his wife for well over an hour. Then he got up and went out to the back yard, where he climbed up into the elm tree and began tearing down the boards. The next day the bird skeletons and insect cocoons disappeared from his daughter's room, and the promised fishing trip on Sunday was cancelled and replaced with a shopping trip on Monday. Karen not only bought a school-bag and pencils, she also set aside time to visit the ladies' clothing shops, where the lavish displays of dresses, ribbons, and shoes made Marianne feel numb.

It was a total transformation. On Marianne's first day of school, a series of loud screams echoed through the house, but the welder did not come to his daughter's aid. He left the house without even looking at Marianne who, after a considerable fight, was ready to enter her new life – wearing a pink dress, white knee socks, patent-leather shoes, and a bow in her hair that was completely ridiculous, to put it mildly. What Karen had been trying to do for several years the welder had managed to achieve in a single day. Marianne felt betrayed by her father, and for the next couple of years an expression of near-hatred could be seen in her previously admiring eyes.

Yet over time she became accustomed to her new identity, and gradually she began directing her admiration towards her mother, who taught her to sew clothes for her dolls. Karen was convinced that learning to care for dolls and stuffed animals would arouse her daughter's feminine instincts, and for that reason she showered the girl with gifts that eventually filled up her room. Only one of them did Karen try to throw out several times – a scruffy old teddy bear that was stained after several falls into mud puddles on the street. It also smelled faintly of fish. It was the green teddy bear – called Gypsy Hans – and Marianne refused to part with him, as if that were her way of clinging to the last remnants of her former identity. But otherwise she soon forgot all about the joyous feeling of slitting open a fish along the arch of its body; she forgot about the blessings of mud puddles and her delight at wandering through the nearby woods. Over time, the only thing left was a distant memory that she had once stood on the highest branch of the huge elm tree, swaying in the wind like a monkey.

As she approached puberty, she conquered new territory in the female terrain and discovered how bows and patent-leather shoes could give her a different and more subtle power than she had achieved by vanquishing the tallest tree in the yard. And as her body swelled in choice places, she noticed that the boys were staring at her white knee socks, and that by casually tossing back her blond hair she could make even the most impudent ones shut up. It dawned on her that she actually possessed a certain attractive force, as if a magic wand had suddenly touched her. Since she also knew that behind every magic trick there was a basic amount of craft, she began to practice new techniques in her evenings – smiles, looks, pouting lips – as she thought: *Here I come, Marianne Qvist. Hold on to your hats and glasses!*

This was not the insecurity that usually characterizes puberty. In other words, everything was going quite well for the Qvist family on Nyboværftsvej until the day when Marianne caught sight of a bicycling mountain-monkey risking life and limb outside her window. It wasn't long

278

before she began faithfully showing up on the street every time he did his breakneck tricks. One moment she would be preoccupied with trying out her newest weapons: looks, smiles, pouting lips. But the next she would be right back to her former childish enthusiasm for all things reckless, which made her feel like casting off the hair ribbons and patent-leather shoes and jumping on to a bicycle herself. This new enthusiasm disturbed her. Mother and daughter started fighting again. And after attending Jug Ears' birthday party, the welder began to show an interest in the newcomers; he thought there was something gypsy-like about them, since they had spent their whole lives moving from one place to another. *And now I'll be damned if he hasn't started to babble about that filthy Greenland again*, thought Karen, quite upset. *What am I supposed to do up there? I'll shrivel up. I'll die of cold.*

One day in the fall of 1962 Jug Ears carried out his long-planned bicycle tour through Ålborg wearing a blindfold. Neither Askild's threats, Bjørk's pleas, nor the ridiculous letter from Mamma Randi could stop him. And Marianne Qvist rode her bike behind Jug Ears so that she could direct him around the rushing cars, playing children, and unsuspecting pedestrians. He fell only once and quickly got back on his feet. 'Don't take off the blindfold!' shouted Marianne, but a possible crash had also been part of their planning, so Jug Ears merely brushed off his trousers with the scraped palms of his hands and climbed back on his bike to complete the ride. The sight of her injured son wobbling along Nyboværftsvej half an hour later instantly made Bjørk think that the plan had failed, but both Jug Ears and Marianne were so elated that

Grandma soon realized the crash had just made the whole experience more thrilling.

That evening a change occurred in the unwritten rules, because now Jug Ears was suddenly standing in the welder's yard while Marianne hung out of the window. Bjørk wanted to know what they were up to, and she gradually got into the habit of sneaking out of bed at night to observe the crazy sweethearts. She would sit for hours in the cold kitchen without turning on a light, her eyes fixed on their every move. One moment she would feel it was her right to keep a vigilant eye on her son; the next she felt like a mother hen, and eventually like a spy peeking under the covers. From what Bjørk could see, the two spent a great deal of time holding hands, kissing, and taking turns pinching each other on the nose. Of course Grandma Bjørk couldn't hear that they also spent oceans of time telling jokes, and that in between fits of laughter they would make plans for formidable new schemes such as climbing up power poles, balancing along water pipes, and venturing out on to the brittle ice floes in the Limfjord. These were all plans that they actually carried out during the course of the winter. Now they both played the role of the daredevil, and a certain sense of competition quickly developed between them.

One ice-cold January night Bjørk noticed that her son was no longer standing outside Marianne's window; no, he was hanging over the windowsill, halfway out and halfway in, flailing both legs in the dark. *Crazy monkey*, she thought, sighing loudly. Spying on the teenage couple had made her think a lot about her own youth. All the effort she had put in to finding the right man, and yet she had still ended up here, in this suburb of Ålborg. And her thoughts swiftly moved on to Doctor Thor. Bjørk knew that Thor was not her great love – no, her great love was a different, and a less cubist, version of Askild, but *he damn well got us on to a sidetrack awfully quickly*, she thought. And she took solace in the idea that she could always divorce him when the children were old enough. But then she pushed those thoughts out of her mind because over in the neighbour's window a new game was being played.

'Won't you let me come inside for a minute?' asked Jug Ears as he dangled from the windowsill. And Marianne, who still thought of herself as a magician with a number of tricks that it wouldn't be wise to reveal all at once, giggled and shoved him back out as he kept trying to push his way in. But each time Jug Ears noticed that Marianne was relenting and that one last small exertion would allow him to fall into her room, something made him hesitate.

'Wait until summer,' said Marianne when she noticed this hesitation. 'When I turn sixteen you can come inside.'

He didn't draw lines on the wall to keep tally. He didn't cut off pieces of a tape measure, one centimetre after another. Nor did he count the days. Yet he was looking forward to the first time he would be allowed to crawl into her room like some Ali Baba entering the thieves' den. Then spring arrived – the day was approaching – and the welder started talking more and more about Greenland. 'Over my dead body!' shouted Karen in the house on Nyboværftsvej whenever she wasn't fighting with her daughter, who had grown very impudent lately. *Not at all Mother's sweet girl any more, and now Erik has also started filling out applications. What does he think he's doing? I'm not going to Greenland. Why are all these misfortunes pouring in on me all at once?* Karen cast a glance out of the window and instantly caught sight of the cause of all her problems. A drunken Norwegian, who had resumed his old habit and was now staggering around with Kai, the parrot, on his shoulder, as he talked out loud to himself about various types of dogs.

Pink Letters

IN THE LONG RUN, it wasn't the welder's dream about Greenland that ended up separating the young couple just a few weeks before Marianne's sixteenth birthday. No, it was the same old story that everyone in the family was getting quite tired of: *those damn engineers, they don't know shit about reality*. To be accused of not knowing anything about reality was probably the worst insult anyone could fling at Askild. As an old man, he was fond of saying that he had seen more than most people and knew more about reality than the rest of the family ever would.

'But what did you see in reality, Grandpa?' my sister Stinna and I would often ask at the same time, prompting Askild to give us a surly look and reply: 'Reality is not for children.'

Of course, he might be right about that. Reality is not for children; life is not for the squeamish. Making use of this philosophy later in his life, in the late 1970s, Askild began locking me, his grandson, in the wardrobe because I was afraid of the dark. 'Just wait until you have to go out into the real world,' he would say afterwards. 'People are only scared of the dark when they don't have real things to be scared of.'

During that time when Mum was going to school and Dad was leaving in his black Mercedes each morning, not returning home until long after dark: that's when Grandma Bjørk and Grandpa Askild looked after us, until the day when Stinna declared that she was now old enough to look after both of us on her own. And besides, she knew of a different method for conquering my fear of the dark – light.

Curing a fear of the dark with light is an excellent solution. The shadows are kept in check by the glowing light bulbs, and over time you might be lucky enough either to forget what they look like, or else you get used to the constant light. In my case, over time I got used to the light bulbs always being on. Even in Amsterdam I was sometimes tempted to leave a light on all night, though it was more out of habit than fear. But back then, when my fear of the dark was more intense, Dad had a different idea.

'Don't let the darkness go through you,' he said one day, slightly rephrasing his uncle Ejlif's line about tree spirits, and then he added, 'It's much better to go through the darkness yourself.'

Afterwards he took me by the hand, and together we went out to the nearest woods. It was a moonless autumn night, and the first thin layer of red leaves crackled under our feet. That image of a father and son wandering through the forest can make my heart overflow even today. He didn't cure my fear of the dark with a single walk in the woods, but as we walked, he did start telling me about his own wandering in the enchanted forest. He told me about a lynx, lit up by the Northern Lights, about an orchestra of tree spirits that suddenly appeared before his eyes, and about two enchanted girls who once came dancing towards him. One of them he met the following year in Ålborg, spying on her through a telescope and courting her with the help of a stolen bicycle until they were separated because of Grandpa Askild's new job in Odense. And the other girl . . .

'Who was she?' I asked.

And he replied, 'She was your mother.'

The move to Odense was the last in a long series of moves. Several years later when Askild was fired from the shipyard in Odense, he found work at the Lindø shipyard and needed only a motorbike to cover the extra distance between his job and home. Later, when he was fired, in turn, from the Lindø shipyard, he discovered to his great surprise that he had reached the age of retirement. The move to Odense was also the only time that Askild didn't promise his family that they would be living like counts and barons – the bitter lines around his mouth had hardened in place. That afternoon, when he came home drunk from the shipyard and had to tell them that he had once again ruined everything with his cubist point of view, he stopped expecting anything good from the future. And yet Odense would end up being the one place where Bjørk actually did feel as if she was treated like a count or a baron. At the age of forty-six, she got a part-time job working in the office of a sawmill, and for the next twenty years whenever the alarm clock rang in the morning she felt an intoxicating sense of freedom stream through her. It was a perfectly ordinary job, but with her sense for

285

magic, Grandma Bjørk soon endowed it with such an aura that there was very little left over for her lost childhood summers in Nordland.

In the removal van – on the way from Ålborg to Odense – a morose Askild sat with his eyes stubbornly fixed on the road until he cast an irritated glance at his older son and said, 'In the real world you have to learn to take a broken heart in stride.' Jug Ears gave his father a look that expressed nothing but contempt, and he promised himself that he would live in the same house for the rest of his life when he and Marianne one day moved in together. Bjørk, on the other hand, didn't make a sound because, if the truth be told, she was shaken. Not at the sudden firing, not at the idea of having to start over again – she had grown accustomed to that – but because of something quite different, a disturbing drama that she had witnessed the night before.

On their last night in Ålborg, true to form, she was sitting in the kitchen keeping a vigilant eye on the wrestling match going on in Marianne's window. But to her great surprise, the crazy pair hung on the windowsill for only half an hour. Then Jug Ears suddenly turned around and ran back to the house, and the light in Marianne's room was switched off. *Final curtain*, thought Bjørk, heaving a sigh of relief. *So that's the end of that story.*

Then she went to the toilet and was on her way back to bed when she felt a craving for a glass of milk. She was standing once again in the dark kitchen when the light was switched on in Marianne's window. The curtains were open, the room was bathed in light. In the middle of the light, which seemed to Bjørk as bright as if it were coming from fifty spotlights, stood Marianne Qvist like any other hussy, firing off her whole arsenal of magic tricks: the pouting lips, the secretive smile, the special way she had of tossing back her hair as she got undressed until finally she was standing stark naked in the middle of the room *with shamelessness painted on her face*, thought Bjørk, who had also noticed the telescope in her son's room. And those two components: a naked Marianne engaged in an insane performance, and her son sitting on his own windowsill with his eye glued to a telescope, made Bjørk swallow the milk the wrong way. This prompted a violent coughing fit that didn't stop until the girl got into bed with her green teddy bear and did things that were simply not decent for a girl her age . . .

There's something unnatural about that girl, thought Bjørk in the removal van on her way to a new life in Odense. *She hasn't even turned sixteen yet; that's just not a proper way to behave!* What Grandma Bjørk feared she had seen, and what she more than a quarter of a century later was positive she had seen, was not a girl who was almost sixteen and rather awkwardly trying to claim the life of a grown-up. No, Bjørk feared that she had seen a dyed-in-the-wool demon, one of those creatures who determine a person's fate. And Bjørk was soon casting uneasy glances at the letters that arrived each week in the new house on the outskirts of Odense – scented letters, pink envelopes covered with hearts on which it frequently said: *I'm supposed to send you many greetings from Gypsy Hans.*

Fortunately, Bjørk didn't know that Gypsy Hans was the name of the green teddy bear. Nor did she know that the crazy pair had put together a plan: to run away together as soon as one of them turned eighteen. In other words, when Jug Ears was eighteen, and that would be in less than a year.

Good thing we got out of there, thought Bjørk instead. And back in Ålborg, Karen gradually came to the same conclusion because her daughter stopped behaving impudently. Now she would sit quietly in her room, writing words on pink stationery, as was only proper for a real girl. And once again things were going quite well for the Qvist family on Nyboværftsvej – that is, up until the evening when the welder called Karen out to the kitchen and pulled the rug out from under her feet. 'Things have got to change, or it's all over, *finito*! I too have certain dreams of my own.' In a last desperate attempt to escape her husband's dreams, Karen tried to ally herself with her daughter, who wasn't wild about the prospect of moving to Greenland either, not now, only a few months before she was about to run away. The letters that arrived in Odense gradually took on a tone that seemed more and more desperate.

We're going to have to push our plans ahead. We have to run away right now! Jug Ears read. *My father is insane, my mother is crazy, I can't stand it any more.* Jug Ears wrote back with golden promises, but even though they were old enough to run away, he never got around to actually doing it. At any rate, the Qvist family did move to Greenland before anyone succeeded in running away, and shortly afterwards, Bjørk noticed a sharp decline in her son's mood. Not even the pink envelopes that arrived from Greenland seemed to cheer him up any more. He didn't care for the tone of them: the obvious enthusiasm, the overly elated euphoria that bore witness to the fact that Marianne had found someone else with whom she could do wild things.

288

That someone was the welder, who took his daughter on hunting trips in the mountains, let her drive the dogsled across the ice, and took her out to see polar bears. Jug Ears' own story about the lynx illuminated by the Northern Lights paled in comparison. *If we're still going to run away*, wrote Marianne Qvist, *Greenland is a fabulous place for it!*

A different tone began to slip in between the lines of his letters too. *Is your father the only one who goes along on those hunting trips? You're not seeing other boys, are you?* And even the grand finale that Marianne had performed, tying the final knot to link her to Jug Ears before he moved away, now became a cornerstone in their foolish bickering. *Has anyone else seen that trick you do with the teddy bear? You won't forget to close the curtains, will you?*

And Marianne replied, *Of course you're the only one who knows what I do with Gypsy Hans. What about you? Who are you drooling over at night these days? And why don't you come here? You promised that we would run away together when you turned eighteen. That was months ago!*

I have a feeling that I would just be in the way, wrote Jug Ears.

The tone of their letters didn't get any better when the jealousy and distrust they were already feeling became exacerbated by maternal interference. Bjørk felt strongly that things had not gone in the right direction for her son during their first days in Odense. Shortly after they arrived, the superintendent of the new school had summoned Bjørk and Askild to a conference. He demanded that Jug Ears repeat a grade in school because his problems with the Danish language had prompted a significant drop in his learning curve. In addition, Jug Ears was always sitting in his room and staring off into space whenever he wasn't writing letters, which he often ended up throwing out. *He hasn't made any new friends*, thought Bjørk, and she decided that something had to be done. The first time she stood with a pink envelope in her hand was undoubtedly the hardest. How could she defend stealing his letters? Bjørk convinced herself that it was for his own good, and then she simply crumpled up the pink letter and threw it away.

Why don't you write to me any more? wrote Jug Ears. *Have you found someone else?*

Of course not! Marianne wrote back. *You're the one who never writes!*

Bjørk didn't take all the letters. She pinched every other one or so, and unlike the first time, she now hid them away in a box stored at the bottom of the big cupboard in the bedroom. Sometimes she also pinched one of her son's letters. 'Let me post that for you,' she would say. 'I'll pay for the stamps.' Not suspecting a thing, Jug Ears would hand the letter to his mother. Finally she had inserted so many silent gaps, so many unknown factors and broken promises between the two that one day the last pink letter arrived from Greenland.

You're an unreliable jerk, not at all the sweet boy I once knew, wrote Marianne Qvist. *I can't stand you any more.*

You're not yourself any more either, wrote Jug Ears. *I bet that trick with the teddy bear was all a fake.* Marianne never had a chance to read these last words because Grandma pinched the letter and hid it in her cupboard. Jug Ears stopped writing. Now he merely sat and stared into space, and without sounding very convinced, Askild said that a broken heart was always mended in the real world.

But Grandma was not so sure. She thought her son

looked even more miserable than before. It wasn't until one afternoon when she caught sight of the big bonfire that Jug Ears had lit in the farthest corner of the yard that she breathed a sigh of relief. *Final curtain*, thought Bjørk for the second time as she watched him poking around in the fire with a stick to make the last charred scrap of pink stationery rise up to be carried away by the wind. *Now that story is over, once and for all.*

A Chrome-Plated Horn

OVER THE PAST couple of years Knut had grown accustomed to the sight of his father dragging home one bicycle after another. The bikes often had flat tyres, and the fenders and frames were bent, but Askild would patch the tyres, pound the frames straight, and remove the remnants of old locks. Then he would put the bikes in the shed, where they eventually took up all the space.

'It's not stealing,' Askild liked to say. 'I'm just taking care of them.'

These were bicycles that had already been stolen and abandoned by unknown thieves, left behind in ditches and hedges. Askild was in the habit of letting the bikes lie there for at least a week before he took them home. For a couple of beers his neighbours and colleagues could buy a spare part, and for a bottle of aquavit they could get a whole bike. At the same time Askild supplied every member of his family with a bicycle. Knut had one too, but it was a stupid bike. The front wheel was crooked, and he didn't like the brown paint. Nor did he like the fact that the younger kids in the neighbourhood had got used to shouting after him every time he rode past.

'Hey, Knutie!' they would yell. 'Where did you steal that bike from?'

In situations like that Knut would instantly jump off his bike, roll up his sleeves, and shout, 'Who wants to touch the bell?' He was daring them, but the kids on the street would all shut up as they remembered the first time an insolent kid had gone over to ring Knut's bell.

'What's so dangerous about that?' he said, but no sooner had his finger touched the rusty bell than Knut punched him so hard in the stomach that he collapsed on the asphalt. Then the Norwegian jumped back on his bike and rode full speed right into the bunch of kids, who fled in panic – and all the while he was ringing that bell like a madman. It made a great sound, even though Knut had long wished for one of the proper chrome-plated horns that his classmates had.

When Askild wasn't home, Knut would sometimes go out to the shed and borrow one of the other bicycles. Then he would ride down to the harbour, which of course was no match for how he imagined the fabulous harbour in Bergen. Odense was, after all, just a sleepy harbour town. And there he would sit, staring lazily at the few ships that put in at the dock – most often to unload animal feed or to be treated for rust. The steady clients at that harbour in 1969 soon grew accustomed to the sight of the thirteen-year-old boy who, rain or shine, would squat a few metres away from the dock; he seemed introverted and a bit morose, but he also had a faintly dreamy expression on his face. Knut had always longed to be out in the world, but now he also started dreaming of getting away. Away from school, away from the annoying brats on the street, and away from his father, who was always after him and constantly praising his older brother. 'Niels Junior was also a real lout at one time,' Askild was fond of saying. 'But now he's come to his senses and started thinking about his future.'

After burning a whole box of pink letters, Niels Junior had recalled the old promise that he had made to himself about not ending up like his father. That very same day he took out his school books, and a few weeks later he announced at lunch that he wanted to go to business school. Now he was always in his room, bending over his books in the glow of the gooseneck lamp, and his yearning for the dream girl of the enchanted forest started to fade as credits and debits began taking hold. But whenever Askild mentioned Jug Ears' brilliant example to his younger son, Knut would always stubbornly dig in his heels. '*Him?*' Knut would say. 'He's so boring.'

After their move to Odense, Jug Ears mentally withdrew from the family, and it was now Knut who took up the battle and, unlike his brother, began talking back to Askild. Knut thought of his big brother as the type who always slipped away. If Askild was in that mood, Niels would disappear into his room and leave Knut standing in front of his father, paralysed by internal fury, incapable of moving or of ignoring his father, as Bjørk always told him to do. On the other hand, if he tried to enter his big brother's precious room, Niels would merely say: 'Get lost, I'm reading.'

Only rarely did his brother take him anywhere. Once Jug Ears took him to the bowling alley where he worked as a pin boy. For one whole evening Knut sat with a soda in his hand, watching as his brother set up the bowling pins with a look of concentration on his face. Another time Jug Ears took Knut along to spend his pay-cheque because whenever he got paid, he immediately spent all his money. That was because of the theft of his pot at the end of the rainbow.

'Lend me a tenner,' Askild used to say. 'Just until pay day.' By the time Askild finally did get paid, he would have forgotten all about the money he had borrowed, and he would accuse his son of being miserly. But if Jug Ears refused to lend him any money, Askild would go through his son's pockets and then take refuge behind his annoying motto: 'If I find any money lying around, it's mine.'

Oh yes, Knut could certainly understand why his big brother always went out and spent his money on pay day. He'd come home with bags filled with clothes, books, and records. And then he'd throw out his hands and, with a nonchalance that Knut had never been able to muster, he would say: 'I'm sorry, Pappa, but maybe I could tempt you with a little lint from my pockets?' What Knut didn't understand was why he was the one who always had to play with Anne Katrine.

'Play with your sister for a little while,' Askild would say. 'She needs to get out for a bit.'

In the past Knut and Anne Katrine had been as thick as thieves. They drove Bjørk crazy with all the pranks that Knut dreamt up. Eventually, when Knut became his sister's intellectual superior, they got tangled up in a web of reciprocal favours, secrets kept from their parents, and golden promises so amazing that they could make Anne Katrine drool with glee. Knut was always promising to take her with him on a ship when he became a sailor one day. He said he would show her jungles and tropical shores, and she would be allowed to sit all day in a deckchair, drinking sodas. In gratitude for these golden promises, she would clean up Knut's room and refrain from telling their parents about his latest pranks, sometimes even taking the blame for him without flinching. But lately all those promises had begun to backfire, and he no longer liked the fact that Anne Katrine was always running after him. She would be eighteen on her next birthday, and it was embarrassing to have that fat idiot following him. 'Get lost!' Knut had started yelling whenever she ran after him on the street. 'I don't want you to come with me!'

Chewing on her thumb and carrying an old rag doll, without giving a thought to straightening out her bowed legs, which were starting to wobble a bit under her weight of nearly 80 kilos, Anne Katrine would stop and stare at her little brother in disbelief. Each time he rejected her she was surprised all over again.

'You have to – Pappa says so!' she would protest, as if she were referring to some higher power that could not be refused.

But Knut would simply reply, 'I don't give a damn, you stupid tomato.' Then he would jump on his bike and leave Anne Katrine behind on the pavement with a wounded look on her face that made Knut clench his teeth – until the sight of a red brick house less than a kilometre away turned his thoughts to other things.

But he didn't see the girl who lived in that house anywhere. *If only I had a chrome-plated horn*, he thought, and continued on to the harbour to see if any new ships had arrived. As usual, it was not his own brown bike that he rode down to the harbour. He always took one of the others. Swiping one of the other bikes was a nerve-wracking experience, and one time Askild caught him at it. Knut knew that if his father had been sober, it was likely nothing would have happened, but Askild's breath stank from far away. He furiously demanded to know whether his son thought the shed was some sort of gift shop, all the while yanking at the little hairs behind Knut's ears. 'Why don't you just hit me?' Knut shouted right in his father's face. 'Why don't you just break my nose, for instance?'

Knut had never forgotten the incident with the forest fire which had ended with a broken nose. His father was quite simply the sort of man who would break his son's nose with a cane. He was also a liar. How many times had Askild promised that Knut could come with him to the shipyard when the newly built ships were about to be launched for the first time? And how many times had he cancelled at the very last minute by saying, 'Next time. I just don't feel like it today'. So my father is the type who doesn't feel like doing anything, Knut thought.

That's what crossed his mind that day when, at the age of thirteen, he stood in the bicycle shop on Skibhusvej, staring at the long row of shiny bike horns. The shop assistant had already asked him twice what he was looking for, and Knut had replied, 'Nothing'. The assistant was the teacher type – he could see that immediately. Nobody knows where Knut had got the habit of dividing people up into various types. *Teacher types poke their nose into everything,* he thought as he let one finger slide over the chrome-plated horns. And suddenly – he didn't really know how it happened – he grabbed a horn and dashed out of the shop with the assistant running after him. He ran as fast as he could, all the way to Fredens Church, where he crossed over to the footpaths and finally slipped through a hole in the hedge, which the assistant couldn't see. 'Doot-doot' was heard half an hour later when the horn gleamed like a beautiful jewel on his rusty handlebars. 'Doot-doot, doot-doot . . .' *Some day I'm going to steal a brand-new bike*, thought Knut as he rode around the neighbourhood of the red brick house until he caught sight of the girl down the street.

'When I'm old enough to decide for myself, I'm going to come for you,' Knut shouted, and the girl gave him a suspicious look and said, 'What makes you think that's what I want?'

'Just wait,' replied Knut. 'I'm sure you'll change your mind.'

The girl was two years younger than Knut, and he pictured himself sailing into some unknown harbour town as she stood on the dock, watching him with admiration. He also dreamt secret dreams about the tattooed dick that he would pull out when the girl came on board. So far he had measured it at 13 centimetres in full erection, using Askild's ruler, *but it'll happen some day*, he thought, *and now at least I've got a chrome-plated horn.* Those were the thoughts swirling through his mind when he got home and found two police officers and an agitated shop assistant talking to Askild in front of the shed. 'There he is!' cried the assistant, pointing.

Whereupon Knut turned his bike around and Askild shouted, 'Come here, you little thief! Come here right now!'

'You should talk!' yelled Knut as he zoomed away from the four men. 'Just take a look inside the shed!' But neither of the police officers thought it necessary to look in the shed. After all, it was only a matter of a bike horn, and everyone had seen the chrome-plated horn on the culprit's rusty bicycle. Knut headed for the harbour. On the way he saw the girl again, and he cried, 'One day I'll come for you. You can count on it!' She stuck out her pink tongue to show her contempt for anything he might have to say.

'And I'll kiss your tongue!' shouted Knut as he continued on towards the harbour, his feeling of desperation growing stronger and stronger as it began to rain. What was he going to say when he got home?

'Why the hell did I take that horn?' he cursed, seeking shelter from the rain under the eaves of a building. 'I can't ever have anything for myself.' It seemed to him that Askild had been spying on him all his life. His father poked his nose into everything, even barging into the room he shared with his sister without knocking. He rummaged through his son's things and threw open the door to the bathroom with no regard for anyone's private life or the fact that he might catch his son with his trousers down, in the process of measuring the length of his stiff dick with a ruler. 'Ha!' Askild had said.

I don't want to go back home, thought Knut. But later, when he gathered his courage and asked a skipper he happened to meet whether he could spend the night on his ship, the man peered at him with red eyes and exclaimed, 'Do you think I'm running some kind of hotel here, boy?' His clothes were soaked, his thoughts were whirling, and the chrome-plated horn was laughing in his face. It was very late by the time the drenched Knut finally crept into the house on Tunøvej.

* * *

'With a stupid grin on his mug,' cried Askild, who was in an unusually bad mood; he had been through an unpleasant experience that very same day. He had stopped in front of a little framing shop on the edge of town and fallen into a reverie as he looked in the display window. The shop was known for its traditional craftsmanship, and Askild was actually seized with a desire to have a couple of his paintings framed, until he noticed a man was standing on the other side of the window, staring at him. A moment later the door opened and the tall, lanky man, evidently the proprietor of the shop, came out on to the street. 'Have you ever been to Germany?' he asked.

And Askild, who didn't care to be reminded of anything relating to Germany, not even the happier times when he had enjoyed shore leave there between the wars, replied at once, 'No, by God, I haven't.'

'I see,' said the lanky shopkeeper, who seemed quite bewildered. His speech did not flow easily but came out as a halting stammer, as if he were rediscovering each word as he spoke. 'Then I must be mistaken.'

Is he someone from the camps? thought Askild on his way home. *What does he know about me?*

It's no understatement to say that the encounter with the lanky man had set his mind churning. On the way home, Askild took a detour to the Corner and downed six shots of aquavit in a row before he set off again, still with the feeling that something had started to unravel. And when he reached home and saw the two police officers standing in front of the shed, he was suddenly convinced that his past had caught up with him, and in an insane vision he pictured the next day's headlines: *War Criminal*

Exposed After Twenty-Five Years. Killed Friend With His Bare Hands.

What a relief when he realized that the whole thing was just about some stupid bicycle horn! Grandpa Askild felt like laughing right in the faces of those sombre men, but the next second Knut had come riding up on his bike. It was bad enough that he hadn't obeyed Askild, but then he also shouted something about the bicycles in the shed. What an embarrassing situation. What did his son think he was doing? And maybe it was just a matter of time before the police were once again standing at his door, but this time with more serious accusations – organized bicycle theft, for instance, or premeditated murder . . .

That's why Askild took a firm grip on the small hairs behind his son's ears when the drenched Knut turned up at home again. He tore off the boy's trousers and gave him a spanking on his bare behind. That was as far as he could go – it was the limit that had once been established in a secret agreement in Nordland over two cups of coffee. And while Knut fought a losing battle against a superior power, not to mention shame, Jug Ears disappeared into his room and put on an Elvis record. Anne Katrine tried to crawl under her bed but her body was so fat that she could only get halfway in. And Bjørk stood nervously in the doorway, wanting to ensure that her spouse wouldn't breach their secret agreement by resorting to a strap, for example, or by hitting the boy anywhere except on the rear end . . . But Knut wished he had been given a beating instead of being treated like a child. *When I'm grown up enough to decide for myself*, he thought later, *it's going to be his turn for a beating, by God.*

At the breakfast table the next day, no one in the family

dared make eye contact with the boy, who sat and stared at his plate while Askild launched into a lengthy sermon. Afterwards, instead of going to school, Knut swiped a bicycle and rode down to the harbour to have another talk with the skipper with the red eyes. This time Knut was a bit more determined. He refused to release his grip on the skipper's arm. He blocked the man's way and would no doubt have fallen to his knees if the red-eyed skipper hadn't taken pity on the boy and invited him into the galley for a cup of coffee.

'But I'm afraid I can't help you,' he said, throwing out his hands. 'I'm only going as far as Ålborg.'

Askild couldn't put the incident out of his mind, either. All day long he kept picturing the lanky man from the framing shop, and ghosts from his past, which he had tried to bury under twenty-five years of silence, began rising up from the depths. By late afternoon they started getting mixed up with the image of the insolent shop assistant who had shouted about Knut's poor upbringing. *Damn it all, it's my own business how I bring up my children*, thought Askild on his way home from the shipyard. And a little while later he marched into the bicycle shop on Skibhusvej, cast an arrogant glance at the shop assistant, and said, 'Spare me your petty concerns and get me a bicycle.' Askild had just been paid, and he spent the majority of his wages on the shop's most expensive bike. Knut was going to have a birthday soon, so why not give him what he had always dreamt of? Why not be generous for once? Askild took particular pleasure in seeing the asssistant's superior attitude transformed into a polite bow, and it was even more pleasurable to hear him speak of the previous day's horn-theft as a misunderstanding.

'Not even worth mentioning, Herr Eriksson. I'll throw in a splendid horn with your purchase, so let's just forget all about it.'

Half an hour later Askild was back home with the new bicycle. An oversized horn gleamed from the handlebars, and Grandpa was actually quite pleased with himself. If the past had decided to catch up with him, at least he would have performed one last good deed. He sat down in the living room, poured himself a beer, and began drumming his fingers on the table in anticipation. He sat there like that for a couple of hours, getting more and more impatient when his son failed to turn up, and at last he sent his older son out to look for his little brother Knut. It had been a long time since Jug Ears had been sent out on such a mission, but he instinctively headed for the harbour. There he started asking passers-by until a red-eyed skipper told him that the little brother in question might very well be the boy who at that very moment was sitting in the galley of his ship, refusing to leave. 'We sail in half an hour,' he told Niels, throwing out his hands. 'So you'd better do some fast talking.'

But Knut could not be budged. 'I don't care where this ship is headed,' he said when his big brother asked him what he planned to do in Ålborg. 'I don't give a shit,' he said, after hearing the story of the new bicycle that was waiting for him back home in the drive. 'I'm not coming home until I'm big enough to give him a kick in the ass. You can tell him that from me.'

Half an hour later, when the ship steamed out of the harbour, both brothers were still sitting in the galley. The skipper shook his head in resignation, and for one whole evening and half the night Jug Ears tried to talk some sense into his little brother. But then a strong wind came up and the ship began rolling ominously. For the rest of the night Knut had to empty his big brother's vomit out of a bucket, wipe his sweaty brow, and assure him that no one ever died from seasickness. Jug Ears was horribly sick, and the sight of his brother whimpering like a child soon removed any remaining doubts that Knut may have had. This was where he belonged. This was the moment he had been waiting for all his life. Whistling, Knut ran back and forth between the ship's head and his seasick brother, trying to calm him. He strongly advised against jumping overboard, which Jug Ears, in a moment of delirium, wanted to try. In the meantime, Knut also found time to serve coffee on the bridge and to repair a companionway step that had come loose. In other words, Knut managed to impress the red-eyed skipper so much that the next morning the man took the boy over to another ship that was significantly bigger to introduce him to the captain. It was a big day for Knut – yes, in fact it was his greatest day; but Jug Ears would always remember that morning in Ålborg harbour as a defeat because he hadn't succeeded in talking sense into his little brother.

'Tell Anne Katrine that I'll come and get her some day,' was the last thing Knut said before he went on board the new ship. But that was just something he said. He knew that he could never take Anne Katrine out on to the seas of the world. He also knew that he didn't want her along, and he cast one last glance at his big brother, who staggered out of the harbour area, found the nearest main road, and began waving his thumb at the passing cars.

On the way from Ålborg to Odense, in the company of

various truck drivers, two little words kept circling in Jug Ears' mind: *going downhill*. It was discouraging to acknowledge that his brother, nine years younger than himself, had moved away from home before he did; the last years of studying under the gooseneck lamp suddenly filled him with loathing. After all, he had once owned a pot of gold at the end of the rainbow, he had been promised a shower of gold and a brilliant future. Yet here he now sat, without even a krone in his pocket, as usual, because he had to spend all his damn wages before he went home to Pappa. When would it be his turn to leave?

As he got closer to Odense, the thought of telling his family the sad news took over, diverting the focus from himself. He knew that Bjørk would be sick with worry. He knew that his little sister would take it as a lifelong blow. And last but not least, he knew how Askild would react: obstinately, defiantly – with an ever-increasing habit of asking 'Knut who?' whenever the conversation turned to his runaway son. Because even though Askild came from a seafaring family, he did not at all care for the idea that his own son had followed the family tradition.

When Jug Ears came home without Knut, very few words were exchanged. The following day the bicycle was put in the shed. Bjørk was not allowed to touch it; the children were not allowed to touch it; and the grandchildren, who always cast yearning looks at the unused deluxe bike with three gears, were not, under any circumstances, allowed to touch it. 'Keep your hands off,' Askild would always growl in his laconic way whenever Stinna and I got too close to that monument to a divided family. For once Askild had shown some generosity – the boy had stolen a horn, shouted about the bicycles in the shed, and yet Grandpa had rewarded him by buying a new bike. In Askild's opinion, that was more than other fathers would have done in a similar situation. And what thanks did he get? His son ran away! A few weeks after Knut disappeared, Askild got so mad at his son that he took down *Bergen Is Burning* from its place of honour in the parlour – he had painted it after the incident with the forest fire and the flailing cane. Several days later Askild took out another painting: *The Doctor and the Scalpel*, that vile and highly flawed work that he had painted in an emotional state after hearing his daughter's diagnosis fifteen years earlier. It was now going to hang where *Bergen Is Burning* had once been.

'At least *she'll* never run away, damn it,' said Askild, and then he added with a gloomy look, 'But first it has to be framed.'

Jug Ears was the one who was sent over to the framing shop. Before he went, Askild spent half the day giving him instructions about the frame, but he also gave his son some other, highly confusing instructions. It almost seemed as if the frame was of secondary importance and that his father was sending him off with a hidden agenda.

So Niels Junior headed for town with *The Doctor and the Scalpel* under his arm. He suddenly felt as if he were walking into a void between 'before' and 'after' – a void that Knut had already traversed when he went on board the big ship. *But I haven't got that far yet*, Jug Ears thought. Susceptible to the phenomenon that we call 'fate', he threw open the door to the framing shop half an hour later and caught sight of a female figure at the far end of the room, standing with her back turned.

'May I speak to the proprietor?' he asked, and she turned around, pointing her finger at a spot between her breasts.

'She's right here.'

It's no understatement to say that Jug Ears was completely dumbfounded. Not at the sight of a female shop owner, even though Askild had said that a confused older man was in charge of the daily operations at the shop. ('Totally nuts,' Askild had said, 'he probably doesn't even know what the going rates are, so there's no need to handle the fool with kid gloves, my boy.') Nor was it because Jug Ears could hardly ask her about things that had happened twenty years ago ('Find out what he was doing during the war. Ask him – just casually, you know – whether he was ever in Germany; I don't want to do business with him if he took part in any shit.') And it wasn't because the young woman, who now stood less than 2 metres away, giving him an inquisitive look, seemed quite attractive. No, Jug Ears stood there gaping because she reminded him of something he couldn't quite remember, and yet, hadn't he seen her before? Wasn't there something very familiar about her? Hadn't he once lain with his head on her lap, and hadn't she gently stroked his hair?

Hell and damnation, he thought as a sudden memory of those early pubescent dream forests knocked his feet from under him. *Is it really her?*

Among Angels and Stepmothers
– My Mother's Family

'GOD CAME LAST NIGHT to get your kitties,' Hans Carlo Petersen, the former proprietor of the frame shop, once said to his six-year-old daughter Leila as he patted her head to comfort her – using exactly the same hand which, the night before, had tossed his daughter's seven kittens into a sack and drowned them in the creek behind the house. Leila, whose father had just given her a big ice-cream cone, noticed something bitter mixed in with the taste of the ice cream. Five years later her father came to get her from her aunt's house and drove her down to the forest lake where he bought her the biggest cone the ice-cream stand had to offer. Then he said, 'God came last night to get your mother,' thus imparting to his daughter not only a great sorrow but also an unremitting loathing for God and sweets.

Hans Carlo Petersen had met his deceased wife at a family gathering. She was a distant relative, and he was instantly struck by her delicate beauty as she sat there in the midst of the guests, allowing kind uncles and jealous aunts to wait on her. After dinner he invited her out to the garden, where he asked her to marry him. At the time he was twenty-three years old. Elisabeth was nineteen, and when she heard his proposal, she burst out laughing, causing my young maternal grandfather to turn pale. Before the evening was over, everyone knew that Hans Carlo was in a courting mood, and jealous uncles and kind aunts gave him the nicknames Courting King and Herr Sneak Thief. Blushing with shame, he decided to risk everything to win her. Two days later he had a messenger deliver a bouquet of white lilies to the delicate Elisabeth, who had taken to her bed after the exertions of the weekend. But when a single bouquet had no effect, he kept on sending flowers in such quantities that it undermined his finances and filled the home of his future parents-in-law with perfume. That's how the image of my other grandmother, Elisabeth, whom I never met, was passed down to me: lying in her sickroom, pale as an angel, and surrounded by a forest of flowers, which my maternal grandfather had carefully selected as appropriate for his future wife's temperament. This meant no roses or sunflowers, but rather lilies, pale tulips, and white Solomon's seal, which had such a sweet fragrance that they made her gasp for breath during her migraine attacks.

A whole year passed before he was allowed to accompany her on a walk around the nearby forest lake, and another year before he was permitted to take her hand in his. But one spring day, walking hand in hand at the forest lake, Elisabeth suddenly stopped and said, 'So, Hans Carlo, now you may ask me again.' Hans Carlo was so happy that he forgot all about asking his question, but the wedding was held all the same. When it was time for the wedding night, she lay pale as death in the bridal bed, gasping from a migraine, unable to give her husband so much as a single little kiss.

Hans Carlo turned off the light, disappointed, and lay down to sleep, but early the next morning he couldn't hold back any longer. Cautiously he let his hands caress her pale body, whispering loving words in the morning light and showering her with all the affection and passion that had accumulated in his body after three long years of courtship.

And Elisabeth actually livened up; colour appeared in her face and she showed a certain taste for the joys of a sexual life and an awkward devil-may-care attitude which no one in her family had known that she possessed. A mere two weeks after the wedding, she asked for a ride on her husband's motorcycle, which up until then had been banned from her parents' drive because the sound of engine noise through the windows could keep her in bed for days.

'Good Lord, it's fast!' she shouted excitedly from the sidecar, and before three months had passed, she was just as often the one driving, while Hans Carlo rode in the sidecar as they roared all over the countryside on weekends and holidays. And so two brief but colourful years passed in the lives of my maternal grandparents. The high point was a motorcycle trip to Berlin between the wars. There they were accosted by a drunken Norwegian who was rash enough to be wandering around Potsdamer Platz with a Nazi flag covered with insults and obscene drawings. Only the quick action of Hans Carlo saved the Norwegian from serious trouble when some Hitler Youths turned up. My grandfather tore the flag right off its stick and stuffed it in his pocket. When they later sat in a smoky pub with the infamous Norwegian, who was telling pirate stories to his pork-faced German drinking companion, Elisabeth leant back, bit Hans Carlo on the ear, and whispered, 'Life is beautiful.' Later that evening the Norwegian and his companion disappeared into the city. The young couple went back to their rented room, where they undressed each other and surrendered to wild and ardent love-making, stopping only when the first rays of sunlight seeped through the curtains and they had convinced each other that life truly was beautiful.

But then the sudden blossoming came to an end. Shortly after, it was clear to everyone that Elisabeth was pregnant, and she, who had been sickly most of her life, began once again to suffer from migraines. Periods of sleeplessness made her totter around the house, pale as death; a low blood count caused her to feel dizzy, and a racking cough started to reverberate in her delicate chest. At first everyone hoped that her health would improve after the birth, but instead, after giving birth to little Harry by Caesarean section, she got worse. The motorcycle was put out in the back behind the shed, and Hans Carlo started bicycling to work so as not to disturb his wife with engine noise. The defaced Nazi flag that he had brought home as a souvenir from their Berlin trip was put away in a cupboard in the basement. And malicious gossip within the family began to undermine his reputation, claiming that Hans Carlo, with his reckless ways, had almost been the death of his delicate wife. Family members began invading their home, ordering the windows closed and the curtains drawn – and above all: silence.

Before long the house was filled with mute old ladies

cooking food and whispering aunts who frightened little Harry out of his wits with their sinister stories about river spirits in the creek and black pits in the basement – yes, they even whispered about two-headed dragons that would come out of the walls and cut off his little dick if he didn't behave properly and stop bothering his mother. A reek of illness, a stench of putrid water in flower vases hovered over the house, and at the same time the income from Hans Carlo's framing shop began to decline. It was wartime – who cared about buying frames for paintings when the Germans had occupied the country?

But after a few years had passed, Hans Carlo decided to oust the horrible old ladies and the whispering aunts from his home. He took over his son's upbringing himself, and for a while things went quite well. One evening in the spring, shortly before the war was over, Elisabeth suddenly got out of bed and surprised Hans Carlo, who was sitting in the living room with his newspaper.

'Damn it all,' she cried. 'I've been lying in that bed for six years now.' And she asked him to open the windows and get out the photo albums from their motorcycle trip, which my maternal grandfather did, as happy as a little boy on his birthday. 'I wonder what he's doing today?' said Elisabeth when her glance fell on the picture of the Norwegian, arm in arm with the pork-faced German in a smoky pub in Berlin. Hans Carlo replied that he was probably not walking around Potsdamer Platz with a defaced Nazi flag. After lingering over their memories, my grandfather went out to the privy to take a piss before bedtime. He thought about a leak in the roof that he hadn't had time to repair.

'Life is beautiful!' he exclaimed, apropos of nothing,

and went back to the house, where he undressed his wife with gentle hands before they abandoned themselves to fierce love-making that was almost as overwhelming as back in those happy days in Berlin.

But before long more malicious gossip began to undermine Hans Carlo's reputation. 'Pregnant again! What is he thinking of, that scoundrel! Is he trying to kill his poor wife?' That was what was heard at family gatherings, and mute old ladies and whispering aunts started invading the house once more. They crept in through the windows when Hans Carlo was at work, they coaxed open the locks, frightened little Harry with their litanies, and in the end they again took over the house. The fact that Elisabeth was having a difficult pregnancy did nothing to reduce the number of family members in the house. After giving birth to little Leila by Caesarean section, Elisabeth was so exhausted that the mute old ladies and whispering aunts immediately installed the newborn infant in a remote attic room – the same one to which Harry had been confined in his day. But while little Harry had lain there quietly, little Leila screamed like a stuck pig, stopping only a few times a day when she was allowed to rest at the breast of the pale angel.

'The child is possessed,' whispered the maternal aunts, exchanging ideas with the silent paternal aunts who saw to it that the little girl got her share of the family's mythological inheritance: river spirits, black pits, everything necessary to break the spirit of an ill-mannered child. And they sang scary lullabies and recited weird rhymes. 'If you scream, your tongue will shrivel up. If you protest, you'll never be a sweet little girl that Mamma Elisabeth will love. If you don't stop hissing at your aunts, you'll be unlucky in love. And if you lie, your stomach will turn black inside.' Yes, they had even heard of cases in which a person's teeth fell out and boils appeared all over her body. When Leila, at the age of three, asked why her mother was always lying in bed downstairs behind closed blinds, she was told that it wasn't proper for a little girl to ask too many questions. But there was always a question mark hanging over the house, which was enough to make any little girl wonder.

Hans Carlo didn't get involved much in the lives of his children, and a couple more years would pass before he succeeded, using harsh methods, in ridding his home of the burdensome family members. Then the windows were opened again; but unfortunately, by then it was too late. One spring night a short time later, a little cluster of red flowers erupted on Elisabeth's pillowcase. At first she hid it away at the bottom of the dirty laundry basket, but before long it was obvious to everyone that this was not merely a springtime cold rattling in her chest. No, death had clearly taken up residence in the angel's lungs. No matter how many windows were opened, the smell of putrid water in the vases could not be exorcized, and red flowers could not be stopped from spreading across the pillowcase each night.

'Damn it all!' whispered the delicate Elisabeth when she heard the doctor pronounce her death sentence. 'I've been lying in this bed all my life!' After that she asked Hans Carlo to bring the photo albums up from the basement for the last time, and for one long evening and half the night they leafed through their memories together. But when the last photo album was closed, she seemed to have lost her courage. The next day the windows were shut, too, and they remained like that for the next five years.

Even though all the family members were now gone, their spirits still seemed to linger over the house. Hans Carlo found himself making use of the mythological creatures whenever he attempted to reprimand his children. He talked about the river spirits in the creek, about the Lord God who came to get Leila's little kittens in the gloom of night. Three years later, when the family doctor said, 'It won't be more than a month now,' his words came almost as a relief, and nine-year-old Leila was sent on holiday to stay with her mother's sister, without knowing that she would end up living with that aunt for two long years. That was how long Elisabeth's battle with death would last. During this period Leila visited her mother only on Sundays and in the same surroundings where she had always seen her: an angel in her sickroom, a mother with one foot in heaven and the other on earth. Elisabeth would pat her daughter's cheek. Later, when she was in the hospital, she would merely pat the girl's hand, and usually she didn't manage to say much before a violent coughing fit would wrack her body. Then worried-looking nurses would take little Leila out to the hallway so she wouldn't see her mother coughing red flowers, and so that the sight of red flower-water bubbling out of her mouth and running down her chin wouldn't frighten the poor child.

'The Lord God always calls the best ones home,' her aunt would say when Leila came back from her Sunday visits. Leila would reply, 'God is an idiot,' and then run up to the guest room with the whispering aunt on her heels.

'That's no way to talk! Are you out of your mind,

315

child! Your tongue is going to shrivel up and fall out!'

Leila would slam the door in her aunt's face and shout, 'You stupid cow!' She kept on like that, giving her aunt so many grey hairs that the woman felt a certain relief when the eleven-year-old girl's father came to collect her on that sad summer day in 1957. Elisabeth had died that morning, but her long illness, the atmosphere in the house, everything that had turned Leila's big brother Harry into a nervous young man, had made the girl as spiteful as could be. After eating the most nauseating ice-cream cone of her life at the forest lake where, twenty years earlier, the young Elisabeth had given Hans Carlo permission to propose, Leila defiantly refused to shed a single tear in front of her family.

Instead, she said, 'That woman,' referring to her father's newly hired housekeeper, 'she's not to touch Mamma's dresses and she can keep her hands off my things!'

The housekeeper was named Lillian. She was twenty years younger than Hans Carlo, and she had been hired immediately after Elisabeth's death. The framing shop, contrary to all expectations, had become a respectable business during the mid-1950s and Harry had just been called up for military service. Lillian stared with horror at her new employer's ill-mannered daughter, at first offended that the apathetic father failed to reprimand Leila. But then she decided to use cunning to win the little girl's heart. 'You are such a sweet little girl,' she whispered ingratiatingly.

Leila replied, 'I'm not sweet at all, and you'd better not think that you can bag my father!'

This last remark made Hans Carlo sit up, maybe because it held a grain of truth, and he responded by giving Leila a stinging slap, causing her to utter a tiny, wordless cry. Then she turned on her heel and ran down to the basement. Shortly after Elisabeth's death, flood waters had transformed the lowest level of the house into a submerged cave where frogs, toads, and tiny water spiders sloshed around among the photo albums and other relics from the past. Now this water had receded, and Leila, who had heard about the flooding from her aunt, went around looking for the pit that her aunts had whispered about in her early childhood and from which she imagined the water had risen. But she found only a muddy drain cover, so instead she decided to inspect the flood damage, which had left everything in a terrible mess. That same evening she asked her father if she could clean up the basement, and Hans Carlo gave his permission, relieved that he wouldn't have to do the cleaning himself and face those painful memories.

And so the eleven-year-old Leila began shovelling out buckets of mud from the basement. She found photographs from which the water had almost entirely erased the images, turning them into unrecognizable caricatures. She found letters whose perfectly formed script had been washed into mysterious hieroglyphics. And she found a number of other things, including a defaced Nazi flag that was so spotted with mould that for a moment she considered throwing it out. But convinced that every piece of wreckage contained a piece of her mother's soul, Leila washed off all the photographs, pressing them flat with an iron and putting them into photo albums, which the housekeeper, in an attempt to ingratiate herself with the daughter of the house, had bought using her housekeeping money, without Hans Carlo's knowledge.

Before long, Leila's efforts bore fruit. She began imagining that the water-damaged photographs revealed scenes from her mother's new, heavenly life on the other side of death. At first she was astonished by the merriment that seemed to characterize this angelic existence. She saw her mother drinking with pork-faced angels; she saw her roaring past on a motorcycle, straight through the Garden of Eden with her blond hair flying in all directions; and a little later she also saw her in more or less obscene situations in which Elisabeth surrendered to angels with rosebud lips and let hairy satyrs kiss her white neck and squeeze her thighs while she carefully enunciated remarks such as: *Life is beautiful* and *How lovely heaven is*.

Convinced that her mother was living the sweet life up above, Leila continued to clean the basement, though she gradually noticed certain depressing changes. The tableaux in the photos altered, becoming frozen and despondent. Facial expressions became distorted, and she kept thinking she saw Elisabeth in the company of weeping angels.

Not for a moment did Leila doubt where this misery was coming from. Her mother was suffering in heaven because a certain housekeeper had invaded their home. Recently Leila had noticed a creaking in the house late at night, and she resolved to be her mother's deputy here on earth. She started sneaking out of bed as soon as the lights were out. At first she didn't observe anything abnormal, but then one night she suddenly heard a creak coming from the housekeeper's door. She huddled under some furniture and there, coming down the stairs and wearing a see-through nightgown that shimmered in the moonlight, was Lillian, dancing in her bare feet like some sort of elf girl. That terrible sight – the utter transformation that the otherwise ordinary housekeeper had undergone – stripped Leila of all courage. Instead of blocking Lillian's way, she simply crept further under the furniture and watched with a trembling heart how the bewitched housekeeper smiled at herself in the mirror before tiptoeing into Hans Carlo's bedroom to take the place where Elisabeth had once slept.

From that moment on the housekeeper was not just an annoying element in Leila's daily life – she was also a mortal enemy. And Leila did her utmost to discredit Lillian in her father's eyes. She turned up the gas on the stove to burn the food. She sprinkled dye in the laundry basins when Lillian wasn't looking. She put thumbtacks in Lillian's shoes, and once, when her father had decided to take the much-maligned housekeeper to the movies, she took a bottle of laxative tablets out of the medicine cabinet, crushed up seven of them, and put them in Lillian's coffee. The result was predictable. The couple came home in the middle of the film. Hans Carlo seemed a bit bewildered, while Lillian, bright red in the face, rushed for the bathroom where she tore off her dress, shouting, 'I'll die of shame!'

That evening Leila went down to the basement to study the water-damaged photos, and noticed encouraging changes in her mother's heavenly life: a certain merriment, a heavenly glee among the angels. And in this way Leila used the photo albums as a release for her own feelings. But as happened every time she played a prank, the merriment didn't last long. The expressions in the photos soon became despondent again, and the weeping angels returned.

In the long run, neither thumbtacks, laxative tablets, nor secret curses could ward off catastrophe. Two years after Elisabeth's death, Hans Carlo told Leila that she was going to have a new mother. 'I know it will be difficult,' he said sympathetically, adding with some firmness: 'But you'll have to get used to calling her Mother.'

'Never!' screamed Leila.

In the weeks before the wedding, Leila was witness to harrowing scenes whenever she examined her mother's life among the weeping angels. In the photos there was great despair, sorrow, and teeth-gnashing. And by the time the wedding day finally arrived, Leila had been so affected by this heavenly unhappiness that it weakened her resistance. After several hours of fierce coaxing, she finally addressed the housekeeper in the manner that was expected of her. But no one could get her to omit one little word which she, in protest, inserted in front of the forced declaration of love. 'Say it,' the guests kept urging.

And Leila would clench her teeth and whisper, 'Congratulations – Madam Mother.'

That's how the title 'Madam Mother' came about, and later Stinna and I changed it to 'Madam Grandmother' to address that silent, slightly melancholy figure who always showed up at family dinners but otherwise never made much of a fuss. Childless, shrivelled up from adversity, she usually went home early to dream of a time when everything was different and she had danced through my maternal grandfather's house like a bewitched elf girl in the moonlight.

Just as certain stories tend to cling to certain people, the story about Madam Mother shitting her pants at the movies clung to Lillian all her life, making her an object of ridicule in the family. 'Well,' Grandpa Askild used to say after we had made the usual Sunday rounds, 'I guess she didn't shit her pants at the coffee table this time' – to Stinna's and my great amusement. Even Grandma Bjørk, who was always correcting Askild's language, couldn't help giggling a little at the comic figure, whom Mum rudely continued to call Madam Mother all her life.

On the night after the wedding reception, Leila dreamt that the winds of change blew through the heavenly world and altered her mother's life among the angels. Now Elisabeth was once again roaring around on a motorcycle, straight through the Garden of Eden; now she again surrendered to the angels with rosebud lips and to the hairy satyrs. When Leila awoke in the morning, she noticed an unfamiliar pain in her abdomen and caught sight of a red spot on the sheet and a slightly bigger spot on her knickers. In other words, she had got her first menstrual period. But without giving it much thought, she put on her bathrobe and ran down to the basement to see whether her dreams in the night had been true.

Leila leafed through the neatly arranged photo albums with growing bewilderment and surprise. She found nothing but water-damaged pictures, their images ruined beyond recognition, along with letters that she couldn't read, and a sorry-looking Nazi flag covered with childish drawings. Her magical world was gone. After leafing through the albums several times, she was left with only two photos that were not completely damaged; they showed utterly ordinary drinking scenes. Leila realized that her mother must have moved to more distant parts of the heavenly realm of the dead, and that, from now on, she would no longer be able to use the photos to get a sense of her mother's life in the hereafter. She stuck the two photos in her pocket, locked the rest of the things in a cupboard, threw the key down the drain that she had once thought was a bottomless pit, and went up to ask Madam Mother for a sanitary towel.

Lillian smiled with delight and showered her step-daughter with good advice. At the dinner table there were suddenly two women who had a secret they weren't going to share with Hans Carlo. They kept giving each other sly winks. Happily surprised at the sudden camaraderie between the two women, Hans Carlo realized that a new era had begun in his life – over were all the years of illness and family invasions, over were the last few years of tension in the house. Now, at the age of forty-eight, he was beginning his second youth. *Life is beautiful*, he thought. *I'm going to go out and find that motorcycle* . . .

But of course his daughter's first period and her startling loss of the magical universe in the basement photos didn't prevent the two women from endlessly fighting for Hans Carlo's attention. 'Your Madam Grandmother,' Mum liked to say to Stinna and me, 'has always thought she could just come here and ruin everything.'

As time passed, it became clear to everyone that the former housekeeper had drawn the longest straw. She had succeeded in gaining entrance to my grandfather's bed-room. The taciturn widower's gentle, craftsman hands had received her young body, just as she had dreamt they would ever since the first time she sat in the kitchen with him. *But I won't settle for being his lover; I don't want to be a housekeeper all my life*, thought Lillian, and she was not the only one to regard the narrow gold band on the ring finger of her left hand as a victory trophy.

Leila often cast disapproving looks at that ring, but as the next battle approached, it suddenly occurred to Leila that Madam Mother was an unusually beautiful woman. That was simply something she had never noticed before. The realization came as a shock. It shattered Leila's confidence, inducing a state of resignation not helped by the striking contrast with her own development as a woman. Pimples appeared, her skin became rough and oily, her breasts ached, and in the mirror in her room she often saw an awkward teenage girl who reminded her unpleasantly of a fat pig. Unlike Marianne Qvist, Leila started avoiding mirrors. She didn't practise pouting her lips, and she never thought, *Here I come!* Instead, she sullenly locked herself in her room.

After winning her first victory, Lillian quickly managed to take over the house. At the same time it dawned on my grandfather Hans Carlo that his young wife was a bit moody. She didn't always wake him in the morning to serve him coffee in bed, and when he came home from work, he would often find her lounging on the sofa with a book.

'Cook your own dinner, Sweetie-pie,' she said when Grandfather asked her why she hadn't made dinner. 'Or get your daughter to do it. I'm not your kitchen maid any more.'

Hans Carlo went out to the kitchen with a foolish grin on his face, and in a matter of minutes he had managed to get so muddled that he finally had to ask his daughter for help. 'But she was the housekeeper,' complained Leila to her girlfriends, 'and now she acts as if she's the Queen of Sheba!'

And so Leila quickly assumed a number of new duties: cooking and cleaning. The elf girl had defeated the pig, even though inexplicable bouts of diarrhoea occasionally forced Lillian to spend whole evenings on the toilet. On those evenings, Leila would have her father Hans Carlo to herself, but no sooner had the last drop of excrement poured out of Madam Mother's intestines than she was back, ready to draw her husband to her with a beauty that made Leila blanch and Hans Carlo melt.

'You're the most beautiful Madam Mother in the whole kingdom!' he would exclaim.

One day Madam Mother opened the medicine cabinet and worked out that the mysterious malady which had plagued her intestines might have a simple explanation. She threw out the laxative tablets, and Leila lost her last weapon in the bitter battle. Then one day Madam Mother announced that she wanted to have children of her own. That was a disappointment to Hans Carlo, who had no intention of throwing himself into the exhausting job of being a father again. He had turned fifty that summer, and he said 'no' three times while pounding the table and giving his wife his familiar foolish grin, which meant that he couldn't be taken seriously.

'Come on, Sweetie-pie,' Lillian replied, pinching his nose. 'When the most beautiful Madam Mother in the realm is on heat all the roosters have to do is crow.'

And so Hans Carlo started to crow, and it didn't take long before Madam Mother was pregnant and began to use a more diplomatic tone with her stepdaughter. Again she tried to win the girl's trust, this time by referring to the new little sister or brother, but Leila refused to be infected with Lillian's enthusiasm.

'Just because she's going to have a stupid kid she thinks she'll be able to get me to baby-sit for nothing,' Leila told her girlfriends. And that's how a couple of months passed, with quarrelling in every corner, until Hans Carlo was awakened early one morning by heart-rending sobs, which also woke Leila in her attic room. Madam Mother had lost her baby . . . And no, it was *not* poisoning from laxative tablets that caused the miscarriage. But that didn't make much difference, because in Madam Mother's subconscious, a terrible suspicion was born. The atmosphere in the house became so strained that Hans Carlo stopped walking around with a foolish grin on his face. He asked his wife and daughter to show a little courtesy, but it did no good, and before long Hans Carlo began to suffer from migraines.

'Shut up, both of you!' he would shout and retreat behind his newspaper, which is what he had done in the past during the invasion of the whispering aunts.

After a couple of years of trying, when Madam Mother had failed to get pregnant a second time, Hans Carlo announced one day that he felt too old to bring more children into the world. This time it didn't help when Lillian called him 'Sweetie-pie'. My grandfather no longer had a foolish grin on his face; he simply let the bomb fall and then ensconced himself behind his newspaper. In other words, the long battle had created two losers and no winners, and Leila soon thought she could detect a lurking malice in her stepmother's eyes – as if it was Leila's fault that Madam Mother had miscarried and couldn't get pregnant again. Leila was showered with hostile looks, and she started to fear the worst: assassination, conspiracy . . .

A few weeks before Leila had finished school, Madam Mother called her into the living room and banished her from her childhood home.

That was how it felt to Leila, at any rate. 'I'm positive it was her idea that I should be a maid,' she told her girl-friends. 'She has always wanted to have my father all to herself.'

Before long Hans Carlo had found a suitable family, and in 1963 Leila was sent away from home. Now she was supposed to live in the house of strangers, cooking, cleaning, and taking care of the strangers' screaming brats all day long. Leila often imagined that she was a princess who had fallen into disfavour because her evil stepmother had cast a spell over her father. Only on her days off did she visit her former childhood home, and not even then could she have her father to herself. Madam Mother seemed to fill the whole house, and she was also constantly correcting Hans Carlo.

'Your memory isn't what it used to be,' she would say, giving him an annoyed look.

'Yes, your muddled father forgot our wedding anniversary,' she would announce, turning to Leila.

Hans Carlo would throw out his hands apologetically, and their constant bickering would continue, poisoning the atmosphere. But aside from Lillian's bitterness, there was a grain of truth in her complaints. Hans Carlo *was* starting to be forgetful. He would often sit and stare into space absentmindedly, as if a switch inside his head had been turned off. 'Hans Carlo,' Madam Mother would cry, 'pull yourself together, for God's sake!'

* * *

One day in 1966 Leila's big brother Harry came home and announced that he didn't want to take over the framing shop, which was what Hans Carlo had always intended. For many years Harry had worked in a grocery store on the island of Sjælland even though at regular intervals he would tell the family that he was learning the framing trade in a carpenter's workshop. When Hans Carlo realized that Harry had been lying, a dark expression slid across his face. The next day he didn't ride his bike straight to the shop. No, to Madam Mother's deep regret, Hans Carlo headed in the opposite direction – out to a stranger's house, where he knocked on the door and apologized to the harried father of the family but, unfortunately, he would have to take their young maid home at once.

Then he took Leila along to the framing shop and said, 'Take it if you want. It's yours.'

That same day Leila moved back home. Hans Carlo furnished a little apartment for her on the second floor. She was twenty years old at the time. Even though Hans Carlo made a great effort to teach his daughter the craft of his profession, it soon became clear to him that she had very little talent for it. 'I just don't understand,' Leila would often complain, not knowing that in reality her lack of talent could be blamed on her incoherent teacher, because Hans Carlo had begun to talk gibberish. Sometimes he had to search hard for the words, or he would switch them around so that 'wood glue' became 'glue wood'. Fortunately, many years ago Hans Carlo had hired a carpenter by the name of Ib, who was familiar with all the routines of the shop.

'Ib will take care of all the practical matters,' said Hans

Carlo reassuringly. 'So let's forget about the craftsmanship and concentrate on the accounts and ledgers.'

Then he started instructing his daughter in the art of setting up an account, but he soon discovered that she also lacked all talent for bookkeeping. 'I still don't understand,' Leila would moan whenever Hans Carlo began confusing credit and debit, babbling so much that it gave him grey hairs.

'When I die,' he then replied, sounding suddenly quite lucid, 'you need to find someone who can take care of the accounts for you. All you need to do is be the boss and make sure everything runs smoothly. Forget all about the damn books!'

So Leila set out to learn how to be the boss. It was easy enough, because she didn't have to lift a finger – and if she needed help, she could always ask Ib. And Ib was remarkably helpful, because even though Leila still saw a fat pig every time she looked in the mirror, Ib saw something quite different when he looked at the boss's daughter. It didn't take long before they made love on the workbench in the back room, in a blizzard of sawdust. Afterwards, Leila, who had always been plagued by speculations about what it would be like the first time, couldn't believe how easy it had been. Whistling, she walked home through the streets of the city, and when she awoke the next morning, she cast a cautious look in the mirror and saw, to her great astonishment, a real woman. The curse had been broken. The evil stepmother who had once changed Hans Carlo's daughter into a fat pig had lost her magic powers. And from that day on Leila regularly made love with Ib in the workshop whenever Hans Carlo, as his headaches grew worse, decided to go home early.

* * *

The first time it occurred to Leila that there was something very wrong with her father was when he came into the framing shop and said, 'Harry is at camp school. We need to get him back home before the angels arrive.'

Leila knew that Harry's decision to enter the grocery trade was still upsetting her father, but why did he say 'camp school'? And why was he talking about angels?

'What angels?' said Hans Carlo later on. 'I never said anything about angels.'

But my maternal grandfather really had begun to babble about angels. In strange visions, he saw them coming nearer: angels with rosebud lips, hairy satyrs, and of course the archangel of them all: the delicate Elisabeth, who carefully enunciated remarks like *Life is beautiful*, and who often roared off on a motorcycle, straight through the Garden of Eden, with her blond hair flying in all directions.

'Your father is an old fool,' Madam Mother complained to Leila. 'Pretty soon he'll even start believing in elves.'

The situation did not improve when Hans Carlo one day caught sight of a heavyset man with a cane standing outside the shop's display window. 'The Norwegian has arrived,' he announced that evening at the dinner table. 'Now Elisabeth and I will be going to Berlin.'

That last remark was the straw that broke the camel's back for Madam Mother. She immediately ordered Hans Carlo to see a doctor, and a few days later it was determined that his worsening headaches, his stammering speech, and his strange visions about angels and mysterious Norwegians were not due to incipient insanity or senility but to a tumour in his cerebellum the size of a tangerine. Surgery was not an option. 'It simply can't be done,' Leila heard the doctor say over and over. And while it had taken Elisabeth many years to die because she clung to life, it took Hans Carlo no more than three weeks. By the time he heard the death sentence, he had already peered into the hereafter, and it wasn't long before his body succumbed to the pressure of the tumour on his central nervous system and became afflicted by spastic paralysis. During this time – as he lay in a hospital bed with tubes going in and out of his body – unexpected transformations occurred in the tissues of Hans Carlo's brain, and he suddenly refused to accept any visits from Madam Mother.

'I don't want to see her,' he told his daughter. And when Madam Mother came to the hospital all the same, bringing him flowers, he merely said, 'Who are you? You're not Elisabeth!'

In the advanced stages of his illness, Hans Carlo didn't realize that a blow delivered from a deathbed could cause wounds that would never heal. Deathly pale and mortally wounded, Madam Mother retreated to her chair in the hospital corridor while *the man who never gave me any children, though I loved him unconditionally,* rapidly wasted away.

It was little consolation to Leila that a few weeks before his death Hans Carlo had suddenly shown the true nature of his feelings for Lillian and herself. To her great surprise, Leila began to feel sympathy for the silent Madam Mother who sat in the hospital corridor day and night, banished by her husband from his deathbed and with tears streaming down her face until, a few days before Hans Carlo died, she simply dried up. If was as if during those days

330

Madam Mother's psyche underwent a transformation that was just as radical as the transformation in the tissues of Hans Carlo's brain. The moody, domineering, and unruly sides of her personality withered away. In other words, Leila was about to win a victory she had never thought possible. *But that's not how it was supposed to happen*, she thought. There was also something unnerving about Hans Carlo's stammering talk about a mysterious Norwegian with a defaced Nazi flag who had been present on one of the happiest days of his life. 'What Norwegian?' Leila asked. 'What's his name?' But Hans Carlo couldn't remember since it was more than thirty years ago that he and Elisabeth had sat in a smoky pub in Berlin with the Norwegian and his pork-faced German friend.

In the last stage of his illness, my maternal grandfather roamed even further back in time, as he started babbling about river spirits in the creek. And the last words to cross his lips were random phrases from sinister lullabies that seemed frightening to both Harry and Leila. 'If you scream, your tongue will shrivel up; and if you lie, your stomach will turn black inside.' Only when Madam Mother occasionally appeared in the doorway would he raise his voice. 'Get out of here!' he would scream, tearing at his hair as if he had seen something completely unbearable.

The worse Hans Carlo behaved towards Madam Mother, the greater Leila's feeling of solidarity with her stepmother became. This feeling was not diminished by Hans Carlo's constant babbling about Elisabeth, who was now sitting on her motorcycle outside the window, ready to transport him across the river of death. The fact that an old and familiar angel was about to steal her father away from her dislodged all of Leila's childhood images. It was suddenly clear to her that throughout her entire childhood she had lost a considerable portion of Hans Carlo's attention to Elisabeth the angel. Because what sort of father had Hans Carlo actually been? A distracted father, burdened by concerns for his sick wife; a father whose eyes were closed in sorrow. If Leila had not been standing in the shadow of an angel her whole life, would she have fought so fiercely against Madam Mother?

In other words, as she was about to be orphaned, Leila was tormented by the idea that she had always been an orphan. With whom had she actually shared her greatest confidences? *It was none other than Madam Mother*, she thought uneasily, noticing that her legs were buckling beneath her. Who had initiated her into the mysterious world of women? Who had given her well-meaning advice about hygiene and birth control? And who, from the very first glance, had called her a sweet little girl? That was, after all, more than her real mother had ever done; that was greater intimacy than even Hans Carlo had shown. In short, it was the closest Leila had ever come to having a real parent: a Madam Mother! Damn it, how that stung! By God, it made her run back and forth in bewilderment between Hans Carlo in his hospital room and Madam Mother sitting in the corridor, while it dawned on Leila that Elisabeth was nothing more than a void that she had filled with angels and songs of paradise. *Poor Madam Mother*, she thought, casting nervous glances at the dried-up Lillian, who never had any children of her own.

On the night after the funeral Leila heard the mono-tonous sound of Madam Mother restlessly pacing back and forth downstairs. 'I've forgotten my helmet,' was the last thing Hans Carlo had said. That was three days before he died, and the phrase kept whirling through Leila's mind because it seemed absurd that anything as prosaic as a motorcycle helmet should play a major role when he was about to go out riding with an angel. Even so, Hans Carlo had constantly babbled about his forgotten helmet. Wouldn't Elisabeth take him along without a helmet? Angels and satyrs, kings and princesses . . . *What the hell is that about?* she thought. And while Madam Mother was roaming restlessly around the living room downstairs, Leila decided once and for all to exorcize any mythological creatures. It was not God who had taken her mother home on that sad summer day twelve years ago. It was not God who had once taken her kittens. And it was *not* an angel on a motorcycle who had transported Hans Carlo across the river of death and on to the kingdom of angels. *Hocus pocus*, chanted my mother Leila. *There are no supernatural beings; there is nothing mysterious between heaven and earth . . .*

Or to put it another way: if she were going to get anything out of life, it was simply a matter of getting started and putting all the debris from a shipwrecked childhood behind her. And as the first rays of sunlight seeped through Leila's window, an unexpected and highly liberating thought occurred to her: *Fuck everything*, she thought, *now I can do whatever I like!* After she took a bath she realized to her great surprise that she was in an exceedingly inappropriate good mood. Madam Mother scowled at her, giving her reproachful looks. Good Lord, the newly orphaned Leila was standing out there in the kitchen, on the day after her father's funeral, *whistling*!

After eating a breakfast that consisted of four eggs, six pieces of toast, and a large serving of oatmeal, Leila went off to the framing shop with the clear intention of finishing with Ib. It was true that he had broken her stepmother's curse and stopped her from feeling that she was a clumsy pig; on the other hand he had also kept her confined in the princess role that she had once eagerly chosen for herself. 'Tell me why you like me,' she used to say, and Ib would praise her figure, her beautiful eyes, and her elegant hands. But she was done with being a princess.

Filled with an extraordinary sense of purpose, Leila arrived at the framing shop, where she immediately threw herself at Ib and made love to him in a blizzard of sawdust because she knew that this would be the last time. Afterwards, she went into the shop and began picking sawdust out of her hair as she composed a brief classified ad stating that she was looking for an assistant skilled in accounting. At that very moment the first customer of the day appeared in the doorway: a thin young man. Under his arm he had the most horrible-looking painting that Leila had ever seen, and when he asked to see the proprietor, she realized that he had a speech impediment. Since she had mistakenly taken his Norwegian accent to be a linguistic handicap, it was not only with triumph in her voice but also a touch of maternal concern that she pointed vaguely to a spot between her breasts and said, 'She's right here.'

Those were grand words, of course. She was not only the boss of the shop, she was the boss of her own life. But no sooner had she uttered those triumphant words than the poor man fainted. He lay there like a jellyfish that had washed up on the shore of her new life. The sight of the poor unconscious wretch with that horrible painting partially covering his body summoned up a flood of emotions in the orphaned Leila. She knelt down beside him, placed his head on her lap, and cautiously caressed him with her hands, which still smelled of love-making.

The Mistakes

IT DIDN'T TAKE LONG before Madam Mother's grief was disturbed by an inconsiderate commotion on the second floor. It was one thing for Leila to decide to throw herself into a dissolute life after Hans Carlo's death, but the fact that Madam Mother was forced to be a witness to her stepdaughter's debauchery was simply too much. The sound of shrieks, creaking bedsprings, and voices chattering half the night rode her like an incubus, and when the thin Norwegian came downstairs in the morning with his hair dishevelled, she glared at him with disgust and reproach.

'If looks could kill,' Dad used to say, 'neither one of you little baboons would ever have come into the world.'

They were the same looks that Stinna and I would later call *Madam Grandmother's looks*. After the death of Hans Carlo, it was rather puzzling to Lillian that other people could enjoy themselves. She started wearing sunglasses, which she lowered only to send those reproachful looks of hers over the rim of the dark frames. A pair of cheap sunglasses provided the only cover she could find for hiding her secret sorrow: betrayed at her husband's deathbed, forced into a childless state, shamed by the family, and ridiculed by an impudent stepdaughter, who didn't seem the slightest bit upset by Hans Carlo's death. 'That's a pretty bookkeeper you've found,' she said in her dried-up voice, 'but doesn't he have the wrong idea about what his duties involve?'

'He's not on the clock after four,' replied Leila, giving Madam Mother a superior smile. The so-called book-keeper had truly aroused unfamiliar new feelings in her.

'When I die,' Hans Carlo had said, 'you need to find someone who can take care of the accounts for you.' And that's exactly what she had done on the day after his funeral, when the poor man with the speech impediment fainted and then woke up to catch sight of the newly composed job announcement.

'That's the job for me,' he had said, but Leila hadn't decided to hire him because he had gone to business school. No, it was more likely because my twenty-three-year-old mother saw in my unconscious father the personification of that helplessness which she had cast off the night before, in an attempt to become a new person.

For Jug Ears' part, there was absolutely no doubt. He considered himself lucky to have met a dream girl from the enchanted forest once in his lifetime, but to encounter two dream girls had to be proof of the most improbable good fortune. And after their meeting he walked home through the streets whistling. Like his little brother, he felt he had stepped on board a big ship, and the next destination was the future. In his mind he pictured an enormous rainbow rising above him and leading the way. Without giving a thought to Askild's secret agenda, he wasn't in the slightest hurry to get back home, nor could he know that Askild was waiting for him on tenterhooks.

'So,' said Grandpa Askild when his son finally turned up, 'what did you find out?'

'Find out?' said Jug Ears, who had forgotten about his espionage assignment.

'The proprietor,' said Askild impatiently, 'what's he like?'

With a foolish grin on his face, Jug Ears stared in astonishment at his father; then he suddenly doubled over with laughter.

'You must have seen a ghost,' said Jug Ears at last before he went off to his room, chuckling. 'The proprietor is a young woman. And starting tomorrow morning, she's also my boss.'

The terms of Jug Ears' employment were rather hazy right from the start. My maternal grandfather's framing shop wasn't big enough to support a full-time accountant, but even so, Jug Ears went over to the business school and returned all his textbooks. After that he showed up each morning at the framing shop, sat down less than 3 metres away from his enchanting boss, and proceeded to go over the accounts. In the dusty books and ledgers he found antiquated systems and hopeless business practices. He found accounts receivable that were thirty years past due and had never been collected; he found bills that had been paid several times over. In short, he found an enormous mess. The accounts were suffering from an incurable cancer. Occasionally, when he glanced at Ib in the workshop, he also saw craftsman traditions that seemed idiotic to him. 'Why don't you just pound in a nail there?' he would ask. 'Why don't you have a machine to do that? It's absurd to stand there polishing that board all day long.'

Ib gave him a resigned look, but he might just as well have said: 'Who the hell do you think you are, Herr Greenhorn?' Jug Ears could take a hint, and he went back to his improvised desk where he did so little work and spent so much time bantering with the boss that Ib started deliberately slamming his tools about. Ib too found Leila's reaction to Hans Carlo's death rather strange. And when he heard those two romping around, shrieking and squealing like an entire kindergarten, he came to the troubling conclusion that it was not just a talent for crafts-manship and accounting that Leila lacked. She was also a hopeless boss, who had no idea how to separate work from play. *If they keep on like this*, thought Ib, *I'll be out of a job before the year is over.*

The whole framing shop now began to bear the mark of this unrestrained atmosphere, and everywhere in the anti-quated systems there were signs of an undermining love: love in the order books, love in the ledger, love between the lines in the accounts, love in every nook and cranny. Nor did it take long before the boss and the bookkeeper began giggling behind the customers' backs, making fun of the paintings that were delivered. 'It looks like a lady-bird that was run over by a steam roller,' they would say, or, 'It looks like someone's tousled hair in the morning.' The customers didn't much care for the idea that their paintings were being ridiculed. Nor did they care for the fact that the new proprietor was more interested in kissing the bookkeeper than in providing a decent service for her customers, and so they started going elsewhere to have their paintings framed. One by one the regular customers stopped coming in. On the rare occasions when Madam Mother turned up at the framing shop after hours to go over the order books and accounts with Ib, the two of them became aware of their own hair-raising situation. Instead of orders they found an enormous number of crudely drawn hearts, and instead of revenues there were comments such as: *This painting looks like a smashed porcupine. The customer has obviously not made love to his wife since last summer.*

'We'll go bankrupt,' groaned Madam Mother, casting a reproachful glance over her sunglasses at Ib. 'Do something, man.'

But what was Ib supposed to do? For seventeen years he had spent his work days in the framing shop, first as Hans Carlo's apprentice, later as his trusted carpenter, and finally as his daughter's lover, even though he had a wife and children at home. But he still had no say in matters. When he tried to talk some sense into the young people, they just laughed in his face. *Ib looks like someone who has hit his finger with a hammer,* Jug Ears noted afterwards in the ledger. And so my young parents continued to undermine the business. That was before their nightly arguments began, before children started making claims on their time, and before Dad was seized by the Fang fervour.

There was only one fly in the ointment, and that was when Leila discovered, to her disappointment, that the newly hired bookkeeper didn't suffer from a speech impediment after all; he simply pronounced his words with a faint Norwegian accent. She found this out the first time she was invited to dinner at the home of Niels's parents, whose Norwegian pronunciation briefly made

340

her feel dizzy. Norwegians also belonged to the category of mysterious creatures that she had banished from her world. In an attempt to forget this, she cast a quick glance around the dining room, caught sight of the newly framed painting, and exclaimed, 'There's that disgusting painting.'

She was talking about none other than *The Doctor and the Scalpel*. And while Askild gave her a disapproving look, Bjørk saw a chance to acquire an ally. Even before dessert was served, she took Leila out to the kitchen and let her whole backlog of secrets come tumbling out.

'If you only knew what I have to put up with . . . If you only knew how he acts . . .' By that time Bjørk's sister Lina in Bergen had said 'enough' long ago. So when my young mother Leila simply listened and listened, she instantly won my paternal grandmother's heart. At the same time Bjørk seized the opportunity to pat herself quietly on the back for her theft of the pink letters in the past.

'Why didn't you tell me that you were from Norway?' Leila asked Jug Ears on their way home, casting disapproving glances at my young father until, without provocation, he kicked a lamp post. It shook slightly and the light went out, and Leila cheered enthusiastically. The next lamp post they passed received a good kick from Leila. Then, kicking all the lamp posts and leaving a dark trail in their wake, they arrived at Hans Carlo's old home. They dashed upstairs to the second floor, tore off their clothes, and threw themselves into a noisy wrestling match.

No one could know that Dad had slept in his parents' home for the last time. Every single morning he now awoke in a house that had twice been haunted by mythological beings, and it was here – less than 3 metres from the sleepless Madam Mother – that my sister Stinna was conceived one November night in 1969.

'A mistake,' Mum liked to say, 'but it was the best mistake in the whole city.'

Nine months later the city's best mistake was witness to the disconcerting sight of a heavyset man with a cane bending over her crib. And using the index finger that was still intact, he tickled her affectionately under the chin until the infant started bawling. Then it was Bjørk's turn. And the city's best mistake was treated to a real downpour of tears. Next the baby's view was completely blocked by a giant, a trembling mountain of flesh, behind which a retarded girl by the name of Anne Katrine was hiding. At first her face lit up with anticipation, only to be replaced by dismay when she realized that this was not a new little brother lying in the crib, not a new little Knut who, in the future, would serve her sodas on the deck of an enchanting ship. And as the mountain of flesh vanished with a look of disappointment on her face, the infant felt a reproachful glance directed at her over the rim of a pair of sunglasses. Madam Mother had shown up at the maternity ward, and she too wanted to tickle the baby under the chin, but there was something half-hearted about the way she did it, a sense of cold envy that made the infant start bawling again.

'What a cry-baby,' exclaimed Askild, shaking his head. 'You're certainly going to have your hands full with her.'

The new family member heralded a new era because as Mum rested and nursed the baby after a successful birth, Dad started making such drastic changes at the framing shop that Ib threatened to resign and Madam Mother turned pale. A bolt of lightning had struck. Dad was possessed by the Fang fervour and decided to grow a thick moustache – I think it was the best mistake that had lit the fuse. In less than three weeks he had pounded on 447 doors in the city and sent out twice as many bill reminders. It was a matter of all those old accounts receivable, and when the money came in, he invested all of it in kitsch: pictures of weeping children and bellowing stags, and film-star posters in simple metal frames. 'Why should we settle for just providing the frames when we can also sell the images inside?' he said, revealing with his choice of 'insides' an incredible contempt for art.

At first the framing shop had been a sanctuary for proud craftsman traditions, then it had been the setting for a particularly undermining type of love, and now it was simply a horror chamber of bad taste. But before Leila even returned to work, Niels had tripled their income and transformed Ib from a solid craftsman into a sales assistant dressed in a cap and T-shirt bearing the image of a moustached Mona Lisa. 'Isn't that funny!' exclaimed Niels, who didn't have the slightest clue who Marcel Duchamp was. 'The woman has a beard!'

Leila, carrying the city's best mistake in her arms, could see how amusing Ib's transformation was. But later she discovered that the hearts had vanished from the account books along with the snide comments from the ledgers, and that Niels was no longer interested in sitting around making fun of customers all day long. Then she was struck by a feeling of disappointment. This was not the poor man with the speech impediment who had fainted and caused her heart to overflow. On the other hand, he was a much more decisive man, who now ordered Ib around and filled the pavement outside the shop with sale signs, banners, and flags. *What's going on here?* thought Leila. *I'm the one who's the boss, damn it all!* That was a little detail that my father seemed to have overlooked. He was acting as if he alone had recently inherited a framing shop near the centre of town. But Leila found it difficult to object in the face of increased profits, just as it was difficult to reclaim the boss's chair with a screaming child in her arms. 'You've certainly been busy,' she noted with a frown, and then went back to their flat. And a few months later – in consultation with Bjørk – she fell in love with a small house with an enormous basement no more than 500 metres from where Askild and Bjørk lived. On the outside it looked like a perfectly normal single-family home from the sixties, but it stood on a foundation of darkness that could be entered by means of a winding basement staircase.

Naturally Niels had dreamt of having a house that was a little further away from his parents, but right now other dreams had captured his attention. With Fang fervour he ravaged the former framing shop and started buying up cheap shares of just about anything. My maternal grandfather's shop was only the first of many businesses ripe for redevelopment that my father would tackle. Over the years the former pot-of-gold enthusiast became an expert consultant to firms on the brink of closing. At first he would join a company to get it back on its feet. Later, after he had made more money, he would buy companies cheaply, divide them up into failing and financially viable sections and then let the failing departments go bankrupt while he reaped the benefits of the profitable ones. Flitting, as he did, from one foundering company to another, it was impossible to keep track of the work he was doing. Stinna and I could never answer the simple question: 'What does your father do?' In the end, not even the tax authorities could make head or tail of the complicated tax forms Dad would submit on vast quantities of hand-written pages, using such an illegible script that everything reeked of fraud. Dad, who even in his days as a dealer of crabs had made use of shady methods, finally lost all grounding and could no longer stem the tide of rumours claiming that, over time, he had become a modern-day Fang – or to put it more bluntly: a swindler, plain and simple.

'Didn't I tell you so?' Askild used to say in that laconic tone of his, signifying the disappointment of old age. 'He has never thought about anything but money.'

But before things got that far, another mistake arrived at the back door. Early one morning in June 1971, my twenty-five-year-old mother awoke with a terrible feeling of nausea, staggered out to the bathroom, and threw up all over the floor before she could make it to the toilet. Then she went back to the bedroom and said with an expression in which Dad could see a certain loathing for the creature that had invaded her body, 'I guess I'm pregnant again, damn it.'

That gave rise to a great deal of discussion within the family because Leila and Niels were not yet married.

'You've certainly been in a hurry,' muttered Askild when he saw Leila's swelling belly. 'How about fornicating less and seeing about getting married?' Askild didn't like the fact that his son was living in sin, and his ill-tempered grumbling soon acquired an echo so that everyone who came to visit could hear the way Grandpa Askild talked under more private circumstances.

'Less fornicating!' could be heard out in the kitchen where Kai the parrot still sat on his perch. 'Knut who?' he also said, and 'Shut up, you stupid parrot!' By the time my sister and I reached puberty, we could still hear fragments of the heated discussions that had marked the period before we were born every time we approached the kitchen with the irascible parrot. 'Asger!' the bird would cackle. 'What kind of a damn name is that!'

Only nineteen months after Leila's first pregnancy, another circus took place in the maternity ward. There's no reason to repeat it all. I too felt the brunt of Madam Mother's reproachful glance, I too was tickled under the chin by Askild, and I too was bathed in Bjørk's sentimental tears. But when the previously pale and vegetative Anne Katrine approached my crib, it was clear to everyone that not every infant was the same in her eyes.

'Can I hold it?' she asked, pointing at the baby. And then, in a voice filled with childish enthusiasm, she added, 'He's sweet.'

At the memory of that jiggling blubber, that body without clear boundaries, which at first filled me with joy and later with anxiety, I suddenly start to hesitate. I pause at something as banal as the memory of her heartbeat – an irregular rhythm that skips a beat and makes her utter a strange sort of hiccup. And with that hiccup I once again find myself in the dark under the stairs. Anne Katrine is giving me an accusing look, death refuses to release its grip on her heart, fear shines in her eyes, and the darkness is getting worse and worse all around me.

I've had that darkness in my thoughts ever since I left Amsterdam. Many times I've promised my nephews to do a painting of that Doghead, and yet I've tried to get out of it because there were so many other destinies that crossed paths and wove their way into my own modest story. There was Anne Katrine, who was robbed of her mother's love. There was Leila, who lost both her parents. There was Niels Junior, with his ears and his corset. There was Knut, with his broken nose. There was Madam Mother's reproachful grief, Grandmother Elisabeth's lifelong illness, and Grandfather Hans Carlo's galloping tumour. There was Great-grandfather Thorsten's bankruptcy. There was Grandma Bjørk with her alcoholic husband, and there was Grandpa Askild with part of his index finger missing and those bloodhounds on an eastern German plain . . . Occasionally I've asked myself what my story about Doghead matters compared to the stories that would later unfold.

'Don't let the darkness go through you,' my father once said. 'It's much better to go through the darkness yourself.'

So allow me to beat the darkness to the punch and confess to my big sister, now listening attentively, that I, Asger Eriksson, dealt the family if not its worst blow then at least *one* of its worst blows . . .

'Oh, that old story about the pee,' exclaims my sister Stinna. 'But it all turned out okay. Can't you leave that until later?'

But this is not about how I, under the expert guidance of my sister, once induced Grandpa Askild to drink a whole glass of pee. No, it's about how I, Asger Eriksson, also known as the Latchkey Kid, the Bastard Boy, the Liar, and a number of other names, murdered my mentally retarded aunt.

'Now wait,' Stinna says. 'The Little Bitch died of a heart attack. She was so overweight that her poor heart finally just gave out. It didn't have anything to do with you at all.'

PART SIX

PART SIX

The Liar and the Letter Vandal

THERE WAS A GREAT deal of quarrelling after I was born. Askild demanded, in accordance with family tradition, that I be named after him. Mum flirted a bit with the name Benjamin, and Dad refused to rule out the idea that Elvis might be an excellent choice. When Dad vetoed Askild, when Askild grumbled enough about Benjamin, and when Mum refused to accept Elvis, Bjørk conjured up the name Asger. It was a compromise that everyone except Askild accepted. Askild regarded Bjørk's suggestion as a personal insult because, for generations, the names Askild and Niels had alternated among the firstborn sons in the family.

'Askild and Niels,' said my sister Stinna many years later, casting a teasing glance in Grandpa's direction. 'Now how exactly do those names fit in with your roots in the French aristocracy?'

'Shut up,' grumbled Askild, whose proud French nose had swollen considerably as the result of his extravagant use of alcohol. 'What do the two of you know about anything, anyway!' By that time he had recovered almost

351

unscathed from his disappointment, and he had started calling me Asger. But for the first five years of my life he refused to utter that name. Instead he indiscriminately made use of names such as You There, Little Baldy, and Number Two. Whenever he was drunk he would make a big deal out of the fact that he couldn't see his own proud French nose on his grandson's face, and then the name Bastard Boy would occasionally cross his lips. If Dad heard that offensive nickname he would react quite fiercely. It was a recurrent theme in our family: Grandpa Askild baiting his prosperous son, while Dad's disarming smile would get more and more strained until he couldn't help flying into a rage. For Dad there were never any stages in between, so Askild would head for the door, leaving the expert, who was in such demand by crisis-ridden companies, in a state of childish spite.

'That's it,' Dad would snarl, 'your grandfather is never setting foot in my house again.' But often it wasn't more than a week before Askild was back, or before we would set course for his house on our usual Sunday rounds.

But Askild was insulted, and Bjørk had to use all her powers of persuasion to get him to come to my christening. Her daughter, on the other hand, needed no persuading. By six in the morning on that Sunday, Anne Katrine was already at the door, dressed in her very best. She was supposed to carry the child to the baptismal font, and she hadn't slept all night because she was going to be God's mother, as she insisted on saying.

'Godmother,' said Bjørk, 'not God's mother. There's a difference, dear.' But her daughter was so happy that Bjørk didn't have the heart to insist on correcting her

352

impression that on a brilliantly sunny June day in 1972 she was actually God's own mother for a whole day. And as the child was christened in a church ceremony during which the parents were also married in order to prevent any further discord in the family, God's mother beamed like a gigantic sun weighing 100 kilos because she stood there holding a new little nephew, a mini-version of her younger brother Knut. And this time he wasn't going to be allowed to cheat her and run away to sea. A few days after the christening, she came knocking on the door of our house on Birkebladsvej, asking permission to take the baby out in the pram. And that's how I took my first journeys out into the world: up the street, down the street, in all kinds of weather, pushed by a beaming mountain of fat. The Little Bitch (as we later dubbed her) and the Bastard Boy (as I had been dubbed even before my christening) quickly became a familiar sight in the neighbourhood. She brought me anything I pointed to: earthworms, dirt, leaves, even cigarette butts and colourful flowers, which I contentedly consumed. 'Tastes good,' she would say, handing me the most amazing creations in the world as I sat in my baby pram. 'Sweet, just like honey.'

At first, my sister Stinna didn't feel like coming along, and that's how it happened that I ended up visiting our grandparents' house on Tunøvej more often than she did. Acrid turpentine fumes tickled my nose, and the sound of clinking glasses and the shrieks of a crazy parrot formed a background to the earliest years of my childhood. Bjørk's gentle voice was also part of this as she sang songs about a brilliant future and chattered away about her enchanting childhood summers in Nordland – until Askild got too drunk. Then Bjørk would order Anne Katrine to take me back to Birkebladsvej, and we would arrive just before Dad came home for dinner. 'Huh,' said Stinna, 'why is Asger always so lucky?'

In response to this unfair division of attention, Stinna began a silent protest: she started ripping up letters. Like a dog who lies in wait for the postman, she would stand each day at the letter box and grab the letters, newspapers, and advertising circulars right out of the hands of the startled postman, only to rip them to shreds and hide the pieces in various places around the house. 'Stop that!' my mother would cry. But once Stinna had worked herself into a bad temper, nothing could stop her. My sister's letter-vandalism continued right up until she hit puberty, and it was a contributing factor to Dad's growing problems with the tax authorities. He didn't realize how bad the situation was until it was almost too late, because the friendly enquiries that were sent during the first few years had vanished into thin air.

'The little vandal,' Askild called Stinna the first time he witnessed his granddaughter's peculiar bad habit, and he set about devising a secret plan. Early one Saturday morning in 1975, he took up position outside our front door shortly before the postman was due to arrive and stuck an empty envelope through the letter box. Stinna showed up at once. But instead of tossing the envelope through the slot, Askild pulled it back out so that Stinna's eager little hands were visible in the letter box.

'Aha!' cried Askild, taking a firm grip on her left index finger. 'Caught you! Ha ha!'

It was never his intention to sprain his granddaughter's finger, but that's exactly what happened. The Letter Vandal yanked back her hand and woke the whole household with her shrieks. That was one of the few times that Grandpa Askild was thrown out even before he had set foot in the door. Full of indignation, he went back home to Tunøvej, and it took him less than a morning to paint *The Vandal Gets Stuck in the Letter Box*. He was very proud of that painting, and rightfully so, even though it would always remind him that he had failed to put an end to his granddaughter's bad habit.

That sort of climate – with one child bathed in the golden glow of attention while the other was relegated to the loneliness of letter vandalism – was not the best environment for nurturing sibling love. I have a vague memory of Stinna occasionally pinching me when Mum wasn't looking. At other times she would come running after me and Aunt Anne Katrine as we walked hand in hand along Birkebladsvej. 'I want to come too!' Stinna would shout, throwing dirt and pebbles into the air.

'No,' Anne Katrine would reply. 'Not possible today.'

A little girl with her grandfather's dark complexion and proud French nose would be left behind on the pavement. *What a little bitch*, she would think, giving Anne Katrine an angry glare.

So it wasn't until I was three and started developing a harmless fear of the dark that my sister and I became close. 'There are no moles living under the beds in my house,' my father was fond of saying at bedtime whenever his son voiced dubious theories about the diffuse nature of the dark.

'Dogs won't come out of the walls when I turn off the light,' my mother assured me. But not everyone agreed that we lived in a perfectly harmless house.

'Down in the basement, in the space under the stairs, you know,' said Stinna, 'that's where Doghead lives, you know, and it's VERY DANGEROUS.'

'Doghead?' I stammered. 'What does it do?'

'I have no idea,' replied my sister. 'But it's very dangerous, you know. It's so dangerous that I don't even know what it does.'

'Doghead?' said Dad, giving me an enquiring look.

'Doghead?' said my mother. 'Don't be silly. There's no such thing.'

'Then what's that thing that sits on the front of a dog?' Stinna asked, giving my mother an innocent look. 'And who lives in that space under the stairs?' she went on, until Mum said she'd had enough of all her babbling. 'Stop scaring your brother,' said Leila, and she sent Stinna to her room.

But in conjuring up Doghead, Stinna had demonstrated a stroke of genius, and the invisible connection between the Doghead in the space under the stairs, Grandpa Askild's mysterious talk about German shepherds and bloodhounds, and all of Mum's mythological creatures soon began disturbing the peace in my parents' bed. It wasn't long before Dad got tired of the third party who kept slipping in between him and his wife at night, drowsily murmuring incoherent phrases about a doghead. Dad started out cautiously by having a serious father-to-son talk; later he issued a firm prohibition – and when that didn't help, he at last resorted to locking the bedroom door before he went to bed. Looming large in my childhood was that locked door, not only as a monument to a lost land, but also as a new beginning. Standing there – at once so close and yet so far away from the promised land of my parents' bedroom – it suddenly occurred to me that I had a sister.

'Okay,' she said and lifted her quilt, 'but then you have to take me along with you and Aunt Anne Katrine tomorrow.'

When Anne Katrine, as usual, came over later in the day, huffing and puffing from exertion and red in the face with sweat, Stinna shouted, 'Today I'm coming with you!'

But Anne Katrine thought Stinna wasn't the one to make that decision. 'Not possible,' she replied, looking around for me, but I was hiding behind a chair until the situation was resolved. It wasn't always easy to be someone who was in such demand. With butterflies in my stomach I watched as the two parties launched into a noisy argument.

'He's not going without *me*!' cried Stinna.

'Oh yes, he is,' snapped Anne Katrine as she continued searching for me.

'No, you stupid tomato,' snarled Stinna just as my aunt found me and started tugging on my arm.

'He's not going,' Stinna went on, yanking on my other arm. 'Just ask him yourself!'

When it dawned on Anne Katrine that I had no intention of going anywhere without my sister, she turned on her heel and walked out of the door. 'Don't care!' she shouted, determined to boycott both of us. But it wasn't long before she forgot all about being offended, and without hesitation took both of us on her rounds of the neighbourhood. Without a trace of resentment, she went back to searching through the yards of strangers, tramping through their flower beds and poking through their hedges.

'Get out of here, you retard!' shouted the angry property owners, brandishing their rakes. But no one could stop her from bringing us butterflies, earthworms, and slippery little frogs that always hopped out of her hands before she reached us.

'Tastes good,' exclaimed Anne Katrine, even after we got too old to want to sink our teeth into her gifts.

'Blech!' said Stinna. 'That's disgusting!'

When Anne Katrine wasn't rummaging around in strangers' yards, she would take us down to the swamp and initiate us into her wild stories about the seafaring Knut. He had recently sent a postcard from the Caribbean, where he had gone ashore to lie in a hammock and drink sodas all day long. Normally no one said much about Uncle Knut, so Anne Katrine's stories would always make us prick up our ears, and his adventures would go on and on. First he was in the Caribbean, then in the South Seas, next in Polynesia. Like some sort of Sinbad the Sailor, Knut survived all kinds of dangers: attacks by pirates, sea waves the size of skyscrapers, sharks with gleaming teeth – and in his wake he left behind a flood of unhappy girls whose fate would end up in Dad's hands and to whom Dad would send off small envelopes containing crisp Danish banknotes. 'Knut thinks he's still a boy,' Dad liked to say, while Grandma Bjørk would blush at the sight of those banknotes. 'But this is the last time I'm going to save his ass.'

The fact that Uncle Knut was still a boy merely served to increase our admiration for the seafarer, and we often tried to get Anne Katrine to tell us more about his unhappy girls. 'I don't know anything about that,' she told us.

'Do you know what I think?' said Stinna. 'Those hammocks – I bet he screws all the unhappy girls in those hammocks.'

'He screws in tons of soda water!' I cried.

'No,' objected Anne Katrine.

'Let's ask Grandma Bjørk,' said Stinna.

We immediately went over to the house on Tunøvej to resolve the question of the unhappy girls, but when we went into the living room, we found Grandma sitting in the big armchair, crying.

'Did you hurt yourself?' asked Anne Katrine, looking with alarm at her mother, whose brother had called her at work that morning.

'My mother is dead,' whispered Grandma, staring vacantly into space.

'You have a *mother*?' said Stinna, looking at Bjørk with astonishment.

At that moment Grandma Bjørk was determined to go back to Norway to attend the funeral. She was almost sixty, and she hadn't seen Mamma Ellen in seventeen years. Now all the memories came flooding over her, instilling her with so much energy that she even called a travel bureau to hear about departure times for ferries and planes. But, as always happened with regard to Norway, her efforts came to nothing. A sense of unreality slipped into her plans, and in the end she and Askild made do with sending a flower bouquet. Then they arranged to have Bjørk's third of the inheritance stored in the ware-house of a removal company. This inheritance comprised the salvaged remnants of the bankrupt Svensson family empire: mahogany furniture, meerschaum pipes, leather-bound books, rare porcelain plates, and all sorts of souvenirs brought back from the seven seas, including a shrunken head from Borneo and a number of other rare items dating from Rasmus Fang's day.

'Grandma had a mother,' Stinna announced that evening at the dinner table. 'But she's gone away now.'

'What!' shouted Dad. He ran for the telephone and then started yelling. It was typical of Bjørk not to tell her son the news. 'She's always been so devious,' he complained later that evening to his wife. 'Did she think she could keep my grandmother's death a secret from me?'

But after Mamma Ellen's death Bjørk began to behave in even more devious ways. While her inheritance gathered dust in the warehouse – just waiting for the day when the storage fee was overdue for three months in a row – Bjørk started taking a detour home from work. Just as she had done in Bergen, she often went out to do the shopping but came home without any grocery bags. And when Askild asked her why she was so late coming home, she had any number of excuses or claimed that she simply needed some fresh air.

'I bet she's met a man,' Stinna once heard her mother whisper in the living room.

'It wouldn't surprise me,' Dad whispered back, picturing to himself the naughty troll who had once leapt out of Doctor Thor's old mahogany cabinet.

When Stinna, at the age of eight, received her first stolen bicycle from Askild, our world grew suddenly bigger, and we didn't always have time to go exploring in strangers' yards with Anne Katrine. But our aunt would still show up every day, and after a while we started thinking of ways to avoid her. If our lies and attempts to slip soundlessly out of the back door and through a hole in the hedge failed, it was always easy to run away from Anne Katrine, whose breathing was so laboured and irregular. She would often have to give up after only 20 metres. Then she would stand there on the pavement, watching us disappear at a furious speed down the street.

'You have to!' she would hiccup. 'Your mother said so!'

'We don't care, you stupid tomato!' Stinna would shout, but one time when we were roaming around by the swamp, Anne Katrine suddenly came rushing through the bushes, her face fiercely contorted.

'Aha!' she cried, and as I was firmly gripped in her jiggling arms, I could hear the eerie sound of her heart pounding wildly.

'Let go of him!' cried Stinna. 'Let him go, you stupid tomato!'

'Uh-uh,' gasped Anne Katrine, pressing me closer to her flabby breasts.

'Let me go,' I croaked, squirming in her arms until I gave up struggling and turned my pleading eyes towards my big sister, who suddenly threw herself at our fat aunt. She knocked her down on to the grass and bit her hand so hard that Anne Katrine finally loosened her grip.

'I'm bleeding!' wailed Anne Katrine, staring at her hand. Blood was in fact dripping from the imprint made by my sister's perfect teeth. 'It hurts,' she whimpered, and finally she dissolved into tears and we had to take her home to Grandma.

'A poodle bit her,' I told Bjørk later when we stepped inside the door of the house on Tunøvej. Grandma looked me in the eye for a moment with a sombre expression on her face. Then she shrugged her shoulders in resignation, as if she accepted my explanation. And that was most likely how they began – my little lies that would grow bigger over the years and inspire Grandpa Askild to paint the last in a series of paintings dedicated to his children and grandchildren. There was *New Life in the Old Privy* for Dad; *The Doctor and the Scalpel* for my fat aunt; *Bergen Is Burning* for Uncle Knut; *The Vandal Gets Stuck in the Letter Box* for Stinna – and finally, in 1979, *The Liar Trips Over His Own Story* for me, his grandson.

I might as well tell the story right now. 'There's a dog in the basement,' I said, at the age of eight, to my paternal grandfather during a family dinner. And Askild couldn't help smiling when I challenged him to go down there himself in five minutes and take a look around.

It was all Stinna's idea. She was the one who had found the badger skull; she was the one who nicked the two candles; and she was the one who spent half the evening persuading me to lie down in the space under the stairs where the badger skull was already waiting, with two lit candles flickering in its empty eye sockets.

The space under the stairs was the scariest place in the whole house, but I crawled in through the narrow passageway leading to the large space, got under an old blanket, just as Stinna had told me to do, and waited with my heart in my throat.

'Woof!' barked Stinna from the next room as a chuckling Grandpa Askild came down the stairs, and she instantly switched off the circuit breaker for the basement. 'Woof, woof,' I squeaked from the space under the stairs.

'You little brats,' grumbled Askild, who was inclined to go back upstairs. But instead he tottered after Stinna, who dashed back and forth between his legs, crying 'woof,

woof', until he was finally enticed over to the passageway next to the space under the stairs. There he could see a faint light and he heard my pitiful 'woof', which immediately made him smile.

'You were supposed to blow out the candles and run off in the dark when he went in there,' Stinna later complained. 'He was only supposed to catch a glimpse of the skull.'

But when the big figure of Grandpa Askild came into view in the space under the stairs, I lay there, frozen in terror and unable to move. Askild was scared too. When he caught sight of that shining skull, his face went rigid and for a couple of endless seconds he didn't look like himself. Maybe he remembered the sight of the pulverized Pork Face in a similar basement light years away. At any rate, the horror I saw painted on his face made me jump up, kick the badger skull with my foot, and run at full speed towards the wall. I would undoubtedly have run right into it if my grandfather hadn't grabbed me by the hair.

'Ow!' I howled.

'He's pulling Asger by the hair,' shouted Stinna when my father came downstairs to see what all the commotion was about. 'He's out of his mind!'

That's how it happened that Askild, once again, was thrown out of our childhood home. 'Your grandfather is never going to set foot in my house again,' Dad announced, even though we knew full well what that meant. He'd spend a week on ice, just like the big toe on my left foot, which had swollen up by the next day. It turned so blue that I had to be taken to the emergency room, where my whole foot was put in a cast. When Grandpa Askild found out about the cast, he set up a canvas and painted *The Liar Trips Over His Own Story*, in which a frightened troll stumbles over a glowing skull while an old, disintegrating grey man looks on.

I like that painting. I like the frightened troll with the huge round eyes, and I like the old man who is falling apart. Bjørk, on the other hand, couldn't stand it. 'That doesn't look like Asger,' she said. 'It looks like a stupid troll.'

'What on earth were you doing, children?' whispered Grandma Bjørk as she bandaged Anne Katrine's hand and gave all of us a searching glance. None of us said a word. We stuck by our story about the mean-tempered poodle that had attacked Anne Katrine, and Grandma didn't ask any more questions. Maybe she had her own ideas about what happened. Maybe the whole family did, but no one ever commented on the bloody battle that was played out between my sister and our fat aunt. After that first incident at the swamp, Anne Katrine was forever after known as the Little Bitch whenever we talked about her.

'The Little Bitch is on her way,' Stinna would say, scowling out of the window. 'We'd better get out of here.'

And we'd run down to the yard, straight through the hole in the hedge, which the Little Bitch couldn't fit through because she was so fat, and then off into the world without the family's dark shadow, who, unlike her brothers, would never be able to move away from home. Every day she wandered alone through the neighbourhood, hunting for her nephew and niece.

* * *

At that time Mum had started studying to be a nurse. After seeing her ancestral framing business transformed into a junk shop, she decided to take charge of her own life again. Dad had also lost interest in the framing shop, which he was thinking of selling to Ib. 'That old store,' he was fond of saying with a laugh, purposely avoiding calling it a workshop. 'How did that place ever bring in enough money to support your family?'

But there was nothing wrong with my grandfather's former framing shop. According to Leila, Niels had started disparaging it only because he had grown so cocky. Over time he had created a reputation as an expert on companies on the brink of bankruptcy and he was now so successful that he had his own office next door to the framing shop, along with an attorney by the name of Jesper Slotsholm. Jesper was a short, stout man – Stinna labelled him the Bath Plug because his shape reminded her of one, and after that he was never called anything else – with a penchant for colourful women, as Mum called them, and with an increasingly pronounced weakness for my sister. He often brought her little gifts: stickers, hair ribbons, paper dolls, and later on perfume and tiny boxed soaps. His own children were boys, and, according to Mum, he was little more than an overgrown boy himself because he changed cars every three months. He made such a fuss about Dad's old Volvo that Niels finally traded it in for a black Mercedes.

'What a show-off,' muttered Askild when he first saw the Mercedes, which reminded him of the time when Lina's oh-so-marvellous husband once, in the far distant past, had arrived at their old house in Bergen with a new Volvo and driven Jug Ears and Knut around the neighbourhood.

Since Mum and Dad were both gone during the day, Stinna and I started going to Grandma and Grandpa's house after school. That was not a great success because Askild quickly decided that he was going to cure my fear of the dark by locking me in a cupboard. Eventually we ended up having our house on Birkebladsvej all to ourselves after Stinna announced that she was old enough to take care of both of us. When that happened we were each given our own house key, which promptly led to a new nickname: the Latchkey Kid, as Askild insisted on calling me, griping about my irresponsible parents who were too busy with their own interests to give their children a proper upbringing. 'You should talk,' grumbled Dad, refusing, with good reason, to discuss childrearing with Askild.

As Mum got smarter and Dad richer, Stinna and I started waking up in the night to the sound of arguing voices. They were not the type of fights we were used to hearing between Grandpa and Grandma. Their voices weren't particularly loud, and when we crept out to the hallway to listen, we often saw the unpleasant sight of Mum sitting on the sofa – sometimes she was crying – and Dad standing with his back turned, staring out at the dark beyond the big windowpanes, while he dropped ash on to the floor. 'It's the Bath Plug,' Stinna once said. 'He always comes first.'

She was probably right. According to Mum, Dad had married her and not the Bath Plug with all his fancy cars. Mum said that sometimes it seemed as if Dad had forgotten who was actually wearing the other gold wedding band, and she started talking disparagingly about the money he earned. 'We don't spend it anyway,' she whispered.

'That money is paying for your education, you know,' Dad replied. The ash dripped soundlessly from his cigarette, and he had the same remote look on his face as he had that day when Stinna and I came in dragging a box filled with pink letters. We had found them at the bottom of a cupboard in the attic on Tunøvej.

'Grandma,' Stinna shouted. 'What's this?'

We were at the usual Sunday coffee gathering, and Askild was in the midst of bragging about the parrot Kai's latest phrases.

'Larsen is a country bumpkin,' cackled Kai. Larsen was Askild's former boss – the one who, a couple of years earlier, had got him fired from the shipyard in Odense. That's why Askild could no longer stand the man.

'Larsen!' Kai continued when we came into the living room, bringing the box with us. 'What an ass!'

But our attempt to rummage through the family archives was not a success. The sight of the old cardboard box containing the pink letters made Grandma Bjørk blanch. The pupils of Dad's eyes took on a dark and distant look, but he didn't say a thing. In fact, he didn't say a word to Grandma for the rest of the day or for the next two weeks, as the remote look in his eyes became more and more pronounced – until one morning when it suddenly disappeared.

'Stinna,' said Grandma Bjørk with an unfamiliar sternness in her voice. 'Please put that box back where you found it.'

At that time we didn't know anything about Marianne Qvist. Of course we had heard about the time Dad bicycled straight through Ålborg wearing a blindfold, but we didn't know anything else about the reason for his grand prank. 'Why did he do it?' Stinna once asked, and Grandma Bjørk replied, 'Well, I suppose he was in love.'

'In love with who?' Stinna went on, rolling her eyes.

And then Bjørk conjured up the reply that was simultaneously both clear and vague. 'In love with life.'

'Ha!' whispered Stinna. 'I'll bet it was some girl, don't you think?'

At that time Grandma Bjørk was getting more and more preoccupied with her devious goings-on, and Stinna wasn't any better. 'Okay, I'm going out now, so you can just play with our stupid aunt all by yourself, if you like,' she would say, and then vanish through the hole in the hedge, wearing the hair ribbons and necklaces that the Bath Plug had bought for her. That same year Mum's brother Harry opened a grocery store only a few kilometres from our childhood home, so Stinna started spending time with our ginger-haired cousin Mia. 'What exactly do you do?' I often asked them, but Stinna would just give me a sly smile and roll her eyes.

I, in turn, became a member of the Hunters' Club, which roamed the area around the swamp. The group also included Bjørn and Mikkel, boys from my street, and it had three clearly defined areas of interest: one, to hunt and capture all living animals in the vicinity of the swamp; two, to run away from a retarded aunt weighing 100 kilos; and three, to shout at the older boys, such as Jimmy from Birkebladsvænget, whom we were always ready to shower with curses as we hid behind the safety of the hedges along the street.

Whenever I opened my mouth, I discovered to my great surprise that it was full of ugly words that took over and kept pouring out until it was too late. By then the bigger boys would have grabbed me, twisting my arm behind my back and making me beg for mercy. 'Are you trying to pester us?' they would yell. 'No, no,' I would wail. 'I'm sorry!'

Going anywhere soon proved to be a risky affair. After discovering that I was some sort of clearing-house for swear-words, a storage place for impudent insults, I could never be sure when the older boys would take it into their heads to implement their revenge. Nor did I ever know when my retarded aunt might come running up and make me the laughing stock of the Hunters' Club. Only when I was with Stinna did I feel relatively safe. The big boys kept their distance, and the Little Bitch had started feeling scared of my sister. But Stinna seldom took me out with her. That's why I started staying indoors for long periods, and it was there – while Stinna was off somewhere with Cousin Mia, while Mum was getting educated, while Dad was working, and while Grandma Bjørk kept missing her bus – that I would often hear a door open, even though I had tried to lock it. I would hear footsteps in the pantry, and then the Little Bitch would come in, hungrier than ever and quite pleased with the situation. I was, after all, her future soda-provider, and she was God's own mother, who had been chased away by a bad-tempered letter vandal. But now the situation had suddenly changed, and she began tickling me, as she had done so many times before while I squirmed in her fat arms. In spite of my frantic squirming and hopeless attempts to escape, I won't hide the fact that sometimes I let her catch me. Or that her jiggling softness could fill me with joy, and I got a certain pre-sexual satisfaction from our wrestling matches, which quickly moved down to the basement, which was far more suited to that sort of game than the bright daylight of the ground floor. As she pursued me among the furniture in the cellar, a sudden terror might seize me, and I would run through the narrow passageway into the space under the stairs. My fat aunt could just manage to squeeze through, and then she stood inside where the invisible Doghead had been living my whole childhood.

For three years she played that game with me. For three years we would end up in the space under the stairs where she pressed me into a corner or squished me flat as a pancake on the floor while her fingers found ticklish spots, until we were interrupted by inquisitive family members.

'What exactly are you doing down there?' Mum asked us one day when she came home early from school.

'Nothing,' we replied in unison.

Another time, not only Stinna but also my ginger cousin came tiptoeing down the stairs to surprise us in the middle of our secret wrestling match.

'Admit it, Peewee,' Stinna said afterwards. 'Aunt Anne Katrine is in love with you.'

'Shut up!' I shouted.

'So the question is,' said Stinna, laughing, 'whether you're in love with her.'

'Not on your life!' I yelled, casting a nervous glance at my ginger cousin, whose quiet giggling hit me right in the stomach.

'Asger and the Little Bitch,' Mia said, making a shrill sound with her tongue.

And so what? It was one thing for my sister Stinna to make fun of me, but the fact that my ginger cousin joined in, murmuring lewd insinuations, was more than I could handle. After that my disgust with our games began to overshadow my joy. The shame of rooting around in the basement with my fat aunt and then allowing her to catch me began to outweigh my budding sexuality. Once again I started running away in earnest, shouting 'You stupid tomato' after her out on the streets. 'You fat cow, you ugly idiot.' At the same time disturbing fantasies began streaming through my mind – strange tableaux showing a lifeless Little Bitch. It had something to do with death and murder and a traffic accident when Anne Katrine pulled me into the darkness under the stairs, lay down on top of me so I couldn't move, and exhaled her warm breath on me as she whispered about ships and tropical shores – all those places we would go, all the sodas we would drink, and all those hammocks we would lounge in.

'When Knut comes home,' she would say, hiccuping, 'he'll take both of us with him. And nobody else.' Just as if my ginger cousin hadn't appeared on the scene. But the Little Bitch had noticed that I was falling more and more in love with my ginger cousin.

And she started to suffer from heartache. Sometimes she would put her hand to her heart, gasping for air. And in the space under the stairs I became a witness to the unpleasant sight of the Little Bitch, all 100 kilos of her, suddenly going rigid. Her face turned red from lack of oxygen, while she whimpered with fear, as if her big, fat heart were being crushed because I had taken to shouting at her on the streets again. But I refused to change. I became violent and recalcitrant. Part of me still felt a certain joy at the forbidden contact with her jiggling flesh, while the other part fought a real battle to get free.

So when I wasn't surrendering to her embraces in the dark, I was struggling to be free to run after Cousin Mia and Stinna, who would turn around halfway down the street and yell, 'Get lost. Go back home to your stupid aunt!'

'Asger,' Stinna went on in a tone that made my ginger cousin double over laughing, 'it's okay for an hour, but you'll have to go home if you start feeling that urge, if you know what I mean.'

Yes, that's how much things had started *going downhill*, with so many insults to my budding sexuality. And in the neighbourhood the big boys were still roaming about – the ones who were scaring me more and more because the smart-ass insults kept pouring out of me in a steady stream. And then there was the Hunters' Club, which had begun to tire of Anne Katrine. 'If she's coming,' said Bjørn, 'and if there are any girls around, then you'd better just quietly take off.'

All right, yes, okay! To compensate for this I started making up lies, weaving a web of falsehoods wherever I went. I told the Hunters' Club that the Little Bitch was sick in bed with pneumonia even though that very afternoon she had come rushing out of the bushes. I told the kids at school that I would soon be leaving on a long trip – maybe to Norway (if only I had known!), maybe all the way to the South Seas. 'It hasn't been decided yet,' I told them. And then one day Mum got wind of her son's travel plans and called me out to the kitchen. 'No,' I told her, 'I never said that.' Nor did I ever say that my cousin had once given me a kiss behind the school's bicycle shed, or that my aunt suffered from a fatal disease, or that my grandfather had been a secret agent for the Allies during the war, or that my father was the richest man in town, or that I was once attacked by a gang of rockers on my way home from school.

Worried glances were exchanged in the family, plans were made behind my back, and even at school my teachers looked startled because wasn't this boy, who was previously so quiet, heading down a slippery slope? That was when Grandma Bjørk, during a Christmas lunch, pulled out a crumpled postcard from her handbag and told us that Knut was coming home from Jamaica for a visit. The son who had promised not to return home until he was strong enough to give his father a good beating; the son who had a long-admired three-gear bicycle waiting; the son who had promised his sister an endless supply of sodas under the heavenly vault of the South Seas. No one had seen him since 1969. Who knew, we thought, maybe he was just coming back to get his bicycle . . .

'So that's that,' says Stinna. 'That's the end of that story. Fat Aunt Anne Katrine died of her heart attack. I still don't believe that you killed her.'

She shook her head and added, 'Heartache,' before she went off to bed. 'A likely story.'

Dogheads Under the Stairs

THE TINS ARE piling up next to Grandma Bjørk's sickbed, and the fresh air from Bergen that seeps out of them has created an enchanting freshness in the room where she has spent the last few months, getting increasingly thinner and more muddled. The fresh air from Bergen has put a glint in her eyes that we haven't seen since the last third of Askild's ashes were scattered in the fjord and brought back memories from the old country, prompting her to tell us stories. In this way I'm gathering up the last threads as I listen to Grandma Bjørk, noting that she keeps returning more and more often to that day several years ago when Askild came home from a routine check-up at the hospital. On that day she suddenly had the urge to stroke his white hair – something she hadn't felt like doing for decades. But he wasn't home more than a few minutes when the urge came flooding over her, mixed with a fear that they might not make it to their golden wedding anniversary. 'But we did,' Grandma Bjørk says with a satisfied smile. 'We just managed to make it.'

Fresh air from Bergen. Hmm ... Combined with a

vaguely fishy smell, since Applehead wasn't always very careful about washing out the tins before gluing them to a postcard and writing those inventive words. He must be in his early sixties by now. Grandma Bjørk still thinks that it's not her nephew but her older son who has been sending all the tins. 'In our old house,' writes Applehead, 'everything is the same as usual. Ida is still fighting a losing battle with the monster in the kitchen.'

'What pranks he used to think up,' says Grandma, giving me a nervous smile.

Tomorrow she's going into the operating theatre to have something removed, something that I imagine comes from that splinter of ice in her heart, that cold wind that blew through Doctor Thor's consulting room, even though more prosaic words have been used in my conversations with the various doctors. My grandmother, with her partiality for stethoscopes and white coats, has the greatest trust in all of them. I was rather alarmed when I heard about the extent of the operation, and I've mentioned my concerns several times, but Grandma Bjørk refuses to budge, and the doctors seem determined to give her what she wants. So I leave her safely in their hands, because I have to go back to my sister's house. I have to make it through the story about my aunt's death and come out on the other side.

Knock, knock, we heard on 2 June 1983, and there he was – the seafaring Knut who had flung around all those easy promises and turned the head of his retarded sister. There he stood, looking like a faithful copy of the impressive Applehead who in 1959 returned home from three years at sea. Knut had been gone for fifteen. His tattoos were no longer new, and he was not carrying a duffel bag but a worn-out suitcase instead. And Dad, who had picked him up at the airport, had already cast several disapproving glances at his long hair.

'Oh hell!' Knut said when he finally stood in the living room. 'I forgot to buy some presents.'

It was of course a blow to the family to discover that Knut had inherited his father's reckless relationship with drink. 'He was drunk for the whole three weeks,' Dad said later, shaking his head in resignation.

'He's turned into a real lout,' said Askild, snickering.

'But he wept at the funeral,' said Grandma Bjørk, and on that day she put away her knitted sweaters for good.

Like Applehead, Knut immediately tried to toss his family members up in the air in our living room on Birkebladsvej, but unlike his cousin, Knut was so drunk that it undermined his show of strength. Everyone except Askild noticed that he smelled of alcohol and that he slurred his words a bit when he turned to his father and said, 'For fifteen years I've been looking forward to giving you a kick in the ass.'

'Go ahead and try it,' muttered my equally drunk grandfather. So, laughing hysterically, Knut took a firm grip on his father's arms and tried to force him to the floor. Grandpa Askild fought back with all his strength, laughing at first, but then more fiercely as their scuffle developed into a regular wrestling match.

'Now stop that, both of you!' exclaimed Grandma Bjørk, trying without much luck to separate them.

Fighting with his father in Birkebladsvej, Knut found strength by remembering the smell of grease from the ship's engine room, the monotony of the routines during the long voyages, and the familiar feel of a rope sliding through his hands, until Dad finally yelled, 'That's enough, damn it all! Stop behaving like a couple of babies!'

By then they were both rolling around on the floor, and even though they obeyed on command, relieved to be able to leave the field of battle before a winner and a loser were declared, they were both annoyed at being admonished by the oh-so-successful big brother and son.

What Knut had envisioned as a triumphant homecoming turned out instead to be a strained affair. 'Not a damn thing has happened here. It's just the same as it's always been,' he grumbled, and then laughed even more hysterically, until he caught sight of his weeping sister.

'Tell Anne Katrine that I'll come back and get her some day,' Knut had said fifteen years ago, in 1969, when he said goodbye to his big brother on an enchanting morning in Ålborg Harbour. He thought that his big sister would have forgotten all about his childish promises by now, but Anne Katrine had never forgotten how she had always taken the blame for him whenever they played a prank as kids. Nor had she forgotten that he, in response to her devoted love, had made a promise which often made her drool with glee. And under no circumstances had she forgotten that he had promised *to take her with him*.

No. During the two weeks Knut had originally planned to spend in Denmark, the Little Bitch never forgot a single detail, and her disappointment was immortalized in the countless photographs that Mum took. Anne Katrine at the very edge of the picture. Anne Katrine turning her back on all of us in protest. Anne Katrine with defiant tears in her eyes.

After a strained dinner at Birkebladsvej, the mood thawed, and Uncle Knut proudly showed us the three scars he had received from the razor-sharp teeth of a shark. He told us about the headhunters in Papua, New Guinea. He bragged about all the unhappy girls while he made an impressive dent in Dad's whisky and talked on and on about the tattoos that covered most of his body. 'Even my you-know-what,' he said, smiling slyly until Mum and Bjørk pestered him so much that later that night he got up from his chair, unbuttoned his fly, and placed his dick on the table.

FOR MY BELOVED, it said.

It became a standard family joke that Uncle Knut's dick, unlike Applehead's, was too small for the tattoo artist to include someone's name. Over time, it also became our only explanation for why he never had any lasting relationships but only short-lived flings with women who were as sweet as chocolate and as brazen as whores, as he would say with a laugh. At regular intervals he would also cast a searching glance at Askild, who didn't seem at all impressed. No, while Knut might impress his nephew and niece, he could not impress his father. *And why would I want to anyway?* he thought, drinking more than usual in order to endure the situation. His inscrutable father who had never given him an approving pat on the back. His oh-so-successful older brother. His mother who, in spite of her tears at his homecoming, was more worried than proud. And his big sister, who couldn't understand that he wasn't a child any more, damn it. He was constantly aware of her look of disappointment, which he couldn't bear.

She interrupted his conversations; she followed him everywhere, even when he went to the bathroom. Three days after his arrival, Knut had finally had enough. When Anne Katrine leant over him as he sat in the living room reading the newspaper, he stood up and pushed her away so hard that she fell on her behind with all her 100 kilos.

'Stop hanging over me,' snarled Knut. 'Get away from me, you stupid tomato!'

Anne Katrine was shaking as she got to her feet. I saw it, but no one else in the family did – her face simply disintegrated. In all the fuss over Knut's return home, no one noticed that Anne Katrine could never be found in the same room with him any more, and that she turned up only at the beginning of each meal in order to assuage her insatiable hunger. Nor did anyone notice that after she had licked her wounds, she became more aggressive, haunting the basement, where she would grab hold of me every time I was sent downstairs to get more wine. She would also rush from the garage to the bushes whenever I tried to go off with Cousin Mia and my sister Stinna. 'Aha!' I would hear, and find myself clamped between her arms.

'We'll be going now, okay?' Bjørn would say, setting off with the Hunters' Club.

'Have fun, you two!' Mia and Stinna would giggle before they disappeared down the street.

I tried to kick myself free. I tried to bite my way to freedom. I tried to scratch my way out of her jiggling arms. If she couldn't get Knut to take her along, as she had dreamt about for the past fifteen years, she could at least make me toe the line, and she hit me so hard on the back that it took me several minutes to catch my breath. She would grab for my nuts, and when she had a good grip, she would keep on squeezing them until I did whatever she said. She would pull me into the bushes or into the space under the stairs so she could lie on top of me, using more force than before, and knowing full well that I was having trouble catching my breath.

And it was there, in the space under the stairs, that her fragile heart finally burst. It was there that she hiccuped for the last time. That hiccup that was so typical of her, sounding as if her overtaxed heart was skipping a beat. 'Stop hiccuping at the table,' Grandma Bjørk used to say. 'Don't sit there belching.'

It was the day before Uncle Knut was supposed to go back to Jamaica. Mum had cooked a fancy dinner, and we were all sitting at the table eating except for Anne Katrine, who was hiding in the basement. Everyone was in high spirits until my sister, in the middle of dessert, asked Knut to tell us the story about the forest fire. In the past, the story of the forest fire had been one of our favourite tales, and at the time we knew almost nothing about the cane that ended the story and broke the nose of little Knut. But we had a feeling that we hadn't heard the whole truth, and that was undoubtedly why Stinna asked the question. Knut stared at her in astonishment and Grandpa Askild told her in a more surly voice than usual that she shouldn't bother the grown-ups, which merely led us to interpret this as proof that our suspicions were correct. One of Knut's eyes began flickering nervously as he peered at Stinna, and I noticed that it had a tendency to turn inward, towards his crooked nose. But maybe that was just because he was drunk.

'The forest fire,' he said at last, looking at all of us. 'You want me to tell you the story about the forest fire? You bet I will!'

But it didn't take long before he started talking more about his nose than about the fire, more about his father than anything else. And then Dad began to smile in a strained manner – and it so happened that he started clearing the table, and finally he told me to go down to the basement for more wine.

'No,' I said. 'Tell Stinna to do it.'

'Uh-uh,' replied Stinna, who didn't want to miss any of the truths that Uncle Knut was suddenly starting to fling at Askild: saying that he had never been a proper father . . . that he had always behaved like a scoundrel towards Bjørk . . .

I knew that the Little Bitch was in the basement, so I crept downstairs as quietly as I could. As soon as I reached the bottom, I dashed for the storeroom, snatched up two bottles of wine, turned, and ran right into her stomach.

'Let go of me!' I shouted, trying in vain to get free of her all-enveloping embrace. She was panting like a wild animal.

I couldn't understand how I could ever have enjoyed romping around in the basement with her. I found her disgusting, and as thanks for all the abuse that had been showered on her by strangers when she poked around in their yards looking for gifts for her sweet little nephew, I now bit her hard on the arm. Her body flinched as my teeth punctured her skin, but she didn't let go. Normally Anne Katrine would have started crying at such treatment. But now she didn't make a sound. With one hand she frantically grabbed for my nuts as she tried to shove me through the passageway into the space under the stairs.

I didn't want to go in there. I never wanted to go with Anne Katrine into that space under the stairs again, and I clamped my teeth together until the sweet taste of blood filled my mouth. I could feel her whole body shaking with agitation. But she didn't let me go. She kept on grabbing for my nuts. Finally she found them and squeezed so hard that my breath was knocked out of me and my teeth let go of her arm. She pushed me through the narrow passageway even though she could barely make it through herself. Her breathing sounded ragged, and I was starting to feel scared. She had been acting strange ever since Uncle Knut had given her that shove that landed her on her backside. She hiccuped and belched and uttered weird sounds that she didn't usually make. When we were all the way inside the space under the stairs, she put one arm around my neck and twisted me around so that I landed on the cement floor. My coccyx hurt. The back of my head felt numb. I was just about to scream when she lay down on top of me for the last time, exhaled her warm breath on me, and squeezed my balls until I lay there motionless with cold sweat pouring from my forehead. And then she uttered her last hiccup . . .

In other words, she loosened her grip on me, rolled on to her side, and clutched at her heart. I could see that she was bleeding from her arm where my teeth had punctured her skin. And in her eyes, in the faint light that was coming through the passageway, I saw that she was paralysed with fear. I sat up, and everything swam before my eyes. I wanted to hurry up and get out of there, but suddenly I saw it. I saw Doghead – that sinister creature that Stinna had told me about so many years ago. Doghead was lying right next to me.

I shrank back in terror and crept into the farthest corner where I sat as if frozen, listening to her laboured breathing, until a little while later when I heard Dad's footsteps on the stairs. 'Asger!' he called. 'What's happening with that wine?'

I hurried out of the passageway and ran right into him. 'What a family,' he said, trying in vain to make eye contact with me.

I should have told him that fat Aunt Anne Katrine was lying paralysed in the space under the stairs. I ought to have said that he should call an ambulance. But I simply gathered up the two bottles of wine from the floor, handed them to Dad, and followed him back upstairs to the living room, where Askild was in the middle of a long story, saying strange things about Grandma Bjørk that none of us could believe. Who had stamped on his finger? Who had come toppling out of Doctor Thor's dark mahogany cabinet like a jack-in-a-box? Who was this person that everyone believed to be a gentle angel?

This was all incredible news, which kept my sister spellbound, coloured my Grandma Bjørk's cheeks bright red, and made Knut fall silent for a moment, until he gathered his strength for a new attack. Everyone shouted at once, except for Dad, who just sat there with a strained smile on his face.

A short while later, I went back down to the cellar, sneaked through the passageway, and discovered to my horror that Doghead was still there. It was gasping for breath. It had crawled over to the passageway and was staring up at me with an accusatory look in one half-open eye. When it tried to come all the way out to the passageway, I took a swing and punched it in the face with my fist.

Doghead retreated. I hit it a couple more times until it lay there motionless on the cold cement floor.

Later on, when my mother came down to the cellar to get a cold bottle of mineral water for the stupefied Bjørk, she saw me standing in the next room, fumbling with a chair. In a casual tone, with her attention still focused on her poor mother-in-law Bjørk, she asked me, 'What are you doing?' When I didn't answer, she went back upstairs. I dragged out the chair. Beads of sweat were streaming into my eyes as I jammed the chair into the passageway to prevent Doghead from returning from the shadow realm to which it had been banished, once and for all . . .

'That's a lie!' exclaims my sister Stinna. 'It's all lies!'

After that the stairs lifted me up; after that I disappeared into the bright evening streets and ran through the neighbourhood looking for the other members of the Hunters' Club. I found them down at the swamp, and Bjørn was the first to start the usual griping, 'If *she's* coming, then—'

'All right, yes, okay,' I replied.

For the rest of the evening I ran around playing cowboys and Indians, as if nothing had happened. For the rest of the evening I caught toads in the waters of the swamp, darted through the streets, and was only once disturbed by my mother who came out to ask me an uncomfortable question.

'Do you know where Anne Katrine is?'

'No,' I replied. 'I haven't seen her tonight.'

Bjørn was quite happy that my fat aunt hadn't turned up. The other members of the Hunters' Club were also happy with me, and I convinced myself that I had once and for all banished my problems – until the evening darkness of the neighbourhood was suddenly lit up by flashing blue lights that were tossed back and forth between the walls of the houses. All the kids on the street quickly gathered around Birkebladsvej 2. It was just like six months earlier, when two medics had entered our living room to gather up Grandpa Askild, suffering from an ulcer. But this time there was a difference. The sight of the flashing lights, the curious children, the slow-moving medics, *who didn't seem in the least bit of a hurry*, made my legs buckle under me. Suddenly I threw up, striking Bjørn's trouser leg with my partially digested dinner.

'Blech!' he cried, giving me a look of disgust.

I walked up the drive, stumbled my way up the steps, and caught sight of Grandpa Askild, who was standing in the doorway, crying. That was something I had never seen before. It was only then, standing in front of my weeping grandfather, that I understood what I had done. In an icy flash I realized that my fat aunt was dead. That I was an evil and inconsiderate boy. And that I was the one who had done it.

Mum was the one who found Anne Katrine in the space under the stairs. She was the one who manoeuvred the chair out of the passageway. It was her shouts they heard upstairs in the living room, and she was the one who tried to pump life into a broken heart and blow air into a pair of lungs that had already breathed their last an hour earlier. And once all life had left my aunt, the fat began bulging out in strange places and they couldn't get her through the passageway until the medics arrived to help. But I heard all that later, because when I stood in front of my weeping grandfather, the whole world stopped, and I didn't wake up until I was lying in bed in my room, where

Dad had carried me. An oppressive silence had invaded the house, and I didn't dare go into the living room. Nor could I keep lying in bed, and so I crept into Stinna's empty room, crawled under her quilt, and breathed in the reassuring scent of hand soap while the whole house remained in a state of upheaval until daybreak.

But aside from the oppressive silence, aside from the grief and guilt that struck the whole family, there was something else in the air that night: a certain uneasiness, a feeling of we-have-a-suspicion-but-surely-it-couldn't-be-true. And when the other family members had gone home, that vague feeling was turned inside out. A chair in the passageway was studied by a worried mother in the role of detective; a suspicious remark was remembered – *I haven't seen her tonight*; and the strange behaviour that had been observed by both parents was discussed over and over until the first rays of sunlight struck their weary faces and all evidence seemed to point in one direction. Was it possible to kill without using a weapon? Can someone commit murder by refusing to act? Can an eleven-year-old boy be *evil*?

The next morning, when I was summoned to the living room by my parents, I knew instantly what had happened: the liar had tripped over his own story. And in my mother's face I saw an expression of estrangement, as if I was suddenly someone who had nothing to do with her whatsoever.

But they didn't go to the police. They didn't send me to an orphanage or to prison so that I could serve out my well-deserved sentence. Dad didn't take out the belt from the cupboard, nor did Mum's mythological creatures step out of the wall to cut off my dick. No, they methodically questioned me.

Had I seen my aunt? Had I put the chair there to block the passageway? Wasn't I as fond of my aunt as everyone in the family believed? Had she done things that I didn't like?

No, no, and again no.

The liar tripped over his own story. The liar cried and said he was sorry and *it wasn't me*.

'But why are you saying you're sorry?'

'I don't know—'

'You're going to have to make up your mind!'

After that the jury took a week to deliberate. Uncle Knut postponed his trip to Jamaica, Askild was pale and drank more than usual. Bjørk was pale too, and she put her knitted sweaters aside because that hypersensitivity to cold, which had plagued her ever since the diagnosis was pronounced in Doctor Thor's consulting room, disappeared the day she saw her daughter lying on the basement floor with lifeless eyes. Suddenly we saw my grandmother walking around outside wearing a T-shirt – something we had never seen before – but there was nothing liberating about her flight from the prison of her knitted sweaters. And when she came home, Askild would be sitting in his chair, staring vacantly into space. *It's so quiet in our house,* she thought, *so terribly empty and quiet . . .*

The day before the funeral there was a knock at the door of the silent house on Tunøvej, and on the steps outside stood a little old lady. 'Sweet Mother of God, that poor child,' squeaked the old woman, and only then did Askild realize that it was his mother, formerly so overweight,

387

who was standing there on the stairs with six suitcases. She was as wrinkled as an old apple, her back was bent, and her eyes had almost disappeared into her head. But she didn't seem to take the frailties of age as a personal insult, because she gave her son a hug, nearly robbing him of breath, and immediately set about cooking the fish balls that she had brought in her handbag.

'People steal like gypsies. You can't trust anyone nowadays.'

And once again Mamma Randi stood among the pots and pans, cooking for the family the way she had in the old days. She quarrelled with Kai the parrot while she prepared the fish balls even though she was now so deaf that she had to guess at the insults uttered by the bird. For seventy-five years she had spent her days among pots and pans, and she was also the one who was in charge of the food for the dispirited funeral guests who stood in Fredens churchyard on a rainy summer day to say farewell to Aunt Anne Katrine. All eight of us were there, each with our own unique sense of guilt, and when the pastor cast the first handful of dirt on the coffin, Askild started to cry and couldn't stop. He cried for three days straight while Mamma Randi served him vitamin drinks and Bjørk grew more and more concerned. But suddenly he pulled himself together, straightened his back, and the usual expression returned to his face: the bitter lines around his mouth, a mean look in his dark eyes.

When Grandpa Askild once again looked like himself, Knut went back to Jamaica and we all expected that Mamma Randi would soon announce her return home – until one evening when she blurted out that she had come to Denmark on a one-way ticket. It was not for nothing that she had brought along six suitcases; it was not for nothing that she had mentioned people who steal like gypsies, because she had brought all of her savings in her handbag along with the fish balls. In other words, Mamma Randi had come to Denmark to die, though that's not how she expressed it.

'I'm too old to go back to Norway,' was all she said.

Maybe she was afraid of how her daughter-in-law might react, maybe she was nervous that Askild wouldn't let her stay, but no one objected. Both Grandpa and Grandma were grateful not to be left alone in the silence on Tunøvej, and Mamma Randi quickly settled into my aunt's old room. She hung the family portraits on the walls and found a place of honour for Pappa Niels's shabby first mate's cap. She had also brought along an old black book in which all of Askild's pranks had been neatly written down:

Cursed at the table. Went through his mother's pockets. Got into a fight . . .

And everyone settled back into their routines. When the jury had deliberated for a sufficient amount of time, when all the evidence had been looked at from all sides – backed up by my teachers' statements of concern, and the neighbours' complaints about the impudent lad who often stood on the street shouting insults – the accused was once again summoned to the living room by his parents, who gently stroked his hair. But that was just camouflage. I stood there all alone, awaiting my sentence: *in the judgement of this court, the murderer,* as we might as well call him now, *is sentenced to indefinite exile.*

The Era of the Suitors

Y SISTER STINNA has stood up and is now wandering around the guest room, shaking her head in bewilderment. The kids have gone to bed; Jesper is working late; and from the kitchen we can hear the faint sound of Kai's chattering, which got significantly quieter after Stinna put a sheet over his cage. 'It's a lie, it has to be a lie!' she keeps on saying, shocked but also astonished that one of the family's biggest scandals went right over her head. 'You locked Anne Katrine in there? You hit her when she tried to get out?'

There's no reason to repeat myself. I look down at my hands, which are spattered with paint. For years I've imagined how Doghead would look on a canvas, but now, as it stares down at me with its whole ugly face, I'm not sure that I've captured it properly. I don't like what I see. It's not especially pretty, but it's not ugly either in that tough sort of way . . .

'She really did do it,' Stinna decides at last, sitting down on a chair. 'She molested you.'

The paintings all around me speak for themselves, loud

and clear, but I think it's the combination of desire and dislike that is confusing me. The fact that great dislike does not necessarily mean an absence of desire. When I saw Doghead in the space under the stairs, I was not seeing the ghost that Stinna had once invented to frighten me. I saw a figment of my imagination which my fat aunt had endowed with flesh and blood.

'But exile?' Stinna says. 'Was it that bad? Didn't you have a good summer up there?'

Three days after being sentenced to exile, I cautiously made my way down the gangway from the big ship. Dad had driven me to the ferry, and I was wearing a bright red sweater so that I could be identified by strangers – such as the giant man, 2 metres tall, who suddenly grabbed me by the arms as I stepped ashore. His beard was sprinkled with grey, his eyes were smiling, and before his strong arms tossed me up into the air, I caught sight of a pin fastened to his shirt pocket with the logo: *Bjørkvig's Elastic Bands – Best in All the Lands*. It was none other than Applehead who had come to pick me up at the ferry dock and was steering me towards the cubist house on the other side of the slum district, which had now been re-developed. 'Your grandfather built this house,' he said. 'I know you're going to like it here.'

The official story was as follows: young Asger Eriksson was so upset by the death of his fat aunt that he needed to get away for a while and think about something else.

Inside the cubist house, no fewer than twelve children and six grandchildren had gathered around the table, all of them staring with curiosity at the Dane, whom Applehead promptly took out to the kitchen. There, to my great astonishment, I saw on the floor the outline of a gigantic monster, which Ida had never managed to scrub off. Not even Applehead's attempt to paint over it had been much of a success. The monster kept breaking through, and there – in the middle of the monster, in the middle of the faded contours of my father's imagination when he was just about my age – stood a woman with hair so red that it hurt my eyes. 'What a shrimp,' she said. 'It looks like you could use some meat on your bones.'

'And colour in his cheeks,' said Applehead, pinching his wife on the behind.

They called me the Danish Shrimp, and I rather liked the name. It was not at all the same thing as the Liar, the Bastard Boy, or the Latchkey Kid. My new name invited gentleness and concern. And as I sat at the coffee table in the living room, feeling very anxious about the situation, I decided never to tell another lie. Never to shout abuse at people and never intentionally to make anyone feel bad again. Mum and Dad would be pleasantly surprised when they decided one day to let me come back home . . .

I also had to remember to write to them so that they wouldn't forget about me. What a fine thing that would be if I ended up spending the rest of my life in the charge of my uncle Applehead – that's what he wanted me to call him – eating free meals at his big dinner table when there were already plenty of mouths to feed. They had so many children because Applehead was so enamoured of Ida's rear end, and because, as he said, he was in the elastic-band business, not the condom business.

'And what about you?' he said to me two days later. 'A handsome little guy like you is bound to make the Danish girls swoon.'

So as not to disappoint him, I said that my cousin was wild about me. Before long I was also telling him that I had been given a choice between going to Norway and staying with Uncle Knut in Jamaica for the summer – I had chosen Norway because Grandma Bjørk had always talked so much about it. And I also told some of Applehead's grandchildren that fat Aunt Anne Katrine was dead because she'd been shot by a bank robber.

That was a fine beginning to my new life. I hadn't spent more than a couple of days in exile before I started lying again, and not even my impudent remarks could be easily reined in. Soon I was once again spewing out childish insults as I roamed through the neighbourhood, and it wasn't long before I had the boys from the redeveloped slum district on my tail. 'Go back to your own country, you Danish Shrimp!' they yelled. Yes, the neighbours scowled, the postmen cursed. Though it was not my intention, after a few weeks I was well on my way to ruining Uncle Applehead's good reputation.

But the more neighbours who turned up to complain to my well-meaning uncle, the more slum kids who gathered out on the street to throw rocks and dog-shit-on-a-stick into Applehead's yard, and the more grandchildren who decided they'd had enough and refused to play with their Danish relative any more, the more fishing trips my uncle would take me on. I couldn't help noticing that Applehead was trying to get me back on the right track, yet as thanks for all the time he spent with me, I started bothering him at night so he could no longer lie in bed and pinch his wife's behind.

'It's that monster,' muttered Ida, half asleep. 'It's giving the boy bad dreams.'

'It's Doghead,' I muttered. After my fat aunt's death, my fear of the dark changed. In the past it had been a more diffuse fear of scary creatures in the dark. Now it seemed to have changed, to a large degree, into a fear of myself and the forces concealed inside me. The dark put me in a state of terror, and I had an almost panicky fear of seeing Doghead again.

Since Applehead could no longer have his wife to himself at night anyway, he took me and the grandchildren on mountain hikes, pointing out animals and flowers to us, making cocoa on the campfire, putting up tents, and grilling trout as he told us pirate stories from the darkest alleyways of Singapore. In other words, he managed to distract my attention so much that the slum kids finally forgot all about me. 'Now all we need is that Doghead,' he said with a laugh.

Before the summer was over I had acquired another nickname in addition to the Danish Shrimp. They called me the Bandit, but unlike so many other people, Applehead didn't seem to have anything against bandits. Nor did he take it personally that, as thanks for the free room and board, I broke his ankle during a soccer game. It happened out on the lawn in front of their house, where a small crater from an exploded privy still marred the hillside. It was on a Sunday, when the whole family, true to custom, had gathered for one of the many soccer matches that Applehead organized over the course of that summer.

I was the goalie, and my team quickly fell so far behind that the grandchildren started to complain. 'Go after him!' they shouted each time an opponent took control of the ball. 'You're supposed to tackle him. Don't just stand there gawking!'

So when Applehead came rushing up with the ball, about to kick it, I dashed out of the goal and kicked as hard as I could. But instead of kicking the ball, I struck his instep. There was a loud popping noise, and Applehead toppled over. For the rest of the summer he hobbled around leaning on a ski pole, grimacing if anyone tried to touch his foot but merely saying, 'It's nothing. I'm sure it'll be better tomorrow.'

In early August, leaning on two ski poles, Uncle Applehead accompanied me down to the harbour, where a big ship was waiting. I didn't even have a chance to thank him for the room and board; I never told him that he was my favourite uncle, or that I was sorry about his foot.

I was back home again, hooray! But I still had a lot of work to do. I was, after all, an exile granted a temporary reprieve, and I had to make it through my probation before I could breathe freely. At the same time I discovered that during my absence the stories had all gone their own way. From one day to the next my big sister had stopped tearing up letters, and the first serious letter from the tax authorities had arrived through the letter box, making everything swim before my father's eyes for a moment. He immediately notified the Bath Plug, who came roaring up in one of his fancy cars. Then they started spending long nights together, going through the accounts and spouting legal paragraphs. If Mum had previously grumbled that Dad was not married to the Bath Plug, she now had every reason to explode, but she was too busy herself, taking exams and training in a paediatric ward, where the tiny patients made her orphaned heart ache.

A new era had begun for my sister and our family: the era of the suitors. Endless knocking at my sister's window, a constant stream of flowers, letters with crudely drawn hearts and asinine words that flowed in a steady stream into our house. That was the reason my sister had stopped tearing up letters – because to her great dismay she happened to tear up a love letter that was addressed to her.

Helped along by a number of tenacious French genes, a magic wand had touched my sister that summer. Without me around, her budding breasts had grown into a pair of nicely shaped oranges, her face had the graceful look of a greyhound, her figure was unbelievable, and she could suddenly give me such a ravishing glance that I felt totally confused. Even Grandpa Askild had stopped harassing her. Drunk as always, he merely staggered around in a stupor with Kai the parrot, who in my absence had learnt to say, 'Hansen is a swine!' Hansen was Askild's latest boss, the one who, shortly before my return home, had summoned my grandfather to his office and for the last time in this particular story, accused him of lacking all sense of reality. Now Grandpa Askild would have to retire. Mum told me that it was because Askild had been drunk out of his mind ever since Anne Katrine's death. Needless to say, I had quite a lot on my conscience at the age of eleven. Every time I saw Grandpa Askild staggering through the neighbourhood, I would shudder and swear to myself that I was going to mend my ways, but there were certain things that were beyond my control.

During 1983 and for the next five years, the suitors never left us in peace; they invaded our house in every shape and form. There were fat suitors and thin suitors. There were the shy suitors, the dandies, and the idiots. I gained a certain status in the Hunters' Club because over the summer my sister had become the best-looking piece in the whole town, as Bjørn said. And I could now offer them a front-row seat, meaning a place on the roof above Stinna's window. There we sat, pouring water on the heads of countless blushing young men who stood below with their flowers and asinine letters.

'Stop staring at me,' said Stinna when she came with Mum and Dad to pick me up at the ferry dock. 'I *know* I have boobs.'

It was mostly because of her so-called boobs that Mum didn't want me to sleep in Stinna's bed any more. She was barely two years older than me, but she suddenly seemed grown up, while I was still a baby, as my sister said when I woke up in the night, my head hollow with fear. What had I done? How could I have done that? I never told my sister the exact content of those dreams, but she quickly started calling them my Doghead dreams. By that time she had completely forgotten who had first planted the image of Doghead in my mind, but I was still allowed to sleep in her bed, even though I usually went back to my own room before Mum came to wake us in the morning.

At the same time stories started circulating about Grandma Bjørk, who was sneaking around town. Six months after my return home, I went with Grandma on one of her frequent trips into town. She liked to go to a cafeteria and act like an elegant lady. She would put on her best clothes and head for the cafeteria in Magasin, the department store, where she had coffee and a pastry while I drank hot cocoa. But that afternoon she took me past Magasin and continued down a narrow side street, stopping in front of a sleazy looking basement place with

Venetian blinds on the windows. 'You don't need to tell anyone about this,' she said. 'This will be our little secret, all right?'

'Sure,' I replied, and the next second I stepped into Grandma Bjørk's secret world. There stood twenty-eight slot machines, lined up seven to a row, flashing their coloured lights. In the very back of the room stood a couple of pinball machines. Over by the cashier where a stout man was changing money and selling coffee, was an automated poker machine, which for the past few years had become the object of my grandmother's secret passion. I can't hide the fact that I was a little disappointed when it dawned on me that all her lies had served only one purpose: to conceal her membership in a gambling club. She changed a fifty-krone bill and gave me a cherry soda and a handful of coins, which I quickly spent at the pinball machines. Then she sat down to play poker with the machine until she had spent the fifty kroner she had budgeted for each visit. Initiated into her hidden passions, I raced home to reveal Grandma Bjørk's secret.

'She belongs to a gambling club,' I told Stinna, who was also a bit disappointed. Maybe she was most disappointed because Bjørk had never taken her into town, while I had been invited many times. On the other hand, Stinna was really too busy with her suitors. A bunch of them were frequently sitting in her room. My cousin Mia was often there too, and in those situations it wasn't particularly interesting to have front row seats on the roof above Stinna's room. Instead we would try to spy on them through the keyhole, and over the next few years we also made many tape recordings of their ridiculous voices.

Some of the words exchanged in that room were so shocking they made us cringe, and Bjørn thought we could sell them to the neighbourhood kids or use them for the purposes of blackmail.

So I started hammering a hole in the wall between our rooms whenever Stinna wasn't home. Before long I broke through. The hole was above the headboard of my bed – covered with a poster from the time when Dad worked in Grandfather's framing shop. It went through the wall to the narrow gap between the outer wall and the clothes closet in Stinna's room. To camouflage the hole on that side, I had attached a piece of wallpaper to a stick that could be pushed into the hole. It was a perfect place for the microphone I had been given for my birthday. Later on it was also an excellent peephole into foreign worlds, a magic show that was revealed to me as I lay in bed at night, unable to sleep.

Through that hole I became the silent witness to both her triumphs and her tragedies. Dad had his telescope; I had a peephole through which I could see a third of my sister's bed. But back in 1984, I made that hole exclusively for recording the ridiculous voices of Stinna's visitors on tape. I had no plans to antagonize my sister, who was still my best defence against the Doghead dreams. That's why I refused to let the tapes out of the house. My high sense of morals in that regard did not please the other members of the Hunters' Club, who each wanted a tape so they could take it home to copy. 'Hey, why do you get to have them all?' they often said.

The Hunters' Club was transformed into the Peeping Tom Club whenever we crowded around Stinna's room, sneaking past, snickering, and of course making tapes, until she sent the suitors after us and they came pouring out of her room to scare us off. The one we liked best was named Peter. If he caught us he would just shake us by the arm a bit, but there were others who didn't settle for just giving us a shake. Jimmy Madsen from Birkebladsvænget, for instance – he was the one at whom I had hurled the most impudent remarks when he came biking over from his father's house. If he caught sight of us, he would go completely berserk; once he even split Bjørn's lip. Jimmy definitely belonged to the category of dim-witted suitors while Peter was the shy type – the kind who surprisingly often would show up again after going home. There he would be, outside Stinna's window.

'Go on home, now, Peter. Okay?' Stinna would say, while we were up on the roof, trying to pour water on him. Gradually Peter, hunched over and with water dripping down his face as a sign of his hopeless love, became a familiar sight in our drive, and Mum commented several times that he must be hard hit.

'Why don't you invite him into the living room for tea?' she said, but Stinna wouldn't hear of it.

'He's just so childish,' she replied with a giggle.

Even our father, who was increasingly absent from home and who had his head full of vaporous dreams about a pot of gold at the end of the rainbow, noticed the presence of the suitors. But otherwise his participation in the family had become reduced to the news he heard after dinner from my mother: 'Stinna had the whole bunch over all day long. Asger was apparently up on the roof again—'

'It's okay to have a sweetheart,' Dad said one evening, 'but you don't need to have more than one at a time.'

In Stinna's opinion she wasn't sweethearts with any of them, but that didn't stop her little brother from discovering that she did have a weakness for those suitors that we in the Hunters' Club had labelled *the dim-wits*. Yes, before puberty Stinna had planned to be a lawyer so she could work with Dad, but by the time she grew up, she was so disappointed by his lack of involvement that she no longer wanted to be a lawyer. At the same time she started falling for the guys that she knew Dad didn't like. That was Mum's theory, at any rate. That's what I heard them arguing about at night, which meant that eventually I stopped waking up Stinna whenever I heard their quarrelling voices.

But one time something did rouse Dad to action. For once he forgot all about pots of gold at the end of the rainbow and the letters from the tax authorities, which had begun to disturb his sleep at night.

'They've caught Asger. They've tied him up! They've lit a bonfire!' shouted two members of the Hunters' Club when Dad came driving up to the house one evening. They were talking about a bunch of suitors in the dim-witted category who had grown tired of having their letters recited out on the street by an impudent little brother. *I think you're pretty, hee, hee . . . I like your hair, ha, ha . . .* Out of the car jumped my father, off towards the swamp he ran, as he suddenly felt his ears vibrating in the wind and saw in his mind a series of images from those daily ear treatments. By that time I had discovered that there were certain things you couldn't share with your parents. So when Dad showed up and started stamping out the fire that Jimmy had lit in front of my feet, and when he untied the rope that the dim-witted suitors had used to tie me to a tree, I tried to make light of the whole thing.

'They were just playing around,' I lied. I mostly felt nervous at his sudden appearance; I hadn't felt that way since the time before my exile when he had said, 'It's much better to go through the darkness yourself.'

By now I was fourteen and still didn't have even a trace of hair around my dick. Plenty of the other members of the Hunters' Club were already a head taller than me, and now I rarely slept in my sister's bed. Not because my Doghead dreams had disappeared, but because nightly suitors had started showing up. Knock, knock, I would hear at her window after bedtime, and when I moved aside the old poster of Mona Lisa with a beard, I would see two figures standing in Stinna's room, whispering to each other. What had previously been innocent guessing and kissing games soon changed into scenes that made my heart pound loudly. My sister's voice changed so that I hardly recognized it. Instead of the usual giggling I heard her speaking in a terse adult voice, which was immortalized on the countless tape recordings I made. I watched them roll around on the bed like a couple of hungry puppies. I saw my sister unbutton the visitor's pants and touch his thing in the same way that I touched my own at night. I saw tongues wriggling into ears, and I saw hands slipping under clothing until my sister's hoarse voice stopped the secret films of the later part of my childhood.

'No, don't take my pants all the way off,' she would say in her new voice.

But let me be perfectly honest: it was never a matter of hordes of guys. It was almost always Jimmy, and if she was

402

fighting with Jimmy for a while, then, on rare occasions, it was a guy named Kim.

And when Jimmy wasn't allowed to take off Stinna's pants, I saw something else. Something that made everything swim before my eyes. What kind of person was I, anyway, sitting there like that, glued to a hole in the wall, unable to sleep at night and losing my ability to concentrate in school, all for the chance to see Jimmy spurt his white seed along my sister's arm? The first time I witnessed that disturbing sight, it occurred to me that I might be getting off on the wrong track again. I really had to try to pull myself together, but the hole in the wall had become an opportunity I couldn't pass up. Like a magic 'open sesame', it allowed me to peer into other worlds, and my voyeur genes were not to be denied.

But did my sister know that I was sitting there? Did she know about my silent, tape-recording presence?

'Back then I didn't know anything about it,' Stinna says and then leaves the room because her sons have started throwing around artificial noses upstairs.

'But I had my suspicions,' she continues when she comes back. 'So what?'

Yes, well, what does it really matter that I, at the age of fourteen, was a little infatuated with my own sister?

'So shut up and keep going. If you really have to include all this, don't drag out the torture. Just tell what happened!'

I'm going to have to tell the whole story. Stimulated by the magic world I had discovered through a hole in the wall, I confessed to my ginger cousin Mia one day that I liked her. She worked in the afternoons in Uncle Harry's store.

There was no one else in the store at the time, and so no one saw how she leant over the counter. Did she want to whisper something in my ear? Was I going to get my first kiss? – and then she laughed so hard at me that I had to pretend that it was all a joke. That I just wanted to see how she would react.

But my sister was right. I'm dragging out the torture to hide the fact that, unfortunately, I've reached the point in the story where I lost control of all those tapes I had made. To compensate for my lack of pubic hair and my discouraging experiences with the opposite sex, I allowed myself to be enticed by the prospect of easy success. A few tapes leaked out; they were copied and distributed via a complicated network of reciprocal favours between friends until my sister's sweet sounds were being heard in the rooms of countless boys after dark. Bjørn was the first to get a tape to smuggle home in his pocket, and with that he reaped the benefit of the increasing pressure on me from the Hunters' Club.

Jimmy's voice was also recognizable. But he seemed to be proud of his sudden fame. If anyone had any doubts, he made a point of announcing that it was his voice on the tapes. But he didn't tell my sister that the soundtrack of their nightly rendezvous was circulating with lightning speed among the boys of the neighbourhood. No, none of them told my sister a thing. Neither did I, and by the time it dawned on me what forces I had set in motion, it was too late. The tapes that I tried to retrieve had been lent out to other boys, and when I finally managed to get my hands on an original, it had already been copied countless times.

At first only my bad nerves were affected. Stinna could

still silence most of the boys with a simple twitch of her face, but what had been recorded in secret started turning up again in secret.

'Why can't *I* when you let the others do it?'

'Stop being such a prude.'

'Don't worry, I won't take your pants all the way off, hee, hee.'

Slowly the tone of those conversations I recorded at night began to change. The first time I overheard some older boys in the neighbourhood talking, with great amusement, about my sister as a whore and a sperm silo, a new era began. The cold-sweat era. What had I done *now*?

The sweat drenched my quilt, made big patches under my arms, and finally enveloped me in such a stench that my sister one day gave me some deodorant, which I accepted like a grinning traitor. She also gave me practical advice, telling me to take a bath and change my T-shirt every day. And after the cold sweat had worked on my skin for a long period of time, causing my face to break out in pimples, she also gave me acne creams and admonished me not to pick at the spots. This was exactly what I had long been hoping for, but my delayed puberty missed the touch of a magic wand; instead, it was like a bubonic plague or a guilty conscience. Where were my proud French genes? Stinna had never had a pimple, but even so, and in spite of her attempts to preserve her facade, I noticed that her mood had changed. Through the hole in the wall I would sometimes see her sitting on the bed, staring off into space. Did she know what they were saying about her? Did she realize what I had done? We started growing further apart, and it didn't take long before my sister let Jimmy take her pants all the way off.

'Give me the tape,' he said the next day.

That was on the way to school, and when I got back home I stuffed all my cassette tapes into a couple of plastic bags and biked down to the swamp. There I buried them behind some bushes. Back in my room I plugged up the hole in the wall with some old newspaper, swore that I would never look through it again, and went in to confess to my sister. 'Get out,' she said, 'I'm doing my homework.'

And so she gave me the perfect excuse to keep my treachery to myself. But a couple of days later the buried cassette tapes came back and hit me in the head like a piece of bad news. Someone had dug up the bags. Jimmy had got his mitts on them and was now going around the neighbourhood with a ghetto blaster, playing the tapes for anyone who cared to listen. He really was. After biking all through the neighbourhood I finally caught sight of a crowd over on Tunøvej, outside the house where my Grandpa Askild and Grandma Bjørk lived. Jimmy was standing in the middle with his ghetto blaster. With my heart pounding, I picked up speed and rode right into the crowd.

'What the hell!' I heard Jimmy shout.

When I opened my eyes I thought at first that I was seeing double. I had split his ghetto blaster in two by running it over with the front wheel of my bike, and Jimmy's face was pale with rage. His father had given him that ghetto blaster, he shouted at me – I was going to have to buy him a new one, what the hell was wrong with me, and the next instant he was sitting on my chest, hammering me with his fists. 'Help!' I cried, trying to protect myself from his punches. 'Help!'

Sitting in the rocking chair in my aunt's old room, Mamma Randi heard me shouting, even though she was actually deaf. Through the window she saw the fight going on, even though by now she was also blind. And suddenly there she stood, right behind Jimmy. The others in the group saw her, but Jimmy was completely blinded by fury, and so he didn't notice the stooped old woman, whose lips were quivering with such menace that her three remaining teeth were clearly visible. Undaunted by her age, she swung her cane a couple of times through the air and struck Jimmy on the ear. He tumbled off me, turned around, and proceeded to howl. Without giving him so much as a glance, Mamma Randi started lashing out at the others in the group until they had all scattered, along with the two halves of Jimmy's ghetto blaster. Then she sat down in the street.

'I'm too old to get up,' she said, and a short time later, when Askild came home drunk from the Corner, he had to help me carry her to the house.

After that Mamma Randi started sitting down in the most peculiar places – behind the curtain in the bathroom, in the shed with the stolen bicycles. 'I'm too old to go back to Norway,' she had said several years ago. Now she was also overwhelmed by the effort it took to stand up, and Grandma Bjørk had to cut back on her activities at the gambling club in order to take over the cooking.

Stinna still didn't know anything. 'Hey, handsome!' she had started saying after the pimples had begun their work on my face, and now I was also the lucky owner of a black eye, but I refused to tell her why.

'Come on, tell me,' she kept saying when I walked past her to my room.

'Why the hell are you always so grumpy?' she cried.

But I wasn't grumpy. I was uneasy, and the uneasiness changed to horror one evening not long after, when I heard a familiar soundtrack through the wall of my sister's room. A much too familiar soundtrack – I had actually heard it before – and I tore the newspaper out of the peephole and stared inside Stinna's room. They weren't fucking. They were sitting rigidly on the sofa – Stinna with her eyes on the floor, and Jimmy with a smirk on his face. His ear was still swollen.

What sort of weird scene was that? Fucking noises without any movement. Words issuing from mute lips. Lustful sounds without a trace of lust on my sister's face . . . But there was really nothing mysterious about it, because Jimmy had repaired the tape, spooling it back inside the cassette after his unfortunate collision with a furious bicyclist, and he was now sitting on the other side of the wall, playing the tape for my sister.

After he left through the window, I could hear my sister crying. Through the peephole I could see a third of her face, a quarter of her upper body, and a close-up of one hand, which she slowly moved up to her throat . . .

'Get the hell out of here!' she screamed when I went into her room. 'What the fuck have you been doing, you little shit!'

While the cassette tapes circulated like rare trade items, while Mum passed the last of her exams and got a job at the city hospital, while a hostile silence arose between sister and brother, I was witness to a disturbing development in my sister's love life. Previously Jimmy had been her steady boyfriend, though she supplemented him with a couple of other guys whenever they were having a fight. But now she threw herself into a life of abandon, and a real parade started entering through her window at night. At the same time I noticed certain abrupt changes: her laughter turned cold, and she used every opportunity to drive her nightly visitors out of their minds.

One day when Jimmy was there – yes, she was still allowing him in – she kept on saying that his dick was the smallest and most crooked she had ever seen. Through the peephole I could see him blushing, and he left without knowing that I had recorded the whole conversation on tape. That very evening I made secret plans to circulate the tape in the neighbourhood, and the next day I gave a copy to Bjørn. I figured that it was only a matter of time before everyone knew that Jimmy had the smallest and most crooked dick in the whole town. But for some reason, nothing happened. My revenge didn't materialize, and so it was up to my sister to defend the family honour by saying demeaning things to her visitors. She let them have a taste of her duplicitous contempt and cold laughter, as if in that way she could take her own revenge on all the lewd gossip. Stinna still exerted a certain power over those boys, even though the cassette tapes had now restricted its effect to a very specific room. So out on the street she kept a low profile, no longer sending out ravishing glances. And it wasn't until many years later that she told me she really had been in love with Jimmy – with his crude manner, his boyish charm – but at the time, in 1987, it seemed as if she had put all her loving feelings on ice and in protest had transformed herself into the image that others had created for her.

'Stinna isn't herself any more,' said Mum, giving my

father an accusatory look during their nightly arguments.

'She's not to have any more visitors after midnight,' my father objected, but the prohibition had no effect on my sister. She was at high school, after all.

'That wasn't my intention,' said Jimmy. He was trying to make amends. In some sense he probably was in love with my sister, and to his great frustration, she no longer wanted to go steady with him.

Back then the only one who had anything good to say about her was Peter. He still arrived carrying flowers and then he would sit on her bed and sigh because he was nothing but air to his beloved. 'Peter is so sweet that he makes me want to throw up,' Stinna often said to Mum. 'All he wants to do is play Mum, Dad, and kids.'

And as for my ginger cousin and our non-existent love affair, I was . . .

'Forget about all that shit,' my sister interrupts me. 'Get to the point!'

Mum had the night shift at the hospital, Dad was in Copenhagen to take care of some business, and the Bath Plug was so nervous about several new letters from the tax authorities that he had rushed off in one of his fancy new cars, when I heard a scream.

The Bath Plug had been on a secret date and didn't remember that Dad was in Copenhagen when he climbed into his car. A Danish–Canadian female mountain-climber had turned his head a bit, even though she had slipped away from him like a flitting butterfly right before things got interesting. 'Damn it,' cursed the Bath Plug when he was alone in his car. The very next day his mountain-climber would be sitting in a plane on her way to the

Himalayas, and the Bath Plug felt a strange mixture of irritation and infatuation. All evening long, at five-minute intervals, she had made him feel alternately like a big shot and like a little boy. As if that weren't enough, there were those threatening letters from the tax authorities, containing words like 'possible indictment' and 'tax evasion'.

But the scream was not the first thing I heard. No, first I heard someone pounding on the front door and agitated voices asking for an impudent little brother who'd had the gall to let a tape circulate through the neighbourhood on which Stinna said that the smallest and most crooked dick of all dangled between the legs of Jimmy Madsen. 'Where is he?' they demanded, and when Stinna blocked their way, they shoved her aside and headed for my room.

'Asger!' Stinna yelled. 'Lock your door!'

I had already recognized one of the voices. It was Jimmy's. The other two I didn't know. 'Open up!' shouted Jimmy, pounding on my door. 'We want to talk to you.' But I had absolutely no desire to get into a discussion with those unexpected visitors. It was almost a year since I'd given Bjørn that infamous tape, but it was only today that several younger boys had called Jimmy over to play him the tape that was supposed to have been my perfect revenge. Not all the kids understood the meaning. 'Jimmy is laughing himself crooked,' they had shouted. 'He smokes too much shit!' But others did understand the insults behind my sister's ambiguous remarks.

'Watch out for the seagulls!' they shouted. 'Jimmy's got a worm, not a dick!'

Standing there behind the locked door with my heart pounding, I had no clue about the unfortunate fate of that tape.

411

'When are your parents coming home?' they said on the other side of the door.

'Soon,' lied Stinna.

'How about giving us a beer?'

'Uh-uh.'

'Bring us some beers,' said a voice I didn't recognize. Then there was total silence on the other side of the door for several minutes until my sister hinted that the tape in question very possibly could be telling the truth. What was going on out there? Glaring eyes, silence, the sound of flesh striking flesh. I heard: 'Or else we'll smash in the door,' followed at once by a swift 'okay', which didn't sound very encouraging.

So Stinna brought some beer for our unexpected visitors. Through the peephole I could see half of one of the boys I didn't know sitting on Stinna's bed, dripping cigarette ash on to the floor. 'Stop that!' yelled Stinna, and I promptly switched on the tape recorder just in case I might get something that I could use later on.

'It's damn nice in here,' said the boy I didn't know. 'This is quite a famous place, hee, hee . . . I've heard a lot about it . . . So this is where it all happens, hee, hee . . .'

What I remember best from that night was the 'hee, hee'. The laughter that rippled back and forth and was immortalized by my tape recorder. A malicious laughter that only got worse when one of the unknown boys pulled a bag out of his pocket and started rolling a joint.

Even Stinna smoked the hash after they pressured her long enough, but she wasn't laughing. 'Keep your hands off!' she cried instead. At one time my sister was famous for throwing a good punch. At one time she could make anyone shut up with a single glance, but on that evening she couldn't stop her visitors from getting more and more unpleasant.

'Maybe your parents aren't coming home tonight at all,' I recorded. 'That means we've got the whole night to ourselves. Hey! Where are you going?'

'I have to pee,' Stinna protested, but Jimmy blocked her way. I heard the sound of a key turning. 'Give me that!' cried my sister, as the key was passed from one grinning boy to another. Every time Stinna was about to grab the key, they would pinch her breasts and toss the key to the next boy. 'Jimmy, damn it all,' said my sister. 'What the hell is going on here?'

But it wasn't her usual self-confident voice that I heard that evening. It was the sound of someone who had lost both her magic wand and her control of the situation. Someone who suddenly was struck by the memory of a drunken Askild reaching out to touch her budding breasts while he laughed so hard that we could see his yellow pirate teeth.

'Let's see it,' I heard an unknown voice say. 'Let's see if it's really that little.'

'What?' said Jimmy. He no longer sounded mad; something hesitant had slipped into his voice.

'Don't touch me,' whimpered my sister.

'Come on!' I heard the unfamiliar voices say, and on the other side of the wall I was starting to feel a little desperate. Should I jump out of the window? Should I try to run for help? I had to pee too, and I was fumbling with an empty Coke bottle when, for the second time that evening, my sister spoke directly to me.

'Run over to Bjørn's!' she shouted.

'Don't worry, we won't take your pants all the way off—'

413

That last remark was imprinted on my mind – it was the key phrase from the treacherous tape that had prompted so much amusement in the neighbourhood. For a moment I stood there, frozen. I saw two hands grabbing hold of the waistband of Stinna's pants and pulling her down on the bed. In one last desperate attempt, she lashed out at Jimmy's face with a clenched fist, but hands grabbed her wrists and pressed her face against the mattress. When a person screams with her face against a mattress, it sounds much worse than a scream in the air, and the sound of my sister's sudden terror instantly released all paralysis from my body. *Should I or shouldn't I?* I turned the key and threw open the door. Hovering out in the hallway like a piece of lint that could be blown in any direction, I wasted several valuable moments wondering whether my fifteen years and ten months could make any difference. *Yes or no . . . No, no, no—* I rushed out of the front door, skidded down the drive, regained my balance, and dashed out into the street at the same instant that a fancy car came zooming up at high speed, heading for our drive. It was a sports car with wide tyres, its red paint job gleaming in the glow of the street lamp. I closed my eyes, and when I opened them again, I was lying on the hood of the car.

The Bath Plug jumped out. 'God damn it!' he swore. 'Are you crazy!'

I had hit my forehead on the windscreen, but I didn't break it. *The Bath Plug is very protective of his cars*, I thought irrationally as I climbed down from the hood, noticing something swelling on my forehead. Was I bleeding? Was I even conscious? Yes. But I couldn't say a word. I merely pointed, and the Bath Plug didn't understood me.

'Does it hurt a lot?' he asked, peering at the lump. 'Did you hurt yourself anywhere else? Can you feel your feet? What the hell is wrong?'

I don't know how much time we wasted there. I was down on all fours with stars dancing before my eyes, and the Bath Plug was bending over me, trying to get me to say something. Thirty seconds? An eternity? Valuable time passed while my sister was fighting a futile battle on that bed.

But it was the Bath Plug who rescued her. It was the Bath Plug who finally threw his compact body against my sister's door so that it flew open and rammed Jimmy right in the face. And it was the Bath Plug who froze for one brief moment at the sight of my sister lying on the bed with her pants down around her knees (in accordance with my taped manuscript, they had not taken her pants all the way off). It was also the Bath Plug who pursued two fleeing shadows out of the window, stumbled over a bench, and got grass stains on his shirt while the unknown boys vanished through the hole in the hedge and dispersed into the dark night. We could hear the Bath Plug swearing outside, but to our great surprise, Jimmy didn't budge. He was still standing behind the door with a lump on his forehead that no doubt looked a lot like mine.

'Get out!' screamed Stinna. 'Get out of here!'

He wanted to say something, but no words came out of his mouth. Stinna pulled up her pants and spat several times on the floor. Had they been inside her? And how long . . .

Not until the Bath Plug came back in the house did something happen with Jimmy. The Bath Plug took hold of his collar and head-butted him so that he fell to the floor with a bloody nose.

'You're staying here,' said the Bath Plug, breathing hard.

'Get out!' shouted Stinna, as blood dripped out of Jimmy's nose, forming a little dark puddle on the carpet.

'Yes, but—' gasped the Bath Plug.

'Get the hell out!' howled Stinna.

'We know who you are,' snarled the Bath Plug when he reluctantly let the culprit go. Still pale, with his bloody nose dripping, and without turning his back to us, Jimmy disappeared out of our story as his lips tried to shape the words that never came out. Later he would be transformed into a shadow that kept slipping out of my field of vision, disappearing around corners, and hiding at random intersections whenever I went past. The other two boys were Jimmy's friends. Stinna knew one of them, but not very well, she told me many years later. We didn't know the other one, and the only thing that I remember about him today is his laugh.

Jimmy closed the front door after him, dripping blood all the way down our drive, and the next moment an agitated Bath Plug was standing in the living room, about to call the police.

That's how Stinna prefers to see it – as if it were just a matter of a lost battle, a lump on the forehead, a rare defeat among many victories. And at last she managed to persuade the Bath Plug not to call the cops. She also made him promise not to say anything to Dad.

'I let them into the house myself,' she said many years later. 'I smoked hash with them. How would that look?'

Half an hour later Stinna had also persuaded the Bath Plug to go home. He was insisting that he should sleep on the sofa, but my sister wanted to get rid of him at all costs.

'We'd like to be alone,' she said apologetically. Feeling

rather bewildered, the Bath Plug got into his red sports car. 'Thank you,' Stinna whispered before he closed the car door.

Then we were once again alone in the house. Where were Mum and Dad? Why did they take up so little space in our story? An unpleasant silence enveloped us, and we sat down at the dining-room table, like two automatons expecting their dinner. I couldn't meet Stinna's eyes, and she was not the one who finally broke the silence and started crying that evening, after the Bath Plug had left. It was her little brother.

'Does it hurt?' Stinna asked me at once. She was not lucky enough to have a lump on her forehead. The next day I noticed two small bruises on her wrist. 'Did they—?' I asked. 'Did they get all the way—?'

'Only one of them,' she told me and then a moment later she added with that familiar scornful tone in her voice, 'Premature ejaculation.'

That made us both laugh a bit, but then we fell silent. What if she got pregnant? Stinna put her hand to her throat. 'I'm going to take a bath,' she said at last. I nodded.

'And then I want to be alone.'

The lump disappeared. My sister's bruises faded. Even the scratches on the hood of the Bath Plug's car disappeared after a visit to the body shop. But that laugh did not. It was a laugh that I had recorded on an infernal tape; I didn't dare listen to it, but I also refused to part with it. Even if I never played that tape again, I would still hear that laugh. It slipped into my Doghead dreams and got mixed up with the sound of my sister taking baths. Our heating bill soared, our water usage reached astronomical heights. In all that dripping and splashing, in the rushing of water through the pipes I heard the sound of a new era – another era over which I had no control. It was the sound of my sister trying to wash the degradation off her body. My sister, who several times a day would sink into the steaming water in the bathtub. Once she forgot to lock the door and I burst in on her to see a pale body lying at the bottom of the tub with open eyes, staring into space, her dark hair floating in all directions. When she pulled out the plug, she wrapped a towel around herself and left wet tracks all the way back to her room, like a dripping mermaid.

A few weeks after the rape she told Mum and Dad that she wanted to transfer to a different school, and after that she was rarely seen in the neighbourhood, except during the time it took for her to bicycle to classes. That was how she tried to make herself invisible. And the suitors also disappeared from our life. Many times I would hear a tentative knocking on her window, but Stinna never let them in. Finally they gave up. No more flowers, no more asinine words. The only one she allowed in was Peter. He would often sit in our kitchen, slurping his tea. He could also make her laugh, but he was never allowed to touch her. 'As long as he drops all that Mum-Dad-and-kids shit, he's sweet enough,' said Stinna. For some unknown reason she was no longer friends with Cousin Mia, and so my ginger-haired cousin remained the non-existent love affair of my early youth.

The Bath Plug never let the story seep out, but he no longer brought gifts of hair ribbons or little bottles of perfume. Instead, he would bring Stinna books which, without the knowledge of our parents, he put on her bookshelf. Books with titles such as *Woman, Know Your Body*, and *Rape and Therapy*. But my sister never read them. 'What do I want with that crap?' she said, purposely creasing the spines of the books so that the Bath Plug would think she had read them.

'What did you think of the book?' he would ask when they were alone.

'It was all right,' was Stinna's standard reply. 'But also a tiny bit boring, don't you think?'

And as the wet footprints revealed that my sister was in the process of changing herself into a mermaid, old stories were at work behind our backs. At that time we didn't know, of course, that a Danish–Canadian female mountain-climber was preparing her entrance into this story.

Late one night a quarter of a century earlier, Grandma Bjørk had seen a real dyed-in-the-wool demon, and as everyone knows, three is a magic number. The first time the demon appeared was at the end of a telescope. The second time it made an appearance in an unknown number of pink letters. And the third time it would step out of the ladies' room in a fashionable restaurant with a newly powdered nose and make two shady businessmen lose their heads.

The Female Mountain-Climber

EARLY ONE MORNING in June 1989 my father opened an insignificant-looking letter from the tax authorities and was brought to his knees by the strongest attack of dizziness he had yet experienced. And that was saying a lot. Lately he'd had numerous dizzy spells. Two days earlier one of his usual arguments with my mother, Leila, had escalated and, contrary to custom, Niels refused to settle for turning his back on her and peering out of the dark windows. Instead, he suddenly turned to face her and in one long tirade delivered his own version of his story for the very first time. The official story was that he was a workaholic who thought more about his business ventures than anything else. Whenever Leila, twice a month, found it necessary to say this, he always agreed with her. He promised to change. He would cut back on his work hours, he would be a more attentive husband and father ... He made these promises with both irritation and sincerity – and always with a disarming smile because deep inside he was convinced that she was right. But standing with his back to her on that ordinary

June evening in 1989, something made him fly into a rage, and he turned around and let a completely different story pour out of his mouth.

It was a story about a boy with big ears. Born in a privy. Mistreated by the kids on the street. Instructed in the art of nut-kicking . . . A boy who, with the help of equal parts of brutality and a savvy business sense, had conjured up a pot of gold at the end of the rainbow. The pot of gold wound up getting stolen, but never mind that. He bore no grudge. Nor did he surrender to gloomy thoughts. No, tree spirits had never gone through him. Did he ever run away, like certain other people? Didn't he still see his parents in spite of all their bickering and squabbling? Hadn't he paid for his sister's funeral? Of course he had!

But once upon a time he had been a very retiring young man, and everyone knows what that means. Such people surrender to vague daydreams. They sit in their rooms reading books in the glow of a gooseneck lamp, even though they really ought to run away. They're the type that needs a kick in the rear. And that's exactly what Niels got one day back in the early sixties, when he stepped through the door of a framing shop with *The Doctor and the Scalpel* under his arm and caught sight of his future wife. He was struck by a lightning bolt. All of a sudden the retiring young man grew up – jubilant at finally stepping into life and finding the strength to pursue his old dream about the pot of gold at the end of the rainbow. Nothing about ending up as his father. Nothing about allowing himself to be cheated by life or about sitting around swilling strong beer from bottles with gold labels.

But when he finally started to make money and could come home each evening and say: such and such orders were filled, and we have so and so much money in the till today, Leila started to say denigrating things about money – and she was the one who had set the whole thing in motion! She began discussing socialist ideas at business dinners and snapping at the Bath Plug who, aside from being an excellent business partner, was also his only friend. As if it were a crime to make money. As if there were something wrong with pursuing one's goals! He was, in spite of everything, a man who had provided for his family so that they were never forced to move from place to place and live a pitiful gypsy existence, the way he once had.

Of course he had made a few mistakes. For instance, investing too much effort in the framing shop. It's very possible that he got a bit of a swelled head and suffered from a temporary bout of arrogance at being the boss. But in the end he listened and let it go. Yet even after griping about the way he ran that business, Leila didn't feel like holding on to it. No, she sold the shop to Ib and started studying instead ... And during that time, while her attention was focused on her books and her time was filled with classes and training, Niels wasn't the one who grew apart from the family. She was the one who grew apart from him. She was the one who backed away. She found other friends, with whom he could never carry on a proper conversation. A different life, and all he could do was stand on the sidelines and watch. She was the one who finally became so absorbed in taking care of sick children in faraway hospitals and jabbered so much about Médecins Sans Frontières that she didn't notice that her own daughter was having problems. Or that her son, at the age of seventeen, still couldn't stop fantasizing about dogheads. Couldn't she see it? It was just the opposite! She was the one! It wasn't him! 'Damn it all!' bellowed Niels with such force that he woke both Stinna and me.

Fragments of Dad's story seeped through the walls, but neither of us felt like taking the trouble to go out in the hallway to listen. We were done with spying; our world wasn't going to fall apart just because our parents couldn't agree. Their fighting simply meant that we couldn't sleep, so Stinna decided to take a bath. I heard her turn on the taps, and in my mind I saw a mermaid sink down to the bottom of the bathtub with open eyes. She had washed off so many layers of her former self that occasionally I had a hard time recognizing her. I, in turn, put on my headphones and stared up at my reading lamp. Fragments of a story about a young man who could use a good kick in the rear made me think he was talking about me, and I got out an art book and began leafing through it. It was my first art book – Grandpa Askild had given it to me for my birthday because, unlike so many other people, I actually liked his cubist motifs, even though back then I already had my eye on the few symbolist art books that I found in an out-of-the-way place on the bookshelf in the house on Tunøvej.

'It's just the opposite!' shouted my father in the living room. 'Can't you see that?'

When the fight was over and my sister was as clean as she could possibly be, neither of us knew that my father had been struck by a dizzy spell that forced him to his knees in the living room after my mother had gone to bed. Nor did we know that he sat on the sofa downing coffee all night long while this new story about himself settled inside him. *Where did that come from?* he thought. *And why now?* Beneath the official story about Niels Jug Ears Junior as the absent father, an underwater mountain had shot up. But the story wasn't done yet. It was still creaking and groaning.

The following morning, one day before he opened that letter from the tax authorities, he awoke after only a few hours of sleep on the sofa and had no desire to get up. He lay on his back with his hands under his head and let his gaze roam over the ceiling. Leila had left without waking him. The kids were at school. He was alone in the house for the first time in a very long while, and the silence filled him with a strange feeling. Something was wrong. He let his gaze continue roaming over the walls: the brown hessian wall-covering that framed the room, the hideous painting that he had hung up to avoid any trouble, and all that worn furniture – for a successful businessman, he certainly didn't live very stylishly. The house was truly in need of a loving hand, he thought, and then he opened his eyes wide because, lying on the sofa at the age of forty-three, it suddenly dawned on him what was wrong: he didn't feel like going to work. That was a completely new sensation, and it bothered him because he had always felt such inexpressible joy each morning when he got into his Mercedes, switched on the cigarette lighter and the radio, and drove to the office, no matter what the weather. But right now he didn't have the slightest desire to go to work. A moment later he picked up the phone and lied to his secretary, saying he was sick while making a big show of coughing.

'A sore throat,' he said. Then he put on an old pair of

jeans and a tattered sweater and drove down to the local paint store to buy some white paint. Before long he had dragged most of the furniture out of the living room, and then he set about covering the old hessian wall-covering with big strokes of the brush. But he didn't really pay much attention to the painting he was doing. Leaping on to a ladder, waving around the brushes and buckets of paint, which dripped on to his hair and made countless splotches on his clothes, the story of the night before kept on churning inside him. Before Stinna came home at three, Niels realized that he had come to the wrong conclusions. He had never freed himself from his own story, and it was all Askild's fault. Askild had always been in the back of his mind, casting his relentless shadow over his son's life and sending Niels off to work every single day with only one goal in mind: not to end up like his father. Was that something on which to build his whole life?

That's how the stories began working on him as our dark living room was transformed into a big bright room. And, according to Stinna, Dad's behaviour was very peculiar. 'Hey! Want to help me paint? What did you do at school today? How are things going, anyway?'

Stinna replied, 'No. Nothing special. Okay.' And then she went off to take a bath. I dropped by Tunøvej on my way home from school and helped Grandma Bjørk feed Mamma Randi and listened to her complain about her own dreary existence since retiring. That was why I didn't see Dad leaping around the living room leaving spots of white paint on everything.

Mum came home too, but the mood between my parents had not improved. She retreated to the kitchen and started banging pots and pans. Why was she always

425

the one who had to do the cooking? Not a damned thing had changed since Madam Mother, back at the dawn of time, had transformed Leila into a kitchen maid! Niels kept on painting the living room, and then early in the evening the phone rang.

'A sore throat, huh? That's a good one. There's someone you have to meet,' said the Bath Plug, sounding slightly drunk. 'Come on, get over here.'

'Not today, okay?' said Niels Jug Ears Junior. He wasn't feeling sociable. The living room was only half finished, everything was a mess, and he knew quite well that it was the Bath Plug's female mountain-climber that he was supposed to meet. For the past year the Bath Plug had been talking about her non-stop. On the wall of the partners' office hung a postcard showing a snow-capped Everest, but even though it had always reminded Niels of a picture from Greenland, he had never taken the trouble to turn the postcard over.

He didn't change his clothes. He didn't think about the fact that he was on his way to one of the city's most fashionable restaurants. Nor did it occur to him how idiotic he looked: the old clothes with spots of paint everywhere; even his face was splotched with paint. He could see white beads of paint in his eyelashes whenever he blinked. But he didn't care, and he told himself that he wouldn't waste more than half an hour on one of the Bath Plug's fluctuating lady friends; then he would go back home.

'Where is she?' asked Niels a little while later when he stepped inside the restaurant, annoyed at the way the waiter was staring at him.

'Powdering her nose, of course,' snickered the Bath Plug.

'My God, you look like shit! A sore throat, huh? A likely story. Are we planning to invest in the paint business?'

But Niels was in no mood to banter with the Bath Plug. He sat down and began drumming his fingers impatiently on the table. The waiter was still staring at him. Was that the way people stared at his father? The waiter knew quite well who he was. Annoyed that the man's goodwill was apparently limited to his clothing, Niels stared back until the waiter looked away.

'This female mountain-climber of yours,' said Niels, 'what exactly is her name?' He had heard a good deal about the Bath Plug's latest lady friend, even though he had listened with only half an ear. He'd heard about her marriage to an elderly, wealthy Canadian who had died a few years back. About her youthful expeditions across the inland ice of Greenland; about her dream of reaching the North Pole with her dogsled. She failed the first time because of a snowstorm, but later succeeded in spite of a sprained foot and a minor quarrel with a polar bear. She did reach the North Pole, but that was just the start, because that's when her obsession with mountains began.

First the puny category, as she used to say, shaking her head indulgently – Kilimanjaro, Cotopaxi – and later the more daredevil expeditions: Mont Blanc, Aconcagua . . . The mountain-climber had never forgotten how she had once stood on the top branch of an elm tree in the back yard on Nyboværftsvej in Ålborg, swaying in the wind like a monkey. She discovered the Himalayas – Ganesh Himal, Langtang Lirung, Cho Oyo – getting closer and closer to the decisive elm tree, the roof of the world, the most daredevil venture of all, the ultimate bike ride wearing a blindfold, which was successfully accomplished when she, at the age of thirty-six, climbed Mt Everest without the use of oxygen along with her old friend McWalter. They made it to the summit. They stood up there at the top. The world lay at their feet – triumph, triumph. But beyond the intoxication, which made them both crazy, she also felt an unexpected sense of disappointment. Now she couldn't get any higher. And the descent that awaited them was also a descent in a metaphoric sense. But she pushed the thought aside, and on their way back down they wound up feeling so giddy – as frisky as a couple of puppies, as silly as a pair of sixteen-year-olds making daredevil plans – that on the third day McWalter misjudged a glacier crevasse in the icefall. It was a foolish mistake; it was so unnecessary that, far away from the peak, he should plunge 30 metres down to where it was impossible to fish him back out.

McWalter's Final Descent was the name of her book, which had enjoyed reasonable success in Canada. There was something disturbing about the way in which she dealt with the loss of her old friend. Grief was not the only thing that could be read between the lines of her book. *Maybe we both should have ended up there. Maybe it was a mistake that I continued down to base camp. Why not accept the consequences? The ultimate descent after the ultimate ascent.*

Yes, people thought that there was truly something daredevil about her. But she found new elm trees. There were other mountains in the world, and she didn't care if people talked. Grandma Bjørk had known it all along. For her, Marianne Qvist had always been a demon.

'What?' said the Bath Plug, staring impatiently in the direction of the ladies' room. Before he managed to say another word, the door flew open and out came Marianne Qvist with her nose newly powdered. She tossed back her hair, puckered up her lips at the Bath Plug, who instantly got to his feet and smoothed out his shirt. Then she walked without hesitation over to their table. Her face, formerly so plump, was now sharply accentuated; her nose seemed bigger, and a network of fine wrinkles surrounded her eyes. But having recently returned from the cold peaks of the Himalayas, she was in the best condition of her life, and the frost, which a few weeks back had threatened to devour her cheeks, had now given them a ruddy, healthy appearance.

'Hi,' she said, as if it were the most natural thing in the world to find Niels Jug Ears Junior sitting there. 'Weren't the two of us supposed to run away together?'

My father didn't say a word.

'Do you *know* each other?' asked the Bath Plug.

'Have you gone grey already? Oh, it's just paint. If Slotsholm here hadn't told me so much about you, I'd think you had ended up in the wrong place. You look like some sort of house painter. By the way, how's it going with that parrot? Have you been spying on any naked girls? And how about your father – did he drink himself to death?' said Marianne Qvist without stopping for breath. And then she coughed.

'I think your friend here is trying to get me drunk. He thinks that an extra glass or two will make an old lady like me drop my knickers, but as I've said all along: keep your mitts off, Slotsholm. After a good dinner I'm willing to go so far as to say that you possess a certain charm, but you'll never get my knickers off . . . And what about you?' Marianne Qvist went on, a little tipsy, as she gave the two shady businessmen a ravishing glance that hit them right in the gut. 'Are you happily married? Kids and all that, I hear, and you've started wearing a moustache. Surely that must be a mistake.'

My father was struck by his second dizzy spell in twenty-four hours. The walls were spinning, the floor was pitching, and in the midst of that revolving carousel sat a forty-two-year-old female mountain-climber.

'Cat got your tongue, huh? I actually had a feeling that it was you – Slotsholm, you know. He talks about you all the time. Listen here! Slotsholm, order some champagne. I think our friend could use something fortifying to drink. It's not always pleasant to have your past catch up with you.'

She was right about that. But as Marianne Qvist kept up her ceaseless chatter, bewildering fragments from half a lifetime ago were swirling around in Niels's mind. Opportunities that were passed by but had lived on in his subconscious suddenly came bubbling up from the depths in a fashionable restaurant at the sight of a female mountain-climber with a newly powdered nose. Images of an exciting life filled with genuine challenges, which, for his part, had come to a halt with a bicycle ride wearing a blindfold, while others possessing a more vigorous nature, like *her*, for example, had taken up the challenge . . . But why hadn't he run away? A familiar story, even though for Niels it was only a day old, provided the answer: Askild had made him stay. Askild was the one who had made certain that Niels Junior stayed on safe ground. At least in the beginning. Business school instead of adventures in Greenland, framing shops instead of ice-bergs. *What the hell was all that?* he thought, but suddenly

430

an image, sharp as a razor, appeared in his mind's eye: a green teddy bear rose up from the depths and started to laugh. 'Gypsy Hans!' were the first words Niels uttered, as he stared off into space. 'Wasn't that his name? Gypsy Hans?'

'Gypsy Hans?' queried the Bath Plug.

'Gypsy Hans?' said Marianne Qvist, giving him a smile. 'I can't believe it! Is that the only thing you can think about? After twenty-five years?'

'What the hell are you two talking about?' snapped the Bath Plug, but then the waiter arrived with the champagne, and the Bath Plug definitely didn't care for the look in Marianne's eyes. He didn't like the way she was staring at his partner. Here he sat in his expensive suit, a man in his prime with a firm grip on his life, and then Niels shows up in a pair of old jeans, and what happens? Suddenly he says 'Gypsy Hans' and immediately wins so many points that everyone else might as well pack up and go home. Niels had waded right into her life, disguised as a simple tradesman. Or at least he had aroused something in Marianne, and the Bath Plug had no clue what that might be.

Afterwards, while the two turtle doves sat and talked at the table without giving him a single glance, the Bath Plug thought Marianne actually seemed a bit patronizing towards him. Of course, he was used to her crude tone, but all the same . . . She also kept refilling his glass, and it seemed as if she were challenging him outright to a child-ish drinking competition. Bottoms up, don't be a wimp . . . That champagne cost two thousand kroner! But he wasn't stingy, and before long the man with a firm grip on his life was getting more and more drunk. Finally he ended up tipping over his glass when he stood up to go to the men's room. That's when the two turtle doves decided to send him home in a cab.

'I can drive myself,' said the Bath Plug, slurring his words.

'Uh-uh,' said Marianne, fishing the car keys out of his trouser pocket.

He received a kiss on the cheek from his female mountain-climber and a slap on the back from his partner, who now seemed to be in high spirits. 'Don't worry about the bill. I'll take care of it—'

What the hell was all that? thought Slotsholm. Did she get me soused on purpose? What are they doing now? Isn't Niels a married man, the father of two children – one of them a pimply boy, the other a beautiful young girl with whom I've always been slightly infatuated? Unfaithful? It just wasn't like him!

There they sat. The Bath Plug was out of the way. *I can't stand you any more*, were Marianne's last words to the great love of her youth. *I bet that trick with the teddy bear was all a fake* should have been Niels's last words, but now it seemed as if the discord of the past had been replaced by enthusiasm. They stayed at the restaurant for another hour. They took turns reciting asinine words from their letters while they laughed boisterously. They went further back in time, pausing at various things they had done: bicycle acrobatics, wrestling matches on the windowsill, daring performances with Gypsy Hans as the guest star. But each time they finished telling a story, they would draw parallels to the bike ride with the blindfold, and their first big project infused them both with a mood of pensive enthusiasm.

'Those were the days, weren't they?' said Marianne.

After going over all the daredevil ventures of the past in distant Ålborg, it seemed to Niels as if the future were bending over him and tapping him on the shoulder.

'Let's run out without paying the bill,' Marianne whispered in his ear. 'I bet you've never tried that.'

'Okay,' replied Niels, thinking that it would be a suitable revenge for the waiter's patronizing glances. So Marianne went out to the ladies' room, and by the time Niels joined her a few minutes later, she had already opened the window above the toilet and was standing there smoking a cigarette in the breeze of that warm June evening. She really did look like a dream girl from the enchanted forests. Niels stepped up on the toilet seat, kissed her on the neck, which was sinewy and strong, and suddenly he couldn't understand how twenty-five years could have passed. What had he been doing all this time? Why had he been so absent from life? He wanted to share his thoughts with her, but by then she had already crawled halfway out of the window. 'Don't just stand there gawking,' she giggled. 'Help me get my fat ass out.'

Niels shoved her the rest of the way out of the window, and when he too crawled out, they both collapsed on the grass. Then they stood up and ran down the middle of the street giggling, following the traffic lanes. They continued down to the harbour jetties, where they leapt from rock to rock, pausing at the sight of their reflections in the black water. Behind my father lay all the bickering and squabbling of the past; ahead waited the triumphs and victories of the future. Even though they didn't mention it, they both knew where they were headed: to the first hotel that would provide lodging for their long-dormant love. Niels threw open the hotel door and woke the night porter, who stood there gaping at the middle-aged couple running up the stairs like two foolish teenagers. Not until he was lying on his back in the wide double bed did Niels realize how drunk he was. The last thing he noticed was his stiff dick rising into the air, and the soft sensation of a woman bearing down on him. 'Hell and damnation,' Marianne murmured ten minutes later, waking him up with a slap on the cheek. 'You're certainly not young any more, are you?'

When Niels awoke the next morning, it was seven o'clock and his head was pounding. Next to him lay a snoring Marianne Qvist. And even though he ought to have hurried home, he stayed where he was, looking at her. A little blob of spit had gathered at the corner of her mouth, and he couldn't take his eyes off it. Finally he cautiously licked it away and then went off to take a bath. But he kept coming back into the room to see if she was still there.

'I'm going to have to go home now,' he said when he woke her an hour later. 'But are you doing anything tonight?'

'Oh, is that *you* again?' replied Marianne, staring at him with bloodshot eyes. 'Go on home to your wife, Niels. Take your kids to the zoo. I'm leaving for Canada next week. God, how my head hurts.'

'I may be married,' said Niels, 'but that doesn't mean I'm going to let you go.'

Back at home, having called in sick to his secretary, Niels Jug Ears Junior shaved off his moustache, which had adorned his lip ever since he, as a new father, was struck by the Fang fervour. Out in the hallway, he cast a swift glance at himself in the mirror and at the same instant heard the soft plop of a letter falling through the letter box. It was one of the usual letters from the tax authorities, and without giving it much thought, he opened the envelope and let his eyes slide absent-mindedly over the page. *After innumerable notifications, etc. etc. have not repudiated suspicions regarding a host of inaccuracies blah blah . . . it has been decided to turn the matter over to the police . . .* On 7 June 1989, Niels Junior Eriksson was brought to his knees by his third major dizzy spell in two days. The walls swayed, the floor spun, and a short time later, some children who were playing soccer out on the street heard a man shout *Fuck!* They looked in our yard but saw no one. They kept an alert eye on the deserted yard, and half an hour later they saw an agitated Niels Eriksson running out of our drive, looking like a bad-tempered little boy. It could have been the lack of his moustache that made the forty-three-year-old man suddenly look like a boy, or it could have been something else entirely, because five minutes later he yanked open the door to the house on Tunøvej.

There stood his mother with a tea towel in her hands; yes, there she stood – the LETTER THIEF, who was so infatuated with doctors that she let him spend his child-hood wearing that *shitty contraption*. And there stood his father – the alcoholic, the tyrant, the THIEF – who had just emerged from the bathroom – the one who, all his life, had been so thirsty that he stole the pot of gold at the end of the rainbow and afterwards beat his son with a belt.

And there stood the son . . . Both parents gave Niels a strange look. He promptly opened his mouth and began shouting so loudly that even Mamma Randi awoke from her stupor in the room that had once belonged to fat Aunt Anne Katrine. He accused them of old crimes, of long-forgotten missteps. Forty-three years of bile came pouring out of the son's mouth; spittle, uncompromising words, and accusations never before voiced were all jumbled together. The gaping parents didn't understand a thing. Hadn't there always been food on the table? Didn't they love their son, and weren't they proud of him when he came driving up to their house, by this time quite dilapidated, in his fancy Mercedes? Hadn't Bjørk bragged about him at her gambling club? Hadn't Askild always wished that just once in his life Niels might drop by the Corner so that his drinking buddies could have a look at his son? But Niels refused to set foot in the place. He had always been embarrassed by his parents, and over the past couple of years he hadn't visited them very often, to put it mildly.

Not until later – when their son, after a delay of twenty-five years, had run off – did Bjørk find out that the whole thing was the fault of the demon whom she had once seen performing obscene acts with a green teddy bear in Ålborg. And Askild knew that it was because his son, at that moment, in that situation, could think only with his dick. But half an hour later, when the door slammed shut with a bang and their son vanished as suddenly as he had arrived, they both sank on to the sofa and stared morosely into space. Grandpa Askild with his fly open and Grandma Bjørk clutching a tea towel in one hand. Not until much later did they muster enough strength to get up.

Dad continued on his rounds. Other people also received a visit from Niels Eriksson on that day: banks, for instance; bankrupt businesses; companies ripe for re-organization ... Niels shut down and closed up, hiding away documents, packing his suitcase, and behaving in a particularly loving manner towards his children, even though he would give no reason for it. And a week later he was sitting next to Marianne Qvist in a plane headed for Canada. It was late one evening in June, shortly before Midsummer, and all the way across the Atlantic they were flying towards the dancing evening sun. 'We're finally doing it, damn it all,' she whispered in his ear. The fact that Dad, a few days earlier, had initiated her into his problems with the tax authorities, did not make their reunion any less joyous. Technically, she was now travelling with a wanted criminal. 'Here *we* come,' she went on in her distinct, clear voice. 'Hold on to your hats and glasses!'

And so – his eyes on the sun that refused to set – Dad disappeared from our story. The living-room walls were only half painted, everything was in a mess, Mum didn't understand a thing, and the Bath Plug didn't receive the infamous tax letter until a couple of days later. He too was struck by a dizzy spell, but unlike certain other people, he did not simply give up. He tried to salvage what he could. He sat up for nights on end, the sweat dripping on to the vast accounts, but finally he had to conclude that he was sitting in shit up to his neck. Several times after Dad disappeared, he showed up at our house on Birkebladsvej and spent hours rummaging through boxes and enormous piles of papers. If we tried to offer our help, he would get annoyed, because there he was – a man with a firm grip on life – on his knees in Dad's office while everything was collapsing all around him.

But as the weeks passed, he became more approachable. He also had many conversations with Stinna in the kitchen while Mum worked the night shift. 'I know where he is. I'll find him, all right,' the Bath Plug would moan.

Mum got a letter a couple of weeks later. She read it quickly, then hid it away and said, 'Your father has replaced me with a younger model. That's how men are. They can't stand to get old.'

That was her way of explaining the whole wretched affair – even though Marianne Qvist was only a year and a half younger than Mum, but she found that significant.

'Your father isn't the one behind all this,' lamented Bjørk. '*She's* the one, that hussy.'

'Sweet Mother of God,' whispered Mamma Randi when she realized in a lucid moment two months later that Niels Junior was no longer in Denmark. 'Has he run off to sea too?'

By that time Dad had finally pulled himself together enough to write to the Bath Plug. The same day that the Bath Plug was supposed to put in an appearance at the police station to begin the first of a long series of interrogations, he drove instead to Copenhagen Airport, left his fancy car at a random parking spot, and climbed on board a plane for Montreal.

From the interrogations that were begun a good year later, it became quite clear that the two suspects had withdrawn large sums of money from their bank accounts. There were even rumours that up until the very last minute they had been milking a number of companies that were either bankrupt or ripe for reorganization. Angry creditors tore at their hair, employees feared for their jobs, and CEOs had to confess openly that they had been no match for the situation – they had been roundly duped by the two con men . . . In hindsight, maybe we should have known. In hindsight, everything always looks quite clear, provided the rear-view mirror isn't misted over.

PART SEVEN

Mt Blakhsa

O UR STORIES WERE dripping with water; yes, the rear-view mirror was covered with mist, and one fine day I could no longer distinguish my story from the haze rising up from the swamp behind our old house, or from the dense cloud of steam that came pouring out of the bathroom whenever my sister threw open the door and left wet footprints all the way back to her room. That's how it was for years, until the fresh air began to arrive in tins from Bergen, and Grandma Bjørk's confused chatter spun new threads and wove tapestries that appeared on our retinas, giving a new perspective to my hazy tales. But by convincing herself that Dad is the generous sender of all that fresh air, Grandma is ignoring the fact that sixteen months after Dad's sudden disappearance the darkness went through us.

The darkness was a phone call that came late one evening.

And after it went through us, Mum saw God, Stinna started at the university, and I myself swiped six tubes of paint from the shed with the stolen bicycles and painted

443

a dripping mermaid, which made my sister give me a disapproving look. It was my first painting, but she didn't much care for it. 'I don't take that many baths any more,' she said.

The Bath Plug was the one who made the call. On his way up a mountain that we'd never heard of, in a country we didn't even know Dad had gone to, their sherpa, in a dream vision, had caught a glimpse of a black woman with a red tongue and a belt from which dangled several decapitated heads. Marianne Qvist had seen a dog, which she thought was her old friend McWalter. The Bath Plug had caught a glimpse of a crow that spread its wings and flew higher up Mt Blakhsa, and Dad heard a voice that hadn't been heard since it was banished from the enchanted forests of Nordland in 1959. *Hey, sonny, things are going splendidly, but maybe we should see about turning our noses in the other direction* . . . Marianne had prepared them for the fact that people often saw ghosts up on the slopes because of the lack of oxygen, but their sherpa refused to go any further, and so they continued on alone, while the sherpa and the rest of the expedition set up camp.

A few hundred metres from the top they had a quarrel. Slotsholm wanted to go back down; he was afraid. Doubt overcame him, and he abandoned the two insane turtle doves. He didn't think he would have trouble finding his way down to camp, but he got lost in a snowstorm, broke his sun goggles, and began roaming around on the mountain, blindly and frantically, until the two lovers, with their arms wrapped around each other, appeared before him in freefall. In an icy vision, they fell from the sky, and after the vision came a faint rumbling from up on the mountain. Masses of snow came loose and ice started rushing down the slope. The Bath Plug blacked out, and when he regained consciousness, it was night. The stars were sparkling and the snowstorm had subsided, leaving a cold and clear wind that howled in his ears. His nose was swollen, and ice had made its way deep inside his bones. *Maybe I'm already dead*, he thought, closing his eyes again. But no sooner did his eyelashes touch and, mixed with his tears, freeze to ice than the Bath Plug was dazzled by his second vision within a few hours. This time the vision was a bit more prosaic, because he saw my sister standing next to a shopping cart in a supermarket, buying groceries with his two boys. The sight of those three shoppers made him open his eyes; the ice cracked and his eyelashes snapped in half.

On that night Grandma Bjørk dreamt that a bird had strayed into her living room and was striking its head against the windowpane because it wanted to get out. It was the same bird that Applehead had seen as a little boy, back when strange things were happening out in the privy. But this time the bird lay on the floor until Askild gathered it up and threw it into the rubbish bin. Bjørk woke up, went out to pee, and then went in to cast a quick glance at Askild, who was sitting in the living room with a glass of milk. In Aunt Anne Katrine's old room, Mamma Randi was sleeping with her eyes open, and in the living room on Birkebladsvej, Mum was drinking red wine with a newly trained doctor, whom we later would dub 'Madam Father'.

* * *

But at the camp farther down the mountain, the mood was not quite as relaxed. The wind was singing, the tents were fluttering, and several hours later the sherpa, unable to sleep, was shaken from his torpor by an abominable snowman, who came bursting into the tent. *Him*, of all people? The fat one? It couldn't be true!

But the snowman didn't see their horror-stricken faces. His eyes had vanished inside his swollen head. His nose looked like a cracked pumpkin spewing out frozen bits of vomit and blood. They tried taking off his gloves, but when they saw the frostbite on his fingers they instantly put them back on. Next they tried removing his boots, but the result was the same. He couldn't possibly be alive. There were only a few hours left until sunrise, and he undoubtedly would never see the first rays of the sun climbing up over the mountain. And that turned out to be true, because the Bath Plug could see nothing when the sun appeared. His eyes were still buried deep inside his suppurating potato face when half the expedition prepared to transport the dying man while the other half went out to search for Marianne Qvist and her companion. But it was as if they had vanished into the earth. Not a single footprint could the search party find, and later, when they stood before the mountainside showing the deep scars of an avalanche, they gave up.

The other half of the expedition was promised a helicopter farther down in Bhanjsang for the man who was apparently not dying after all, but he didn't see the metallic bird coming to rescue him. Nor did he see the doctors in Kathmandu who later received him and removed the sorry remains of his nose. Five and a half fingers had to be amputated, four toes were beyond

446

rescuing, half of one ear was sliced off, and when the man finally awoke, he hardly looked human at all. Kind doctors took away all mirrors. Even so, early one morning he caught sight of the noseless monster reflected at the bottom of a metal dish.

He wept when we picked him up at the airport. He cried during the lengthy interrogations, confessing to everything, personally taking all the blame, even though many matters were never resolved and rumours would always be the most important witnesses in the case. *Con Artists on Their Asses in Himalayas* said the worst of the newspaper headlines. But there's no reason to go into detail or to mention how Grandpa Askild and Grandma Bjørk began fanatically reading the daily papers. They devoured everything they could find, sitting in their living room on Tunøvej and staring at the growing pile of newspapers as they searched for the last truth about their son.

Nor is there any reason to dwell on the fact that Askild started showing up at Birkebladsvej at all hours because he thought we were in need of some paternal authority. After the death of my fat aunt, he had gone to the dogs, but now he reacted quite differently. He got his drinking under control, he shaved, he ironed his own shirts, and he started turning up at Birkebladsvej every morning. He was afraid that our lives would fall apart. He thought that it was his responsibility to make sure we went to school, that the house was cleaned up, and that Mum bought groceries so there would be a hot meal on the table every evening. Tranquillity and regular routines seemed to be Grandpa's answer to the darkness that had gone through us, but during that time we mostly felt like falling apart.

'It's none of your business,' shouted Stinna whenever Askild started telling his granddaughter, who was now a university student, why she should come home in the evenings.

'He was the one who left me,' snarled my mother whenever Askild spoke disparagingly about Preben, her new boyfriend. She would often sit and drink red wine with Preben until the wee hours of the morning.

'Leave me alone!' I yelled whenever I was in my room with all my painting supplies and Grandpa pounded on my locked door because he wanted me to go to school.

Several years later I often wondered whether our common interest in painting might have restored the connection between us if I had allowed him in. But back then Grandpa was both too much and too little at the same time. We couldn't stand to see him arrive every morning, wearing his newly ironed shirt, with his hair plastered down and those bitter lines around his mouth. It was unbearable that Grandpa Askild, who had fought his own endless battle against falling apart, should teach us anything about order and structure. In short, he poked his nose into everything. He examined my report cards and called the high school to find out why I'd been given such low marks in Latin. One day he called my mother's office because he thought they should give her fewer shifts at night and at weekends. But that was also the last straw. When Askild arrived the next morning, Mum had just come home from the night shift. We were having breakfast when she caught sight of Grandpa, and she stood up to hurl a milk carton at him. She didn't say a word. She merely screamed – one shrill, sustained scream, astonishing us with how loud it was and how long it lasted. The milk carton struck the wall just behind Askild's head. The blow knocked out the bottom of the carton and sprayed the left side of Grandpa's face with milk.

The next day he didn't show up, nor did we see him on the following days. Not until a week later, when I was biking through the open areas around the swamp, did I catch sight of him. He was lying under one of the newly installed benches with a bottle of aquavit in his hand. I biked right past him, hoping he wouldn't see me. Two hours later I went back to make sure that he wasn't dead. But by then Grandpa Askild was gone. He must have got up and staggered home in a drunken stupor. Maybe somebody helped him.

None of us had seen Dad for a year and a half. We hadn't even talked to him on the phone, and so it was difficult for us to surrender to the grief. Nor were there any great outbursts of emotion at the church service we held in his memory. Grandma Bjørk cried a bit, but most of the time she seemed silent and withdrawn, just like the rest of us.

Slotsholm was the only one who gave his emotions free rein. One day Stinna remarked that he had apparently decided to produce enough tears for the whole family. He sobbed in front of the assistant chief of police, who wanted to record his nasal voice, and in front of the newspaper photographers who wanted to immortalize his noseless swindles. His tears made big dark splotches on his leather briefcase when his sentence was handed down in court: fifteen months in prison, confiscation of all mortgage deeds, stocks, and bank accounts, as well as a ban on starting any new businesses. But the Bath Plug didn't seem to care. At that time my sister had already become a regular visitor at Horsens State Penitentiary. Every Wednesday she would skip her classes at the university and catch a train, fixing her gaze on the passing landmarks, to spend a couple of hours in the company of the noseless man. At first, she mostly wanted to pump him for information. What had they been doing for the past year and a half? How was Dad during that time? Did he ever talk about his daughter? Dad's last year of life was like a puzzle that only slowly fell into place, and every Wednesday evening I waited anxiously for the latest news. But later, after all the information had been pumped out of him, Stinna kept on visiting.

She had never forgotten how, long ago, he had smashed open the door to her room, chased the uninvited visitors out into the dark, head-butted Jimmy, and started putting books on her bookshelf. But now the roles were reversed. Now it was Stinna who sent the Bath Plug's ghosts fleeing. She was the one who lent an ear to his Chagall-like visions, his sudden confession that he had always been a sceptic, a half-hearted husband, a bad father. In between the tears and the snot that poured out from under the patch hiding the sorry remains of his nose, secrets were passed on, and finally the pact was sealed. Stinna knew something about the Bath Plug that no one else knew, and he knew something about my sister that only I and three others knew. She shared his grief, wandering with him through the dead ends of memory, up and down Mt Blakhsa and all the way back to his childhood – back to when he was a fat little boy running through the streets selling newspapers and dreaming of fame. And he did find fame, but not the kind he had imagined. But eventually his candour began to be a little too much for my sister, and she tried instead to get him to think about other things. 'You could get a new nose – one made of plastic. And that's just as good, isn't it?' she said, patting his shoulder to cheer him up. 'So what are we going to do when you get out?'

But the Bath Plug was not easily diverted to other thoughts, and before long it wasn't enough for Stinna to offer him encouragement, gently stroking his hair and whispering sweet words into his half-ear. No, Stinna was overcome by a sense that something was missing; a gaping hole had started to grow inside her, and it wasn't just the empty place once occupied by a father. That wasn't what was tormenting her. It was something else, an increasing void, a vague longing, a hunger that could not be satisfied. *Oh no, not the Bath Plug, damn it!* she thought as she sat in the train on her way home. *Not a middle-aged man without a nose! Oh God, I'm going to die!* But by then it was already too late, and the longing began to produce strange visions: the Bath Plug in her nightly dreams, the Bath Plug absolutely everywhere. In the visitors' room at Horsens State Penitentiary, as he lay on a bench with dishevelled hair, her attempts to cheer him up became more and more clumsy. She started spouting angry accusations and tugging at his shirt. One afternoon she spat right in his face, and another time she said that she wished he too had died on the mountain.

'Stop all that blubbering!' Stinna screamed at last, pounding on his chest. 'Take off your clothes, act like a man, and do it with me!'

For the first time since Mt Blakhsa a smile appeared on

Slotsholm's face, making its way through disbelief and wild astonishment. *What? Is she talking to me?* Then the smile emerged fully. At least his nuts hadn't frozen off.

Askild's Landscapes

GRANDMA BJØRK is standing on the corner of Tunøvej, waving. Grandma Bjørk is running towards the prison in Oslo, even though Askild has already been sent to Germany.

Over the years countless stories arose, but on that night when my mother Leila stood on the stairs in her nightgown to deliver the news from a mountain that Grandma had never heard of, Bjørk stopped telling stories. And no one ever urged her to break her silence again. Neither Stinna nor I had any desire to hear any more stories. There was something painful connected with them, and also something hypocritical. At that time none of us realized that the stories were the glue holding our family together, because it was only after they vanished that everything began to disintegrate, and slowly we were scattered to the winds.

That's how things were for about ten years until Bjørk broke her silence and started sending fragments of our story to Amsterdam by mail. But there are still some stories she refuses to tell again: how she lost her older son to a crazy woman. How his only earthly remains were some clothes that they placed in the coffin along with Pappa Niels's first-mate's cap and a handful of pink letters, which her grandson tossed into the grave at the last minute. He had swiped them from the cupboard, and suddenly they were drifting down towards the darkness like a pink snowstorm as the pastor began the graveside ceremony. Grandma Bjørk didn't know if he did it in recognition of the love story contained in those letters or in anger over the treachery they symbolized, but, no matter what the reason, it created a minor uproar. Askild wanted to fish them out of the grave. Mum wanted to leave them there; she just wanted the ceremony to be over so she could go home. And Grandma Bjørk . . . well, she didn't know what to think. Her world no longer made any sense. People were dying in the wrong order. Her feeling that there was something unnatural about the whole thing didn't diminish when her mother-in-law, now 103 years old, got up from her rocking chair, demanded elk meat, and proceeded to cook for the dispirited funeral party that had stood at the grave quarrelling over a handful of pink letters. But that was only a brief flowering. The following week Randi had again slipped into lethargy.

Nor had Grandma Bjørk said anything about how she gradually lost contact with Mum, who found a young doctor called Preben, saw the God she had denied ever since the death of her father Hans Carlo, and finally left to fulfil her mission in life and take care of the world's orphaned children. That didn't happen until Stinna and I had moved away from home, but Bjørk still couldn't understand it. She had seen the crucifix glittering on the thin silver chain around my mother's neck. She had also seen the love-bites that the young doctor had given Leila. And she had heard Mum tell the story about the night in the living room when God had returned to her life. But for Grandma Bjørk, God had always been something inside people and not the motorcycle-driving fop that she pictured whenever Leila talked about Him. Nor did Grandma Bjørk realize that at the funeral Leila had felt like a Madam Mother.

In spite of the huge quantity of divorce papers in our cupboards, Mum had not divorced Dad. And so she was technically a widow and now stood like any other Madam Mother in the cemetery, saying goodbye to a husband who had plunged to his death with another woman. There were countless parallels with Madam Mother's situation, and in the next few months Leila was haunted more and more by ghosts from the past. Maybe it was her unresolved grief about her father Hans Carlo that caused this. Or maybe it was triggered by her feelings about her mother Elisabeth or the expression in her children's eyes. Apathy engulfed her; insomnia made her wander restlessly through the house. She no longer even had the energy to put Askild in his place when he arrived to instil our family with a little patriarchal authority. Her children became peripheral. They had their own lives independent of hers, and she often felt like a little girl standing all alone near a forest lake, trying to eat the world's biggest ice-cream cone.

Nausea and a cold sweat and dancing stars. For all of this she could find a natural explanation. But what she couldn't explain were the visions that started to overpower her in broad daylight: glimpses of a flooded basement; mud-covered furniture; loud roars, as if from a motorcycle revving up in the distance. Soon these visions began to coalesce into a film; brief scenes passed over her retina and convinced her that she was about to go mad – until suddenly she understood. These visions showed her the same world that she had once seen in a series of water-damaged photographs in her religious childhood. They reflected worlds of consensus and coherence. Worlds that could give orphans courage. Worlds radiating with an energy she had lost when, the night after Hans Carlo's funeral, she had uttered a defiant vow: *Hocus pocus, there are no supernatural beings; there is nothing mysterious between heaven and earth.*

Her life collapsed. She started snapping at Preben. One day she tried to hit Askild with a milk carton, and that very night the shutters gave way to the surging waters. Cascades of water, dissolved letters and blurred photographs sloshed around her until she felt she was swimming in a sea of debris, and believed that she was about to drown. But then she heard the roar of a motorcycle; then she noticed the light; then He stepped inside. And when she awoke the next morning, she knew immediately what had happened. *Hocus pocus, all sorts of supernatural beings exist; there is much that is mysterious between heaven and earth.* She found Elisabeth's crucifix in a drawer; she polished it and put it on. Standing in front of the mirror in the bathroom she now saw an older version of her own mother, but she felt no anger towards that woman. *No, never any anger again, I'm done with all that shit.* Of course she told us about it, but the very essence of it – what He had whispered before He vanished on His motorcycle – she told only to Preben. The rest of us didn't find out until three years later when she sold the house on Birkebladsvej and, along with Preben, left for Burundi to join Médecins Sans Frontières.

'They're all savage and insane down there,' moaned Bjørk.

'She's the one who's insane,' Askild remarked. Neither of them understood that orphans have to stick together. Or that Leila, on that night, had embraced a rejected world, and in reward had been given a mission. Bjørk preferred not to talk about that.

Nor did Grandma Bjørk ever return to another distressing story, the one about the youngest in a series of children and grandchildren. Yes, the boy who was scared of the dark and who had inherited his grandfather's penchant for painting ran off one day. That was the last thing she had expected. Applehead, Knut, yes, even Niels had apparently had it in him. But that youngster? She remembered the day he knocked on the door of their house on Tunøvej. He was beaming all over and talking about Amsterdam as if it were a golden city, equal to her own Bergen. Bjørk felt invigorated by all that talk of foreign cities until it dawned on her that he was talking so much because he was on his way there. Then Amsterdam lost some of its magic, but the boy didn't seem to notice her lack of enthusiasm. He leafed through Askild's art books, spilling coffee on Picasso and Georges Braque and talking a good deal about the academy where he had been accepted. He left a couple of hours later with a stack of art books under his arm, after his grandmother had admonished him to write to her regularly.

'Stop all that blubbering,' Askild said to Bjørk when he closed the door. 'I give him a week, at most. Then he'll be back home.'

They waited and waited. They waited for the boy who was scared of dogheads, thinking: *all alone in a foreign country; he'll never last.* But a week passed, a month passed, a year passed, and the youngster still didn't return.

Grandma Bjørk once again began to feel like an inhabitant in a foreign land. Still, she had her gambling club. Stinna and her husband, about whom she'd read so much in the newspapers, visited them regularly, but whenever that noseless swindler stepped through the door, the mood would become a little strained. And even though the man was polite and cleared the table, even praising all the hideous paintings, Grandma Bjørk couldn't help thinking: *What an old pig. How could Stinna, with her proud French genes, fall so hard for a noseless fatso when she could have had that sweet boy Peter?*

On the other hand, the one thing she kept brooding over to the very end was the day that Askild came home from the hospital. He had been kept overnight for observation due to growing problems with an ulcer, and he sat down at the dining-room table. That was five years after Dad had disappeared on Mt Blakhsa. Askild didn't say a word. Nothing about the doctor's verdict or any of the things he usually grumbled about. No complaints that the coffee was too strong or too weak – and that's when Bjørk started to worry. That's when she gently touched his arm and asked him if there was anything else wrong besides the ulcer, which had been bothering him for decades. 'What did the doctor say? It's nothing serious, is it?' But Askild still said nothing, nor did he complain about the prudish nurses or the conceited doctors. He didn't utter a single curse, and not once did he pound the table so the cups and glasses danced. Then Grandma Bjørk was even more worried. She hovered over him, feeling an urge to touch his white hair – and out of the blue came a desire to pamper him with a really good dinner. *Maybe some wine*, thought Bjørk, *and candles* . . . So she took the bus to town, went to the speciality shops and bought everything that she knew he liked.

But when she returned home that afternoon, Askild was out in the yard – in exactly the same place where an unspecified number of pink letters had gone up in flames thirty years earlier. *Final curtain*, she thought at the time, and now she thought it again, as the grocery bags slipped out of her hands. *They must have said something at the hospital* . . . Grandpa Askild had dragged all his paintings out to the yard, sprayed them with petrol, struck a match, and now he stood there, staring into the flames that rose up with a great rush, practically taking off half the hedge.

There went *New Life in the Old Privy*. There vanished *The Doctor and the Scalpel*. There was *Bergen Is Burning*, finally coming into its own. There fell *The Vandal Gets Stuck in the Letter Box* right into the sea of flames. There the liar tripped over his own story for the last time.

They all went up in flames, all that cubist shit which had taken so much of his attention, all those hideous paintings that had filled the shed and outbuildings. Paintings populated by disintegrating people, those who were knocked off balance or who had merged with buildings and ships in an inferno of fractured shapes and sharp edges. They all vanished in one furious moment, while Askild stood there as if turned to stone. The flames made his eyes glitter, but he didn't reply when she said: 'But what are you doing, man, are you out of your mind?' Nor did he protest when she picked up a stick and tried to rake the charred pieces out of the fire. But it was too late. Grandma Bjørk started to cry. She gave him a hard punch on the chest. She kept on hitting him until she collapsed. Then, as if nothing had happened, as if the cubist paintings had been a mere curiosity for the past fifty years, he walked back to the house, poured turpentine into metal containers, and began painting his first landscape with such ease that it made Bjørk gasp. A mist like those in Turner paintings, an impressionistic shimmer, a Nordic simplicity that took her breath away.

Slowly it took shape – not at all with the same mad tempo as before – no, it took several weeks; and before her eyes Bjørk gradually saw a landscape emerge which they could have entered together, if it hadn't been for his cubist intransigence, his jazzy penchant for the bottle, and his bloodhounds on an eastern German plain. Standing there at the age of eighty, he painted an opportunity they had never seized, a love she had barely tasted during those first years of the war when Grandpa Askild was a shy young man with imploring eyes. He painted meadow-filled valleys and mountain plateaus; he painted Danish rapeseed fields and Norwegian birch forests. But that was not the strangest part.

The strangest part was that the paintings quickly began to change their creator, erasing the bitter lines around his mouth and the mean look in his dark eyes. The landscapes seemed to be talking back. They took on a life of

460

their own and began changing Askild – repainting him – whenever she looked away. She noticed the gentleness that suddenly came over him. She couldn't help noticing how quick he was to cry whenever they sat in front of the TV in the afternoons, watching sitcoms and soap operas. One day she discovered that she was serving him dinner without wondering whether a few burned patches in the bottom of the pan would prompt a fit of rage.

But the more gentle he became, the less there was of him. In the end he looked like the skeleton who, fifty years earlier, had stepped through the door of the house on Skivebakken – except that his back was not as straight, his hair was not black, his eyes were not as brown, and his nose was no longer as proud. He actually looked more like a wrinkled fledgling that had fallen out of a nest. His footsteps were silent, his presence nearly invisible, and the strong Giraffe beers were replaced by ordinary beer. One day Bjørk discovered that the bag he was fumbling with in the hallway held only light beer. Another day she couldn't help noticing the spots of blood on the toilet, but that was not something they talked about. Instead, they looked at landscapes. For the first time Bjørk began to meddle, giving him advice and telling him her opinion regarding the patina and choice of colours. She pointed out dead spots in the paintings and incompatible colour combinations, which Askild without the slightest hesitation changed.

Yes, they would stand there together for hours, getting lost in the strange world that emerged on the brown canvases, staring into them, at all the rapeseed fields and meadow-filled valleys, which became more and more abstract and blurred. And at times Bjørk felt as if she were actually living in them, until early one morning Askild sat in the rocking chair and began vomiting blood. Then the bubble burst, and Grandma Bjørk called the doctor and had Askild taken to the hospital. There they gave him an IV and filled him with morphine even though he never complained of any pain or about the slop they fed him: gruel, fruit porridge, liquid nutrients in a bottle . . . It was there that Bjørk first heard the diagnosis of stomach cancer, but it didn't come as a shock. Nor could she reproach him for refusing any form of treatment when he simply sat there like an infant, sucking on his bottle.

If only Niels could see him now, thought Bjørk, *if only Knut would come home to say goodbye to his father*. But no sons – either dead or gone – turned up. Nor did a retarded daughter weighing 100 kilos jump on to the bed to greet her father. On the other hand, Stinna and the noseless man did show up on occasion. Letters arrived from Burundi, a single one from Amsterdam, and a handful from Bergen. Grandma Bjørk read them all aloud, and if it hadn't been for the deaf and blind Mamma Randi in my fat aunt's old room, she would undoubtedly have moved to the hospital. But she had to go home three times a day to feed her mother-in-law. In her old age Bjørk was once again the mother of two children in diapers.

Time passed, and she couldn't get herself to tell Mamma Randi that Askild was in the hospital. Her mother-in-law didn't seem to notice, because her life had become reduced to what went in one end and what came out the other. Even on the day when Grandma Bjørk brought flowers to a man who was no longer there – although he still lay in his bed in a remote private room, looking like an unconscious fledgling – she couldn't say anything to Randi. It was all so unreal: the glances of the nurses, Askild's dead body. Of course he should be laid out at home. And that's how it happened that the dead Askild was laid out in one of the rooms on Tunøvej. In another sat the blind old lady, and every time Bjørk went from one room to another, she would pass a landscape painting and pause, enchanted and paralysed. *Who should I call? Should I get permission?* Askild wanted to be cremated and have his ashes scattered in the North Sea, but how would all that be arranged?

Standing in the hallway – weighed down by the news which she never did manage to convey to the old lady – Bjørk was struck by paralysing doubt. And all the while, the sweet stench of rotting flesh began to spread through the house. It seeped into the carpets and curtains, clung to her clothes, and it did not disappear until the day when Stinna and the Bath Plug came bursting through the front door after a vain attempt to pay a visit at the hospital. 'Uff!' groaned Stinna, pulling her T-shirt up over her nose. 'Why the hell didn't you tell us he was dead?'

First she went to Dad's old room to see Askild, but the stench made her turn on her heel, slamming the door behind her. Then she went to fat Aunt Anne Katrine's old room, and there she had another shock. Mamma Randi may have been deaf and blind, but there had been nothing wrong with her sense of smell. She had inhaled his stench. She had stood up for the last time, and now she lay dead on the floor. Her eyes had sunk so far into her head that Stinna couldn't tell whether they were open or closed.

* * *

463

'What a madhouse!' Grandma Bjørk often said afterwards, thinking about the drinking buddies who suddenly turned up after reading the death notice that Stinna had put in the newspaper. A vast number of unknown men came rushing into the church where only the closest family members were sitting. What a commotion there was! And what a shock to discover that Askild had not been as friendless as we had thought. *Cheer up, there's better beer in heaven*, one of them had printed on a banner – an offence that the pastor would have responded to at once if Grandma Bjørk hadn't said, 'Now that they're here, just let them stay.'

So there sat Grandpa Askild's unknown drinking buddies, with whom he had caroused for more than thirty years – both old and young, a real motley bunch, and they all lined up to kiss the coffin, showering it with flowers and little notes written on the back of beer labels.

'He was certainly full of surprises,' said Bjørk, thinking about the unfortunate incident with the ashes. It was the following week, after the cremation had occurred and the ashes were to be scattered in Odense Fjord – the North Sea was, after all, too far away in Bjørk's opinion. But no one had ever told her that Grandpa Askild had once promised each of his unknown friends a share of his dead body. That he had donated, so to speak, over half of his body to social causes. She had never seen him sitting in the Corner, flinging around his imaginary ashes while he laughed loudly and at the same time made use of the occasion to sponge a few beers.

'If you buy me a beer,' Grandpa used to say to new pub guests, 'I'll give you a little piece of myself in return.'

So when his drinking buddies turned up and strolled

with us down to the harbour and out towards the fjord, Bjørk was once again caught by surprise. It was a warm and cloudless summer day, which prompted several of the drinking buddies to shed their shirts while others sang drinking songs, and Grandma Bjørk was almost starting to feel at ease in the company of these good-natured boozers. But then the solemn moment arrived. Applehead, who had come from Bergen to attend the funeral and also to take Mamma Randi's ashes back home to Norway so that she could rest next to Pappa Niels, wanted to say a few words.

Grandma Bjørk stood there, holding the urn. Applehead spoke of all the good and all the bad, but when he was finished with his fine speech, she was suddenly accosted by those unknown men who lined up in front of the urn, each with a little plastic bag. 'Where's the spoon?' shouted one, and a spoon was instantly produced, and then they started helping themselves. Grandma Bjørk stood there as if stunned, while plastic bags were filled with Grandpa's ashes and disappeared into the pockets of shirts and trousers – as if she were holding a bowl of candy and not the earthly remains of her deceased husband, only one-third of which ended up scattered over the fjord. Grandma Bjørk was on the verge of tears; her hands shook as she scattered the last dregs of his ashes. On the way home we tried to console her, saying that in spite of everything, those were Grandpa's last wishes.

Bjørk would not have been as outraged if, during the last year of Askild's life, she hadn't discovered a different man behind the cubist facade, a gentle and loving man who looked at her kindly in the morning over a cup of tea and half a breakfast roll. A man who gave her one enchanting landscape after another. Landscapes that she dreamt about during the next few years and which meant that she didn't liven up the way she had thought she would. She didn't let herself cut loose at the gambling club, she didn't throw herself into all the things she had planned to do, such as dancing and singing. Instead, she felt herself slowly languish, she felt a yearning to step into the same landscapes that Askild had at last stepped into. Everything became so difficult – all that cooking and cleaning. She started letting things go. 'Pull yourself together, Grandma,' cried Stinna. But in Bjørk's nightly dreams she began following Askild more and more often into his landscapes. She walked through the rapeseed fields, she wandered around in misty, meadow-filled valleys, she got lost in foggy winter landscapes, birch forests, and mountain plateaus. And when she awoke in the morning, her greatest desire was to close her eyes again. *Pull yourself together!* She tried. She did everything Stinna told her to do: exercise classes at the senior centre, for instance, but when the classes were over, she didn't feel like going back home. Her legs felt heavy.

'Couldn't I just stay here?' she asked, and when she had asked that question often enough, people started moving her personal possessions.

In the end she couldn't figure out where she actually lived, but she still promised Stinna that she would soon have everything under control again. She believed it too, until one day when she got a letter from Applehead in Bergen, telling her that Doctor Thor had died on his ninety-fourth birthday. Grandma Bjørk sat for a long time, staring out of the window. She saw hikers scattering across a field and vanishing into the birch forest in the distance. When the nurse arrived later and found Grandma Bjørk sitting in her armchair with a letter that had fallen out of her hands, it dawned on Grandma that she had been staring into a huge painting.

After Thor's death she began to get seriously muddled. She thought Stinna was her sister Lina, and she told the nursing staff that her deceased husband had also been a respected doctor; he had written a book entitled *517 Ways to Break Your Neck and One Way to Become Human Again*.

'And he *did* become human again,' said Grandma Bjørk to anyone who would listen. 'He escaped from the camps.'

Even she could tell where things were headed, and so she started writing postcards to her grandson in Amsterdam. *Somewhere in eastern Germany, your grandfather is running across a plain. I've begun to fear that he may never come back home.* But Askild was not the one she was talking about. It was me. As she was about to die, Grandma Bjørk felt that it was enough to have one son in the family who never came back home. Come home, she wrote. *The bloodhounds are dead . . . Not even Doghead is alive any more.*

It was then that her older son suddenly rose up from the dead and started sending her fresh air from Bergen. It was at that time, too, that she once again noticed the splinter of ice in her heart, and when the doctors finally offered to do something about it, well, she could no longer feel the familiar pressure in her chest. It was as if everything flowed out and was transformed into an enchanted landscape, and she would undoubtedly have vanished into it if one thing wasn't still bothering her. One thing made her wake up at night and crawl around in bewilderment among all those tins. *Fresh air from Bergen*. She sniffed at them. She played with them. She sat on the floor in the dark and inhaled that familiar scent from Vågen, Fisketorget, Skansen, and the newly developed neighbourhood. She saw in her mind the patrician villa on Kalfarveien. She got completely lost inside the widow Knutsson's old room, but she also noticed something else: an icy wind, a dizzy plunge from the peaks of Mt Blakhsa . . . Doubt began spreading. Doubt grew inside her like a heavenly city and made her consent to the operation. She had to buy time. She had to solve the mystery about the fresh air from Bergen. But every time she got close, every time she saw an unspecified number of pink letters drifting down into a dark grave, she would lose her train of thought and feel unable to make head or tail of her own story.

'There's something that doesn't fit,' said Grandma Bjørk.

But at last he came. Just as it dawned on her that we were fooling her and that it wasn't her older son who was the generous sender of the fresh air from Bergen, there he stood in front of her, smiling. Little Jug Ears had returned, and at his side stood Leila. 'Thank you for the fresh air,' said Grandma Bjørk. And they replied, 'It was nothing, Ma.'

Yes, there stood the happy pair, and then the landscapes came sliding in. And all of a sudden Askild was there, waiting for her off in the distance, inside a misty composition – he was standing under a birch tree. In one hand he held his cane, in the other an old paintbrush. *Now we've waited long enough*, he said. *Yes, little Askild, now we're home, now we've finally come home*, whispered Grandma Bjørk. And then she closed her eyes and didn't open them again.

* * *

Oh yes, she did open them one last time. 'The smuggling money!' she said, staring up at us. 'I've buried it behind the shed.'

The Pot of Gold at the End
of the Rainbow

'SO THAT WAS THAT,' said Stinna. 'Now there can't be any more to tell.'

Stinna's right. There's *almost* nothing more to tell. No more pictures to paint, no more empty canvases to stretch. Each story has been given its own canvas, and while the last of them were drying as they hung in Stinna's guest room last week, Grandma Bjørk died in her hospital bed. The doctors had rooted around so much in search of that splinter of ice in her heart that her systems were thrown into disarray, and after the operation she awoke only once. We were able to talk to her for a couple of minutes. She was convinced that I was Dad and that Stinna was Mum. She babbled a good deal about fresh air from Bergen, and finally she gave us a hint about where we might find our inheritance. Then she closed her eyes for the last time. No mob of drinking buddies turned up at her funeral, but a few souls from the gambling club did find their way there. A Fru Meier and a Fru Nielsen came, and both of them asked so earnestly about Bjørk's older son that for a moment we froze.

Hadn't Grandma ever told them that Dad was dead?

'And what about the younger son?' they went on. 'The Jamaican businessman? Was his plane delayed?'

I remembered Grandma Bjørk's words the first time I stepped through the door of the nursing home: 'In this family it's apparently fashionable to run away.' She was right about that. Many have run away, few have returned. And where would be the appropriate place to end? With the pastor's words? With my sister's hand, which completely unnoticed slides down inside my jacket pocket? Or with my own homecoming? I spent a good seven years in Amsterdam. Seven years in which Grandma Bjørk waited for the boy who was scared of dogheads to return. That's the amount of time it takes to regenerate, but the boy couldn't get rid of his own dogheads, and he had no desire to return home to his inheritance of cubist motifs. But sniffing around in the old house on Tunøvej, I found nothing more than the hazy winter landscapes of old age, until I caught sight of the charred remains of the mighty bonfire that was still disfiguring the hedge.

And then I understood what Grandpa Askild had done. He had cleared the way. I was free to recreate the burned paintings and in that way present my own version of the story. And nearly six months ago, in the guest room of the house belonging to Stinna and the Bath Plug, I took out my supplies: turpentine and linseed oil, palette and paintbrush. What I hadn't brought with me from Amsterdam I could find in the shed on Tunøvej. Using the new and the old – that's how I set to work. I painted *A Dripping Mermaid*; with my paints I conjured up the *Doghead in the Space Under the Stairs, Askild's Flight Across an Eastern German Plain, The Ship* Amanda *in the Morning*

Fog, A Monster in the Kitchen, A Troll Jumping Out of Its Box.
I painted *Triumphs and Tragedies Seen Through a Peephole.*
The Fall of the Mountain-Climbers. The Defeat of a Swindler.
I painted quickly, making generous use of colour. I often
allowed myself to be sidetracked by pure fantasy. And in
between *Untitled* and *Omitted Paintings*, more prosaic titles
turn up: *Self-Criticism* and *Searching*. Why does my mother
take up so little of the story? Is there too much red in the
pictures of my sister? What happened to the seafaring
Knut? Up until the last minute we were expecting him to
come to the funeral.

The questions are endless. I'm not proud of the mess
that I've left in my sister's guest room. Among my titles
there are *Loose Ends* and *False Leads.* There is also a special
mix of paints for various insults. There was Great-
grandfather Rasmus, who suffered the indignity of
becoming Fang. There were paint combinations devoted
to the incomprehensible. I used them to paint *Tree Spirits*
and *Monsters, That Took On a Life of Their Own.* These
colour combinations were my extreme points: they were
what I would turn to when I couldn't find any common
ground in my family stories – and they were also the
colours I used to paint *Mt Blakhsa.* Shall I finish by
revising now and say: *Even I didn't know what was actually
going on?* Should I end instead with the row of empty
canvases that are still in the guest room? A hasty picture of
my two nephews playing Circus Eriksson with the Bath
Plug's discarded noses? He buys a new one every year,
when the nicotine from his cigarettes has stained them
yellow. Then he puts them in a box in the pantry, and the
kids take them out whenever they feel like dressing up. Or
should I be faithful to my story – *take it or leave it; that was*

my only truth – and end by stretching one last small canvas?

Yes, says my sister Stinna. I should hurry up and finish. It was nice to have me visiting, but I can't live in a guest room forever.

'I've buried it behind the shed,' was the last thing Grandma Bjørk said. After the funeral we drove out to the house on Tunøvej, found a shovel, and began digging. After half an hour it started to rain, and Stinna was sceptical.

'It's not here. Why should the money be here after all these years? They were always short of cash.'

The rain made her hair curl and her make-up run; it made us both so crazy that we started throwing mud at each other.

'I still don't believe in it,' she gasped in resignation. But when we finally caught sight of the top of the black plastic bag under the murky water in the mud, we both felt a rush. It was the same excitement that went through Grandpa Askild every time he sewed money into the mattress in the widow Knutsson's old room. The same rush that Dad had felt standing in front of Ibsen the coin dealer's dusty display window, or when the coins rained down on the Skoltegrunn dock, or later when he got lost in the grey zones of the business world, chasing after new pots of gold at the end of the rainbow. The same rush – and the same disappointment – when, a moment later, we stood there looking at a tattered plastic bag filled with mouldy Norwegian banknotes. Since the time when Askild was arrested by the Germans, Grandma Bjørk had lived in nine different houses. Each time she moved, she had taken her secret cargo along with her. She had buried it in yards, hidden it in storage rooms and in attics. Maybe she was so ashamed of having the money that she couldn't bring herself to spend it. Maybe she knew all too well what Askild would have used it for . . . She could have put the money in the bank instead; she could have invested it in something. But in our family we've never been very good at managing our inheritance.

'Fuck this,' Stinna said, staring at the sorry remains.

'Fuck this,' I agreed.

There we stood with the family's real pot of gold at the end of the rainbow, only to discover that it had been devoured by rain and devalued by time. There we stood with the reason for the bloodhounds and everything worse – there we stood, plain and simple. And when Stinna picked up the mouldy banknotes to count them, they began to disintegrate.

'She knew all along,' Stinna kept on saying as we drove home through the city.

The rain came down harder, darkness fell, and suddenly it was all around us. Stinna looked at me. For a moment it seemed as if she wanted to say something, but she changed her mind, turning her focus back to the road. We did what Dad would have done: we drove straight home without letting the darkness go through us.

THE END

THE HOUSE OF THE SPIRITS
Isabel Allende

'A GENUINE RARITY. A WORK OF FICTION THAT
IS BOTH A LITERARY ACCOMPLISHMENT AND A
MESMERIZING STORY'
Washington Post

Spanning four generations. Isabel Allende's magnificent
family saga is populated by a memorable, often eccentric cast
of characters. Together, men and women, spirits, the forces of
nature, and of history, converge in an unforgettable, wholly
absorbing and brilliantly realised novel which is as richly
entertaining as it is a masterpiece of modern literature.

'EXHILARATING . . . POSSESSED BY AN IMMENSE
ENERGY, A FECUND IMAGINATION . . . AN ELEGANT
WAY WITH LANGUAGE'
Newsweek

'THIS IS A NOVEL LIKE THE NOVELS NO ONE
SEEMS TO WRITE ANYMORE: THICK WITH PLOT
AND BRISTLING WITH CHARACTERS WHO PLAY OUT
THEIR LIVES OVER THREE GENERATIONS OF CONFLICT
AND RECONCILIATION. A NOVEL TO BE READ FOR ITS
BRILLIANT CRAFTSMANSHIP AND ITS NARRATIVE
OF INESCAPABLE POWER'
EL País, Madrid

'ANNOUNCING A TRULY GREAT READ: A NOVEL
THICK AND THRILLING, FULL OF FANTASY, TERROR
AND WIT, ELABORATELY CRAFTED YET SERIOUS
AND ACCURATE IN ITS HISTORICAL AND
SOCIAL OBSERVATIONS'
Die Welt, Berlin

9780552995887

BLACK SWAN

THE BOY IN THE STRIPED PYJAMAS
John Boyne

'A SMALL WONDER OF A BOOK . . . A PARTICULAR HISTORICAL
MOMENT, ONE THAT CANNOT BE TOLD TOO OFTEN'
Guardian

What happens when innocence is confronted by monstrous evil?

Nine-year-old Bruno knows nothing of the Final Solution
and the Holocaust. He is oblivious to the appalling cruelties being
inflicted on the people of Europe by his country. All he knows is
that he has been moved from a comfortable home in Berlin to a
house in a desolate area where there is nothing to do and no-one to
play with. Until he meets Shmuel, a boy who lives a strange parallel
existence on the other side of the adjoining wire fence and who, like
the other people there, wears a uniform of striped pyjamas.

Bruno's friendship with Shmuel will take him from innocence to
revelation. And in exploring what he is unwittingly a part of, he
will inevitably become subsumed by the terrible process.

'THE HOLOCAUST AS A SUBJECT INSISTS ON RESPECT,
PRECLUDES CRITICISM, PREFERS SILENCE. ONE THING IS CLEAR:
THIS BOOK WILL NOT GO GENTLY INTO ANY GOOD NIGHT'
Observer

'AN EXTRAORDINARY TALE OF FRIENDSHIP AND THE
HORRORS OF WAR . . . RAW LITERARY TALENT AT ITS BEST'
Irish Independent

'A BOOK THAT LINGERS IN THE MIND FOR QUITE SOME
TIME . . . A SUBTLE, CALCULATEDLY SIMPLE AND ULTIMATELY
MOVING STORY'
Irish Times

'SIMPLY WRITTEN AND HIGHLY MEMORABLE. THERE ARE
NO MONSTROSITIES ON THE PAGE BUT THE TRUE HORROR
IS ALL THE MORE POTENT FOR BEING IMPLICIT'
Ireland on Sunday

'STAYS AHEAD OF ITS READERS BEFORE
DELIVERING ITS KILLER-PUNCH FINAL PAGES'
Independent

NOW A MAJOR FILM

9780552774737

BLACK SWAN

ESCAPE
Heleen van Royen

THE INTERNATIONAL NO. 1 BESTSELLER

I have a husband, we have two children and we own our house. I am in good health and so are they, our lives are good; we have everything we need. Sometimes I look at them and wait, in vain, to be moved, as a mother should when watching her own family. Why do I no longer feel anything?

Julia is thirty-six years old. At first sight she has it all, but actually she feels miserable. Trapped in the monotony of daily family life and fed up with her passionless marriage, Julia wants out. Escape. For once not to be a good mother, a good wife, a good daughter. So for the first time in her life she does something completely irresponsible: she leaves her family behind and heads off into the sun.

When Julia finally meets someone who makes her realize what she's been missing all her life, she is forced to reconcile with her past and confront the crucial question: does she dare to go home?

9780552773799

BLACK SWAN

LAND OF THE GOLDEN APPLE
Eve Makis

Summer has come to this idyllic Cypriot
village, and for Socrates, it brings an open
invitation to indulge in his favourite pastimes; spying
on his brother's girlfriends, setting off homemade
fireworks, tormenting the local pensioners and
generally getting up to no good. Alas, his mother's
favourite pastimes include stopping him from doing
any of these things. An uneasy truce is reached after
an unfortunate incident with a box of matches,
and lazy peace is restored.

But this summer will bring a rude awakening
to all of the villagers. The jasmine-scented breeze
carries with it a threat of danger, and the close-knit
community will be shaken to its very core
by the menace it brings . . .

9780552773256

BLACK SWAN

SISTER OF MY HEART
Chitra Banerjee Divakaruni

'CHITRA BANERJEE DIVAKARUNI IS A TRUE STORYTELLER.
LIKE DICKENS, SHE HAS CONSTRUCTED LAYER UPON LAYER
OF TRAGEDY, SECRETS AND BETRAYALS, OF THWARTED
LOVE . . . [A] GLORIOUS, COLOURFUL TRAGEDY'
Daily Telegraph

Born in the big old Calcutta house on the same tragic night
that both their fathers were mysteriously lost, Sudha and Anju
are cousins. Closer even than sisters, they share clothes, worries,
dreams in the matriarchal Chatterjee household. But when
Sudha discovers a terrible secret about the past, their
mutual loyalty is sorely tested.

A family crisis forces their mothers to start the serious
business of arranging the girls' marriages, and the pair is
torn apart. Sudha moves to her new family's home in rural
Bengal, while Anju joins her immigrant husband in California.
Although they have both been trained to be perfect wives,
nothing has prepared them for the pain, as well as the
joy, that each will have to face in her new life.

Steeped in the mysticism of ancient tales, this jewel-like
novel shines its light on the bonds of family, on love and loss,
against the realities of traditional marriage in modern times.

'DIVAKARUNI STRIKES A DELICATE BALANCE BETWEEN
REALISM AND FANTASY . . . A TOUCHING CELEBRATION OF
ENDURING LOVE'
Sunday Times

'A PLEASURE TO READ . . . A NOVEL FRAGRANT IN RHYTHM
AND LANGUAGE'
San Francisco Chronicle

'DIVAKARUNI'S BOOKS POSSESS A POWER THAT IS BOTH
TRANSPORTING AND HEALING . . . SERIOUS AND ENTRANCING'
Booklist

'MAGICALLY AFFECTING . . . HER INTRICATE TAPESTRY OF OLD
AND NEW WORLDS SHINES WITH A RARE LUMINOSITY'
San Diego Union Tribune

9780552997676

BLACK SWAN